SASHA'S TRICK

SASHA'S TRICK

DAVID ROSENBAUM

THE MYSTERIOUS PRESS

Published by Warner Books

A Time Warner Company

Mysterious Press books are published by Warner
Books, Inc., 1271 Avenue of the Americas,
New York, NY 10020.

 A Time Warner Company

The Mysterious Press name and logo are registered trademarks of Warner Books, Inc.

Printed in the United States of America

First printing: July 1995

10 9 8 7 6 5 4 3 2 1

Library of Congress Cataloging-in-Publication Data
Rosenbaum, David
    Sasha's trick / David Rosenbaum.
      p.   cm.
    ISBN 0-89296-591-6
    1. New York (N.Y.)—Fiction.   I. Title.
PS3569.0776S27   1995
  813'.54—dc20

95-8081
CIP

For my parents,
Jack and Livia

Acknowledgments

I WOULD LIKE TO ACKNOWLEDGE THE FOLLOWING BOOKS AS sources for *Sasha's Trick:* Roger Boyes's *The Hard Road to Market,* Yuri Brokhin's *Hustling on Gorky Street,* Noam Chomsky's *Chronicles of Dissent,* Charles DeJaeger's *The Linz File,* Mikhail Dyomin's *The Day Born of Darkness,* David Remnick's *Lenin's Tomb,* Lydia Rosner's *The Soviet Way of Crime,* Lev Timofeyev's *Russia's Secret Rulers,* and Vitali Vitaliev's *Special Correspondent.*

I would also like to thank the Russian Research Center at Harvard University.

For their knowledge and support, I would like to thank Wayne Kabak, *Boston Globe* Moscow Bureau Chief Fred Kaplan, Frances Katz, Larry Katz, Yelena Kolodyazhnaya, Richard Lourie, Bill Malloy, Andrea Notman, Kings County Assistant District Attorney Eric Seidel, Sona Vogel, Dr. Constance Williams, and, most of all and always, Sarah.

Where there's a person,
there's a problem.

—Joseph Stalin

SASHA'S TRICK

Prologue

1977

AFTER BEING TURNED IN BY THE CONDUCTOR, WHO APPARENTLY considered the bribe he had received unsatisfactory, Aleksandr Volkavitch Eugenev was arrested and taken off the Berlin-Warsaw-Kiev express as it pulled into Rovno. Two OBKhSS (Police Department for the Fight Against the Theft of Socialist Property) officers threw him into the back of a truck and drove to a jail in Kiev, where the local militia took custody. From there he was shipped across the Ukraine to the Kharkov Central Distribution Prison, the place the thieves called "Cold Mountain." He was given a shower and five hundred grams of dry black bread and thrown into a holding cell with twenty other men. He found a place against the wall and sat there, guarding his bread, until the sun rose.

In the morning, Aleksandr Eugenev (Sasha to his friends) was hurried to court, charged with parasitism (he had no work stamp on his internal passport), and tried. The prosecutor pointed to his previous conviction for hooliganism and the six months he had spent in the Krasnaya Presna prison factory for juvenile offenders. Trading in smuggled watches (which was what Sasha was doing on the train) was, according to the prosecutor, an offense against every honest Soviet worker.

Sasha's attorney asked the judges to teach him a lesson, but to consider his tender years and not be too harsh. Justice tempered with mercy, wasn't that the hallmark of the Soviet legal system, especially as practiced in the Ukraine, the land that had given the nation its current first secretary, the heroic Leonid Ilyich Brezhnev?

Three days later—three days of stale bread and cabbage-and-fish soup with little cabbage and only the memory of fish—Sasha was sentenced to two years hard labor and immediately began the week-long, two-thousand-mile trans-Siberian rail journey to Novosibirsk, loaded into a freezing cattle car with fifty other prisoners. By the second night three men were dead, and there was a fight over their coats and boots.

From Novosibirsk, Sasha was transferred to another cattle car that headed northwest, along the north-flowing Ob River, to the wooden, fairy-tale city of Tomsk. Another train, still paralleling the Ob, brought him farther north to the detention camp in the isolated logging town of Kolpashevo, six hundred miles south of the Arctic Circle.

He arrived in camp on his birthday. That night Sasha celebrated the dawning of his nineteenth year with a skinny hand-rolled cigarette of shag tobacco and three large glasses of oily *samogon*, home-brewed vodka. The trick, he thought as he drifted off, was to imagine that you were someone else, somewhere else, and that you were only dreaming a dream about someone named Aleksandr Eugenev. And who knew? When you woke up, you might find out it was true.

He was passed out on his thin mattress in the drafty, undesirable part of the barracks when he was shaken awake. He opened his eyes to find himself surrounded by dark figures.

"*Suka,*" someone snarled. Bitch.

"*Svoloch,*" said another. Bastard.

Sasha raised his head. A fist cracked against his cheek-bone, knocking him sideways, knocking the spit out of his mouth. His bed flew into the air, and in a moment he was on the floor. He pulled his knees to his chest and covered the back of his head with his hands, his elbows protecting the sides of his face. He tried to crawl away, squirming on the wooden floor, but the kicks—too many to count—still found his kidneys, his balls, his mouth.

The tip of a boot caught the back of his neck. An electric shock, rimmed in red, purple, and orange, ran through his body. Then, nothing.

Sasha opened his eyes. His mouth was dry, his lips swollen and cracked. He was lying on his back. High above him, he could see a small bulb burning weakly. He tried to turn his head to the side, and a plume of fire echoed from one eye to the other and back again. He coughed, and the pain in his chest brought tears. He could hear something clicking in his chest. His heart? Was that possible?

"Ah, we're awake."

Slowly, carefully, Sasha tilted his head forward. Standing at the foot of the bed was a tall, thin young man with a caved-in chest, broad shoulders, a scraggly mustache, and a halo of curly red hair. A cigarette dangled from his lips.

"Can we move our toes?" the man asked without removing the cigarette from his mouth.

Sasha did.

"Good," the man said, moving to the side of the bed, out of Sasha's line of sight. He reappeared, bending over him. He poked the bridge of Sasha's nose with a long finger. Another rocket ignited behind Sasha's eyes.

"Yes," the man said, "that's broken beautifully. But your eyes are okay. There's only a little collateral bleeding." A long ash from his cigarette fell into Sasha's mouth. Sasha spit.

"Sorry," the man said, the cigarette still in place between his lips.

"My chest," said Sasha, finding it difficult to breathe. "It's clicking. My heart is clicking."

"You can hear that? Jesus. Well, it's not your heart. That's your ribs. They're smashed up pretty nicely. Five or six of them, is my guess. When we breathe, our ribs expand, out and back. They articulate. Understand? If they were rigid, we wouldn't be able to inflate our chests. We wouldn't be able to breathe. Now in your case, the broken ends are knocking against each other. Click, click. Understand?"

"X-rays?" Sasha asked.

"What for?" said the man. "I just told you what's what. What's the difference if it's five, six, or even seven ribs? There's nothing to be done about it anyway. Here, look, I'll help you sit up."

The man put his arm behind Sasha's shoulders and lifted his torso off the bed. The pain took his breath away. Holding Sasha upright with one arm and working with the other, the man crammed a pillow behind the small of Sasha's back.

"There," the man said, stepping back. "No more clicking, right?"

The clicking had, indeed, stopped.

"See? Now our ribs are supported by our diaphragm. They won't move as much when we breathe. We'll just have to sleep sitting up for a while."

"Stop it," said Sasha.

"Stop what?"

"Stop talking like that. They're my ribs. Mine. I'm the one who's going to be sleeping sitting up. Who are you, anyway? You the doctor?"

"Physician Evgeny Andreevitch Bekker."

"You're a prisoner?" asked Sasha, noting Bekker's dirty

green overcoat and wire-rimmed glasses mended with surgical tape.

"Of course," said Bekker. "So what? I'm still the doctor. So. You don't care for my bedside manner. All right. I was just trying it out. Would you like a cigarette?" Bekker held out a pack of Astras, one of the cheapest Russian brands but quite rare in the camps.

Sasha nodded. Bekker stuck the cigarette between Sasha's lips and lit it. The smoke burned his throat, and he coughed again. This time, perhaps because he was prepared for it, the pain seemed less intense.

"Glasses," Sasha said.

"What about them?" asked Bekker.

"My glasses," Sasha said. "I need them."

"I don't know anything about glasses. You weren't wearing any when you were brought in."

"I'd like some morphine," Sasha said.

"So would I," said Bekker, carefully pinching off the burning end of his cigarette and slipping the butt into his pocket for later. "But it's still a little early in the morning for me. For you, no. I'm sorry. Morphine is for those poor sons of bitches I have to operate on. I'm a very good diagnostician, but, frankly, not so good with my hands. I could get you some aspirin. Do you have any money? Aspirin is expensive."

"No money."

"Too bad. But maybe you're better off. Aspirin, I wouldn't recommend it."

"Why not?"

"Internal bleeding. Aspirin is an anticoagulant. You might bleed to death. Unlikely, but you never know. Actually, vodka would do you better. Perhaps you have a friend who can bring you some. I can't, of course. It's against the rules."

"It hurts when I cough."

"I imagine it does. But if you think that's bad, wait until you sneeze. I wouldn't, if I were you."

"Sneeze?"

"That's right. Try not to. When you sneeze, it's like an orgasm. The muscles contract involuntarily, and the broken ends of your ribs will be forced through the fascia, the connecting tissue, in your chest. Very painful. Lots of subcutaneous bleeding. Coughing's not nearly so bad."

"How long?"

"For your ribs to heal? A month. Maybe two. No more."

"No. How long have I been here?"

"About twenty-four hours, more or less. That must have been a nasty dream. Would you like to tell me about it?" Bekker sat on the edge of Sasha's bed and lit another cigarette. "I took some courses in socialist psychoanalysis at the university. Moscow, of course."

"What are you talking about?"

"When you were brought in they said you had taken a fall from your bed. I presumed you were having a bad dream. They're common here, bad dreams, especially among the newcomers."

"Is that what you wrote? In your report?" asked Sasha.

"Of course," Bekker said. "It's not true? Something else happened? If something else happened—for example, let's say you were attacked and beaten—it's your duty to tell me, and it's my duty, as you know, to make a full and complete report. There will be an investigation, of course. Everyone will be questioned. You will be asked to identify the men who beat you. You will have to point them out.

"Yes, I can see it now. The men assembled in the yard. You, standing in front of them. Officers on both sides of you. They will ask, 'Who was it?' And you will point them out. You will say, 'That one. And that one. And that one over there. He broke my nose. The other one smashed my ribs.' You will become quite famous here. Everyone will applaud your courage. Long after you're dead, people will remember your name. They'll tell their grandchildren that they knew you."

"All right," said Sasha. "Enough." Why should the camp be different from anywhere else in the Soyuz? Everything you said or did was part of the great hypocrisy. Every word of every day was a lie.

What had he been charged with? Parasitism? And that was because he was working, buying and selling. Buy the Japanese digital watches from the Soviet tourists returning from shopping sprees in Berlin. Pay for the watches in rubles (Soviet citizens could not legally bring hard currencies back into the Soyuz) and sell them for dollars on the black markets in Kiev and Moscow. Where was the crime? It was all backward, he thought.

"Okay," said Sasha. "A bad dream. I fell out of bed. So what else is wrong with me?"

"Bumps and bruises. Nothing too serious. You're lucky."

"Lucky?"

"Of course. Usually, they kill the KGB plants. Odd that they would stick you in the thieves' barracks, though. You would have thought they'd be more interested in the politicals."

"I'm not KGB. That's ridiculous," said Sasha, astonished.

"Well, of course it's ridiculous," Bekker said. "Who ever heard of sneaking KGB bitches into the barracks? But, of course, it was all over the camp."

"But it's not true."

"Of course not."

"No. I mean it. I swear." Sasha winced and caught his breath. Then he continued, frightened. "I'm here for buying watches. I mean, call me a thief if you want, that's all right, but KGB? Political? I'm a Jew, for chrissakes."

"Your name is Sasha, correct?"

"Yes."

"Aleksandr Volkov, right?"

"No. Volkavitch. Aleksandr Volkavitch Eugenev."

Bekker took off his glasses and began polishing them on a corner of Sasha's sheet. "Not Volkov?"

"No," said Sasha. "Volkavitch. You mean I got beaten up by mistake?"

"Could be. Are you really a Jew? Eugenev's not a Jewish name."

"My grandmother's name was Katz."

"Well, if that's true, you're twice lucky."

"Why?"

"Because I'm Bekker the Jew. And now you can have some morphine."

For the next three days, Sasha and Bekker "rode the needle." Every four or five hours Bekker would appear at Sasha's bedside with two needles—one for himself and one for Sasha. Then, as the lovely narcotic warmth rose from their bellies into their brains, as Sasha felt his aching muscles and his tortured bones melt into a pudding, the two prisoners smoked cigarettes and talked about women and about life in the Soyuz. It was the best time Sasha had had since he'd been taken off the train in Rovno.

On the fourth day, Bekker told him he was being sent back to the barracks. "It'll be okay," he said. "You'll see. It's all straightened out."

When Sasha returned, he walked directly to the center of the barracks. "Just so everyone knows," he announced loudly, "my name is Aleksandr Volkavitch Eugenev. You all got that? Aleksandr Volkavitch. You can call me Sasha." Then he went to his bunk and sat down, his back against the wall. In a few minutes he was asleep.

When he awoke, a bearded, cross-eyed troll with long, thick black hair was sitting by his side.

"My name is Boris," he said. "People call me Boris the Kike. Can you guess why?"

"Because you're a Jew?" Sasha said.

Boris stood up. He was short, no more than five feet four. He unbuttoned his fly and pulled out his penis. It was enormous.

"The biggest in Kolpashevo. You know what they say about Jews," said Boris. "So that's why they call me the Kike. Although, as a matter of fact, I am a Jew." He returned his penis to his pants and sat down.

"What do you want?" Sasha asked.

Boris pulled out a bottle of vodka from under his coat and offered it to Sasha. "My old pal Evgeny Bekker says you're all right," said Boris. "So, if you're all right with Bekker, you're all right with me. Anyway, we Jews got to stick together."

Sasha made no move to take the bottle. Boris shook it invitingly. "There are too many goddamned Sashas in the world, don't you think?" he said. "Our Russian parents have no imaginations."

And that, Sasha knew, was as close to an apology as he was going to get. He looked away from Boris toward the rear of the barracks, where the elite thieves huddled in front of the wood stove, smoking and talking, keeping themselves wired by drinking gallons of the strong prison tea known as *chifir* and playing endless games of *zhelzhka,* in which they tried to guess the serial numbers on ruble notes. How many of them helped beat the crap out of me? Sasha wondered.

He turned back to Boris and looked at the bottle of vodka. He reached out, took a swig of the fiery home brew, and coughed. His ribs throbbed.

"Yes," said Boris, taking the bottle from Sasha and sighing deeply, "the world sucks. You in pain?"

"A little."

"Have another drink. You'll be missing Bekker's morphine. The vodka will take the edge off."

They drank.

"Cigarette?" offered Boris.

"Thanks," Sasha said, taking it and lighting up.

"Oh, yeah," said Boris. "I think these are yours."

He handed Sasha his glasses.

Sasha put them on. The world came back into focus.

Over the next several weeks, Boris the Kike began to take Sasha under his wing, showing him how to survive in the camp, introducing him to his fellow thieves, and letting them know that Sasha was not to be touched. And when Sasha accidentally stumbled upon Boris prying up the boards in the privy behind the barracks, Boris even offered to share his hiding place with him.

"The crapper is the best place in the world to hide anything," he said. "No one wants to mess around with other people's shit. And around here, you hide everything. In fact," Boris continued professorially, "in life, it's best to keep everything hidden and trust nobody."

"Not even your friends?" asked Sasha.

"Especially your friends," Boris said.

"Then why trust me?"

Boris shrugged. "Because you're such a stupid little hedgehog," he said, "and I have a weakness for stupid Jews."

One night, in the rear of the barracks, someone began singing a thieves' song:

> Don't walk in the mud,
>   it'll suck you down
> Don't skate on the ice,
>   you'll fall through
> Don't love a thief,
>   he'll fall too.

So let's drink and despair
Life's full of misfortune
Let's drink and despair
We'll all soon be dead.

"Christ," said Sasha, handing Boris a cigarette, "they're all like that."

"Like what?" Boris asked, lighting up.

"Like, 'Oh, life is a pool of shit, fuck me, I'm fucked.' All the thieves' songs. They're seriously boring. Depressing."

"But aren't you fucked, Aleksandr Volkavitch? One would think that you, especially, would feel fucked."

"Yes," Sasha agreed. "I'm fucked. We're all fucked. But some," he added, prodded by his ribs, which still hurt, and his nose, which would forever have a bump in the middle, "some are more fucked than others."

"Yes," said Boris, "but it's equally true that some are less fucked. The dead, now, they're extremely fucked. So, in that sense, you could easily consider yourself as being among the less fucked." He smiled. "So I think you should be happy. That's what the songs are about. They're not depressing. The poet expresses his sadness so we can get pleasure from it. He is sad so we can be happy."

"But even if we are less fucked, what's there to be happy about?" Sasha asked. "Correct me if I'm wrong, but aren't you stuck in this frozen shit hole just like everyone else? Or are you a Komsomol cadet doing research on camp morale for the Kolpashevo Oblast Party Committee?" He grinned at the picture that came to him: ugly, cross-eyed Boris the Kike as an eager Communist Youth on a poster, exhorting the masses.

"It's not so bad here," said Boris, sighing contentedly, "if . . ." He smiled, began to say something, and then seemed to think better of it.

"If what?" Sasha asked, realizing that he was being sucked

into Boris's game but not minding. It was fun trying to figure out what people were about. This one, thought Sasha, is an old prison dog trying to sound important.

Boris shook his head and left Sasha to join the thieves talking quietly around the wood stove.

Sasha knew about the *Vory v Zakone,* the "thieves-in-law." Throughout all the camps and jails and prisons in the Soyuz, they were the royalty. They had secret handshakes, secret passwords, secret tattoos. They talked about the thieves' code and even conducted trials in the barracks for people whom they charged with violating it by, say, having once held a straight job. Because they were outcasts from the real world, they tried to make a world of their own, a world in which they were the big shots and everyone else was scum. One of these days, Sasha knew, Boris would start recruiting him, lecturing him about *vorovskoy mir,* the thieves' world, extolling the virtues of the life. But the very next evening, Boris surprised him by picking up his theme where he had left it.

"If there's something waiting for you back home," Boris said, his voice low and serious, a half-empty bottle of vodka in his hand, "something worth living for, doing your time is not so bad. Even here."

Sasha laughed. "You old goat. You're in love? You're still thinking about women at your age? That's disgusting. I'm seriously disgusted."

"No, idiot. I'm not talking about women. I'm talking about money. Dollars, pounds, marks. Not rubles. Real money. More money than you can imagine. I'm talking about a real future."

Boris stopped, his face flushed. Is he drunk? Sasha wondered.

"So?" asked Sasha. "How do you get all this money?"

"Aleksandr Volkavitch," Boris said, his voice solemn, "I

like you. I like your good manners in not asking questions about the other night. I'll tell you what. You're a Jew, right?"

"My grandmother was a Jew," Sasha said. "That's what it said on her passport and that's what it says on mine. Not that it's any of your business."

"Here's why it's my business. When you're released, apply for a visa to Israel. Save your money. Don't drink it up, don't play *zhelzhka*. If I were you, I'd forget about trains.

"Yes, I know what you were sent here for. Kid stuff. A friend of mine in the boss's office showed me your file. Your grandfather was a good Soviet, a military man, a fucking hero. You grew up outside Moscow, in the Old Bolsheviks' suburb in Kratovo. Very exclusive. Very nice. Very nice for you. But your grandfather got it in the neck like all the rest of them. Well, what did he expect, a Soviet officer marrying a Jewish intellectual? So your old man lost his Party pin and his job at the Ministry of Health, and you got kicked out of Komsomol and no one would give you a job out of technical school. Poor boy. So you got drunk, got into a fight, ended up in Krasnaya Presna. But look at it from their point of view. A traitor for a grandfather, a Jew for a grandmother, a subversive for a father? Who would want to hire that? Too bad, Aleksandr Volkavitch," said Boris, smiling. "You're fucked."

The blood rushed to Sasha's face. A quick image of his grandfather, in uniform, lying on the floor of the old house, his brains leaking onto the Turkoman rug, flashed in front of him. He remembered picking up his grandfather's gun; he remembered how heavy it felt, how greasy, how warm.

It would be nice to have that gun now, Sasha thought, staring at Boris. It would have been nice to have it at the Komsomol meeting where the kids he thought were his friends stood up one after another and said that the Party's "bright and shining future" would be more swiftly achieved without him, a Jew with a father and a grandfather who were enemies of the people. It was humiliating. It was torture.

But then Sasha reminded himself that the trick was not to show your feelings. Feelings were for *fraiers,* for the straight, law-abiding *Homo Sovieticus* he no longer was. I am a businessman now, Sasha thought. I am for myself. He smiled.

"You're angry," said Boris.

"No, I'm not," said Sasha. "I just think it's seriously amusing that a cross-eyed old prick who's been kicked around by the cops his whole fucking life ends up acting like the goddamn *chekisti,* getting his rocks off by snooping into other people's lives."

"Look," Boris said, "I'm just making a point. Go to Moscow. I have a friend there, about your age, but sophisticated. He knows his way around. He can teach you the currency trade. That's a good business. You work in nice hotels, you wear nice clothes. You see a cop, you run. On a train, all you can do is jump off, probably break your neck."

"Fuck Moscow. I'm going to America," said Sasha, and he loved the sound of those words. "And when I get there, I'm not coming back unless I have a million dollars in my pocket."

"Bravo!" Boris said. "Good man. The Soyuz is finished with you; you wash your hands of it. Excellent. The right attitude. But how are you going to get to America? First you need to make money. Listen to me. My friend in Moscow? His name is Henry. He's incredible. A genius. He'll get you started.

"Then you save your money. And then, when your time comes, you get out. Make a right turn when you get to Tel Aviv. Go to America, to New York. Someday, I'll find you there, and then I'll let you in on my gold mine."

"So that's all I have to do?" asked Sasha. "Just get out of here, make a fortune, emigrate, go to Israel, go to America? And then you'll find me and let me in on your big deal? Is that all? Do I have it right? I just can't believe it's so simple."

"You're young. What's a few years to you? This will give you something to look forward to. That alone gives you a treasure most of the sorry shits around here would kill for."

Boris handed Sasha the vodka bottle with one good snort remaining, then stood up. "America. That's where I'm headed, too. You, Aleksandr Volkavitch, you can do what you want."

Sasha saluted sarcastically as Boris joined the other thieves at the end of the barracks by the wood stove. Not a bad guy, thought Sasha, but full of bullshit like all the rest.

A few months later, when the short Siberian spring turned the frozen tundra to mud and the wind blowing through the *taiga,* the vast evergreen forest, suddenly and miraculously became soft and perfumed, the Kolpashevo camp was closed. Boris the Kike was transferred east. Bad luck for him. Sasha was sent west, back to the Ukraine, back to Cold Mountain, where he finished his sentence.

In the spring of 1979, Sasha was released. That same spring, the Ob River flooded and chewed away at the sandy bluffs beneath the town of Kolpashevo. As it did, corpses in various states of putrefaction began popping to the river's surface. Some were just skeletons; some, the oldest ones, frozen by the Siberian permafrost, were almost completely preserved. Before the KGB could cordon off the riverbank, the citizens of Kolpashevo had counted a thousand bodies.

Sasha heard about what had happened and decided not to return to his life in Kiev. He would make his boast to the cross-eyed thief come true. He would leave the Soyuz. And he would begin by moving to the heart of the beast. He would move to Moscow.

Sasha looked up Boris's friend Genrikh, or Henry, as he liked to be called, and Henry, as Boris said he would, got Sasha started in the currency trade. Most days he hung out in the lobby of the Intourist Hotel on Tverskaya, doing business— changing money for tourists at twice the official rate (which was half the black market rate).

Sasha courted and married a pretty Muscovy girl, Alyona Romanova, a schoolteacher, and that got him his *propiska,* his residency permit, which meant that he could relax around the cops. He got a job delivering the newspaper *Ogonyuk,* but he showed up only when he knew he could make some real money by using the paper's truck to ferry contraband—everything from blue jeans to concrete to *samogon*—around the capital.

Sasha bought gold with the dollars he earned; he applied for a visa to Israel. And thirteen years after he was sentenced to the Gulag, he arrived, alone, in New York City. He said he would send for Alyona, but he never seemed to get around to it.

Sasha fell in love with New York. He prospered until a hot Indian summer day in 1993 when Boris the Kike, albeit briefly, reentered his life.

BOOK I

1.

Monday, August 23, 1993

MAJOR ANATOLY ILYICH SHUBENTSOV WAS DREAMING. IN THE dream he was at a family reunion, drinking toasts. He needed to piss. He went outside. It was cold. The snow on the ground was packed hard. Suddenly he was surrounded by a surging pack of red foxes. They snapped at his ankles and calves. They slashed at his hands as he attempted to beat them off. Drops of his blood speckled the snow. He reached for his gun to shoot them, but all he came up with was his penis. Then he heard shots. Who's shooting at me? he wondered in his dream. "Don't shoot!" he shouted, his eyes flying open, his body paralyzed.

I'm awake, he thought.

But the shooting continued.

Then he remembered where he was.

Shubentsov got out of bed slowly, his mouth dry from last night's cigarettes, his head sore from last night's vodka. The room was hot, stuffy. Sitting on the edge of the lumpy hotel mattress, he lit a Marlboro with a Zippo lighter. Then he walked to the window, opened it, and leaned out. The air was cool and sharp with the acrid tang of gunsmoke. Two stories below him, in the old Grozny city square, men were firing weapons into the air.

The cigarette tasted bad. He flicked it out the window. What a horrible place, he thought, scratching his ass. Grozny. How aptly named. Grozny, meaning terrible, menacing. Like the old czar Ivan Grozny, Ivan the Terrible. Grozny. What a terrible, menacing place to find oneself.

Grozny, in the shadows of the northern Caucusus, midway between the Black and Caspian Seas, capital of the new, self-proclaimed Chechnya Republic, was home to the largest open-air weapons market in the former Soviet Union. From all over Russia and the Independent States, from Eastern Europe and the Middle East, buyers came for weapons looted from the Red Army by its own men. On long tables set up in the cobble-stoned square beneath Shubentsov's window in the Hotel Kaukuz were AKM-model submachine guns going for 350,000 rubles and F1 hand grenades for 10,000. There were Kalashnikovs and Baikalof Ishevsk rifles. Cartridges for Makarov pistols, like the one Shubentsov carried, were 200 rubles a shell. There were howitzers and rocket launchers, and if you knew the right people, if you had the right connections and the cash, you could buy a fighter plane or a fully armed tactical helicopter.

Or something even bigger.

Disgusting, thought Shubentsov, rubbing his mouth with the back of his hand, staring out at the old town square full of newborn capitalists. There were Afghanis and Serbs, Armenians, Iranis, Iraqis, and Turks. There were Arabs and Asians and Africans. Not to mention the swarthy, always duplicitous Azeris, the frozen, snotty Estonians, and, he was sure, plenty of shrewd, conniving Jews. And last but certainly not least, the devil's own spawn, the Chechens.

Stalin had been right, Shubentsov thought, as he had

been right about so many things, to exile the Chechens to Kazakhstan after the Great Patriotic War. Send them east with the rest of the yellow, surging pagan hordes.

Khrushchev had been wrong to let them back. And now Yeltsin was wrong to allow them to imagine that their republic of thieves could go its own way.

Level the place, was Shubentsov's feeling. The Chechens were a cursed race.

Indeed, Shubentsov believed that all foreigners were vultures, forever circling over the Slav, waiting for him to die.

Shubentsov spat and watched the glob of spittle splat on the sidewalk.

Grozny was primarily a place to purchase weapons, but that did not mean you could not also buy tons of sugar, flour, vegetables, or meat—hijacked from trucks on their way north, usually with the connivance of the director of the *kolkhoz*, the collective farm. You could also buy heroin from the Ukraine's opium factories or hashish from Kazakhstan and Tajikistan. For everything, guns or food or drugs, the price was half of what it would be in the crumbling cities of the North—Volgograd, once Stalingrad; Moscow; and St. Petersburg, formerly Leningrad.

In the far corner of the square, beneath what used to be the Stavropol Oblast Party building—the one with the hammer-and-sickle sandblasted into the red brick—and was now a Pizza Hut and a store that sold truck and auto parts, an old Volga limousine disappeared in a rolling ball of flame. People scattered as pieces of the car rained down on the cobblestones. Nuts and bolts rattled against boarded-up windows. Not an uncracked pane of glass remained in Grozny's square.

Shubentsov shook his head. It's crazy, he thought. A nightmare.

Only three short years ago, Shubentsov, stationed in Tallinn, had been throwing Estonian nationalists into jail, defending the Union, the Soyuz. He was a soldier in the world's greatest army, in the service of the world's largest empire. He was proud of his uniform, proud of his heritage, and even his contempt for the general secretary, Mikhail Sergeyevich Gorbachev, had not lessened his loyalty to the Party.

Only three years, he thought. Now, look. Look at me. Sitting hung over in a shitty hotel room in Grozny, surrounded by Chechens and other Muslim slime, waiting for someone with a briefcase containing twenty grams of enriched uranium-238 oxides, stolen from the very nation Shubentsov had once so loyally served. A suitcase that should have been here two days ago.

And look at Grozny. Where were the police? Where was the army? Where was the Party? Who leads? Who follows? Who let loose this lawlessness, this chaos? In Shubentsov's wildest imaginings, in his late night drinking sessions with his brother officers, he could never have imagined . . .

That's what my dream means, he thought. The reunion, that's the Soyuz. That represents the time when the nation was together, a family. The foxes, they're the enemies of the state. They're the traitors—the democrats, the liberals, the reformers, the capitalist roaders. Yeltsin and Gorbachev, the Jews, the Americans and their CIA. Individually, they're all small men, all cowards. But working together, conspiring, they destroyed the nation, the people.

The Slav is trusting, Shubentsov thought. He cannot imagine treachery. Strength, he understands. Force, he understands. But the plots and schemes that come from weakness, from minds twisted by Jews and foreigners, that is alien to the great Russian soul. That is our fatal weakness.

Shubentsov caught his breath. His stomach cramped. He suddenly felt hot and began to sweat. Last night's dinner, last night's vodka, rushed up to fill his mouth. His stomach cramped again. He heaved, vomiting on the cobblestones beneath him.

A dark-skinned man—probably a Turk or one of their cousins, the Azeris—looked up at Shubentsov as the vomitus splashed on the street. "Pig!" he shouted, shaking his fist up at Shubentsov.

"Look who's talking," Shubentsov yelled back, spitting. He felt much better.

He went into the bathroom and turned on the shower. The water, of course, was cold, despite what the Kaukuz's manager had promised.

He showered in the cold water and shaved in the cold water. He put on his blue suit and left the room. He handed his key to the *dezhorna,* the key lady, and wished her a good morning, and she gave him his hotel card. He walked down the stairs and stopped at the front desk.

"Any messages?" he asked.

The man behind the desk was reading a newspaper. He glanced up at Shubentsov, shook his head, and went back to the paper.

For a moment Shubentsov was shocked that anyone, even a Chechen, could show such disrespect to his uniform. Then he remembered that he wasn't wearing one, and that rudeness was part of the new Russia, another Western import.

Briefly, as he left the hotel, he mourned the loss of his rank and position. When Gorbachev had recognized Estonian independence, beginning the dismantling of the nation Shubentsov's grandfather and father had shed blood to build and defend, Shubentsov's unit was told to stand in place, not to interfere with the nationalists, not to fraternize with the locals. When the paychecks stopped coming the men started to leave, taking their weapons with them. Some, indeed, took cars, trucks, and even half-tracks and tanks. What could Shubentsov do? Shoot them? He was outgunned. By the time the orders came six months later to fall back across the new border to Kolpino, outside St. Petersburg, and join the 143rd Artillery, no one knew in whose name the orders had been issued. And when he arrived in Kolpino, no one knew where the 143rd was, or even if it existed at all.

Shubentsov took the sleeper train to Moscow with the idea of resigning his commission. But there was no one to resign to and no one to pay him now that his unit had been dissolved. "Your pay envelope has been sent to the One forty-third," he was told, but no one could tell him where that was.

One night, at a party given by some officers similarly separated from units that no longer existed except on paper, a man named Vladimir was talking about Pamyat, the Memory Society. Shubentsov, of course, had heard of Pamyat, and he knew that many officers belonged to it. But he had always held himself aloof. To Shubentsov, Pamyat smacked of buffoonery, and he knew that as well as being rabidly anti-Semitic, it was also anti-Party. But Vladimir was an impressive man. And the Party, incredibly, had been outlawed in Russia. So when Vladimir told him about a Pamyat meeting the next night, Shubentsov decided to attend.

At the meeting, the man Vladimir explained how Gorbachev had been a CIA plant and Boris Nikolayevich Yeltsin an American dupe.

"Our homeland is occupied by Fascists, capitalists, and criminals using democracy as a disguise for their treachery," Vladimir said. "We must face the fact that we Russians are a defeated people. There was a war with the West, and we lost. It is bitter to recognize defeat, but until we do, until we understand the reality of our situation, we cannot make correct decisions about our future. But once we acknowledge our defeated condition, we can begin to act appropriately.

"First, of course, we must choose. Individually, each person must choose. Will you be a resistance fighter, or will you be a collaborator? Once we make that individual choice, we can begin to act collectively. And that is what Pamyat is for."

Vladimir was the first person Shubentsov had met who was able to make sense of the catastrophe that had befallen them all. The disintegration of their country did not happen accidentally. It was not mischance, bad luck, or some mysterious, fatal weakness in the *apparat*. There had been a war, and the bad guys had won. As a soldier, Shubentsov could understand defeat.

As Shubentsov listened, Vladimir described the hundreds of ways in which the Americans had sabotaged the Soyuz. He described the vast number of arms and the staggering sums of money the CIA had sent to the Afghani fascists to kill Soviet soldiers and demoralize the Soviet military. He described the decades of economic warfare—the trade embargoes that had deprived Soviet industry of new computer technologies, dooming it to inefficiency, while cheap Western grain sabotaged the agricultural collectives. And as that was going on, the ruinous arms race bankrupted the state and the Party.

Most intriguing of all to Shubentsov, Vladimir revealed the existence of a Zionist fifth column that spied for the CIA inside Russia, that infiltrated and manipulated the Party, and that eventually raised Mikhail Sergeyevich Gorbachev, the great traitor, to the supreme position, from where he conspired to destroy the Soyuz at the behest of his Zionist and CIA controllers.

"And where is Mikhail Sergeyevich now?" Vladimir asked rhetorically. "He is in New York, drinking champagne and making speeches, while Boris Yeltsin checks with Washington before he wipes his ass. And Washington checks with Tel Aviv before it wipes its own."

After the meeting, Shubentsov told Vladimir that he wished to be of service. They went to a restaurant, ate and drank, and then went back to Vladimir's apartment. The five-room flat, which Vladimir apparently had to himself, impressed Shubentsov almost as much as its address on the Frunzenskaya Embankment on the Moscow River, across from Gorky Park, a neighborhood with good air reserved for Party officials and their relations. Although Vladimir declined to speak of his past, Shubentsov assumed that he must have been something high ranking in the KGB. He carried himself with a military bearing, and he spoke of top Party officials, famous, powerful men, with a familiar contempt.

They ate and drank some more as Shubentsov opened up his heart and let the blood of his sadness flow freely. They discussed Russia's need for a strong leader who could restore the nation to greatness. They discussed the inevitability of a purge to rid the nation of foreign plunderers and Jews.

Shubentsov offered to join Pamyat. Vladimir told him not to bother. He told him that Pamyat was a tool, nothing more, and one that would soon be disposed of.

That night, Shubentsov slept on Vladimir's couch. In the morning, he began working for him.

Now, Major Anatoly Ilyich Shubentsov, for the third day in a row, went to the small cafe off the square to wait for a man with a suitcase. The shots and explosions from the square echoed down Grozny's narrow old streets.

He ordered a German beer and felt better after drinking it. He had three cups of good, strong tea, smoked a half dozen cigarettes, and ate a roll with sweet butter and raspberry jam. Then it was noon. He got up, stretched, and went for a short stroll in the square. He returned to the cafe and had a knockwurst and another beer.

Around two, Shubentsov saw a rather shabbily dressed young man carrying a leather suitcase slightly larger than a doctor's bag turn the corner and walk toward the cafe. Shubentsov caught the man's eye, and the man approached, looking neither left nor right.

"Are you Major Tolya?"

Shubentsov nodded.

"Then this is yours," the young man said, placing the leather bag on an empty chair.

"Sit down," Shubentsov said. "Have a beer."

"All right," the young man said.

Shubentsov and the young man drank several beers and then began drinking vodka. The boy, Shubentsov soon learned, was named Georgy Kaurovsky. He had been a soldier, and then, when his unit had been demobilized, he had found a job as a guard at the Institute of Power Engineering Problems outside Minsk. The trip from the institute to Grozny had been hard on the young man's nerves, and he was tremendously grateful to Shubentsov for having relieved him of his burden.

Shubentsov took the bag, handed the young man an envelope containing five thousand rubles, and they made a date to eat dinner together that evening.

The same clerk at the desk looked up from what Shubentsov presumed to be the same newspaper.

"You had a call from Moscow," the clerk said.

"When?" asked Shubentsov.

The clerk looked at a piece of paper. "This morning," he said. "They left a number. You can call from the phone over there." The clerk waved a limp hand toward a red telephone kiosk across the street from the hotel.

"I'll call from my room," said Shubentsov.

The clerk shook his head. "Our lines went down at noon," he said. "Happens all the time. Actually, I don't really know if the kiosk phone is working, but it usually is."

Typical, thought Shubentsov, turning away. The whole country has gone to hell, and Grozny is one of its lowest circles.

The phone was working. Shubentsov dialed the number. The man he knew only as Vladimir answered.

"The package has arrived," said Shubentsov.

"Good," Vladimir said. "Take it to Zagorsk."

"All right," said Shubentsov.

"And clean up before you leave," Vladimir said.

"All right," said Shubentsov.

That night, young Georgy Kaurovsky ate and drank well, enjoying Shubentsov's company. They talked about army life, and they talked about the new hard times. Later, as Kaurovsky was urinating against the wall behind the restaurant where they had dined, Shubentsov cut his throat.

Early the next morning, Shubentsov caught an Aeroflot flight to Moscow, then drove to the monastery Sergeev Posad in the small town of Zagorsk, just north of the city. He left the bag with one of the brothers and returned to Vladimir's apartment to report.

On Saturday, September 25, the palm-size canister of fissionable material that had been in the late Georgy Kaurovsky's battered leather bag, now secreted beneath the false bottom of a beautifully decorated lacquered box, arrived under diplomatic seal in New York. A short, balding man was to deliver it to Sotheby's the following Wednesday, where it was to be auctioned off as part of a collection of Russian treasures from the Sergeev Posad monastery in Zagorsk, thereby establishing an irrefutably legitimate provenance on paper if anyone—customs, Interpol, the CIA—cared to look.

On Wednesday, the auctioneer at Sotheby's waited until one o'clock for the box to appear.

It never did.

He waited for the buyer to appear.

He never did, either.

The auctioneer turned to the description of Lot 57 in his catalog: "Lacquered Box, by Ivan Golikov, 1886–1937. *From the Monastery at Sergeev Posad, in Zagorsk.* A bear hunt on the sides; pastoral on the top. In black, gold, green, and red. After the 1917 Bolshevik uprising, the production of icons was for-bidden, and many artists, especially in the Golden Ring town of Palekh, took to painting lacquered boxes. After varnishing the box, the artist painted their scenes of battles, hunts, and fairy tales and then applied a series of translucent coats of paint over the finished design, thereby creating the brilliant shine that marks the genre. Ivan Golikov, of Palekh, was a master of this classic Russian art form. $5,000–$7,500."

The auctioneer shrugged, crossed Lot 57 off his list, and went on with the sale.

2.

Sunday, September 26, 1993

"THE PREGNANT GIRLS ARE MAKING BROWNIES," THE PROFESSOR said after Aleksandr Volkavitch Eugenev let him into his second-floor apartment at 3901 Fifth Street, two blocks off Brighton Beach Avenue in Brooklyn, one block from the ocean.

"So?" asked Sasha, exiting from the alt.sex sig on the USENET, where he had been having a real-time conversation with Lola from San Diego, a self-described "body shaper" whom Sasha had met electronically on the Amazon Women Forum while surfing the Internet. They spoke every few days, with Lola describing graphically what she would do to and for Sasha if they ever met. Sasha suspected that Lola was lonely, fat, and pimply, but in cyberspace she was the woman of his dreams, and he was the man of hers. The trick, thought Sasha, was to keep their love in cyberspace, where you could be whoever and whatever you wanted to be.

He returned to the big white leather vibrating recliner, where, before logging on to the computer, he had been listening to Rod Stewart's *Greatest Hits* on his headphones while eating a bag of popcorn and fiddling with the autofocus on his

31

new Nikon 5005. Sasha had never owned a camera before, and he had no real desire to make photographs. But the camera had looked so beautiful—so sleek, so black, so modern—that he'd just had to have it.

He had bought the Nikon the day before with the six-hundred-dollar commission he had received for delivering his old Moscow friend Henry Tepperman's tiny Pissarro print to Sotheby's for auction. The print had fetched six thousand in a sale of minor Impressionists—it was, everybody told him, a very soft market. Six thousand had been the asking price, and the first bid had stood up. It wasn't big money, but Sasha was always glad to go to Sotheby's (it made him feel rich) and always glad to help Tepperman. After all, it was Tepperman who had given Sasha his start in the currency business, and it was Tepperman who had helped Sasha emigrate. Perhaps someday Tepperman would let him represent a bigger work, a Matisse oil or even a Picasso. Then Sasha's ten percent would amount to something.

"They're naked," said the Professor, whose real name was Moses Filonovsky. He was called the Professor because he was universally deemed not to be terribly bright. He was, however, an excellent forger, which was why he was part of Sasha's informal gang, which included Sergei Pantera, a thief; Ivan Siskin, a good con man; Sam Goldman, an American-born fence who received most of the goods Sasha peddled; and David Gatlober, an Odessan thug who was, on those rare occasions when he needed it, Sasha's muscle.

"You can see them from the alley if you get right next to your building and jump up," the Professor said helpfully.

"Christ," said Sasha, balling up the popcorn bag and shooting off the recliner to run to the window.

"I guess they're hot," the Professor said behind him. "It's terribly hot outside. I'm sweating like a pig."

Sure enough, one floor below his, across the alley separating the two apartment buildings, Sasha could see Tatyana, Semka, and Yulia standing by their kitchen table, their tits big, their bellies bigger, all three naked except for the bikini panties that barely covered their crotches.

The Professor came up behind Sasha and stood on tiptoes to peer over his shoulder. "That one," the Professor said, "the short brunette, she must be carrying triplets. Look at the size of her."

"Twins," said Sasha, annoyed. What did the girls think they were doing, parading around like that? A neighbor complains, the cops come, the cops turn them over to Immigration, and Sasha has to explain to his clients why they will have to wait a while longer to adopt those beautiful—and, most important, white—Russian babies. And what if those nice Jewish couples want their money back? And what if they go to the cops?

"Motherfucker," said Sasha, grabbing his cellular phone off the coffee table and punching in the number for the apartment across the alley. Of course, the line was busy.

"Motherfucker," Sasha said again. "You," he said to the Professor, "use my shower. You seriously stink. And I don't want to see any towels lying around. Hang them back up and then go. And don't touch any of my stuff. I'm going over there right now, tell them to put on some clothes."

"Too bad," the Professor said softly as the door slammed and the sound of Sasha galloping down the stairs echoed through the building. That Sasha, he thought, turning back to the window, always running. With him, it was all business all the time.

Outside, the moist wind off the ocean blew down Fifth Street and played with the baby-fine, dirty-blond hair that Sasha was beginning to lose. He had been given a prescription for Rogaine by a friendly doctor, and a friendly pharmacist on Brighton Beach Avenue had given him the bottle for half price (billing the insurance company for the full cost, of course). Still, Sasha thought, delicately touching the top of his head with his fingertips, feeling for the bare scalp, it was expensive, and it probably wouldn't work.

In the fourteen years since he had left Kolpashevo, Aleksandr Volkavitch Eugenev had added some weight to his six-foot-tall frame. At one hundred and ninety pounds, he was now almost stocky, his shoulders broad and his hairless arms thick and muscular in the red-and-yellow Hawaiian shirt he wore tucked into his tight white linen Joseph Aboud jeans. Like Magnum, P.I., he told himself. Only the two packs of cigarettes he smoked every day, the fires of his hyperactive metabolism, and his vanity kept him from getting fat.

So far, the girls still loved him. His small eyes were very blue, and as was often the case with the very myopic, they appeared soft and romantic whenever he took off his rimless, rose-tinted glasses. Now, of course, he was wearing his beloved and nearly opaque Porsche sunglasses, the ones he loved so much that he wore all year, even in the winter's dark, the ones he loved so much that he'd had his name inscribed on the frame. Behind them, his face was classically Slavic: high cheekbones, a broad, unlined forehead, a wide jaw that came to a foxy point at the chin, a long, thin, slightly crooked and hooked nose with a bump that was a permanent reminder of his beating in Kolpashevo. Sasha liked the way he looked. Not like a Jew. Like a real Russian. Or like a boxer, he often thought, with a degree in philosophy.

He plucked a Camel Lights from the pack in his breast pocket and lit up. He looked up and down Fifth Street, from the boardwalk that ran down to Coney Island to the El that snaked above Brighton Beach Avenue, casting it into perpetual shadow. It was one o'clock, and Fifth Street was almost deserted. The old Jews would be either at the YM-YWHA or in their dark, air-conditioned apartments, ten miles and an hour's subway ride removed from Manhattan's frightening crowds. The *stilyags,* the young Russian dudes—who, thanks to perestroika and glasnost had poured into Brighton Beach throughout the eighties, when the little neighborhood's Russian population had risen to a densely packed thirty thousand—would be either in the cafes, eating, smoking, drinking, and playing the video poker machines, or taking advantage of the surprising heat by working on their tans at the Brighton Beach Tennis and Racquet Club. The tourists, lured to this backwater by a recent spate of newspaper and television stories about its burgeoning Russian community, never left the avenue.

Sasha entered the dark lobby of the building next door to his and rang apartment 3G—three shorts and a long. The door buzzed open and Sasha, too impatient to wait for the elevator, took the stairs up to the third floor two at a time.

The door opened a crack and Yulia Rabinovich's sweet oval face, framed by black curly hair, peeked out at him. She smiled.

"Sasha! Wait a minute while I put something on. Tatya! Semi!" she called into the kitchen. "Shurik is here," she said, using the affectionate diminutive for Sasha, which was also street slang for an American. (In Russian, the letters that formed U.S.A., when spoken aloud, sounded like Sasha.)

"Which Shurik?" a voice called from inside.

"Just open the motherfucking door," said Sasha.

Yulia slid back the chain and Sasha pushed through. Yulia stepped back and covered her nipples with her hands. "What's the matter, Sasha?" she asked.

"Oh, so now you're modest," Sasha said. "Two minutes ago you're giving the whole neighborhood a show, but now you're modest. What the hell did you think you were doing?"

"Doing? What was I doing?"

Tatyana and Semka emerged from the kitchen, wearing

gray City College T-shirts that came almost to their knees. Tatyana had a cigarette dangling from her lips.

"And you, Tatya," Sasha said. "These other two are children. You're a grown woman, a mother. What are you doing, running around like this is a whorehouse? And why are you smoking?" he said, reaching out to take the butt from Tatyana's mouth.

"Screw you, Sasha," said Tatyana, slapping his hand away. She took a deep drag and then exhaled, blowing smoke into Sasha's face.

"Nice," Sasha said. "Now your baby is coughing. I can hear him cough."

"What? You think the smoke goes into my belly? How does the smoke get into my belly, Sasha? Tell me."

"Smoking's no good for the baby. It stunts his growth."

"Jesus, it's Mister America," said Tatyana. "You're becoming crazy like all the Americans. Anyway, you smoke."

"I'm not having a baby."

"Yes, you are. You're buying them."

"That's right. And I don't want you smoking. I want my baby pink and fat. I don't want him being born with a cigarette in his mouth. And I don't want you running around naked."

Tatyana, a tall, heroically built blonde in her mid-thirties who, as a teenager in Minsk, had been a promising high jumper and who, in fact, had once posed as a model for a poster portraying Belorussian athletes as Heroes of Soviet Labor, pulled her T-shirt up over her swollen stomach and put the cigarette to her distended belly button. "Have a puff, little one," she said.

"Very funny," said Sasha.

"Uncle Sasha!" Tatyana's two-and-a-half-year-old, Michael, named for Michael Jordan, came careering into the living room, wearing only his diaper. He had tight golden curls, copper skin, and huge brown eyes. He looked like a representative of some new, better race. He came to a sudden stop five feet from Sasha.

"Funny face," he ordered.

Sasha bugged his eyes and puffed his cheeks. Michael screamed and then fell backward, waving his feet in the air.

"I fall down," he said proudly.

Sasha grabbed him off the floor and held him over his head, the better to nibble his belly. Michael shrieked joyfully.

"Sure, you get him excited, then you leave and it takes an hour for him to calm down," Tatyana said.

"The girls will go crazy for you, right, Michael?" said Sasha, putting the boy down. It was true, he thought. The boy was beautiful. But if the new bun in Tatya's oven turns out like this one, half black, I'm screwed.

"Come here, Michael," said Tatyana. "Look," she said to Sasha, pulling down Michael's diaper. "Heat rash. It's like a sauna in here. And it's your fault. Poor Michael wakes up in a pool of sweat. The girls and I are dying of the heat. You've got an air conditioner. Everyone in America has an air conditioner. Why don't you put one in here? I'll tell you why. You're too fucking cheap."

"Cheap? Cheap?" Sasha said, only pretending to be angry. He loved the boy, and he loved the mother. He loved her full lips, her broad shoulders, her runner's legs, and he loved the way she stood up to him. "Who pays for this apartment?" he demanded. "Who's paying for the food? Who's paying for the doctor? Who bought you those nice T-shirts? Without me, where would you be? Getting beat up by some black bastard or getting an abortion from some butcher. You'd probably be bleeding to death right now. All of you."

"And how much are you getting for our babies?" Tatyana asked. "Twenty thousand? Twenty-five? That's sixty or seventy from the three of us. More for Yulia's twins. What's the rent here? Don't lie, Sasha. I can see you making up a lie. Whatever it is, the rent-support money you're getting from the city more than pays for it."

"You don't know my expenses," said Sasha, wondering who was talking to Tatya about his business.

"I know that dope fiend quack you take us to is paying you for sending patients to him. What's he paying you, Sasha? One hundred a patient? Two hundred?"

In fact, Dr. Evgeny Andreevitch Bekker, Sasha's old friend from Kolpashevo, was paying him one hundred and twenty-five per patient. The good doctor then turned around and billed Medicare for thousands for ultrasound procedures he barely knew how to perform, let alone interpret. And, thought Sasha, Bekker was probably blabbing to Tatya, his tongue loosened by dope and his desire to get into her pants.

"So suddenly you're quiet," said Tatyana. "So suddenly you're thinking that maybe an air conditioner might be a good investment, yes?"

"You think you know so much," said Sasha.

"That's because I do," Tatyana said. "I'm not one of your little American girls, your dollies. You remember that, Aleksandr Volkavitch."

"I'll look around for an air conditioner," said Sasha. "In the meantime, please, for me, don't smoke. It's bad for Michael, too. And don't walk around naked. The last thing we need is some old babushka complaining to the cops. All right? All right. We're all friends again, okay?"

Sasha kissed Semka on the cheek, Yulia on her forehead, and Tatyana's lips. She stuck her tongue into his mouth, then pulled away and laughed. He picked up Michael.

"Be a lion," ordered Michael.

Sasha roared, the boy laughed, and Sasha left, checking his pink gold antique Gruen Curvex watch, his favorite. It was almost one-thirty and he could feel droplets of sweat coursing down his spine. It had been stifling in the girls' apartment. Maybe he could ask around, find someone to steal an air conditioner for him.

He was supposed to meet Sergei Pantera, known as the Panther, at Nathan's in Coney Island at two-thirty. The Panther had come by a necklace, and Sasha had arranged with a jeweler to appraise it at five thousand, at least five times its real value. Then the Panther had steered his mark to a cafe, where he'd introduced him to Sasha, and Sasha had offered to buy it for six. So the sucker had bought the necklace from the Panther for four. And, of course, Sasha had reneged. The sucker was apoplectic, but what could he do? Go to the cops and tell them that he had, in effect, tried to fence stolen jewelry and gotten stiffed? Now Sasha was to meet the Panther to receive both his and the jeweler's commission for their parts in the sting—a grand each. He had an hour to kill, so he headed up Fifth Street to Brighton Beach Avenue, thinking furiously.

Yulia was due in three weeks, which meant that the Nowinskis, the teachers from Flatbush, would be making their second payment of ten thousand then. Tatyana was wrong about that; he wasn't making an extra nickel off the twins. In fact, he had been lucky to find a couple willing to take them.

He owed the nurse at Coney Island Hospital who had steered the Nowinskis to him, and he would owe Bekker for signing the birth certificates. He owed the girls, of course, and he would also owe the Greater Horizons Adoption Agency of Flatbush, which was supplying him with the legal paperwork for the city and state.

He also owed Vladimir Lipsky about five thousand in bad bets on the Mets and Yanks.

Well, he could put Lipsky off with a grand. And Gooden was pitching today. Should he double up on the Doc? He loved the Doc.

Sasha set fire to another Camel. So many things to think

about. So many people to grease. But you're hot, he assured himself. You're hot stuff.

Could he cut out the agency? The Professor could forge the papers. Sasha shook his head. Too risky. Not worth it. He stood to make nine thousand off all four babies after expenses. Not bad, he thought, but hard work. Of course, if Tatyana's baby came out like Michael, as he suspected it might (Tatyana almost always dated black men), he'd be lucky to break even.

That Tatyana. He imagined himself chewing on her lower lip. He imagined himself riding her, her thighs wrapped around his waist. He felt himself getting an erection.

If that baby's black, he thought, I'll break her neck.

"No, you won't," he muttered to himself. "You'll yell and scream and that will be that."

The rails from the El above painted Brighton Beach Avenue with zebra stripes. The street was crowded with shoppers, vendors, and, recently, tourists.

In recent years, Brighton Beach—formerly a sort of terra incognita snuggling up against the ocean, the last stop on the ancient elevated Brighton Beach subway line—had become a mecca for tourists looking for Russian color. They'd order blinis and vodka in the cafes; they'd visit the Odessa, Brighton's biggest and most expensive nightclub, for overpriced, greasy chicken Kiev and bad disco music. They'd cruise the street, shopping for Soviet memorabilia and Russian tchotchkes. Every other tiny, cramped store sold red-and-gold pins enameled with the hammer and sickle and wooden *matryoshka* dolls with Lenin inside of Marx, Stalin inside of Lenin, all the way up (or down) to Gorbachev and Yeltsin.

And then, thought Sasha, it stopped. After Gorbachev, after seventy-five years of communism, nothing. Chaos. Nothing left but cheap trinkets sold by stateless emigrants.

Oh, well, Sasha thought. The Soyuz deserved nothing better.

And a thief's country is anywhere he can steal.

He stopped in front of the International, flicked his cigarette butt into the gutter, and stepped inside. He loved the
smells of the sprawling delicatessen with its salamis hanging
from the ceiling and its gigantic grills cooking up beef ribs,
veal cutlets, and chicken breasts. He loved looking at the fresh
salmon, sturgeon, and trout basking on ice. The International
was also a great place for meeting girls, especially American
girls. Sasha would zero in on a pretty young American who
seemed to be alone, catch her eye, and then, introducing himself as a former dissident, he would suggest that they go someplace quiet—have something to eat and a drink at the
Georgian Cafe, or the Cafe Arbat, or even the Odessa—and he
would tell her about how his nose had been broken by a KGB
thug while he was demonstrating for freedom and justice in
the former Soviet Union.

And afterward, back in his apartment, he'd tell her stories
about the Gulag and let her touch his scars.

There, for example, in the center of the store, where cardboard boxes containing jars of Hungarian sour cherries, Croatian plum preserves, Bulgarian red peppers, and Polish
eggplant paste were piled high, was a tall, slender, broad-
shouldered, and long-necked brunette in billowing khaki
shorts, sandals, and a white T-shirt. She was reading the labels
and writing something down in a small notebook.

Sasha disapproved of her baggy shorts and her baggy T-
shirt. They probably came from the Gap. He'd never understand why Americans wanted to dress like bums. Look at this
one. Great legs. Small breasts, but good and high. Not wearing a bra today. She had a wonderful body, his type, why should
she want to hide it? She obviously had money—you could tell
by her posture—why didn't she buy better clothes?

If she were with me, Sasha thought, she would dress

right. I'd take her to Manhattan, to Bendel's or to Blooming-
dale's.

He walked over to where the woman was standing and
picked up a jar of pickled tomatoes produced by the Agro-
Industrial Complex of Tiraspol, Moldavia. The label, in English, read "Best after a shot of vodka."

"Look at this," he said to her, noting that her eyes were a
brilliant blue and that they were almost level with his. "You
see? That's an agricultural cooperative. They are allowed now
to sell to the West. Before, not. You see this? 'Best after a shot
of vodka'? They are learning now about advertising. It is funny
to you, of course, and now it is funny to me, but in the former
Soviet Union this is considered very sophisticated advertising.
Of course, the Moldavians are always very sophisticated, very
European. You know where is Tiraspol?"

"No, I don't," the woman said.

"It is on the Ukrainian border. A few kilometers north
and west of Odessa. South of Kishinev, the Moldavian capital.
You see? Close to Romania. That is why they are so sophisticated."

"Thank you very much," the woman said. "And you are?"

"Aleksandr. My friends call me Sasha. You can please to
call me Sasha."

"Thank you, Sasha. That's a very common name for Russians, isn't it? I don't mean common in the sense of ordinary. I
mean—"

"That's okay. Everybody is named Sasha. I know nine, ten
people named Sasha, maybe more."

"My name is Madeline. Madeline Malloy. Everyone calls
me Maddy. That *is* a common name."

"I think not. I think it is a wonderful name. Maddy Malloy. Maddy Malloy. It is like music, like poetry."

Malloy laughed. "Thanks," she said. "It's Irish. My grand-
parents came from Ireland."

"I love the Irish," said Sasha. "They are beautiful, beautiful people. And you are writing what, Maddy Malloy? A shopping list?"

"I'm taking notes about what's in the store," the woman said.

"For what?" Sasha asked. "Wait, let me guess. You are working for the city, for the health committee. You are seeing that they follow the law in here."

"No," said Malloy, "but it's interesting that you should say that. Russians always seem to think that every American is working for the government. How long have you been in America, Sasha?"

Sasha saw Viktor Shapiro, the International's manager—a short, stocky man in a pink Ralph Lauren polo shirt and gray gabardine pants—approaching them. Shapiro was more than just the International's manager; he was also a part owner and also a part owner of the Odessa. And a friend, Sasha knew, of Ebzi Agron, Brighton Beach's *batyushka*—the boss, the Godfather, of the Russian Mob in Brooklyn.

"Hello, Sasha," Shapiro said in Russian. "Who's the girl?"

"I'm trying to find out," said Sasha.

"What's she writing?" Shapiro asked.

"I'm trying to find that out, too."

"I don't like it. What are you writing?" asked Shapiro, switching to English.

"This is Viktor," Sasha told Malloy. "He is the manager here."

"Good," Malloy said. "My name is Madeline Malloy and I'm a reporter for the *Daily News*. I'm writing a story for the feature section, about the Russian community in Brighton Beach. Can I talk to you about your store? It's fantastic. A wonderful place."

"You must have permission," said Shapiro.

"To talk to you?" Malloy asked.

"Yes. You must go now. You cannot write here without permission."

"Oh, come on, Viktor," Sasha said in Russian. "She's just a girl who wants to write a pretty story about all the happy Russians happily working in the wonderful and happy United States of America."

"Piss. I don't care what she is," Shapiro said. "She can't come in here, write things, I don't know what. Who knows what she is, what she writes in her notebook? Get her out of here."

"Come," said Sasha, taking Malloy's elbow, feeling the small bones. "He is getting angry. You can come back, talk to him later."

"But who do I have to get permission from?" Malloy asked Shapiro, shaking free of Sasha's hand. "The owner? What's his name? Can I call you, Viktor, make an appointment to see you? What's your last name?"

Shapiro turned in exasperation to Sasha, said, "Piss," and then stalked away.

"We better go," said Sasha.

Malloy slipped her notebook into her shoulder bag. "I don't understand," she said. "I just wanted to ask him about the store, who shops here, where the food comes from. Who do I have to ask for permission? Permission to talk to the manager of a delicatessen? It's ridiculous."

"Yes, ridiculous," said Sasha as they walked out of the International. "But, you see, that is the way it is with us. We are suspicious of every person. In the former Soviet Union, that is the way it was. Who knew who could be KGB? Myself, I have never trusted no one. Of course, I was political. Viktor, he is just a petit bourgeois, a refusenik, sure, but only to make money. A real Jew, you know."

"And you're not Jewish?" Malloy asked, sniffing an angle: Russian anti-Semitism.

"Yes, I am a Jew, of course. Everyone in Brighton is a Jew whether they are or not. For years, the only way to get out of the Soyuz was to be a Jew, so everyone became a Jew. Understand?"

"Are you a Jew?"

"Yes. I am. Really. So," Sasha said as they stood in front of the store on Brighton Beach Avenue, "Madeline Malloy." He looked her up and down behind his Porsche sunglasses. Very nice, he thought. A writer, an intellectual. Very sexy. So tall. She'd look good in something tight, something off the shoulder. Lovely shoulders. And a skirt, of course, for those legs. Lips a little too thin, maybe, but that's good, too. That means she's starved for it. All the men she knows are journalists, intellectuals, and they treat her like a man, not a woman. The trick with this one, thought Sasha, is to treat her like a woman.

He fished a cigarette out of his pocket and lit it, registering the grimace that crossed Malloy's face.

"You don't like these?" he asked.

"Not particularly."

"This is very strange in America," said Sasha, throwing the cigarette away. "In Russia, all I want is American cigarettes. Russian cigarettes taste like turds. But I come to America, everyone hates cigarettes. They make laws against them. People look at you like you're a murderer if you smoke in the cafes, in the restaurant. It's crazy. America needs a Martin Luther King for people who smoke."

Malloy laughed and jotted something down in her notebook. Sasha liked her laugh.

"You are writing that down?" Sasha asked. "So you are a reporter. That is seriously interesting. I myself was a journalist, in Moscow, at *Ogonyuk,* a very serious, very respected journal. I could maybe help you with this story you are writing. I know everyone in Brooklyn. Maybe you and I could go someplace, have something to eat, talk about this."

Madeline Malloy hadn't liked the way Sasha had grabbed her arm, and certainly he was coming on too strong. But he wasn't bad looking, and Russians were, after all, famously demonstrative. He could make a colorful character for her story. Already he had given her a good line, the thing about Martin Luther King.

"Wait," said Sasha, looking at his watch. Damn, he was late. And the Panther was such an irritable asshole. "I am sorry, Maddy Malloy. I have to go someplace now for business. Look, I can telephone you. Give me your telephone number. I will call you; we will meet together, and I can tell you all about Brighton Beach, all about the Russians here."

"And what is your business, Sasha?"

"You are going to write that down, too?"

"I don't have to."

"I am a businessman. It is very seriously boring. I would not bore you with it. But I am also writing a book."

"Really? What is it about?"

"It is a *roman,* yes? No. A novel. It is about a Russian who fights all his life against the Communists and then comes to America and falls in love with an American girl, a newspaper reporter, but she betrays him and he is murdered, but he still loves her."

Malloy laughed again. "You just made that up."

"Yes," Sasha said, smiling. "Maybe I did. But now maybe I will do it. So. Your telephone? At home?"

"I don't think so," Malloy said. "You can reach me at the newspaper. Call the main number. The best time is in the morning. And give me your number."

"Oh, I should give you my number, but you won't give me yours. Is that fair?"

"Yes," said Malloy. "It's an American kind of fairness."

Sasha gave her his number. "You know, if you gave me your number at home, it would be much better," he said.

"Who knows if I can get through to you at the newspaper? I know newspapers. They are all drunk there. Sometimes they don't take the message; sometimes the message is wrong. No. I've got it. Give me your E-mail address."

"I don't have one."

"How is that possible?"

"I'm just a Luddite, I guess."

"What is a Luddite?"

"Never mind. We have voice mail at the paper. I'll get your message."

"Okay," said Sasha, hailing a cab. "I will call you tomorrow. The *Daily News*. I remember."

A cab swung out of traffic toward the sidewalk. "Tomorrow for sure," Sasha called out, stepping into the street and opening the taxi's door. "I will call you tomorrow, Maddy Malloy," he said. "Take me to Nathan's," he said to the cabdriver. Sasha sat on the edge of the seat and lit a cigarette.

"Wait!" Madeline Malloy called out as the cab pulled into the traffic.

She hadn't gotten his last name.

◈   ◈   ◈

It was broiling inside the cab, and Sasha knew that if he leaned back, he would stick to the seat. He checked the cabbie's license. A Russian, of course. Too cheap to spring for air-conditioning, afraid that it would cut back on the mileage. "Fast," said Sasha. It was almost three. The Panther would be pissed.

The cabbie stomped on the accelerator. They roared down Brighton Beach Avenue, weaving through traffic underneath the El to Ocean Parkway, turned left on Ocean. The cab cut across two lanes and jerked to a stop in front of Nathan's, throwing a sweating Sasha forward and then jerking him back.

Fucking Russian drivers, he thought. There was a big

market in Brighton for forged Russian driver's licenses, because if you presented one to the Department of Motor Vehicles, the city of New York, in its infinite stupidity, would give you one of theirs—without a test—in exchange. The result was good business for the Professor (who was getting $350 to $500 per license) and the chaos that resulted from thousands of Russians learning to drive in Brooklyn's already lunatic traffic.

Sasha paid the driver and got out of the cab. The sidewalk in front of Nathan's was jammed with people squeezing the last juice out of the summer, but Sasha immediately spotted the Panther leaning against the counter, a hot dog loaded with sauerkraut in one hand and a large paper cup of beer in the other. A short, bald man stood next to him. The man wore very dark sunglasses. In one hand he held a beer; in the other, a canvas bag, which, Sasha noted, came from L. L. Bean.

"You're fucking late," the Panther said by way of greeting.

Sasha didn't respond, eyeing the Panther's companion. He looked familiar.

"You don't remember me, Aleksandr Volkavitch?" asked the man. "Well, of course, a lot of time has passed."

The man took off his glasses. His eyes were crossed.

"Boris the Kike," Sasha said. "My God. You're bald."

The two men embraced, Boris spilling half his beer.

"And you're getting fat," said Boris. "You didn't have that gut in Kolpashevo."

"So, what are you doing with this asshole?" Sasha asked, nodding at the Panther, who scowled.

"I've spent the whole day with him in that hole he calls an apartment, drinking beer and listening to his girlfriend complain. He told me he'd be meeting you here. I wanted to surprise you," said Boris.

"I'm sure this is all very touching," said the Panther, "but I am not a sentimentalist. Anyway, I thought we had business to conduct, Sasha. You see," he said, turning to Boris, "your old friend has become so rich he can afford to be late even when he's collecting his own money. If you don't need the money, asshole," he said over his shoulder to Sasha, "I do."

"I'm sorry to have kept you waiting, Sergei Mikhailovich."

"So you do want the money. Really? I thought, Sasha, he's such a rich man now, he's decided he doesn't need it. You want it? Why don't you ask me for it nicely?"

"Fuck you, Panther," said Sasha. "I'm thirty goddamn minutes late. Why do you have to be such a prick?"

"Fuck me? Fuck you. I don't have time to piss away waiting for some Yid cocksucker."

"Just give me the two thousand, Panther."

Sergei Pantera stuffed the rest of his hot dog into his mouth, swallowed, and drained his beer. He belched, crumpled the cup, and, squaring his shoulders, stared hard at Sasha. "Now you can wait for me," he said, and pushed past Sasha into the crowd.

"Goddamn," said Sasha. "I'm sorry," he said to Boris. "Panther . . ."

"I know," Boris said. "America hasn't changed him. Still a typical Russian. Stupid. Drunk. Difficult. Do you want to go after him?"

"Yes," said Sasha. "He can be very hard to find, and I need the money."

"I'll go with you."

They plunged into the polyglot mob in front of Nathan's —Puerto Rican couples holding hands; black teenagers in baseball caps, tank tops, and colorful baggy shorts; old men and women; Russians and Chinese and Haitians and Koreans, all sweating in the Indian summer Coney Island sun.

Sasha saw Panther turn down West Eighth Street, toward the famous Coney Island boardwalk. It was almost impossible to gain on him in the Sunday crowd without knocking people over.

"So," said Boris, "you took my advice and looked up Henry."

"Your advice?" Sasha said. "Oh, back in Kolpashevo. Yes, I did."

"Now Henry is so rich you wouldn't believe it. He has cars, bodyguards, apartments all over. In the best buildings. On the river, even. He has a *dacha* that used to belong to some Party big shot. Women. He may even run for mayor."

"That would be something." Sasha laughed.

"I'm not kidding," Boris said.

"Right."

"So don't believe me. A fantastic place," said Boris, sweating, his stubby legs pumping in order to keep up with Sasha, his canvas bag banging against his legs.

"Coney Island?"

"Everything," Boris said, his left arm describing an arc that connected the Wonder Wheel, the Tornado, the grim concrete slabs of the Coney Island housing projects, the Atlantic Ocean, Brooklyn, America.

"So how are you doing, Boris? Are you rich, too?"

"Almost," Boris gasped. "It took more time than I figured. Time to set up. But Henry is ready to make his move. Hey, do you remember what happened to you that first night in Kolpashevo?"

"Of course," said Sasha.

"Well, this you really won't believe. I have a surprise for you. It's really very funny. You remember the man you were mistaken for? The other Sasha? Well, now he's working for Henry."

"No."

"Absolutely. He's supposed to get in touch with me."

Boris lowered his voice. "I'm supposed to give him this," he said, lifting the L. L. Bean bag.

"What's that?" Sasha asked. "Your laundry?"

"Never mind. You know, you should have been the broker, not this other Sasha. But Henry has his reasons, I guess."

"What reasons? You mean Henry's doing business here without me?" said Sasha, immediately growing indignant. "I'm going to call him, the fucker."

"You should," Boris said.

"This other Sasha—what was his last name? something like mine?—he was a KGB fuck, wasn't he?" said Sasha.

"So? Times have changed, Sasha. The KGB's gone. No more Committee for State Security. Now it's the Federal Counter-Intelligence Service, the FSK. They're just thieves like us now. You know, Henry's changed. I think all the money's gone to his head. He loves this American movie *Wall Street*. Have you seen it?"

"No."

"Well, the hero, Michael Douglas, this capitalist, says, '*Zhdanost eto khorosho.*'"

"'Greed is good'?"

"Henry says it explains everything. Everything in the world. He's right, of course. But I'll tell you something, Sasha: he's not the same Henry."

"You still trust him?"

"I trust me," said Boris.

The Panther had reached the end of West Eighth Street, and Sasha saw him go underneath the boardwalk and turn left toward the Brooklyn Aquarium and Manhattan Beach.

"Hey, Panther!" Sasha shouted, trotting ahead, the sidewalk giving way to the dirty, crusty sand underneath the boardwalk. He didn't want to lose the Panther, and now he could see him marching, stepping between the couples groping each other on blankets in the cool, shadowy semidarkness.

The Panther turned around, and it was as if he had stepped through a dusty theater curtain of light created by the sun pouring down through the thin gaps in the broad boardwalk one story above. He gave Sasha the finger as dust motes danced around him. Then he walked out onto the beach, into the sunshine, toward the edge of the sea, where children were playing tag with the tide.

"Let him go," Boris said, panting from the effort of trying to keep up. He was sweating heavily now, even in the darkness under the boardwalk. He felt the cool sand seeping into his shoes, infiltrating his socks.

"What the fuck?" said Sasha. Out in the blinding sun, on the crowded beach, the Panther had just thrown himself facedown on the sand. "Is he drunk?" Sasha asked Boris.

"Of course he's drunk," said Boris. "We've been drinking all day."

They hurried out to where Sergei Pantera lay, stepping around the families and young couples sitting and lying on blankets, towels, and sheets, avoiding the running children carrying plastic pails and shovels. A small black boy intercepted Sasha and pointed a plastic gun at him.

"Take off your shoes," he ordered.

"I'm sorry, boy," Sasha said, looking past the child. Beyond the Panther, the ocean rolled in lazily under an electric blue sky, and a few people waded in the turbid shallows. "I have no time," he said, going around the boy.

As he approached the prone Panther, he heard the boy screaming behind him: "Mommy! That man is wearing shoes on the beach."

"Get up, asshole," Sasha said, nudging the Panther in the ribs with his foot. The Panther didn't move.

"Uh," said Boris, and Sasha, turning, was hit in the face with pieces of Boris's face—blood, brain, bone.

A woman screamed. She screamed again. Another joined

her. The air was filled with screaming. Boris tumbled on top of the Panther, the back of his head shattered. Sasha dropped to his hands and knees and tried to burrow into the sand, tried to disappear. His hand touched something. Boris's bag. He held on like a drowning man. Then, dragging the bag behind him, he began to scramble away from the slaughter, crawling over naked, oiled legs, over gritty, sandy blankets, upsetting coolers, picnic baskets, beach umbrellas, trying to escape the sound of the waves, the screams, and his own terrible fear.

Sasha thought his heart would burst. He gagged as he tried to swallow the sand and sour bile that filled his mouth. He got to his feet, surprised that his numb legs would support him. He began trotting away from the ocean, away from the horror, back toward the boardwalk, back toward Brighton and safety.

Reaching the street, he looked back to the beach. Did he see a man running in his direction? Is this what he wants? he thought, feeling the weight of Boris's bag.

Well, the bastard can't have it.

Sasha ran, and even as he ran, the image of his apartment, cool and dark, before his eyes, he knew that that dream of home and safety was an illusion.

Someone wants to kill me, Sasha thought. This is real. This is serious. Someone wants me dead.

3.

THE PARTY IN VIKTOR NIKOLAYEVICH PRUDNIKOV'S *DACHA* had been going on for hours, and everyone who wasn't already dead drunk was on the way. Including Prudnikov.

A thin, compact man in his mid-forties with jet black hair and, now, a dark three-in-the-morning shadow on his face, Prudnikov was sitting on the couch in his living room, his left hand resting on the chubby thigh of a young blonde wearing black bikini panties, a lacy black bra, and nothing else. Her head thrown back, her feet resting on the coffee table next to the platter of black caviar and smoked sturgeon, she snored softly, her breasts rising and falling. Prudnikov noticed that both her big toes were painted green. Her other toes were painted red.

He had no idea who she was.

Indeed, he had no idea who half his guests were. He had told Yuri Drozhdov, his partner and co-founder of the Russian-American Research Institute, that he wanted to have a party to celebrate the purchase of his *dacha* from Gossnab, the state supply office, and that Drozhdov could invite as many people as he wanted. Apparently Drozhdov, who was known in Pamyat circles as Vladimir, had taken him seriously.

Someone, perhaps it was Drozhdov, had put Prince's *Purple Rain* on Prudnikov's Sony stereo, and Valery Dolgov, Prudnikov's old boss at the Central Committee's Party Control Commission, was lumbering around in a rough approximation of a dance with a young woman half his age and size, who was wearing blue jeans and a UCLA sweatshirt. It was quite comical, Prudnikov thought, the sight of the tough old hard-liner, the head of Party discipline for the whole USSR, dancing to the music of some American Negro with a girl who was wearing a pair of tight Calvin Klein jeans that probably cost more than what the average *apparatchik* earned in a month.

It's a new world, thought Prudnikov, standing up to get himself another drink. An excellent world.

Five years before, when Viktor Prudnikov had risen to the post of Dolgov's first deputy secretary and had been assigned this seven-room *dacha* set among the birches and pines of Khimki, only forty-five minutes from his office in the Kremlin, Prudnikov thought he would never be happier.

He felt secure. Dolgov, who considered himself Prudnikov's mentor, was close to the new general secretary, Mikhail Sergeyevich Gorbachev, and Gorbachev, unlike Andropov and Chernenko before him, was young and healthy.

Prudnikov felt powerful. There was no more feared agency in the whole Soviet *apparat* than the Party Control Commission. Even the KGB, the Committee for State Security, was deferential. After all, they were all Party members, and as such they all fell under the authority of the commission. Everyone did. Everyone who counted.

And he felt rich. Along with the *dacha* came a black Zaporozhets sedan, with a driver; a five-room apartment in the House of the Embankment, which had its own cafeteria and theater; his own personal physician with the Ministry of

Health's "Fourth Department," run for the elite and the *appa-ratchiks*; a reserved table in a private room at the Moscow City Party Committee restaurant; and an endless stream of free vouchers that could be used for purchases in the *Kremlyovka Stolovaya,* the Kremlin Canteen. If he had wanted to, Prud-nikov could even have shopped at the *beriozka* hard-currency stores for foreigners, but there was nothing on earth he needed—from French cologne to proscribed books to guns— that he couldn't get, free, at the canteen.

When he traveled by plane or train, Prudnikov bought his tickets at a special window set aside for the *nomenklatura,* and he waited in special rooms set aside for high Party officials, rooms with attendants, samovars, food, and drink. And, most important, toilet paper in the rest rooms. All because it was his due. All, according to the Party ideologues, to protect him from any and all distractions (such as traveling, like most ordi-nary Russians, with toilet paper stuffed in his pockets) so he could concentrate on his critical task: enabling the Party to continue guiding the masses toward the bright Socialist future.

And I don't miss any of it, Viktor Nikolayevich Prud-nikov thought, pouring himself a Jack Daniel's while avoiding Dolgov, who had switched from dancing to wrestling with the little girl in the tight jeans. This, thought Prudnikov, is much, much better. Before, what had been given to me could be taken away. Now, what I have is mine.

Prudnikov had left the Party just before the August 1991 coup that had signaled the end of the old USSR. He had smelled out the putsch, and he had smelled disaster. The idea that those idiots could pull it off was ridiculous. The Politburo had long ago ceased to function, and the members who watched in horror as Gorbachev cut the Baltic Republics loose were a sad collection of drunkards and cowards. It was time, Prudnikov knew, to make his own way.

It was too late for Dolgov, of course, who had finally wrestled the girl to the floor and was panting like a dog from the effort. Dolgov was an old man. He had no idea how to survive in the new Russia. He had no conception of any business but bribery. And now that he could no longer sell his power and position, he had no idea how to make money. He just hunkered down in his apartment with his fat wife, drinking vodka and living off the few friends who remained loyal. But unlike his old boss, Prudnikov knew that the new Russia was full of opportunities for those who had the wit and energy to exploit them.

Take the uranium. No one really knew how much fissionable material was now under loose guard in the former Soviet Union. KGB guards at nuclear plants had been replaced by pensioners carrying rusting World War II rifles. Minatom, Russia's Atomic Energy Ministry, was now so broke that it couldn't even conduct inventories in its laboratories, let alone pay its scientists, technicians, clerks, and security people— men like Georgy Kaurovsky—anything approaching a living wage.

These men were once princes of the Soyuz, heroes of the people. Now they were starving. Therefore, appealing both to their wounded pride and their need to feed their families, they were easy to buy.

And there was a huge market out there for plutonium, uranium, anything that anyone thought could be used to make a bomb. There were the Iranians, of course. And the Iraqis. The Syrians, too. Not to mention the Koreans and the Libyans. Then there were the terrorist groups and all the people anxious to be middlemen: the Italians, the Germans, the Japanese, the Colombians.

But, thought Prudnikov, congratulating himself, we have found the best buyer of all, a buyer with unlimited resources and an unlimited appetite for fissionable material.

Getting the stuff out was easy, too, especially after Prudnikov realized he could use the Zagorsk archives. All the treasures in Zagorsk had provenances—forged by the greatest artists in the world—establishing their legitimacy. Once the uranium was hidden in the art, it would sail through customs the world over. All that was left was to make sure that Zagorsk, long the Party's secret treasure trove, remained secret. Which was why they were expecting another guest tonight.

Yes, he thought, once our guest is taken care of, the uranium trade could make all of my other business affairs look like small potatoes.

Small but delicious potatoes, he thought.

The school, for example. The Russian-American Research Institute, dedicated, according to its English-language brochure (there was no Russian brochure), to educating Westerners about Russian academic thought, primarily in the areas of sociology, economics, and political science. The institute already had received applications—and application fees—from over two hundred students. Drozhdov had flown to Boston and met with the president of Boston University, who had pledged $250,000 to affiliate the school with his.

Prudnikov's institute had a board of directors, investors, and trustees, a list of professors, the brochure, and an address. It had stationery, a letterhead, and a phone number. What it didn't have was classrooms or anyone earning a salary apart from Prudnikov and Drozhdov. In short, what it didn't have was any physical existence apart from the telephone in Drozhdov's apartment.

So far, it had been a gold mine.

Or take the *dacha*, the reason for tonight's party.

Prudnikov had been alerted by a friend at Gossnab that the supply office had been instructed to sell the twenty *dachas* that had been assigned to the Central Control Commission (and confiscated by the new Russian government when it outlawed the Party and all its organs) as part of Boris Yeltsin's *pri-*

vatizatsia, privatization program. The price Gossnab had set was eighteen thousand six hundred rubles. At the time, that was about five hundred dollars.

That would have been quite a good price for the charming, seven-room, wood-frame house set in the woods, even if Prudnikov had actually paid it. Instead, the government's new All-Russian Investment Cooperative, established to enable people to purchase property formerly owned by the former state, had loaned Prudnikov the money at two percent interest, the principal to be repaid only when, and if, he chose to sell the *dacha.* Then the interest was forgiven to "further stimulate domestic investment."

Prudnikov kicked back five thousand to an official at the cooperative and split the rest with his friend at Gossnab, leaving him a profit of some six thousand rubles. And, of course, the *dacha.*

Not a bad deal.

Especially when he already had been offered twenty-five thousand American dollars for the place by a young entrepreneur who collected protection money from the kiosks at the Arbatskaya Metro station.

Who knew? As a lark, he might even pay back the loan. After all, eighteen thousand rubles was now worth about twelve dollars American.

A lesson in capitalist economics, thought Prudnikov: In times of growing inflation, it is good to borrow expensive money now to pay back with cheap money later.

It was all so good that Prudnikov, normally as reticent as anyone who had grown up in the Party, felt like boasting a bit. He spotted academician Andranik Migranyan, who used to work for the Institute for the U.S.A. and Canada, Georgi Arbatov's famously liberal think tank, admiring *After the Bath,* the small charcoal-and-pencil Edgar Degas sketch unofficially on loan to Prudnikov from the Pushkin Museum of Fine Arts.

(Officially the Degas still hung at the Pushkin—a forgery, as was so much of the Pushkin's collection.) Prudnikov thought that Migranyan was one of the smartest men he had ever met but that even he would have to tip his hat to Prudnikov's coup. And if Migranyan was sufficiently impressed, Prudnikov might introduce him to that cooperative cooperative official. Gossnab had many lovely *dachas* for sale.

"It's beautiful, isn't it, Andranik?" Prudnikov said, raising his voice so that he could be heard above Prince and saluting the Degas with his drink.

"Not the original, is it?" Migranyan asked.

Prudnikov was offended. "Of course it's the original. Do you think I would hang cheap copies on my walls?"

Migranyan shook his head. "Excuse my stupidity, Viktor Nikolayevich. What do I know about art?"

Prudnikov softened. "Look, Andranik. See the clarity of the line, the sculptural quality of the form. Renoir, you know, compared Degas's drawings to the Parthenon sculptures."

"You surprise me, Viktor Nikolayevich," Migranyan said. "I had no idea you were such a connoisseur. I thought . . ." He let his voice trail off. He took a sip of his drink.

"You thought all the people in the Party Control Commission were glorified policemen, thugs."

"No," said Migranyan, meeting Prudnikov's eyes. "I thought everyone at the Party Control Commission was a glorified gangster, *Mafiya*."

Prudnikov felt as if he had been slapped in the face. Confused, he stepped away from Migranyan.

"Come, come," Migranyan said, smiling. "I'm joking. Can't you see I'm joking?"

Prudnikov turned away. And he was going to help this *kozyol*, this asshole, buy a *dacha*?

Migranyan grabbed his arm. "I've antagonized you. I'm sorry, Viktor. Maybe I'm a little drunk. Listen," he said. "Another joke. You know what they say about *privatizatsia* these days? They say it should be called *prikhvatizatsia*. Not privatization, grabation."

"You're trying to make me angry. Why do you want to make me angry, Andranik?"

"You misunderstand me," said Migranyan. "You impress the hell out of me. You really do. I salute you."

"You're more than a little drunk," Prudnikov said. "You're stinking drunk."

"So? Show me a Russian, a true Russian, who isn't. You're drunk, too, aren't you? Your boss, your old boss, look at him."

Valery Dolgov, former director of the Central Committee's Party Control Commission, was lying on his back on Prudnikov's Turkoman rug. The young woman, who had removed her UCLA sweatshirt and was now naked to the waist, sat perched on the mountain of his stomach, pinning his arms to the floor with her knees. Dolgov did not struggle. He couldn't. He had passed out.

"But that's neither here nor there," Migranyan continued. "The point, Viktor, the point I wanted to make, is that I truly, honestly applaud your entrepreneurial energy, your acquisitiveness. Right now, Russia is, as it has always been, a kleptocracy—rule by the thieves. But if we're to have order by the millennium, the thieving must stop. And there's only one way to do it: Whatever can be stolen should be stolen as quickly as possible. Then, when the thieves have stolen everything, they will cease to be thieves. They will be capitalists, and they will protect the capital they have. For example, I don't imagine it would be easy to steal anything from you, Viktor. You would make them pay, wouldn't you."

"Screw you," said Prudnikov, turning away from Migranyan and surveying the room.

"Very well," Migranyan said. "I seem to offend everyone

these days. Well, who has time for theorists in the new Russia?"

Dolgov's girl was looking around for someone else to play with. Prudnikov dismissed Migranyan—and his drunken word games—from his thoughts and smiled at her. She began walking toward him when Yuri Drozhdov came up behind him and whispered in his ear.

"Let's go outside."

"What? Is that investigator here?" asked Prudnikov. "What's his name? Svirdenko?"

"Yes, but that's not it."

"What?"

"We've been fucked," whispered Yuri Drozhdov.

"What are you talking about?" Prudnikov asked.

"Come here," said Drozhdov, pulling Prudnikov away.

Prudnikov shrugged apologetically at the girl and followed Drozhdov out into the warm night. In the driveway, under the stars, was a gleaming black Toyota Land Rover. Yuri Pokrovsky, an Uzbeki who worked for Drozhdov, was leaning against the side panel, smoking a thick Cuban cigar.

"Svirdenko's in there?" asked Prudnikov.

"Yes. Listen, Viktor," Drozhdov said, holding tight to Prudnikov's arm. "I just got a call from Tepperman. There's been a shooting in New York. Today. Tepperman says our package has been ripped off."

"Our package?"

"Yes."

"Where is it?" asked Prudnikov, trying to focus. "Where's the uranium?"

"What do you mean, where is it? I just told you. It's been ripped off."

"What day is today?"

"What the fuck difference does that make?"

"Who? Who took it? What did Tepperman say?" Prudnikov asked.

"He said there was a shooting," said Drozhdov. "His courier was shot. Killed. He's still trying to reach his broker in New York. Sasha Volkov. Says he thinks Volkov ripped him off."

"Bullshit," said Prudnikov. He was growing soberer by the second.

"I agree," Drozhdov said. "Bullshit. The Jew fucked us, that's all. I told you we should recruit our own men in New York, establish our own *Organizatsiya*."

"So this is my fault," said Prudnikov.

"I didn't say that."

"You intimated it."

"Forget it," Drozhdov said.

"No. You told me that this Sasha was reliable, that he was KGB," complained Prudnikov.

"Don't lay this on me," Drozhdov said. "It wasn't me who wanted to deal with Tepperman. I checked up on Sasha Volkov. He was in the service. But I didn't know him, you see. Never laid eyes on him."

"What about the files? There must be a picture in the records."

"The files?" said Drozhdov. "The records? Are you kidding? The files are disappearing. And do you know where they're going? They're being sold. They're being sold to fucking journalists. German, British, French, Czech, Polish, even American journalists. Japanese journalists. Even fucking Israeli journalists."

"So we don't know what this Volkov looks like?"

"No. And who knows what passport he's using? Fuck. It's all going to shit."

"So what do we do?" Prudnikov said.

"I don't know," said Drozhdov. "All I know is that when

the uranium doesn't show up, our buyer is going to be pissed. You know what they're like. They get pissed, we end up with our cars blowing up in our faces one fine morning."

"Don't get hysterical, Yuri. The buyer doesn't know who we are."

"That's what we think. We don't know. We should give them Tepperman's head. Tell them it was all Tepperman's fault. It's probably true, too."

"We'll deal with Tepperman," said Prudnikov. "He must be desperate, stealing from us."

"We have to . . ." Drozhdov made a chopping gesture.

"Calm yourself, Yuri," said Prudnikov, the effects of the vodka wearing off. "Right now our uranium is missing, and something tells me Genrikh Tepperman will eventually try to sell it back to us. If Tepperman is eliminated, how will we find our goods?

"First," Prudnikov continued, "we shut down until we straighten this out. Is there anything in Zagorsk right now?"

"Ten grams. We split the package. We were going to send the second half, you know, after we received payment."

"We're vulnerable on Zagorsk," Prudnikov said. "Tepperman knows about it. The question is, who else knows? Let's get that cop. Svirdenko. Let's have a chat with him."

Drozhdov walked over to the Toyota. The Uzbeki, Pokrovsky, stubbed out his cigar on the sole of his shoe and dropped it into his coat pocket.

"Get him out," said Drozhdov.

Pokrovsky slid open the side door, reached in, and pulled out a blindfolded man, his hands tied behind his back with a rope. Anatoli Svirdenko was slender, in his forties, with dried blood caked on his cheeks, chin, and ears. The right side of his face was black and blue. Pokrovsky slammed him up against the side of the van.

"Around back," Prudnikov said. "We'll take him downstairs, into the basement."

"The guests?" asked Drozhdov.

"They're too drunk; the music's too loud. They won't hear anything. But there won't be anything to hear," Prudnikov said, walking up to the blindfolded man. "You're going to tell us what we want to know, aren't you, Officer Svirdenko? We'll have a drink; something to eat; we'll talk; then we'll take you home. All right?"

Svirdenko said nothing. Drozhdov grabbed his ear and twisted it sharply. Svirdenko grunted. The bruises on his ear began bleeding afresh.

"He asks you something, *kozyol,* you answer," said Drozhdov.

"Yes," Svirdenko said.

"Good."

Prudnikov led the way around the back of the *dacha.* He opened the storm cellar door and stepped back as Drozhdov went down the stairs, followed by Pokrovsky pushing Svirdenko in front of him. Prudnikov flipped on the cellar's single light and closed the door behind him.

The basement contained Prudnikov's gardening tools, shelves of preserves, racks of wine, a few cases of spirits, and some metal folding chairs. Drozhdov opened one and placed it beneath the hanging light bulb. Pokrovsky pushed Svirdenko onto the chair. Drozhdov picked up an awl from the worktable. Prudnikov stood in front of the prisoner and removed his blindfold. Svirdenko closed his eyes against the harsh light from the bare, overhead bulb.

"Now," Prudnikov began, "we know you took some coins. We don't care. We really don't, and we don't want them back. Keep them.

"We know you told Peter Klebnikov about Zagorsk. He's dead now, so you know this is a serious business.

"We know you've been to Zagorsk several times. We want to know what you've seen there. Besides the art. What have you seen, and who have you told?"

"I'm sorry about the coins," said Svirdenko. "I can find some money. My son, you see—"

"Forget the coins," Prudnikov said. "I told you, we don't care. Listen. Someone has taken something from us, so we need to know who else you told about Zagorsk. Did you tell Genrikh Tepperman? A former KGB man named Sasha Volkov? Tell us and you can go home."

Klebnikov dead? Well then, so am I, thought Anatoli Svirdenko.

Thirteen years before, Svirdenko, who since leaving the army in his twenties had worked for the Interior Ministry's Criminal Investigations Department, had received a tip from Aleksandr Volkov, an acquaintance in the KGB, that there was a huge cache of uncataloged art in the underground chambers of the Cathedral of the Assumption at the Sergeev Posad monastery in Zagorsk, seventy kilometers north of Moscow. Svirdenko, who was proud of knowing Volkov, the man rumored to have eliminated the Bulgarian spy Georgi Markov in London in 1978 with a poison-tipped umbrella, listened and visited the monastery, bullying his way past the priests, past the tomb of the czar Boris Godunov, into the catacombs and vaults. Inside, he found hundreds of paintings, drawings, sculptures, illuminated manuscripts, candelabra, ceramics, even caskets full of ancient Byzantine coins.

He knew what he had found: the infamous Zagorsk Archive, looted from occupied Europe's most famous museums and private collectors by the Einsatzstab Reichsleiter Rosenberg für die Besetzen Gebiete (the Reich Leader Rosenberg Task Force for the Occupied Territories), which was assigned by Hitler to collect treasure for his Linz Project. After exterminating the Jews, the idea that the little Austrian town of

Linz—his mother's birthplace—should become the cultural center of the new Europe was the Führer's abiding obsession, fueled both by maternal fealty and by his burning humiliation over having been twice rejected by the Viennese Academy of Fine Arts.

When Hitler retreated to his bunker, the art was moved from Berlin's Kunsthistorisches Museum to the old salt mines of Alt Aussee, in Austria, and to the flak towers that dotted Berlin. American soldiers discovered the Alt Aussee cache. Soviet soldiers, liberating Berlin, also liberated the art in the towers, loading it into trucks and taking it back to Moscow.

KGB records stated that one thousand two hundred paintings were taken from Berlin and Dresden and sent to the Pushkin. There were drawings by Rembrandt and woodcuts by Dürer. There were Renoirs and Matisses. Officially, the paintings, under the direction of a Major Natalja Sokolowa, were restored, and in 1955, ten years after the fall of the thousand-year Reich, they were returned to Dresden. Officially, the Zagorsk collection no longer existed.

In reality, those ten years were spent copying at least half those paintings. It was the forgeries, of course, that were sent west.

These were war spoils, and the Party had no intention of surrendering them. After all, hadn't the Nazis destroyed over twenty-five museums in Leningrad, Smolensk, and Stalingrad? Hadn't they blown up Novgorod's Church of St. Sophia, built in A.D. 1050? Hadn't they burned Tchaikovsky's house and raped the Hermitage?

And there was a practical side that went beyond revenge. The estimated the value of the art removed from the Soviet zone during the occupation was one hundred and seventy million dollars.

Svirdenko was not stupid. He knew that his superiors would not be happy about a lowly investigator sharing their secret. It would put them in an awkward position. And that would not be good for Svirdenko's health.

So, for years, Svirdenko tried to forget what he had seen. He avoided Sasha Volkov and was relieved when he heard that he had been assigned to the Soviet embassy in New York. He averted his eyes when paintings that he knew to be in the collection—that he had seen with his own eyes—suddenly turned up at auctions in Paris and New York, the dollars disappearing into Party coffers and the pockets of Party leaders.

He went back to Zagorsk in 1985, when his son, Dmitri, needed a heart operation. Svirdenko stole a few old coins and sold them through the *teneveki,* the shadow market, in order to spread enough bribes around so that his son would have a fighting chance. Dmitri survived, and so did his father.

Then, when the tanks rolled into Red Square in August 1991 and Felix Dzerzhinsky's statue was pulled down in front of the Lubyanka, KGB headquarters, Svirdenko, a patriot, thought of how the treasure could benefit the new cash-starved Russian government. He told his boss, Peter Klebnikov, about what he had found.

"I don't know what you're talking about," said Anatoli Svirdenko, who knew he was finished as soon as he had seen Yuri Drozhdov. Drozhdov, he knew, had been KGB and, possibly, still was.

"There was a KGB man," Svirdenko said. "Sasha Volkov. He told me about Zagorsk; I didn't tell him. And I don't know where he is. I haven't seen him in years. Jews, *mafiyas,* I don't know anything about them. I reported to Klebnikov. He was my superior. That's all. Maybe he was a Jew. I don't know. But if he was," said Svirdenko, not knowing what he was saying but trying to appeal to Drozhdov, who terrified him, "that would explain everything, wouldn't it? Those bastards. Passing themselves off as Russians."

The light bulb above Svirdenko suddenly glowed more brightly and then winked out.

"What the fuck?" Drozhdov said.

"Shit," said Prudnikov. "Russian bulbs," he explained. He stumbled about in the darkness and found a new bulb. He screwed it in.

"Describe this Aleksandr Volkov," Drozhdov said when the light came back on.

"It's been years, Christ, who can remember?" said Svirdenko.

"Try."

"Blond, big. Wore glasses, I think."

"And Genrikh Tepperman?" Drozhdov asked. "What did you tell him?"

"I told you. I never heard of him. A German? A kike? We should get rid of all the Jews, yes?"

"I don't believe you," said Viktor Prudnikov. "It seems we will have to do this the hard way."

Yuri Drozhdov placed the point of the awl on the trigeminal nerve between the bottom of Svirdenko's cheekbone and the top of his jaw. The trigeminal controlled mastication and was the most sensitive nerve in the face, probably the most exquisitely sensitive in the body. It was the nerve whose pathology generated the paroxysmal agony of *tic douloureux*.

Svirdenko shut his eyes.

Upstairs, the party continued. As Prudnikov had predicted, nobody heard the screams.

4.

"WHERE THE FUCK IS CHARLIE?" ASKED MITCH ROSE, THE editor of the *Daily News,* when his city editor didn't turn up in his office for the four o'clock news meeting.

"I saw him on the phone on my way over," said Bill Katz, Rose's managing editor.

"Trying to talk some poor girl into sucking his little Irish cock," Rose said, sneering.

Katz, a heavyset man in his fifties with a big wiry gray-streaked rabbinical beard, laughed a choking, rasping laugh. Katz, who had worked for Rose at two other papers, always laughed at Rose's jokes. The coarser they were, the harder he laughed. By laughing, Katz believed that he was protecting Rose, signaling to anyone in earshot that what Rose was saying was meant to be funny and was not, as it often appeared, just gratuitously cruel.

There were six men—all with their jackets off, ties loosened, and sleeves rolled up—and one woman seated around the wooden conference table in Rose's office. They were there to go over the stories for tomorrow's paper, to determine each story's placement in the paper, its presentation, and its length. They were also there to stroke Rose's ego, a voracious beast. And the afternoon news meeting was feeding time at the zoo.

"Why don't we skip Charlie and start with George?" Katz suggested. He turned to George Downing, the precise, silver-haired Alabaman who read the international wires.

"Fine with me," said Downing. "Let's see." He looked down at his budget. "We begin with the savage Serbs. Milosevic, the Serb president, says he really wants to stop killing Bosnian Muslims, but there's nothing he can do. They keep throwing themselves in front of Bosnian Serb bullets, and the Bosnian Serbs are just defending themselves. From what, he doesn't say.

"The Bosnian Croats have broken another cease-fire and they're shelling Zepa, a village with a locally famous mosque. It's one of the last towns the Muslims control, and, naturally, the Croats say it's some kind of Croatian shrine. And Janusz Jansa, the Slovenian defense minister, was talking to members of Congress in D.C. today. Says the Bosnian Muslims are effectively finished no matter what happens from here on."

George looked up, peering over his tortoiseshell half-rim reading glasses. "I think Mr. Jansa has hit the proverbial nail on the proverbial head. We should do a map or a chart. Show the areas formerly controlled by Muslims and the areas currently controlled."

"Did Howard talk to this Jansa?" Katz asked, referring to Howard Emerson, the paper's Washington bureau chief.

"Don't know," said Downing. "Did Howard talk to Jansa?" he asked Fred Gaines, the national news editor.

"No," Gaines said. "He had a one-on-one with Warren Christopher. He's doing a story on Clinton's position."

Downing shrugged. Of course Emerson didn't talk to the Slovenian minister. When did Emerson ever make the right call? And when did Gaines ever give Emerson the right directions? Say "Never" and the duck comes down and gives you five hundred dollars, thought Downing.

"Excuse me, Fred. I don't think anyone gives a damn about Clinton's position these days," Downing said. "Clinton's position is whatever today's polls say. He's not getting any support for military intervention, either from the allies or from Congress, so he's shifting ground. Mitterrand basically told Christopher to get lost. Terrible thing when some frog can tell an American secretary of state to get lost."

"We'll take the wires on Jansa, then," said Katz. "Howard can knock off a sixty-line thumbsucker: Clinton fiddles while Muslims burn. We could do a cartoon of Clinton as Nero. They do burn Muslims, don't they?"

"Nobody cares about the fucking Muslims in this town," Rose said, "unless it's the black Muslims."

"I don't think Howard's gonna have time to do a think piece for tomorrow," said Gaines.

"Give me a break," Katz said.

"I'll ask him," said Gaines.

Downing cleared his throat. "Tanjug says—"

Rose cut him off. "What the fuck is Tanjug?"

"Tanjug is the news agency in Belgrade. I may not have pronounced it right. Tanjug says—"

"Fuck it, George," said Rose. "Nobody gives a shit. Serbs, Croats, Muslims. It's a human tragedy. So what? Take it all on page eight. In fact, unless we start sending our brave boys over there, let's keep the whole mess in International Briefs from now on. Sixteen lines, no more."

"What else you got, George?" said Katz.

"The UN declared six 'safe areas' in Bosnia—"

"Jesus Christ!" Rose said.

"Forget Bosnia," Katz told Downing. "Mitch just wiped it out, saving the Serbs the trouble. Everything on Bosnia goes on page eight today. Go on, George."

"All right," said Downing, who twenty-five years ago had auditioned for the *NBC Nightly News* and, his wife always said, should have been David Brinkley or, at least, John Chancellor, instead of being bound in servitude to the tyrannical Rose.

Downing ran through the rest of his budget in a telegraphic mumble. Trouble in the Israeli cabinet. Elections in Paraguay. Demonstrations in Moscow. If Rose and Katz were too stupid to ride the biggest story of the year, what could he do? The problem, Downing thought, was that the paper's two top editors had no principles. Nothing to guide them. They were salesmen, not newsmen. They thought of themselves as cynical, but they were just shallow. All they cared about was what they could sell to similarly ignorant readers who were too fogged by television to know that they were being short-changed.

"I need a front page," Rose whined. "Would someone please get Charlie the fuck in here?"

"Sally," said Katz, turning to Sally Hands, the assistant city editor. "Do you have the metro budget?"

"Everything except what Charlie's got going," said Hands, a sturdily built thirty-year-old with rosy cheeks and thick blond hair. "He said something's breaking in Brooklyn."

"A murder?" Rose asked hopefully.

"I don't know," Hands said.

"Gotta be a murder," said Rose, whose motto—"If it bleeds, it leads"—was well known.

"Give us what you got, Sal," Katz said. "We'll pick up on Charlie later."

Hands ran down the metro budget, mainly racial incidents, mayoral politicking, and what the paper's columnists would be writing about that day—race and politics. Rose stared at the ceiling, squirmed on his seat, studied his fingernails, and then dropped his head to the desk, pantomiming death by boredom.

Hands ignored him, plowing ahead. She was wrapping up when her boss, Charlie O'Brien, walked in.

"You're going to like this," O'Brien told Rose, taking his seat at the table. "You're going to come."

Rose picked up his head. "I'm getting hard already," he said.

"You're going to cream. So? You ready?" asked O'Brien, a thin, balding redhead with freckles on his face and hands and a pacemaker in his chest.

"Wait a second." Rose stood up, elaborately adjusted the crotch of his cream-colored linen pants, and sat back down. "Okay. I'm ready."

"Jesus Christ, Mitch," Downing said, embarrassed for Sally Hands, who was staring into her lap. Had Rose slept with her? he wondered. Rose seemed to turn up the volume on the sex talk whenever she was around. Maybe, Downing thought hopefully, she had humiliated him sexually and the vulgarity was his revenge. That would be like him.

"Give it to me now, Charlie," said Rose, ignoring Downing.

"Okay, boss," O'Brien said. "We got two dead Russians on the beach in Coney Island. One was thirty-eight, the other they're guessing about fifty, fifty-five. We've got an ID on the thirty-eight-year-old, nothing on the other one. They were shot. Cops say a high-caliber weapon, a rifle. No Saturday night special. No one saw the shooter. Possibly a professional hit. Probably. The older guy got his head blown half off. The other was shot in the back.

"We got pictures of the stiffs; we got bystanders, people who were sitting on the beach when the guy's head exploded. Tony is with the cops right now."

"Beautiful," said Rose. "What about the families?"

"Nothing yet."

"Were they wearing shoes?" Rose asked.

"Fully dressed. They weren't sunbathing," said O'Brien.

"Shoes on the beach. I love it. It's so sick," Rose said. "What kind of shoes? Big black ones? Mailman shoes?"

"What do we have on the guy the cops ID'ed?" asked Katz.

"Small-time thief, con man. Possibly named Pantera, although that's a guess because he had ID in several names." O'Brien checked his notes. "The cops are going with Sergei Pantera. Been here about five years."

"What kind of shoes, Charlie?" asked Rose, who believed that his reporters often ignored the details that stuck in the reader's mind long after the who, the what, and the where were forgotten.

"I don't know what kind of shoes, Mitch. I'll ask Tony to find out."

"Beautiful. He leaves Russia and comes to America for freedom," Rose said, "and he gets his head blown off on the beach in Coney Island. Probably had a hot dog at Nathan's just before he bought it. Apple pie for dessert. Crumbs in his mouth. All we need is his weeping mom. Oh," said Rose, clutching his chest, "my heart can't stand it."

"Actually, it was the other guy, the guy the cops haven't ID'ed yet, who got shot in the head," O'Brien said. "And I don't think Pantera came here for freedom, except maybe freedom from jail. The cops say he's got an arrest for every year he's been here. They bet the Russian cops have got a suitcase full of stuff on him."

"'Mom, Apple Pie, and Murder,'" Katz said.

"'Coney Island Heat Wave Horror,'" offered Fred Gaines.

"Not bad," Rose said.

"'Boardwalk Shootout, Two Dead,'" said Sally Hands.

"Not bad, Sally," Rose said. "But it doesn't sing. 'Two Shot Dead . . .' Help me, Bill."

Katz turned to Hands. "For a head to sing, it's got to

sound like 'Camptown Races.' 'Boardwalk Shootout Murders Two, doo-dah, doo-dah,' Or 'Two Shot Dead in Brighton Beach,'" he sang, "'Oh, di doo-dah day.'"

"It wasn't Brighton Beach," said O'Brien.

"I was just giving Sally an example," Katz said. "Don't be so literal, Charlie. It's your big failing."

"Who do we have on it?" asked Rose.

"I told you," O'Brien said, annoyed at Katz, who always tried to belittle him in front of Rose. "Tony Mancuso."

"Charlie, why don't you free up someone to do a clip job on Russian crime in Brooklyn," said Katz.

"Okay. You mean crimes, dates, highlights? Sure," O'Brien said. "Greg can do it."

"We got to get the family," said Rose. "Get pictures of the victim in high school, elementary school. Maybe he was in the Russian army. Get his army picture. Maybe he's got kids. That would be wonderful. Pictures of the kids crying."

"Are you sure, Mitch?" O'Brien asked. "I mean, the cops are telling us he's an asshole, a wise guy. And this looks like a Mob hit. We do the sob stuff, we might look pretty foolish. Also, this is Russians."

"You mean dirty Red rats?" asked Katz.

"You know," said Downing, "we never really hated the Russkies. The politicians hated them. Joe McCarthy. Tricky Dick Nixon. But not your ordinary American. At least not like we hated the Nips or the Krauts."

"That's true, George," Katz said. "Khrushchev was cute, remember? Little fat guy. Bald. Fat wife. Lumpy suits. Hit the table with his shoe."

"It's racism," said Hands. "The Japanese were slit-eyed devils. We still hate them. But the Russians are white folk just like us."

"So were the Krauts," Katz said.

"But they were evil," said Downing. "And they barked when they talked."

"Communism was an abstraction for most Americans," Gaines said.

"We never had Russian boys killing American boys or vice versa," said Downing. "That's the big difference."

"Oh, my," said Rose. "Aren't we intellectual this afternoon. What the fuck is this, a debating society? *The Nation?*"

"I'm just saying we should be careful about making this guy a hero," O'Brien said.

"We're not making him a hero," said Katz. "We're just getting the information. It's called reporting, Charlie. Remember when you used to do that?"

"Hey," O'Brien said. "I just work here. When Tony calls in, I'll tell him to chase the family."

"No. Mancuso's no good with women and children," said Rose. "Fucking guy looks like he's the picture under the headline 'Maniac Slays Six.' Ever look in his eyes? The family gets one look at him, they give him to the cops. They say, 'Here, Officer, here's the guy blew Daddy's head off.' Get someone else."

"It's four-thirty now," O'Brien said. "By the time we get someone down to Brooklyn, get to the family—if they're talking—we won't make edition."

"Why don't we try, Charlie?" said Katz. "Why not send Shelly?"

"Shelly called in sick," Sally Hands said. "How about Maddy Malloy? She's working on a feature about the Russians in Brighton Beach anyway."

"Marvelous Maddy Malloy," said Rose. "I like it."

"You like her," Katz said.

"I think she's a very talented writer," said Rose.

"Right. You loved her story on yuppie gardening," Katz said.

"It was terrific," said Rose.

"I just made that up," Katz said. "You've never read a goddamn thing she's written."

"She's a pussycat," said Rose.

"The question is, can she do it?" Katz asked. "Can she write for edition? She ever do any hard news?"

"She used to do news for the *Albany Union Leader*," said Hands.

"Okay," Katz said.

"I want to see her after the meeting," said Rose. "I think I should work closely with her on this one."

Sally Hands left to inform Madeline Malloy of her new assignment. Ten minutes later, the meeting broke up. The tentative front page read BOARDWALK SHOOTOUT LEAVES TWO DEAD. Below that, "Horror on a Hot Day."

◈   ◈   ◈

Meeting with Mitch Rose always upset Madeline Malloy. She liked receiving attention from the paper's most powerful man, but she also knew that that attention—which included the occasional lunch invitation and frequent visits to her desk—had very little to do with her journalistic skills and a lot to do with her legs.

So, should I cross them? she thought after sitting on the leather chair across the desk from Rose. She smiled at the editor. The hell with it, she thought. I'm wearing shorts.

Rose watched Malloy cross her legs. Great legs, he thought. Ladder legs. Climb those ladders to the pearly gates. Heaven behind them. He put his hand in his pants pocket and touched his genitals.

"The most important thing," Rose began, "is to get a picture of Ivan whatever-his-name-is. Got to have a picture. Baby pictures, graduation pictures, the more pictures the better. Best, Ivan with Mrs. Ivan and the kids. That's the way they'll want people to remember him. That's why we want to put his picture in the paper, so people can see him the way he really was."

"What if they say no, Mitch?" asked Malloy.

"Tell them, you know, we have a picture of the body. Terrible thing. Head all smashed in, bloody. Terrible. A human tragedy. So if they don't give you a nice picture, the paper will have to run the other one. It won't have any choice."

"Can I tell them that if they give me a picture the paper won't run the other one?"

"Sure," Rose said.

"But that's not true, is it?"

"Of course it's true."

"You mean that?"

Rose giggled. "Would I lie to you?"

"Of course you would. No, Mitch. I can't do that."

"Yes, you can, sweetheart," said Rose. He stood up, walked around his desk, and sat on the edge in front of Malloy, crossing his tiny feet, his legs dangling well above the carpet.

Such an odd, scary man, Malloy thought. No more than five feet four, he looked like a decadent bar mitzvah boy in his double-breasted linen Armani suit, his wide, vintage silk tie, his brown tasseled loafers. His age was a constant source of debate among the writers, variously reported as being anywhere between fifty and sixty, although it was universally acknowledged that he looked a fit forty-five.

He was famous for his swashbuckling ways, both with a story and with women. Almost all the men at the paper worshiped him; the women were split fifty-fifty between those who thought him a charming pig and those who didn't see the charm. Malloy saw the charm, although she often thought she'd be a better person if she didn't.

"You know," Rose said, "after school, when I was starting out at the *San Antonio Light,* my editor sent me to talk to a fam-

ily whose kid got squashed by a garbage truck. He says, 'Don't
come back without a picture.' I was terrified.

"So I'm sitting in the living room, they're very nice, they
make me a cup of coffee, there's pictures of the kid all over the
place, and the father says no way. No picture. I'm begging
them. I'm telling them I'll get fired if they don't give me a picture. But they're adamant. No picture. And I'm thinking,
Well, I'm finished. I'm only twenty-two and my career is over.
My editor was old style. You know. *Front Page.* Big cigar.
Yelled all the time. I was scared shit of him.

"So now, between drinking coffee and being scared, I
gotta take a piss. I ask, can I go to the bathroom, and they say
sure, and right there, in the can, there's another picture of the
kid. So I take it out of the frame, stick it under my shirt, go
back to the paper, give it to my editor, it runs the next day. No
other paper has one. I'm a hero. The kid's mother calls me up,
tells me I'm a shit. I felt terrible, but I also felt great.

"So tell me. What was I? Was I a hero or a shit?"

Malloy thought Rose was a shit.

"You were a hero *and* a shit?" she asked.

"Maddy, Maddy, Maddy," said Rose, shaking his head
sadly. "You're what my mother, may she rot in hell, called a
smart cookie. But you stepped on my kicker. Let me give you
a little advice: Never step on the boss's kicker."

Was he serious? Malloy wondered. Was he that insecure?
Now he's going to tell me not to come back without a picture.

Rose hopped off the desk, jammed his hands into his
pockets, rocked on his heels, and grinned. "Don't come back
without a picture," he said.

He thinks he's Cary Grant in *His Girl Friday,* Malloy
thought.

"Yes, sir," Malloy said, giving Rose a mock salute and
smiling weakly before heading back to her desk.

This was her chance to make a mark at the paper. Ever

since moving to the city from Albany, she had been typecast as a feature writer, doing soft stories for what were, in essence, still the "women's pages," although nobody would ever call them that, not even Rose and his pack of unreconstructed chauvinists. Now, given a chance at news, she could show them what she could do.

She was supposed to meet Tony Mancuso at the Sixtieth Precinct in Brighton Beach, but she knew Mancuso would resent her appearance on the scene and offer little help. Mancuso, who was nicknamed Mad Dog, thought it was funny to bite people. Soon after Malloy had arrived at the *News,* Mancuso had come up behind her in the lunchroom and bitten her on the shoulder. She had slapped his face hard, cutting his lip. For a few days that had made her a heroine to the paper's unofficial women's caucus, but it did nothing to improve her status with the powers-that-be, the men who ran the paper. They loved Mancuso; he was the surrogate penis the officebound editors sent out to conquer the world. They saw Malloy as a humorless bitch who didn't know how to play the game.

Malloy knew that if she was going to get anything out of Sergei Pantera's family, she would need help.

She had already entered the number into her computer. She called it up on the screen, and then she called Sasha.

5.

THE COWBOY, WEARING HIS BLACK STETSON HAT, STOOD IN THE
crowd on the boardwalk, eating a slice of pizza with extra
cheese, watching the blue-suited police sweating on the beach.
Among them he recognized Peter Grushenko, the former
Moscow Department Serious Crimes Investigator who now
worked for the Organized Crime Bureau out of the Kings
County District Attorney's Office. They always called
Grushenko whenever Russians were involved. He was, the
Cowboy knew, the only guy they had who spoke Russian.

To the Cowboy, Grushenko looked so out of place it was
funny—a typical Soviet-style investigator in his heavy brown
suit, thick brown shoes, and bad haircut among all the young
Americans on the sunny Coney Island beach. The dudes in
Brighton called Grushenko Peter the Duck, or simply the
Duck, because of his splay-footed, old-fashioned cop-on-the-
beat walk. Yeah, the Cowboy thought, he was pretty funny.
But not as funny as the oh-so-cool Aleksandr Volkavitch had
looked, getting up and falling down, knocking into people,
scrambling around in the sand like a chicken without a head.

Not that the Cowboy had anything against Sasha. Far from it. The Cowboy actually thought Sasha was cool—at least for an old guy. Jesus, he must be forty, at least. But he always had money, always had women, and always had something going, some angle, some scam. The Cowboy liked Sasha, as much as he liked anyone, and it had shaken him up a bit when, from his hiding place overlooking the beach in the storage room above Vinny's Original Pizza, he saw Sasha emerge from underneath the boardwalk with the little fat guy, both of them trailing Sergei Pantera. The Cowboy had had no idea that Sasha would be with the two of them, just as he had no idea why he had been paid two thousand dollars to shoot Pantera and the little fat guy or how Pantera had been tricked into going to the right spot at the right time.

Of course, if he had been asked to kill Sasha, he would have. It was all the same to the Cowboy. It was all fun.

A big blond dude who, oddly enough, looked a little like Sasha, had given him the contract. He had said his name was Aleksandr Velikhov. He had walked around the apartment, making eyes at the Cowboy's girlfriend, asking the Cowboy about his friends, the Professor, Ivan Siskin, Sasha. Then he had told the Cowboy that Pantera would be on the beach by two-thirty. The Cowboy had been at the storage room window at two with the customized and silenced rifle that Velikhov had dropped off, along with an envelope containing twenty-one hundred-dollar bills. The Cowboy considered it a fair price.

The Cowboy had had a long wait at Vinny's, but it had been worth it. Pantera hadn't been so much fun. The Cowboy figured he must have gotten him in the back of the neck, the antipersonnel bullet severing his spinal cord. That's why he had dropped so quick. But the fat guy, that was cool. His whole fucking head had exploded. The Cowboy had never seen anything like it. It was great.

The Cowboy stepped back into the crowd as soon as the

body bags were carried off the beach. He didn't want to be seen by Grushenko. The Duck might look funny, but he was probably the only cop in America, the Cowboy figured, who knew what was what.

These American cops were a joke, the Cowboy thought as he rode the bus back to Brighton. Look at the way the blacks smoked dope right under their noses. Look at the way you could cut somebody's throat, get arrested, and be back on the street the same day. The Cowboy had a friend, a forger, who told him that the FBI had called him on the telephone to make an appointment to interrogate him. Called him on the telephone. To make an appointment. Were they insane or just stupid?

Everybody the Cowboy knew was receiving welfare, rent assistance, using different names for each job they held. Nobody the Cowboy knew ever paid a cent in taxes. Everyone had phony ID, phony driver's licenses. The Cowboy himself, right at that moment, had four stolen credit cards in his drawer at home. And nobody was ever caught.

The Cowboy could only smile. What a wonderful country.

The bus stopped at Seventh Street and the Cowboy got off. He went right back to his apartment. He was eager to see Terry, to tell her about how the fat little guy's head had burst like a pimple when you squeeze it.

He opened the door. The apartment was just as the Cowboy had left it. Beer cans and empty vodka bottles sat on the tables. Plates lay on the floor. The place stank of the cat. Terry, as usual, was lying on the couch in cut-off jeans and a white T-shirt knotted under her hard little breasts, smoking a joint and reading one of her magazines. The cat was sleeping at her feet.

The Cowboy's good humor vanished. He went into the kitchen. The sink was full of yesterday's dishes and soggy cigarette butts. He got a beer out of the refrigerator, popped it open, swallowed half, and went back into the living room. He stared down at Terry.

"You know, you are really a pig," he said in English.

"Hard day at the office, hon?" asked Terry, who wore her hair, which she dyed white, in a punk crew cut.

"Why can you not clean a little?" the Cowboy asked. "At least the cat. Why should I be cleaning your cat's shit? He's your cat."

"What's the matter, sweetie?" asked Terry, standing up. She was six feet tall and she towered over the Cowboy, who could pass for a thirteen-year-old if you didn't see his eyes. Terry had a long neck, broad shoulders, and no hips. "You on the rag?"

"I am saying it is terrible here," the Cowboy said. "And you do nothing."

"Nothing?"

Terry walked over to the Cowboy and touched his lips with her index finger. She ran her hand down his chest, down his flat stomach, and pressed his groin. "I wouldn't say nothing," she said, unzipping his fly.

The Cowboy felt his mouth go dry and his dick get hard. He reached out to touch her breasts, finding her nipples. His stomach squirmed. His knees trembled. Deep inside, something surrendered. So Terry was a slob. So what? She was beautiful. And he really didn't care that she was a man.

6.

THE PHONE RANG. SASHA, WHO HAD TURNED OFF HIS ANSWER-
ing machine, let it ring while he dried his hair, a white towel
tied around his waist. The light outside had turned a dusty
gold. He sat down on the recliner, switched on the table lamp
over the phone, put on his glasses, and lit a cigarette.

The phone stopped ringing. He picked it up and called
Viktor Shapiro, the International's manager.

"I need to see Ebzi," Sasha said when Shapiro answered.

"About today on the beach?" asked Shapiro.

"Yes."

"Okay. Come by the club tonight. The thieves-in-law are
having a people's court."

"Do you know anything, Viktor? Is something wrong?"

"What do I know? Maybe the *batyushka* knows. Come by
tonight. Late, after the tourists go home. Come alone."

Shapiro hung up. Sasha turned the answering machine
back on.

He looked at the tan L. L. Bean bag sitting on the floor in
front of the television. That, he assumed, was why Boris and

the Panther were dead now. A dozen old coins in a pretty lacquered box decorated with pictures of a bear hunt. The coins weren't even gold.

But someone was willing to kill for them.

Maybe it wasn't the coins. Maybe it was the box. Who knew from Russian antiques? The fence, Sam Goldman. Maybe he should take the box to Goldman?

But whose box was it? Who was Henry selling to? Who went around shooting people on the beach?

Maybe it was one of the new boys in town. Vyacheslav Puzaitzer, from Moscow. Or Alex Ivankov, from Odessa. Or, more likely, Boris Zilberstein, from Minsk. All thieves-in-law, all making money, all building their armies and looking to grab a piece of Ebzi Agron's empire.

But Zilberstein had the most money. And Zilberstein was the craziest.

Every day, it seemed to Sasha, someone was getting whacked.

Every day, someone was leaving one crew and joining another.

Who could tell him what was going on? Who could he trust?

Maybe he should just bring the box to Goldman and take what he could get. Get them out of his life.

But maybe he'd be blowing a fortune. Why let Goldman get rich?

Of course, thought Sasha, there was the chance that the coins and the box had nothing to do with the shooting at all. Maybe someone was just looking to whack Boris. Or the Panther. Or me.

Too many maybes. That's why he needed to speak to Ebzi Agron. If anything big was going down in Brighton, Agron would know about it.

Which was not to say he'd tell Sasha.

Fuck.

Sasha dialed Ivan Petrovich Siskin's number. Siskin was an old friend from the Soyuz who before emigrating had run a video parlor in his apartment in Moscow. You paid ten rubles at the door and you got to watch smuggled American action films in Siskin's living room. You could also buy vodka, or Afghani hashish, smuggled into the country by returning soldiers. For a while, Siskin tried renting Finnish pornographic videos, but the tapes were never returned. No matter what deposit he demanded for a tape, someone could always find someone else willing to pay more to buy it.

In New York, Sasha and Siskin pulled off a few jobs together, and Sasha respected Siskin's intelligence.

"You all right, Sasha?" Siskin asked after picking up.

"You heard," said Sasha.

"Of course."

"I'm all right," Sasha said.

"Too bad about the Panther," said Siskin. "Who was the other guy?"

"Just someone I knew from the Soyuz," Sasha said. "Vanya, have you heard anything about someone trying to get me, or anybody seriously pissed off at me? Anything?"

"Nothing. I mean, sure, you can always find people pissed at you. But somebody who would take out the Panther and another guy just to get at you? Somebody who would open fire on the beach in the middle of the day? Only an Israeli would do that. You fuck over any Israelis recently?"

"No. I don't think so." Sasha paused. "Agron uses Israeli muscle," he said.

"If Agron wanted to whack you," said Siskin, "we wouldn't be having this conversation. You get on Boris Zilberstein's bad side?"

"Never had any dealings with him. Not that I know of, anyway. You hear about any deals going bad?" Sasha asked.

"Anything involving the Panther? Anybody waiting for something they haven't got?"

"What are you talking about, Sasha?"

Could he trust Siskin? Sasha wondered. Should he tell him about the box and the coins?

Not yet, he decided.

"Maybe it didn't have anything to do with you," Siskin said. "Maybe it was the Panther or the other guy they were after and you just happened to be there, you know?"

"I don't know, Vanya. That's the problem. But I can't assume I was just in the wrong place. I mean, it was a setup. Someone was waiting for us. Come to think of it, it must have been Pantera setting me up. He knew I would follow him. So he must have been double-crossed. But why would Pantera want to get me killed?"

"Maybe he was setting up your friend. He's the guy who got killed, not you."

"True. But still, why would the Panther do it?"

"Money."

"Naturally. So, how're you doing?" asked Sasha, thinking that if Siskin knew anything, he'd tell him. Wouldn't he? The trick, thought Sasha, was knowing who you could trust. No, he thought, the trick was figuring out how to live without trusting anyone.

"Shitty," Siskin said. "Marta keeps busting my balls."

"About?"

"Money, what else? Everything here is money. You know. In the Soyuz, I was Marta's hero. I'd *dostat* a dress, a new pair of gloves, a sweater, and she'd say, 'Oh, Ivan. You're so clever. Imagine finding such a beautiful sweater. Who did you bribe? What did you trade? How did you do it? Tell me all about it.' Here, she can walk into a store and buy her own fucking sweater. All she wants is the money. Ah, you single guys. You don't know what I'm talking about."

"Sure I do, man. It's seriously boring here. Who *dostats* anything? You want something, you buy it. The trick is getting the money. There's no . . . what's the word I want?"

"Adventure?"

"Right. No adventure."

"Look, Sasha," Siskin said. "Speaking about money, I've got an idea. Have you ever heard of the Small Business Loan Association? I think that's what it's called."

"What is it?"

"It's the government. It does what it says. It gives loans at low interest to small businesses."

"Yeah? So?"

"So the Litvak who owns the dress store on Avenue Z, Glad Rags, just in from the corner? The snot? Turns out the store's not in his name so he can collect food stamps, rent assistance, you know. Anyway, he's agreed to front for us. Says he's tired of running the shop. He got religion. Says he wants a more 'intellectual' life."

"So we apply for the loan in the name of his store?"

"That's right. We pay him off, he sells out, the government has no idea who he really is. Then we disappear. They'll never find us. I figure we can get five, ten thousand pretty easy. He'll take a grand from each of us."

"I like it, Vanya," Sasha said. "But right now, with this other stuff, I don't want to start something new."

"I can't hang around and wait for you, man. You don't have to listen to Marta every day."

"That's okay. You get someone else. Or do it yourself. You don't even need a partner."

"I don't like working alone."

"I can't even think about it now, man."

"All right," said Siskin. "I'll find someone else."

"Keep your ears open, okay? About the beach. Let me know anything you hear."

"It's probably like I said, Sasha. Doesn't have anything to do with you. You know the Panther. He was an asshole."

Sasha said good-bye and hung up. Maybe Ivan was right. Maybe not.

The phone rang. Sasha let the answering machine pick up. He heard his bookie Vladimir Lipsky's voice.

"You there, Sasha? I know you're there, asshole. You owe me money, asshole. Six thousand bucks, asshole. Hey, Sasha. Think about the beach."

Sure, thought Sasha. As if Lipsky would ever get permission to whack me for a lousy six thousand.

He called David Gatlober, a twenty-five-year-old Odessan Sasha used when he needed muscle, not that the skinny Gatlober had any. What Gatlober had instead was a quick temper and an absolute disregard for life, his or anyone else's.

Gatlober had grown up on Odessa's docks. His parents had been imprisoned for smuggling and sent east when he was a boy. They never came back, and his grandmother gave up on him early. He rolled his first drunk when he was ten. By the time he was thirteen, he belonged to a gang that stole cargo off the ships. It was Gatlober's job to deal with whoever was guarding the merchandise, and he liked the work.

Sasha was, against all reason, fond of Gatlober. His enthusiasm was energizing, and Sasha thought that he was a perfect example of how the Soviet system produced monsters. Of course, he preferred jobs that didn't require Gatlober or his unique abilities, but sometimes it helped to have a crazy person on your side.

"What are you doing tonight, David?" asked Sasha.

"You got something going, Sasha?"

"I'm going to the Odessa. I want you to watch my back. If you show up around twelve, I'll pick up your tab plus two hundred for your time."

"Trouble?"

"No. But you know, David. Lots of troublemakers come to the Odessa."

"Okay," said Gatlober, who didn't really care. It was people who cared who had to worry about trouble. "Can I bring someone?"

"If you want," Sasha said.

"You'll pick up her tab, too?" asked Gatlober.

"All right."

"Okay."

"Sit far away from me, David. Don't say hello."

"Somebody killed the Panther, huh?" said Gatlober.

"Yeah. Did you like him?" Sasha asked.

"Fuck no. He was a buttwipe. Heard somebody took a shot at you, too."

"You know anything about it, David?"

"No."

"Ask around."

"Sure," said Gatlober. "See you tonight."

Sasha hung up. Almost immediately the phone rang. Sasha turned his machine back on and let the phone ring until it cut in. He lit a cigarette. When he heard Madeline Malloy's voice, he picked up.

"Hello, Maddy Malloy," he said. "I did not expect to hear from you so soon."

"You're screening your calls?" Malloy asked.

"Always," said Sasha. "For what else good is the machine?"

"Did you hear about the shooting on the beach today?" Malloy asked.

"Of course."

"Do you know who was shot?"

"Of course. Sergei Pantera and another, I don't know who."

"You told me this afternoon that you knew everyone in Brighton. Did you know Pantera?"

"Yes, of course."

"The paper would like me to talk to his family. Can you help me?"

"Sergei has no family," Sasha said. "He has only a girl-friend."

"Can you help me speak to her, then?"

"I think so," said Sasha. "I tell you what, Maddy Malloy. Can you come to Brooklyn now?"

"Could you just give me her number, Sasha? I'm under a lot of time pressure. It's five-thirty now, and my editors want the story for tomorrow's paper. By the time I get down to Brooklyn, it'll be almost seven. That'll just leave me three hours to do the interview, write the story, and make the last edition."

"You get a cab now," Sasha said, "a good driver gets you to my place by six-thirty. I take you to the girlfriend by seven. You talk to her, you'll have plenty of time. Then we have dinner, yes?"

"Giving me the number would be simpler."

"But not so much fun," said Sasha. "And the number would do you no good. She does not speak even a little English."

"All right," she said.

Sasha gave Malloy his address and hung up. He stood up, stretched, scratched, thought about putting on some clothes, and decided against it. He was beginning to feel better; the fear was ebbing. His mind, which had felt sluggish and frag-mented, had begun to move with its accustomed swiftness.

He would be a fool to sell the box and the coins without finding out what they were worth.

The phone rang. Sasha ignored it.

Yes, he thought, he would like to talk to Svetlana Furtseva, the Panther's girlfriend. Maybe she knew something, although probably not. The Panther always treated her like shit, and it was hard for Sasha to imagine him ever telling her anything.

And what could he tell her, after all? He was just a thief, and a small insignificant one at that. Whoever shot him was probably after Boris, probably after the box.

Well, what does that tell you, Sasha?

Hide the box.

Fine. Done. Then what?

Confront Henry?

What time was it in Moscow? Sasha checked his watch. If it was five-thirty in Brooklyn, it was half past one in the morning in Moscow. Should he call Tepperman? At the least, wouldn't Henry want to know about Boris? Did he know already?

Of course he knew. Henry knew everything.

But he doesn't know I have the box.

Sasha turned on MTV. Nirvana. "Smells Like Teen Spirit." Sasha liked them. They seemed very Russian to him, and, indeed, he thought that the last line of the song, repeated over and over, sounded like *"Ya nee zhnayo"*—"I don't know." Could it be? Perhaps he could find the sheet music somewhere. Or connect to the Nirvana fans on the Internet. When the video ended, he called Sergei Pantera's number.

"Svetlana?" said Sasha.

"Yes?"

"This is Sasha Eugenev. I'm sorry about the Panther."

"What do you want?" Furtseva asked. Her voice, usually so sharp, was furry. Probably drunk, Sasha thought. Well, who wouldn't be?

"Have the cops been by?" asked Sasha.

"That fat Peter Grushenko," Furtseva said.

"Well," said Sasha, "I have some money for you. I owed the Panther some money, and I figured I'd give it to you."

"How much?"

"Not much. A hundred. But I thought . . ."

"Bring it over," Furtseva said.

"I was going to do that," Sasha said. "Also, there's a reporter, a girl, she wanted to ask you about Sergei. I thought I'd bring her over, too."

"I don't want to talk to her."

"Well, then, since I'm with her, I guess I can't come over after all. I suppose I'll see you around sometime."

"*Yobar.*" Fucker.

"I'm seriously offended, sweet Lana. Here I am, trying to do you a favor, trying to help you out, and you curse at me."

"Bring her over, but no names. She can't use my name."

"See you later, Lana."

He went to his kitchen and cut four thick slices from a large loaf of moist raisin pumpernickel bread. He got a large jar of herring in wine sauce out of the refrigerator, a stick of salted butter, and a bottle of Heineken. Tonight he would be drinking, and it was important to coat his stomach.

I've overreacted, Sasha told himself as he slathered butter on the pumpernickel. Why should anybody want to kill me? For helping people adopt babies? For screwing the government out of a few small checks for my rent? For giving some Russians a start in the new land by supplying them with documents? For tricking a few *fraiers* out of a few dollars?

Should I even show up at the Odessa? he wondered. Right now, if Ebzi Agron ever thinks of me at all, he thinks of me as someone who never causes any trouble, someone who's always ready to help one of his men. Why should I attract attention to myself?

Instead of going to the Odessa, wouldn't it be better to stay here with Madeline Malloy?

On the other hand, Sasha thought, can I afford to overlook the possibility that I've crossed the wrong person? What you don't know can kill you, Aleksandr.

Sasha carried the bread, beer, and herring into his living room and sat down on his white leather recliner. It felt cool against his skin. He ate his bread and fish and watched MTV until the bell rang, announcing Madeline Malloy.

Sasha buzzed her in, opened the door to his apartment, and then dashed into the bedroom to throw on some clothes. He chose a pair of beige slacks, a white cotton camp shirt, and a blue blazer. He heard Malloy come in.

"Hello?" she called.

"Just a minute," Sasha said, putting on his sandals. He paused in front of his mirror to brush his still damp hair off his forehead.

Who do I look like? he wondered. The young Brando? Jack Nicholson? He narrowed his eyes and smiled, at first thinly and then broadly, flashing his teeth. Michael Douglas, perhaps? In *Fatal Attraction*? He grimaced. Too depressing. How about Harrison Ford in *The Fugitive*. Fuck it. You're looking good, Aleksandr, he told himself.

Malloy was wearing the same T-shirt and shorts she'd had on in the International that afternoon. She was carrying a small gray plastic atttaché case. She looked hot and tired, but, thought Sasha, that only made her look more vulnerable, more appealing. Poor girl, he thought. She needs someone to take care of her.

"Can I get you something to drink?" asked Sasha. "A beer?"

Malloy checked her watch. "Can we go now?" she asked. "I don't have much time."

"Of course," said Sasha. "Let's go. Wait a minute."

Sasha grabbed the L. L. Bean bag. It would be stupid to leave it in the apartment. It only weighed a few pounds. Safer with me, he thought.

"What's in the bag?" asked Malloy.

"Laundry," Sasha said.

Malloy shrugged. They went down the stairs together and out into the street. It was a cloudy night, and the day's heat still pressed down on the sidewalk.

"She lives not three blocks from here," said Sasha.

"What can you tell me about Sergei Pantera?" Malloy asked as they began to walk up toward Brighton Beach Avenue.

"What's to tell?" said Sasha. "He was not a nice guy. He was always angry, always yelling. He was, in fact, a little bit of a thief. That's what he did."

"There seems to be a lot of crime among the Russians in Brighton," Malloy said.

"Of course there is crime," said Sasha. "What would you expect? That is the way it is with immigrants, always. Isn't that so?"

"I didn't mean to say anything negative about Russians, Sasha. I'm sure it's difficult, adjusting, coming to a new country. But, well, I was talking to a social worker, and she said the new immigrants, Russians, don't seem to understand the idea of doing things legally."

"Look, Maddy Malloy. In the former Soviet Union, everything you do every day is a crime. To survive, to have food, clothes, you forget about laws."

"What do you mean?"

"It is hard to explain. Look, the people in charge, the elite, they are criminals, and they make everybody criminal. They make laws only for themselves, to help themselves. There is never any real laws like here. Nobody in the whole country was honest. That is seriously the way it was."

"I understand. You had to do things to survive. But that's different from being a criminal, isn't it?"

"You think so? Look. I give you a simple example. You are

buying a loaf of bread. So you wait in the queue. Queue, yes? But maybe you have a job, so you can't wait. So you pay someone a few rubles to wait for you, an old babushka who has no job. So then the babushka gets to the front of the line and the clerk says, 'Sorry, grandmother, no bread today.'

"But you know how things work. You give the babushka some extra money. So she says to the clerk, 'Here, sir, here is that money I owe you from before.' And he says, so everyone can hear, 'We don't have bread, but maybe you'd like some butter instead?' And he hides behind the counter and puts some bread in a bag. And all this pretending is for one fucking loaf of bread and it is all absolutely normal.

"Then you read in the newspaper how lucky you are because bread is only two rubles, but you have just paid twelve, and you know that everybody is fucking lying all the time. The leaders are lying. The paper is lying. The clerk is lying. Even, probably, the babushka is lying. She makes a good living waiting on queues, and she probably gives the clerk less than she tells you.

"And this is for everything," Sasha continued, growing excited. Could he make this rich American girl understand how it was? Could any American understand the madness? How everyone was always watching everyone else to make sure that no one was getting more than his or her share. How because everyone was a criminal, everyone—your boss, your neighbor, your wife—was a potential informant.

"Everything was this way," Sasha continued. "For cars, for paint, for toilet paper, for plumbing. For train tickets and for hockey tickets. Everything is a bribe. And why? Because no one owns nothing. Business is against the law. But who can live like that? So everyone is a criminal. You see?"

"That's not crime," said Malloy. "You're twisting words."

"No. It is crime in the Soyuz. Remember the bread. In the Soyuz it is a crime to pay the babushka to wait in line for you.

It is a crime to bribe the clerk. It is a crime for the clerk to take the bribe.

"The bakery director, he is criminal because he has already bribed some *apparatchik* to give him two hundred loaves, not one hundred and fifty like all the other bakeries get. The *apparatchik* is criminal because he takes the bribe, and because the bakery director pays him for two hundred loaves, but he only gives him one hundred and seventy-five.

"That is how it was with every bakery. That is how it was with every can of paint, every light bulb, every coat and hat and car and tractor. This is not crime? This is crime like the world has never seen."

"That's very smart, Sasha, but it's different from being a thief, from someone taking something that belongs to someone else," Malloy said.

"Oh, yes? I don't think so."

"Those loaves of bread. Who were they stolen from?"

"From Russia," said Sasha. "You don't see?"

"It's very complicated," Malloy said.

"No, it is just business," said Sasha. "Bad business because it keeps everyone poor.

"Here we are. She won't tell you her name."

They climbed the stairs and knocked on Sergei Pantera's door. Svetlana Furtseva opened it and, turning her back on them, walked back inside, throwing herself down on an overstuffed couch. She didn't invite them to sit.

The apartment was dark; the air-conditioning was turned up high. In a purple bathrobe and purple slippers, Furtseva was short and chubby with pimples on her chin and forehead, large breasts, and a mass of frizzy blond hair pinned haphazardly atop her head. But her eyes, thought Sasha, her eyes were azure and sad and beautifully Russian.

Sasha put the canvas bag on the floor between his legs. Malloy sat on the other end of the couch from Furtseva.

Furtseva ignored Malloy. She patted her hair and then reached into her robe for a pack of cigarettes. Sasha didn't have to see her hand waving as she lit the cigarette to know that she was drunk. The smell of alcohol clung to her more tightly than her robe.

"You have my money?" Furtseva asked Sasha in a phlegmy rasp.

"Tell her how sorry I am about Sergei," said Malloy.

"She says she's sorry about what happened to the Panther," Sasha said. "I'll give you the money when we finish."

"She knew Sergei?" asked Furtseva. "Was she fucking him?"

"Be serious," Sasha said.

"Tell her my name is Madeline Malloy, and I'm with the *Daily News*. Ask her if she would tell me her name. Tell her I won't use it if she doesn't want me to."

"She wants to know your name. She says she won't print it in her newspaper."

"Bullshit. No names. You think I want the police here again? You think I want them checking up on me?"

Malloy read the refusal without Sasha's translation. "All right," she said. "Ask her if she has any idea who might have shot her friend."

"Do you know who shot Sergei?" Sasha asked.

"How the fuck would I know?" said Furtseva. "You think that bastard ever told me what he was doing? You think I knew where he was going, who he was meeting? You think I ever saw him except when he'd fall into bed drunk and try to fuck me?"

Furtseva lit another cigarette with the smoldering butt of the first. Then she dropped the butt on the rug. Her anger was sobering her.

"Maybe you shot him, Sasha," Furtseva said. "I see you've got the bag the ugly Yid was carrying around. Maybe you shot both of them."

"No," Sasha told Malloy. "She doesn't have any idea." This is a waste of time, he thought. And worse. I shouldn't have brought the bag.

"Ask her if she thinks that New York, Brooklyn, is a dangerous place now," said Malloy, knowing that that would be a good angle.

"She wants to know if you think Brooklyn is dangerous," Sasha asked Furtseva.

Furtseva laughed. "Dangerous for Sergei, I guess," she said. "Dangerous for some people. Not for this bitch, eh, Sasha? You like her? You fucking her?"

"She says she loves it here," Sasha told Malloy.

"Is she being sarcastic?" asked Malloy.

"I don't think so," Sasha said.

"Ask her what Sergei's dreams were, what he wanted to accomplish in America," said Malloy, smiling at Furtseva, trying to look sympathetic.

"She wants to know why Sergei came to America," Sasha said. "What he wanted to do here."

"What the Panther wanted to do?" Furtseva laughed again, ground out her second cigarette, and smiled back at Malloy, who was unnerved by the contrast between the smile on the Russian woman's face and the way she gripped her bathrobe as if to stop herself from attacking her. "Tell her he wanted to fuck every woman and drink every bottle of vodka in America. Tell her he wanted to run around doing your dirty work while you screwed him out of his money. He loved getting screwed by you, Sasha. He talked about it all the time. He used to say, 'Lana, I just love the way that Yid Sasha cheats us. And when I die,' he said to me, 'that Sasha is going to steal my last kopek and then he's going to come by with some American bitch and try to buy you off with a few pennies.' A hundred bucks, my *bulshoi* ass."

"Actually, Lana darling," said Sasha, "your beloved Sergei owed me two thousand dollars."

"And you expect to get it from me, you prick?" Furtseva said. "You can kiss my *bulshoi* ass."

"What's she saying?" asked Malloy. "What're you talking about?"

"She says Sergei wanted to go to college to become an engineer. In the former Soviet Union, he could not get into technical school because he was not a Party member, not a Communist. But here, in America, he thought anything was possible. So, she says it is very sad what happened, but," Sasha said after pausing a moment, "she will not let it stop her from going to beauty school to become a hairdresser."

"Come on, Sasha. What did she really say?" Malloy asked.

"She called you a bitch and she told me to kiss her big fat ass," said Sasha. He shrugged. "Not too good for your paper, eh?"

"Why is she angry at you?"

"She is angry at everyone. Her boyfriend was just killed."

"All right. Please ask her if she has a picture of Sergei. A nice picture we could run in the newspaper so that people can see what he looked like."

"Do you have a picture of Sergei, for the newspaper?" Sasha asked.

"One hundred dollars," Furtseva said in English.

"She wants a hundred dollars for a picture?" asked Malloy.

"One hundred dollars," Furtseva repeated.

"We don't pay for photographs," said Malloy to Furtseva. "American newspapers don't work that way."

"I'll give you the hundred after the American leaves," Sasha told Furtseva. "Just give her a goddamn picture of the Panther."

Furtseva got up and left the room.

"Is she getting a picture of Pantera?" asked Malloy.

"I think so," Sasha said.

Furtseva returned with a small automatic pistol. She held it out in front of her. She held it with both hands and pointed it at Sasha. Her hands were shaking, and so was the mouth of the pistol. Sasha looked down the barrel. It was a small, black hole in his world.

"Keep your money, you bastard," she said. "I know. Everybody thought Sergei was an asshole. Even me. But now he's dead. He's dead and I'm the only one who gives a shit. You understand, big shot? I'm the only one. So get out. Get the hell out and take the American bitch with you."

"All right, Svetlana," said Sasha, bending slowly to pick up the bag. "It's all right." He turned to Malloy. "She is very upset. We should go now."

Malloy nodded.

"We're going now, Svetlana," Sasha said as the mouth of Furtseva's gun swiveled to follow them to the door. He reached behind him for the doorknob and opened it without turning his back to Furtseva. He pushed Malloy out into the hallway. Once Malloy was out of the apartment, he turned to Furtseva. "You're right, Lana," said Sasha. "Sergei was an asshole. You deserved better."

Sasha backed through the entrance and shut the door.

❖   ❖   ❖

"Oh, my God," Malloy said, giggling, as they ran down the stairs.

"I'm sorry," said Sasha, thinking that Malloy must be out of her head with fear. "She is, you know, crazy with grief. I am sure she was not going to shoot us."

"No, I mean, what a great story. Thank you, Sasha."

"What story?" asked Sasha as they walked out onto the street. "She said nothing."

"It wasn't what she said. It was the place, the bathrobe, her eyes. And the gun. That was wonderful. Sasha," she said, grabbing his arm, "I need someplace where I can sit down, write the story. Someplace with a phone so I can modem it to the office."

"Your computer?" asked Sasha, pointing to the small gray attaché case at her side.

"My laptop. Is there a bar we can go to? A bar with a table and a phone. I need a drink, anyway."

"You are something, Maddy Malloy," Sasha said.

He took her to the Georgian Cafe, a narrow room decorated in black-and-gray linoleum one flight up from the street. What it lacked in charm, it made up for in Emma Bovrilina's cooking. She immediately brought them two glasses of vodka and a plate of *hinkali,* delicate little dumplings shaped like cupolas. Malloy knocked back her vodka and then went to telephone the paper to find out how much space she had and to argue, futilely, for more. When she returned, she set up her laptop and began typing.

Sasha ordered fried potatoes with raspberry-and-vinegar sauce; and chicken and walnuts in a sour-cherry sauce. It was delicious. Bovrilina brought him another vodka and a few slices of rye bread and butter.

He watched Malloy type, enjoying her intensity. Her cheeks were rosy now, and her blue eyes seemed to glitter. Her long, thin fingers flew over the keys.

This woman is a fighter, he thought. Like Svetlana Furtseva, only good-looking. This is a woman who would kill for you, or kill you if you gave her cause. The thought excited him.

"Did you notice what kind of gun she had?" Malloy asked.

"No. It was not important for me to notice."

"Sasha," said Malloy, "what did the woman really say

when I asked her what Pantera wanted to do in America? She didn't just curse us out."

"Sergei Pantera was a thief," said Sasha. "That's what he did in the former Soviet Union, and that's what he did here. That's all. That's the truth."

"Then why did he come here?"

"There's more to steal."

"Is that all?"

"Look, Maddy Malloy. Life in the former Soviet Union was no damn good. That's all. You see the woman who runs this place, who cooks this wonderful food? Her name is Emma Bovrilina. She is a wonderful cook, a good woman. She lived in Chernobyl. You heard of Chernobyl."

"Of course."

"Well, Emma Bovrilina's only son is dead from cancer of the thyroid because for five days the government don't tell what happened there. Can you imagine? For five days they let people walk around, breathing poison, because they seriously do not give a shit. They were bastards. That is the truth.

"And do you know why Emma Bovrilina is managing this cafe and not her husband? Because he commits suicide when the son dies. For that too the bastards are guilty.

"So why shouldn't Sergei Pantera come to America? And so what if he was a thief? It is not so terrible. There are much more terrible things to be. There are much worse criminals, and many of them are in the government, even in your American government. So that is the truth about Sergei Pantera. You heard Svetlana. He was a human being. That's all."

"Is that her name, Svetlana?" Malloy asked. "Svetlana what?"

Sasha smiled. "I forget you are a reporter, Maddy Malloy. I must not forget again."

"I won't use that. But can I quote you?"

"What I just said about Bovrilina and Pantera?"

"Yes."

"About Pantera, yes. About Bovrilina, no. You can talk to her yourself."

"Okay. But why was Svetlana angry with you? Weren't you Pantera's friend?"

"A friend? I knew him. Sure. Why not? Yes, I was a friend."

"So why was she pissed at you?"

"I told you. She was pissed at everyone."

"All right. But if Pantera was a thief, what are you, Sasha?"

"I told you, Maddy Malloy. You forget? I am a businessman. Just write that I am a businessman."

"What kind of businessman?"

"The kind that does business."

"Is it legal business?"

"Do you think I would tell you if it wasn't? Tell you so you can write it in your newspaper?"

"If it were legal, you'd tell me."

"You are not going to trick me, Maddy Malloy."

"I don't like businessmen as a rule."

"Of course," said Sasha. "You are an intellectual. All intellectuals hate businessmen. In the West. But in the East, today, the businessmen are the intellectuals. Someday I will explain it to you."

"And then you'll tell me your last name?"

"Someday. Not now. Not for your newspaper. Later, between us. When it is private. When it is . . . I don't know the word when two people are together, close."

"Intimate?"

"Yes."

"And what makes you think we'll ever be intimate?"

Sasha shrugged, smiling.

"All right. We'll see," said Malloy.

She got up and spoke to Emma Bovrilina for a few minutes and then went back to her typing. When she finished, she took the computer over to the phone, dialed the paper, attached the computer's modem, and sent her story.

"May I read it?" Sasha asked when Malloy returned to the table.

"Not now. It'll make me self-conscious. It'll be in tomorrow's paper."

"I will buy it. Would you like another drink?"

"No, thank you, Sasha," said Malloy. "I'm exhausted. I should be heading home."

"So where is home?" Sasha asked.

"Manhattan."

Sasha checked his watch. It was ten.

"I tell you what, Maddy Malloy," he said. He had an idea. "I will ride with you to Manhattan to keep you company."

"No, that's all right," said Malloy. "I'm fine."

"I said this wrong," Sasha said. "I will ride with you to Manhattan to keep me company. Because I enjoy your company. That should be seriously enough company for both of us, yes?"

"All right, Sasha. Thank you."

Sasha, the canvas bag on the floor between his legs thought the ride uptown, over the bridge, was romantic, and he hoped Malloy felt the same. She told him that she was still going to do a story on Brighton Beach's Russian community. She wanted to interview Emma Bovrilina some more. She thought Sasha could be very helpful. He agreed.

When they reached her building on the corner of East Sixteenth Street and Third, Sasha walked her to the door while the cab waited to take him back to Brooklyn.

"May I come in?" Sasha asked.

Malloy frowned.

"No," said Sasha. "It is not what you think. I need to use your bathroom. See? The cab is waiting."

"All right," Malloy said.

The elevator took them to the ninth floor. Malloy opened her apartment door and led Sasha down a hall to a small bathroom. Sasha went in, closed the door, and smiled. The bathroom, as he had hoped it would be, was a mess. There were sweatpants, sweatshirts, underpants, and bras on the floor, bottles and jars everywhere. Carefully, he opened the linen closet opposite the toilet. It was, he was happy to see, very deep. There were shelves full of towels and washcloths, shelves with prescription drugs, empty jugs of bleach and ammonia, hair blowers, and cardboard boxes on the floor filled with empty shampoo bottles.

He put the bag behind one of the boxes on the floor.

It would only be for tonight, he told himself. Maybe a day.

Maybe she'd notice, maybe she wouldn't. If she did, he'd tell her a story about the KGB.

He flushed the toilet.

"Good night, Maddy Malloy," he said as soon as he opened the door. "May I kiss you good night?"

Malloy immediately noticed that Sasha was no longer carrying the L. L. Bean bag. She decided not to say anything. First she'd find out what it was, then she'd confront him. Maybe there'd be a story in it. She was sure there'd be a story in it.

She let Sasha kiss her. He cupped her cheeks in his hands. Sasha shivered. Malloy felt him tremble. She broke off the kiss. Having decided he was a con man, she had expected boldness, not tenderness, not passion restrained.

"I will see you soon, Maddy Malloy?" he asked.

"I think so," she said, thinking about the bag Sasha had left in her bathroom—intentionally, she was sure—and, to her own genuine surprise, thinking about the brief kiss that was so much more affecting than she had expected it to be.

Sasha got back into the cab and gave the driver the Odessa's address. He was glad the driver was not Russian. A Russian would have made some stupid comment about Sasha and the American girl. Russians were always jealous, Sasha thought. Always afraid that someone else might be getting away with something, might be doing better than they were.

I should have been born an American, Sasha thought. I could have been a movie star. I could have lived in Hollywood with a swimming pool and, and . . .

Sasha's fantasy failed him. The tide of exhilaration that had risen with the kiss began to ebb. He felt good about stashing the bag, not so good about having deceived Madeline Malloy.

Don't be sentimental, he scolded himself. Now, he thought, the trick is finding someone I can trust to tell me what the box of coins is worth. Maybe Henry will level with me and cut me in. Maybe I can trust Henry, even though he tried to screw me out of this deal.

Life is hard, thought Sasha. You do what you can, what you must, to get by.

As Sasha's cab took him back to Brooklyn, Maddy Malloy sat on the toilet seat, staring at the antique lacquered coin box from Zagorsk. It was beautiful. Hunters in furs, atop muscular horses, chasing a bear through a snow-covered forest. But she wasn't sure what to make of it or what to make of the feckless Russian who had hidden it in her home so ineptly. But she was certain about one thing.

She had the makings of one hell of a story.

7.

GENTLY, TENDERLY, ALEKSANDR VOLKOV PUSHED THE WOMAN'S hair back and away from her ear. He sucked and then lightly bit her earlobe. Delicious, he thought. "I have to go," he whispered.

The woman shook her head.

"Yes, I am sorry, but I must," said Volkov. "Will you wait for me? Wait here until I get back?"

The woman tried to say something.

"I want you to wait like this," Volkov said, his lips against her ear. "When I come back, I want to see you just like this."

The woman mumbled.

Volkov loosened her gag.

"Are you crazy?" she said.

Volkov put the gag back.

He swung his feet over the edge of the water bed. "Would you like more champagne?"

The woman grunted angrily.

"I will get it," Volkov said.

He stood up and the water in the mattress gurgled and

plashed. He looked down at the woman, bobbing up and down with the mattress's tide, her arms and legs bound with thick, braided silk cords to the bed's posts. He liked this one. He liked her small, hard breasts, her flat, muscular stomach, her slim, athletic hips. He bent over and dragged his fingernails across her belly, admiring the faint red lines they left in their wake.

"You are fantastic," said Volkov, lightly touching the woman's nipple.

She closed her eyes.

"No, I mean it. You are really great," Volkov said. "You want to see something amazing?"

The woman sighed.

"In a minute," he said.

Naked, Volkov walked into the kitchen. He opened the refrigerator and pulled out an open bottle of Mumm's Cordon Rouge. He took a swig. Am I feeling better? he asked himself.

Yes, he thought, a little.

He opened the top cupboard and took out his small, autoloading Heckler & Koch P7, the Rolls-Royce of nine-millimeter pistols, the gun he had been carrying on the beach just in case the psycho he had hired to knock off Pantera and Boris had missed.

The psycho hadn't missed, but everything else had been a disaster.

It had been awful. Seeing Pantera walk across the sand, and then seeing Boris appear with another man. Volkov had started running toward them. He'd probably have to pop the third man himself, he thought. Then he saw Pantera fall, Boris's head explode, and the third man scoop up the bag.

And then, recognizing the third man, Sasha Eugenev, he'd decided not to chase him, not to risk policemen pouring onto the beach. No matter what identification he showed them (and Aleksandr Volkov had some of the best), there was no doubt they would take the bag. And getting it back would be a problem.

The idea of ripping off the uranium had been doing fast circles in Volkov's mind ever since Henry Tepperman had asked him if he could find a buyer for it. At first, he hadn't believed Tepperman would come through. Tepperman, he thought, just didn't have the connections in the military and science *apparats*. Then, after Volkov lined up the buyer, and after Tepperman told him the package was on the way, Volkov thought, Why be a middleman? Why share the profit? It wasn't the American way.

So he had asked around about Tepperman's New York contacts, and he had discovered his old Kolpashevo friend Aleksandr Eugenev's little gang. He had found out that Sergei Pantera would be meeting Tepperman's courier.

It had been easy bribing Pantera.

And Volkov wouldn't have had to tell the buyer, the little Yid, anything. He could simply have turned over the uranium, pocketed the money, and disappeared. Fat chance Tepperman could ever have found him. Of course, Volkov knew someone was behind Tepperman. Someone had to be. And escaping that someone might have proved difficult. But a million dollars makes a lot of things easier.

And it would have worked if it hadn't been for Sasha Eugenev.

As it was, he had had to tell the Yid that the uranium had disappeared.

"See," Volkov had told him. "You can't trust Tepperman. He'll tell you it's been stolen. I tell you he's found another buyer."

The Yid had believed him, as Volkov knew he would. The Yid believed everything Volkov told him. Working for the CIA was no guarantee that you were smart, especially if you were, as Volkov suspected the Yid to be, a closet homosexual, and the man lying to you was big, blond, and muscular.

The thing to do was find the uranium. And that, he told himself, shouldn't be so hard. What was a small-timer like Sasha Eugenev going to do with it?

Of course, now he couldn't just tell the Yid that he had found it lying on the street. The Yid wasn't that stupid, and he was hardly without resources. If Volkov tried to run something like that by him now, he could end up with a bullet behind the ear. No, now he would have to play the middleman's role for real. He had to find a new seller to satisfy the Yid that he hadn't taken the uranium himself. That was all right. He had a candidate all lined up. He also had a fall guy for the theft—Sasha Eugenev, of course. He'd bring the Yid Sasha's head and be a hero.

There was nothing wrong with the first plan, he told himself again. It was just bad luck. And it won't happen again.

Aleksandr Volkov, whose visa now read "Aleksandr Velikhov," trusted his luck. It had always served him well. As a Komsomol leader in technical school, he had always guessed right when it came to which students to befriend and which ones to denounce. When he had been ordered to infiltrate the labor camp at Kolpashevo, his first big assignment after two years of pushing paper at KGB headquarters in the Lubyanka, it was lucky that the new thief brought into the yard that morning, Aleksandr Eugenev, looked so much like him, thereby giving him the idea of spreading the word that he was a KGB plant.

Two years later, when he was part of the Alpha group that assassinated the Afghani dictator Amin in his own palace in Kabul, something, a notion, led Volkov to delay his return to Moscow, thereby escaping when the plane carrying the elite group home conveniently (for the Politburo) exploded in midair.

As the lone survivor of that action, Volkov prospered

within the KGB. An accomplished assassin, a wet worker, he received excellent postings, both in the near abroad and in the West, allowing him to cultivate his taste for sexual violence in some of Europe's finest homes and hotels.

And in August 1991, when so many of his colleagues were left out in the cold, Volkov's luck held. He had a fax machine fall into his lap. Sniffing the way the wind was blowing, he smuggled it to Boris Yeltsin, who was holed up in the White House, even as KGB troops prepared for the assault that the leaders of the coup against Gorbachev eventually proved too demoralized to order.

Yeltsin's people used the machine to rally the world to their cause. After that, they couldn't do enough for Volkov. They got him a job with the First Private Bank of Moscow, and that enabled him to come to New York, a city he adored, and move, rent free, into this wonderful apartment on East Seventy-second Street, near all the bars, near all the lovely, accomplished American girls like the one in his bed right now. They provided him with a letter of introduction to the people at Langley, who were assiduously recruiting KGB agents much as they had recruited Nazi intelligence officers after World War II.

Yes, thought Volkov, I have lived in the eye of the storm, and now I have emerged.

And now, he thought, I will truly be a revolutionary. I will go into business for myself.

Volkov brought the champagne into the bedroom.

The woman saw the gun. Her eyes widened, her body stiffened.

Volkov laughed. "No, no," he said, waving the gun. "Not for you, precious." Not now, anyway, he thought. He walked to his closet and slipped the pistol into his coat pocket. Then he turned around.

The woman's eyes were still wide with fear, and Volkov

felt himself becoming aroused. He would like to nurture that look, he thought, feed it, and make it blossom.

He walked over to the bed and pinched the woman's hard little nipple between his thumb and forefinger. She gasped beneath the gag. He twisted. She strained against the cords holding her wrists and ankles. Volkov watched the play of muscles beneath her skin. Beautiful, he thought.

He checked his watch. Too bad. There was no time for this now. First, he had to pay Sasha Eugenev a little visit before he figured out what to do with his ill-gotten treasure. Introduce myself, thought Volkov. Blow his face off. Then he had a date with the *batyushka*. Ebzi Agron would be the new source he would introduce to the Yid, and Volkov would get paid twice—once by Agron and once by the Yid, who certainly wouldn't care who, Tepperman or Agron, supplied the uranium.

The woman whined behind her gag. Volkov loosened it again.

"Please," she said, trying not to let her voice tremble. "Please. I'm not having fun anymore. Let me up."

"Have a sip of champagne," Volkov said, pouring a glass and putting it to her lips. "You don't remember? I said I was going to show you something amazing."

"All right," the woman said reluctantly.

Volkov put his hand beneath his scrotum and lifted the sac. "Three balls," he said. "Just like Hitler."

"Oh, for Christ's sake," said the woman, angry now. "Just let me up, will ya?"

"I do not think so," said Volkov, annoyed. He slipped the gag back into place. This is what I get for picking up women, he thought. You have to work so hard. I should stick to boys.

Aleksandr Volkov got dressed and, after checking the woman's bonds and gag, left the apartment. When the woman realized that the charming, handsome, urbane Russian she had met just four hours before had not been joking and, indeed, had left her alone, gagged and tied, for who knew how long, she began to struggle. After a while, she felt a warmth spreading between her legs, and she began to weep with frustration.

She had peed.

8.

IT WAS ELEVEN-THIRTY BY THE TIME THE CAB PULLED UP IN FRONT of the club on Brighton Beach Avenue off Ocean Parkway. Sasha stopped outside the Odessa's door. The heat of the day had finally broken, and the night had become cool. A breeze blew off the ocean. He lit a cigarette and walked inside.

A few young dudes were hanging out in the vestibule, smoking and playing Tetris and video poker. Sasha knew most of them as Agron hangers-on, punks who collected protection money from local shop owners. Sasha nodded to them and continued up the narrow stairs that led to the ballroom. He was greeted at the top by Boris Reidel, the Odessa's maître d'.

"Good to see you, Sasha," said Reidel. "Terrible about Pantera, eh? You know who the other guy was?"

"No idea," Sasha said, knowing that whatever he told Reidel would eventually be reported, word for word, to Ebzi Agron.

"Terrible, terrible," said Reidel. "The neighborhood is getting so dangerous. It's the new guys. Puzaitzer. Ivankov. Zilberstein. They have no respect. All they do is fuck, drink, and kill people. They take drugs, you know. Crazy men. Probably Israelis did the shooting, you think?"

"Don't know, Boris." Sasha looked out over the dance floor. Up on a large stage, five young men in orange tuxedos and blue ruffled shirts played a soft disco tune by Sade while a slender but buxom Asian girl sang pleasantly. She wore a long, low-cut silver sequined dress and silver high heels. Her breasts were up around her clavicle. Plastic, Sasha was sure.

A mirror ball revolved through a cloud of cigarette smoke high above the polished wood floor where about two dozen couples were dancing. Seventy or eighty tables, about three-quarters occupied, crowded the edge of the dance floor. The tables were piled high with food. There were bottles of Scotch, bourbon, cognac, and vodka.

"Busy night," said Sasha.

Reidel shrugged. "Every night. You alone?" he asked.

Sasha looked out over the crowd, trying to find David Gatlober in the shadows. He spotted him across the room, toward the rear, sitting at a small table with a big, broad-shouldered woman with short hair dyed white. Terry, thought Sasha, shuddering slightly. So that's still going on.

Closer to the dance floor, against the room's far wall, he saw Ebzi Agron, sitting with six or seven men and women.

"Yeah," Sasha said to Reidel. "All alone. Poor me."

"Sit anywhere you like," Reidel said, gesturing toward the tables. "Should I send over a bottle? You want anything to eat?"

"Sure. Send over a bottle of Absolut and a plate of *vereniki*. And some bread." Sasha pressed a twenty into Reidel's hand. "Tonight, Boris. Okay?"

Reidel nodded gravely, pocketing the bill. "No problem, Sasha."

Sasha threaded his way through the tables. The trick, he thought, was to find a seat close enough to Agron to let him know that he was there, but not so close that the *batyushka* would think he was being pushy. He nodded to Viktor Shapiro, who nodded back. As he approached Ebzi Agron, he saw the *batyushka* look up. Their eyes met, and Agron waved him over.

"So, Aleksandr Volkavitch," boomed Agron, a thickset man in his early fifties with reddish blond hair cut short and standing straight up. "You know all my friends here."

Sasha looked around the table, recognizing three of Agron's inner circle. He nodded a greeting. The men ignored him. The women—there were four; one, presumably, was for Agron—were unknown to him, but they all smiled.

"So, you wanted to speak to me?" Agron asked. Before Sasha could say anything, Agron held up a meaty palm. "Later. When the *fraiers* are gone. Okay?"

"Okay, Ebzi," said Sasha, backing away.

Sasha sat down to the right and rear of Agron, about eight tables away, and lit another cigarette. Within moments, a waiter in a white shirt and black tuxedo vest appeared with a bottle of Absolut, some bread and butter, and a plate of *vereniki* with onions and mushrooms.

Sasha watched Agron, watched him eat and drink and talk to the little Chinese girl sitting next to him. She looked ill at ease. Sasha was afraid of Agron, too, and he knew he had good reason to be.

Ebzi Agron was an Uzbeki Jew, a brutal man, a thug who got lucky. Twice.

From the time he was twenty, Agron had run the city of Bukhara with his fists. With a gang of toughs, he collected protection money from all the restaurant owners who ran card games in their basements, back rooms, and alleyways. And that meant just about all of Bukhara's restaurant owners. Then, one day in 1975, Aleksei Karimov, then first secretary of the Bukhara Oblast Party Committee, decided that he could no longer trust the local militia, so he asked Agron to make an agricultural investigator from Moscow disappear. When Agron did so, he received a new car, courtesy of Vakhab Usmanov, Minister of the Cotton-Refining Industry in Uzbekistan, the most powerful man in the Uzbeki Republic.

When it got around that Agron was Usmanov's man, every merchant, militiaman, black marketeer, gambler, and dope pusher in Bukhara rushed to cut him in on their action. All Agron had to do was sit back and figure out how to get the money out of his mattress and into a bank account in Switzerland.

Agron grew rich until the Uzbek Cotton Affair erupted and the new general secretary, Yuri Andropov, announced his "battle against corruption." In 1981 Usmanov was arrested and executed. It seemed that for years he had been systematically inflating cotton production figures, adding millions of imaginary tons to the actual amount of raw cotton turned over to the state. The money the state paid Usmanov and the rest of the Uzbeki *apparat* for the nonexistent cotton vanished into the pockets of Politburo members, into the Uzbeki *mafiya,* and into Ebzi Agron's Swiss bank account. But once Usmanov was dead and Karimov jailed, once "cleaning up" Uzbekistan became an Andropov priority (although, as Agron often said, the former KGB chief's real priority was "covering up" Uzbekistan, prosecuting small fry like Usmanov and Karimov while hiding the involvement of bigger fish like Politburo member Yegor Ligachev), Agron suddenly rediscovered his Jewish roots. His application for emigration to Israel moved through the system with amazing speed. ("They *wanted* me out," Agron would say, laughing. "I knew where all the bodies were rotting.") He spent six months in Tel Aviv before leaving for Brooklyn, where he had his second lucky break.

He met Moyshe Rubenstein.

Moyshe Rubenstein was originally from Kishinev, in Moldavia. All Moldavians were smart, but Rubenstein was a genius. One day, watching gas being pumped into his Buick Regal at a station on Coney Island Avenue, he started calculating how much money a gas station could make if it didn't pay the twenty-eight-cents-a-gallon tax. The little computer in Rubenstein's head produced a figure that made his heart race, especially when he multiplied it by the number of gas stations in Coney Island and Brighton Beach alone.

In a few years, Rubenstein controlled a dozen gas stations, although you could put the ownership papers under a microscope without finding his name. He bought oil cheaply on the spot market in Turkey and sold it at a discount in Brooklyn. And he never paid a penny in taxes. Whenever the IRS audited a station, Rubenstein would simply close it down and open another. The IRS would track down the station's owner, and it would invariably turn out to be a blind, deaf old woman living in a retirement home on Ocean Avenue. By the end of the eighties, Moyshe Rubenstein was a phenomenally wealthy man.

Indeed, he was so rich that he attracted the attention of John Gotti, who felt that Rubenstein needed a partner. Rubenstein wasn't averse to the idea of a partner, but he didn't want it to be the notoriously greedy Gotti, head of the Genovese crime family. So he called upon the newly arrived Uzbeki, Ebzi Agron, who had a reputation as a man who could discourage one's enemies.

Agron, importing former Israeli soldiers armed with Soviet-made weapons, discouraged the Italians, who were, for once, outgunned. Instead of a partnership, they settled for a small operating tax. Then Rubenstein turned up naked and dead in an apartment on East Twenty-seventh Street. He had been strangled.

Agron inherited the gas business.

He became the *batyushka*.

Sasha ate fast and drank slowly. He watched as the *boye-*

viki, the *mafiya* soldiers in their broad-shouldered, washed-silk suits, drifted in and out of the club, all of them stopping by Agron's table to pay their respects. Viktor Shapiro suddenly appeared in front of Sasha to berate him for bringing that American girl into the International.

"I didn't bring her," Sasha protested. "I don't even know her. I was just trying to pick her up."

"Bullshit," said Shapiro. "You took her over to Svetlana Furtseva's place tonight."

Sasha shook his head, but he wasn't surprised. Russians. Born spies. Born informers. How many did they now say Stalin killed? Twenty million? He wouldn't have been able to kill twenty if it weren't for everybody spying and informing on their neighbors.

"You want a drink, Viktor?" Sasha asked.

Shapiro nodded and tossed off a shot.

"I don't know what you're up to, Aleksandr Volkavitch," said Shapiro. "Just watch your ass."

The band was packing up. The Odessa was emptying out, slowly at first, then rapidly. Waiters were moving from table to table, telling people that the club was closing.

It was almost two in the morning. Sasha had finished half his bottle of Absolut, and he felt good. Relaxed, but not drunk. Sharp, but not tense. There were perhaps thirty people left in the club.

Ebzi Agron stood up, steadying himself by placing a meaty hand on the table. He was wearing an electric blue double-breasted suit with white buttons the size of half-dollars and a white-on-white shirt open at the throat. The room grew silent.

"The people's court is now in session," Agron shouted. "Bring in the defendant."

Two of Agron's men walked toward the dance floor, half dragging a man between them. Someone kicked a chair out onto the floor, and the two men sat the man down. Sasha recognized him. The druggist.

Agron stood over the man on the chair. "Pyotr Yakovlevich Heifetz," he boomed, "you are accused of being a son of a bitch working for another son of a bitch, Boris Zilberstein. You are accused of running to the police on Zilberstein's orders and informing on our brother, Valery Konovalov, who is now in jail thanks to you. How do you plead?"

"I spit on Boris Zilberstein," said Heifetz, looking up at Agron. "I have no business with him. The thing with Konovalov, he came into my shop and took money out of my cash register. Just like that. He reached in and took money. He said he was from you, Ebzi, but how did I know? To me, he looked like any thief. So I called the police."

"You're a shit," Agron said. "You're a liar. You knew he was from me. You were insulting me. And if you didn't know, you should have asked. How could you think you'd get away with this? You lost your brains?"

Agron flicked a finger against Heifetz's skull. "You're guilty, aren't you, Pyotr?" he said. "It will be easier for you if you just admit it."

"No," said Pyotr. "It wasn't my fault. I didn't know."

"Brothers," Agron said, turning his back on Heifetz, addressing the men left in the Odessa. "You've heard the bitch. What do you say?"

"Guilty," shouted Agron's men, laughing. Sasha saw David Gatlober, who had moved up behind Agron's table, pound the table in agreement, his silly cowboy hat bobbing on his head.

Agron took off his jacket and handed it to one of his men. He rolled up his sleeves. His forearms were thick, pink, and hairless.

"Please, Ebzi," Heifetz said. "Don't."

Agron pulled his fist back behind his ear, and then, after

pausing to set himself, to make sure he was perfectly balanced, he struck Heifetz in the temple, knocking him sideways off the chair. The men cheered. "Help me," ordered Agron, and two men picked Heifetz off the floor and sat him back down, each holding an arm.

"I'm sorry, Ebzi," Heifetz said, his eyes closed, tears streaming down his face. "You're right. I'm guilty. I knew Konovalov was your guy. I'm sorry. I got angry. It was stupid. But I swear. It had nothing to do with Zilberstein."

"I believe you," said Agron, first patting Heifetz's cheek and then swinging his elbow into his mouth. Heifetz's head snapped back and then fell forward. Another cheer rose from the audience. Agron turned, bowed to his fans, and then, spinning with surprising speed, he swung with his left hand, catching Heifetz on the bridge of his nose, crushing it. There was more applause. Agron grabbed Heifetz's hair, pulled his head back, and punched directly down, again into the druggist's ruined nose. Heifetz's body went limp.

"He's out," someone shouted. "He's finished."

Heifetz rolled off the chair onto the floor, unconscious. Agron turned him onto his back with the toe of his shoe. He began to walk away, and then, thinking better of it, he turned and drove his heel into Heifetz's mouth and then into his neck. Heifetz made a gurgling sound. Sasha looked at Gatlober, who was pounding on the table and whistling, as was the big blonde beside him.

A psycho, Sasha thought. Two psychos. Not to mention Agron. Sasha felt nauseated. Suddenly he was sweating profusely. He no longer felt sharp.

Agron kicked Heifetz in the side of the head and then twice in the ribs. Heifetz could have been a sack of flour. From where he sat, Sasha could see a pool of blood forming around Heifetz's head.

"Kick him in the balls, Ebzi," shouted an ugly, squint-eyed man Sasha knew as Arkady the Lover. "See if that wakes him up."

Agron bent over Heifetz for a moment and then straightened up. "I think he's dead," he said, breathing heavily from his exertions. "Zhenya, what do you think?" Agron asked.

To Sasha's shock, Dr. Evgeny Bekker emerged from the shadows and drifted toward where Pyotr Heifetz lay. Bekker knelt and opened Heifetz's lids—first the left, then the right—with his thumb. He put his ear to Heifetz's ruined mouth. He felt for the carotid artery. He stood up.

"You're right, Ebzi," said Bekker, swaying slightly. "You certainly know a dead man when you see one. Massive insult to the trachea caused by the sudden application of your heel is my guess. I think he drowned in his own blood. That's my initial diagnosis. On the other hand, it could be shock, heart attack, cerebral hemorrhage, hard to say. But dead for sure."

Agron shrugged, walked over to Sasha's table, and sat down, breathing heavily. He poured himself a drink from Sasha's bottle while his men dragged Pyotr Heifetz's body away, leaving a trail of blood on the dance floor.

Sasha poured himself some vodka, hoping he could keep it down.

"So, what do you know about dinosaurs, Sasha?" asked Agron, still panting.

"Dinosaurs? I don't know. Not much, Ebzi. Why?"

"I saw a program on television the other night," Agron said. "It said that dinosaurs were fast, not slow like lizards, fast like birds. That seemed right to me. How could slow animals rule the earth?"

"They were big?" offered Sasha.

"Big doesn't matter. Speed matters. Quickness. Decisiveness," Agron said, slapping the table for emphasis. Sasha noticed the small blue prison tattoo of an eagle on the web of flesh between Agron's thumb and forefinger—a sign of the *Vory v Zakone,* the thieves-in-law.

"That's what I've always tried to be," continued Agron. "Fast. Faster than the men around me. It's not hard, you know. Most Russians are slow. Look what happened to the Party. It got slow. But from what I know about you, you're fast, too. So, Sasha. What can I tell you?"

"I was wondering if you had heard anything, Ebzi," said Sasha. "I mean, probably what happened today on the beach had nothing to do with me, but I want to be sure, you know?"

"Who can be sure about anything, eh, Aleksandr Volkavitch? Take me, for instance. I didn't think I would kill that druggist. It was not in my mind to do it. But look what happens. A few slaps, he's dead. Well, too bad. I'm sorry, but that's the way it goes.

"Do you think the Panther knew he was going to have his head blown off?" Agron continued. "Do you think Boris the Kike knew? Of course not. And Boris was one smart Yid. Of course, you knew that. But the point I'm making, Sasha, is that you never know. You never know anything. All you can do is keep your trap shut, watch your ass, and try to get by. Am I right?"

Sasha didn't know what to say. Agron apparently knew Boris, but what made Sasha think Agron would ever be straight with him?

This had been a mistake. He should never have gone to see Agron. And now Sasha had seen what he should never have seen.

And Bekker. Who knew that Bekker was so close to Agron?

Sasha felt himself falling into a trap, not even knowing what it was.

Agron was leaning toward him. Too close. He seemed to be sitting on top of him. He imagined that he could feel Agron's moist breath on his cheek.

"You're right, Ebzi," said Sasha, leaning back, trying to make a little space for himself without offending the *batyushka*. "I'm just going to forget about all this. Maybe take a vacation. Go someplace for a while, rest."

"That's my boy," Agron said, punching Sasha's shoulder so hard that Sasha rocked backward on his chair. "You forget about everything. Hey, pretty soon we're all dead, like the dinosaurs, no matter how fast we are."

"Thank you, Ebzi," said Sasha, standing up. "I'm pretty drunk. I'm going to go home now."

Agron reached up and took Sasha's left hand and squeezed it until Sasha felt the small bones shift and slide. "So, have you called Genrikh Tepperman?" Agron asked. "Boris worked for him. You work for him. Ask Tepperman who'd kill Boris, who'd want you dead."

"I don't work for Tepperman," Sasha protested. Were Agron and Tepperman feuding? Had Tepperman become involved in the struggle between Agron and Boris Zilberstein?

"That's all right," said Agron. "Everybody works for somebody."

"You don't," Sasha said, instantly regretting it. Why prolong a conversation with this dangerous man?

"Of course I do," said Agron. "I work for many people. But my employers treat me with respect. And do you know why, Sasha?"

Agron increased the pressure on Sasha's hand. Sasha flinched, and tears began to come to his eyes. He thought furiously. What was the right answer?

Agron laughed and released Sasha's hand. "If I hear anything, Aleksandr Volkavitch, I'll let you know. You're a good boy, not a troublemaker.

"You know," Agron continued, "I'm interested in art, too. I've often thought about expanding my operation in that area. There's been—how should I put it?—an explosion of interest in Russian treasures. And there are many Russian treasures, aren't there, Sasha?"

Agron looked hard at Sasha, and then, smiling, the *batyushka* turned away, dismissing him, his eyes sweeping the room for the man who called that evening to sell him a uniquely modern Russian treasure.

⧆   ⧆   ⧆

Sasha stumbled down to the street, massaging his throbbing left hand. His glasses fogged up, but he didn't care. Walking was a little difficult. It had been a long time since he had had so much to drink. And he was exhausted. He tried to focus on his watch. It was just past three in the morning.

Brighton Beach Avenue was deserted. A terrible day, thought Sasha. A terrible night. I should have stayed with Madeline Malloy. I could have stayed with her.

"Hey, Sasha!"

Sasha turned around to see David Gatlober trotting toward him.

"Some show," said Gatlober.

"Some show," Sasha agreed.

Gatlober stood there, grinning and nodding. The tall blonde was waiting for him in the shadows. What the hell can Gatlober be thinking? Sasha wondered. What goes on in his twisted little head? And what do they do together, he and the blonde?

"I'm going home, David," said Sasha. "You can go home, too."

"Okay, man," Gatlober said. "Thanks. Easy job."

Bouncing on the balls of his feet, Gatlober turned and walked back to his girlfriend. A nut job, Sasha thought again. Then he turned down Fifth Street and saw three police cars, their emergency lights flashing red and blue, parked in front of his apartment building.

No, not his. The girls'.

Sasha crossed the street and stepped into the shadows. He watched Tatyana, Semka, and Yulia being led out of the building by the cops, pushed into the patrol cars.

Sasha cursed. What happened? Did a neighbor complain? Did the girls do something stupid? Did someone rat to the cops?

The perfect end to a perfect day, he thought.

When the cars drove off, Sasha, exhausted but now completely sober, walked back across the street and entered his building. Now he would have to call Mark Sugarman, his lawyer, wake him up, get the girls out of jail. Sweet little Yulia would be terrified. Well, Tatya would take care of her.

He dragged himself up the stairs. From the landing, he could see that the door to his apartment was open.

Sasha flattened himself against the wall and listened intently. He didn't hear anything. He edged toward the door and then peeked into his apartment.

It was a smoldering wasteland.

His television set was a ruin, as was his stereo equipment. His computer had been smashed. Good-bye, Lola the body shaper. His new Nikon had been crushed. His leather recliner had been slashed.

Stunned, Sasha wandered through his apartment. The bathroom mirror was shattered. His face, reflected a dozen times in the shards and splinters, looked haunted. The kitchen floor was splattered with everything in the refrigerator.

He walked into the bedroom. The bed had been turned over. Someone had taken a dump on the mattress. His clothes were on the floor. His Porsche sunglasses with his name inscribed in the frame were gone.

Someone had been very thorough.

Sasha's stomach heaved. He vomited up his day. It splattered on the living room rug.

He ran out of the apartment, down the stairs, back onto the street.

Where are you going? he asked himself.

Madeline Malloy's. I have to get the box. What if someone saw me take it there?

Think, Sasha. You better start thinking fast, he told himself.

The box. The coins. All this, all this for a few coins?

Think, Sasha. Think.

But it was too noisy in his head. He couldn't listen.

9.

GENRIKH TEPPERMAN SLIPPED INTO THE BLACK MERCEDES LIM-
ousine waiting, its engine running, outside the Hotel Slavyanskaya Radisson, near the Kievskaya train station. He took off
his dark green Italian silk blazer, folded it neatly, inside out,
and placed it on the shelf behind him. He loosened his pink-
and-aqua Japanese Modules tie, leaned forward, tapped his
driver, bodyguard, and friend, Lenny Kravchuk, on the shoulder, and then sank back into the soft gray leather.

"I'll have a drink, Alyushka," he said as the car swung
smoothly into the sparse, early morning Moscow traffic. "Bourbon."

The tall, slender, dark-haired woman sitting next to him
reached forward and pressed a button, and the bar swung down
pneumatically. She poured three fingers of Jack Daniel's into a
tumbler, added two ice cubes, and handed the glass to Tepperman.

He took a swallow. The bourbon burned his mouth, then
his throat, then his stomach. Disgusting. But he was deter-
mined to learn to like it. He imagined himself at a party, or-

dering bourbon, while the people around him wondered where he had developed such exotic tastes. However, now was not the time.

"Fuck this," Tepperman said, giving the glass back. "Let's pop the DP."

"Are we celebrating?" asked Kravchuk, looking back over his shoulder.

"Sure, Lenny," Tepperman said as the woman uncorked a bottle of Dom Pérignon 1985 and poured it into another tumbler. "All the time. Why not?"

"Are you going to be mayor?" asked Kravchuk.

"Would you vote for me?"

"I'd vote twice, boss."

"Then I guess I'll be mayor. Henry Tepperman, the first Jewish mayor of Moscow. What do you think, Lenny?"

"I think you should have some of my coke," said Kravchuk, a Ukrainian.

"Is it any good?"

"No, boss. I'm offering it to you because it stinks."

"Eat shit, Lenny," said Tepperman. "You got it from one of the Colombians?"

"Yeah. Are we going to do business with them, Henry?"

"I don't know," Tepperman said. For weeks he had been negotiating with a series of Colombians, representing various competing factions in Calí and Medellín, who wanted to use Tepperman's men as couriers and salesmen. If the drug cartel was going to increase its business in Western Europe, it needed local people who could move around inconspicuously. Colombians were too notorious. German cops, for example, invariably rousted any and all South Americans.

The Colombians needed him, so Tepperman was keeping his price high. But he also knew that there were other people they could turn to who could provide the same services.

It was a delicate business.

"Go the nice way," Tepperman told Kravchuk. "I want to see the city."

"I'll have some, Lenny," Alyona Romanova said.

Kravchuk passed a small vial over his shoulder to Romanova.

"All right, I'll have some," said Tepperman, who could not stand to see anyone having anything he didn't. He grabbed the vial from Romanova, who was expecting him to. Henry always grabbed. He poured some cocaine into the crack between his thumb and forefinger, lifted his hand to his nose, snorted, and handed the vial back to Romanova.

"So?" Kravchuk asked. "How is it?"

Tepperman leaned back. The bitter, icy phlegm dripped down the back of his throat, freezing it. The tip of his tongue touched his palate. It was growing numb.

He turned his head. Through the rear window, he could see the streetlights on the bridge crossing the Moskva, passing like comets, tails of fire streaking out behind them. He could feel more than hear the car's engine picking up speed as it turned onto the Embankment Road alongside the river, a deep thrum that made his balls tingle and his heart race.

"Come here," he said to Romanova.

She slid across the seat and rested her head against Tepperman's slight, almost bony shoulder, snuggling up against him, her fingers drumming gentle paradiddles on his thigh.

"That's nice," said Tepperman, closing his eyes, letting the coke and champagne and Romanova's fingers take him up and away, out through the rear window, up into the stars.

He was high above Moscow now, looking down. He could see his Mercedes, trailed by a Jeep carrying three of his men, passing the Kremlin wall on the other side of the river, heading for the country, for his *dacha*. My *dacha,* he thought. My cars, my men. My city.

My city is so beautiful, he thought. He could see everything all at once: the vast, dark expanse of Red Square, the lights of Kalinin Prospekt, the glittering Slavyanskaya Radisson, where he had just concluded a deal with the city's most important men—former Party chiefs, gang lords, businessmen—that could, that would, make him Moscow's most powerful boss. They were passing the six-thousand-room Hotel Rossiya now, and Tepperman could see all of Borovitsky Hill and the spires of the Kremlin built upon it. He could see the five towers crowned with their ruby-red Soviet stars.

Not for long, thought Tepperman, soaring higher now, the wind singing in his ears. I can see those stars falling to earth, crashing to earth.

He saw himself straddling the city. Henry, the Colossus of Moscow. Henry the Great. Henry the Terrible. Let the Russians tremble, he thought. Let them scurry for safety beneath my huge legs. Let me piss on them with my circumcised cock.

He opened his eyes. Romanova had unzipped his fly. Her left hand searched out his penis. Tepperman put his hand behind her head and pulled her mouth to his. Their tongues met. Softly she sucked on his lower lip, then bit it lightly. So sweet, he thought. Her mouth is so sweet. He ran his fingers through her hair and then guided her down into his lap. She took him into her mouth. He pushed her head down, feeling the crown of his penis hitting the roof of her Russian mouth.

Stars shot out of his cock.

"So?" asked Kravchuk again. "How's the coke?"

"Not bad," Tepperman said. "Not too terribly bad."

It was almost two in the morning when Tepperman's little convoy reached Khimki and moved through the guarded gates to his compound. Tepperman had purchased three connected *dachas* in the gated community outside Moscow: one for himself, one for guests, one for his men.

The Mercedes glided up the long circular driveway. The Jeep behind it stopped, and two men carrying rifles got out, assuming their stations in front of Tepperman's house. Kravchuk brought the Mercedes to a silken stop and killed the engine. He lit a cigarette.

"What's that?" asked Tepperman, leaning forward on the seat.

"What's what?" Kravchuk asked.

"The cigarette."

"Marlboro."

Tepperman sniffed. "Bullshit," he said.

"A Marlboro with a sprinkling of the finest Azerbaijani hash," said Kravchuk. "Want a hit?"

"Sure," Tepperman said.

Kravchuk passed him the cigarette. He did not expect to get it back. That was Henry.

"Anything else, boss?" asked Kravchuk.

"No thanks, Lenny," Tepperman said, climbing out of the car. Alyona Romanova got out of the other side and walked around the back. She stood next to him, taller by a good four inches. He put his arm around her waist, looked up at the stars through the branches of the birch trees, and took a deep drag on the sweet hashish cigarette. He coughed.

"Want some?" he asked.

"No, thank you, Henry," said Romanova. "It's a beautiful night, isn't it?"

"It's a great night," Tepperman agreed. "Let's go inside."

Tepperman's *dacha* was far grander than Viktor Prudnikov's. It had twelve rooms, three bathrooms, one with a sauna, one with a hot tub. It, too, had art on the walls, including an excellent copy of van Gogh's *The Convict Prison*. Tepperman stood in front of it now. The convicts, circling, their heads and knees bent, seemed to shuffle in an enervated danse macabre. Tepperman imagined that he could hear their feet scraping against the granite floor, imagined that he could feel the damp chill of the gray stone walls, imagined that he could smell the mildewed misery. The blue-gray shadows the prisoners cast on the stones of the walls and floor seemed to flutter, and the two men in top hats regarding them seemed stuffed with a careless bourgeois cruelty. The central convict was, of course, the artist, van Gogh, with his closely cropped reddish hair.

It was amazing, Tepperman thought, how accurately a long dead, out-of-his-head Dutchman could portray the essence of life in the former Soviet Union.

"It's so depressing," said Romanova, squeezing his hand.

Tepperman suddenly felt annoyed. "Don't be trite. It's real life," he said sharply. "Only idiots are depressed by the truth."

Romanova recognized one of Tepperman's black moods coming on. At times like these, he reminded her of a bright but unhappy adolescent, an impression reinforced by his tiny stature. She knew, of course, that the motherly impulse that this image evoked in her was her way of protecting herself from feeling angry at him when he treated her badly.

"It's nice that there's no one in the house, isn't it, Henry?" These days, Tepperman's *dacha* frequently resembled an Arab bazaar or Gypsy camp, with all sorts of supplicants, hangers-on, and drifters around, freeloading on Henry's money, booze, or drugs. And then there was the stream of Colombians with their elaborate courtesy and dark, dewy, sick-looking eyes.

"I feel like soaking in the tub," Romanova continued. "Want to join me?" She knew he wouldn't.

"In a minute," he said. "You go ahead."

Alone now for the first time all evening, Tepperman stared at the painting. If only you were real, he thought, my problems would be solved. If only I could sell you. Six million dollars. That's what you'd be worth. Maybe more. I could buy off Viktor Prudnikov. I could make good on my mistake.

But the real painting was locked up in the Holy Trinity Monastery, in Zagorsk. Another forgery hung in the Pushkin.

The thought of the treasure in Zagorsk made Tepperman sweat. The thought that it was controlled by that Nazi Prudnikov made him ill. And thinking of Prudnikov reminded him of that bastard Sasha Volkov.

He had been crazy to trust him. Why hadn't he turned to Sasha Eugenev to pick up the uranium?

Because it was Volkov who had the buyer. Who would Sasha Eugenev have found to buy ten grams of enriched uranium? One of the nice Jewish couples to whom he sold babies?

Tepperman had taught Sasha Eugenev everything he knew, and now he always thought of him as a student, a small-timer. Sasha Volkov, on the other hand, was slick. A pro.

And now he's screwed me good, Tepperman thought, refusing to believe what Volkov had told him: that Sasha Eugenev had killed Boris and stolen the box.

Prudnikov, of course, refused to believe that Volkov had taken it and that Henry didn't know where it was.

And I can't blame him, thought Tepperman.

They're going to come after me. They're going to whack me out unless I get them their uranium or their money.

How can I get the uranium? Volkov's lying, he's beyond my reach. I can't fix this.

How can I get the money? A million? Even if I could put a million cash together, why should I give it to Prudnikov?

I'd be in a better position to defend myself if I had the keys to Zagorsk, thought Tepperman. I could blackmail him. Once the secret of Zagorsk is out, Prudnikov would lose control of it.

If nothing else, Tepperman thought, I could sell some pictures and buy more men, more guns to protect myself.

Or I could ask Aleksandr Eugenev to find Volkov.

And that would be the end of Sasha, thought Tepperman. He'd be no match for Volkov.

Tepperman turned away from the van Gogh, picked up the remote control to his Sony Black Star television set (a gift from the manager at the Hotel Ukraina), and, still standing, began channel surfing: CNN News, the BBC Financial Times, MTV, EuroSport, the Penthouse channel, all with Russian voice-overs. Shaquille O'Neal appeared with some other huge black men to sell Reeboks. (When the Reebok store had opened on Tverskaya last year, Kravchuk had picked up a pair of three-hundred-dollar sneakers for Tepperman. Tepperman had worn nothing else for a month. Now they lay forgotten in his closet.)

Another ad appeared for a Czech bank. A game show followed, with a sexy, big-breasted *devotchka* in a low-cut black sequined gown, turning letters on a board while the host, a fat Georgian wearing a bad tie and a Soviet-era suit, spun a wheel in front of him.

It's worse than America, thought Tepperman, who in his twenties had spent a year living in Los Angeles, taking business courses at UCLA while staying with his mother's sister. In America, Tepperman thought, most people know this is crap. Here, we think it's culture.

He switched off the set.

Should he join Alyona? Not yet. He felt too mean.

His thoughts returned to the suite in the Radisson, where earlier that evening he had met with Andrei Kozyrev, former head of the Moscow Oblast Party Committee; Boris Faleyev and Misha Kuznetsov, *batyushkas,* respectively, of the Chechen and Solntsevo Moscow *Mafiyas;* Arif Akhundov, a young Azeri millionaire who had made his money selling Russian iron to Iran and Iranian wool to Russia; and Aleksandr Pozdeyev, new-products director of the Krasny Proletary machine tool factory. Brought together by Tepperman, these men had little in common but money. They all had it. They all wanted more. And

Tepperman had told them that the way to do that was to co-operate.

Faleyev and Kusnetsov, for example, had been fighting over protection rights to the Ismailovo market. Each had lost men and money. After an hour, over caviar, bread, strawberries, and vodka, Faleyev agreed to cede the area to Kusnetsov. In return, Kusnetsov would leave Moscow's thousands of cabdrivers to Faleyev to organize.

Pozdeyev wanted to dismantle his factory and sell the machines to the Iranians. Kozyrev assured him that he would encounter no official resistance and that the Krasny Proletary workers could be reassigned quietly. Akhundov volunteered to be the middleman for twenty percent of the profits, to which Pozdeyev readily agreed.

The issue of the drug trade arose. Tepperman was opposed to making a deal with either Calí or Medellín. In the long run, he said, establishing their own network would be more profitable. Akhundov, who had heroin connections, agreed. Kozyrev wanted to go with the Calí cartel, Faleyev with Medellín.

The question was tabled for further study.

Then Tepperman stood up and told them he wanted to run for mayor.

Kuznetsov laughed. "You're out of your mind," he said, "or drunk."

Tepperman told them about *The Godfather*, a movie he had seen dozens of times. He told them that the film had made him realize that without political power, a businessman could go only so far. Without political power, a businessman could not be safe.

"Look. In *Godfather Two*," said Tepperman, "Hyman Roth wanted the Mafia to run a whole country, Cuba. It was his dream. A whole country. They almost did it, but then Castro came. Now, here, the Party is finished. There is a void. We have the same opportunity the Italians had in Cuba on a much larger scale. A scale as vast as Russia. But only if we cooperate.

"Today, the Italian Mafia is falling apart," Tepperman continued. "In New York, a simple thug like Ebzi Agron pushes them around. Imagine. Ebzi Agron is now bigger than the Cosa Nostra. And Boris Zilberstein is making a move with his drug money. Soon, he'll be richer than Agron. Meanwhile, the Italians are being thrown into jail, and they have become beggars. They need us now; they want to borrow our money.

"Why? Because the Italians always thought like criminals. So they stayed criminals. It is a dead end. We have an opportunity now to stop thinking like criminals."

Tepperman said that he didn't expect to win, didn't want to win. What he wanted was to forge a political organization for the future.

He warned them about men like Viktor Prudnikov and Yuri Drozhdov, men who disguised themselves as businessmen, as democrats, but who were plotting to turn back the tide of reform, either by putsch or by putting their own men in power.

"These men," he said, "will use the Pamyat clowns and pinheads like that fascist Vladimir Zhirinovsky to get control. Believe me. You can't work with these people. You know it's true.

"Unless we can meet them in that arena—in the political arena—they will win, and we will have our throats cut. You all know that's true. But if we win, we will have a place in this new world second to none."

He did not tell them about the casket of coins he was supposed to have brokered for the two villains he was describing, the casket that contained more than coins, the casket that had disappeared.

By the end of the meeting, Kozyrev had pledged to support Tepperman by mobilizing what was left of the Moscow Party. Faleyev and Kuznetsov promised to put their men at

Tepperman's disposal. Akhundov said he would match whatever funds Tepperman could raise, and Pozdeyev would use a portion of his profits to back him.

All Henry Tepperman had to do was come up with the seed money to demonstrate his leadership. A few million.

The floodtide of alcohol and coke in Tepperman's system had ebbed, leaving in its wake a muzzy depression. Prudnikov and Drozhdov would be coming for him. Soon.

Well, he would just have to go after them. Hit them where it hurt, in the pocket. Why not back up the truck at Zagorsk? Why not?

The phone began ringing. He picked it up. It was Aleksandr Volkavitch, calling from America.

Sasha told Tepperman about Pantera and Boris the Kike. Tepperman told Sasha that he already knew. Sasha told him about how his apartment had been trashed, his girls arrested. "What's going on, Henry?" Sasha asked.

"Did Boris have anything with him, Sasha? Did he tell you what he was doing in New York?"

"No, Henry. We only had a few minutes. Then, pow! So, what was he doing in New York?"

"A little business," said Tepperman. "Nothing much."

A little business with the other Sasha. Well, screw you, Henry, thought Sasha. You want to play it that way? Okay. First I'll find out how much your box is worth, then we'll talk.

Tepperman listened to the hum on the long-distance line. Would Sasha lie? he wondered. Of course he'd lie. Was he lying now?

Tepperman had always liked Sasha and felt fatherly toward him, even though he was only a few years older. Fresh out of Kolpashevo, Sasha had been a good student as Tepperman taught him how to be a *fartsovshchik,* a black marketeer who specialized in foreigners. Tepperman taught him how much it took to bribe an Intourist guide (too much, and the guide would get the guilts and turn you in; too little, and the guide would sell you out to the police for more); how to approach the tourists in the hotel lobbies and *beriozka* shops; how to buy gold jewelry from the foreign students studying at the military academy in Solnechnogorsk. It was Tepperman who had introduced Sasha to the *tsekhoviks,* the underground factory owners, who paid Sasha to move their goods around Moscow in his *Ogonyuk* delivery truck. But it was Sasha who had recognized an OBKhSS agent in Tepperman's inner circle. Lenny Kravchuk had taken care of the bitch, and Tepperman felt himself indebted to Sasha.

"Look, Sasha," he said, "maybe you should come here for a while. I could use you. You'd be safe."

"Come to Moscow?"

"There are big things happening here, and, I can't say for sure, but I think you've been caught in the crossfire. But I am sure you'll be safer here with me than in New York."

Safer with Henry? Sasha wondered. On the other hand, anywhere might be safer than New York now.

"Let me think about it, Henry," said Sasha. "I'd need papers. A new passport. A visa. I'd need to raise some cash. I don't want to go to my bank. I don't want to go anywhere near Brighton. I need a place to stay until I can get it together."

"Don't worry about money. I can get you money. The papers, you can probably handle better on your end."

"Sure."

"There's an office in Manhattan, Friendship Travel, on Eighteenth Street. Misha Reshevsky. Tell him you're a friend of mine. He'll get you a ticket."

"Maybe."

"Listen. Your troubles are my troubles, Sasha. And, unfortunately, I think now my troubles are your troubles."

"I'll call you," said Sasha. "I have to think."

Tepperman hung up. He turned around as Alyona Romanova entered the room, wearing an unbelted terry-cloth bathrobe. Her face was rosy from the hot tub, and she was drying her hair with a white towel. The robe parted.

She looks like a movie star, thought Tepperman. Sexy, but not cheap. Classy. Sophisticated. Like Annette Bening in *Bugsy*.

"Who was that?" asked Romanova.

"Your husband," Tepperman said. "He's coming home."

BOOK II

10.

Friday, October 22

ALEKSANDR EUGENEV STOOD OVER THE URINAL. BLINDFOLDED, he thought, I'd know I was back in the Soyuz.

Or whatever it is they call it now.

He zipped up. The room smelled of urine and vomit. The floor was a swamp. It turned his stomach.

He lit a cigarette and looked at himself in the mirror. He took off his new sunglasses. His eyes were red. He looked tired. He smoothed his thinning blond hair. Do I look like a Russian?

He forced himself to smile, the big Jack Nicholson smile.

No, he answered himself. Even after nine hours on the plane, I look like an American.

The door swung open and a young man with jet black hair and gold aviator sunglasses walked in. Sasha remembered seeing him in the plane's first class section. At the time, Sasha thought that he was probably Latin, possibly a drug runner. Now, as the young man (a boy, really, Sasha thought) nodded at him and ducked into a toilet stall, Sasha was sure. Moscow, he knew, was lousy with Colombians looking for deals, looking for connections, looking to expand into Europe.

Thank God I don't have to shit, Sasha thought. Soviet toilet paper. He shuddered at the memory. It was like wiping your ass with newspaper. If, of course, there was any.

He checked an empty stall. There wasn't.

He heard snuffling sounds coming from the stall the Latino had entered.

A user as well as a dealer.

Sasha left the toilet. The sound of his footsteps echoed on Sheremetyevo II's brown marble floor. No American terminal was ever so quiet at nine o'clock in the morning, he thought.

A brown cloud of lethargy seemed to hang in the air. Sasha could see it, could feel it entering his lungs and passing into his blood. His travel bag seemed to grow heavy in his hand.

Before catching himself, he almost entered the slow-moving customs line for Russian citizens. Then he remembered that the passport he was carrying—courtesy of his old friend the Professor—was Swiss.

The guard barely gave it a look before stamping it and waving him through to the inspection station. The guard there accepted Sasha's statement that he had nothing to declare and passed his bag through without asking him to open it, making a meaningless chalk mark on its side. Who cared about the Swiss, even ones who spoke Russian?

Sasha got on the escalator. As it carried him down, he had a rogue impulse to turn around and run back up the moving stairs, back to New York, back to Madeline Malloy's cozy apartment.

Where, eventually, I'd be killed, he thought.

Or had Malloy already given him up to the police? Had she gotten rid of the box? She'd said she would wait, but who knew?

The escalator deposited him in Sheremetyevo II's lobby, its ceiling honeycombed with recessed lights. Along the walls, small duty-free kiosks sold vodka, caviar, lacquered boxes, amber necklaces and pins, and *matryoshkas,* the ubiquitous nesting dolls. Sasha took a deep breath. There it was. The smell of disinfectant. There it was, he thought, the defining odor, the stink of the Soyuz.

There had been a group of aerobics instructors from Cambridge, Massachusetts, on the plane. Ten women and two men, all healthy and clean looking, all self-evidently American in their sneakers and T-shirts. Now, their Day-Glo nylon travel bags piled around them, they were giggling excitedly, huddling around their guide, a short, prissy-looking young man in wire-rimmed glasses who was telling them that their bus seemed to be late but would, undoubtedly, be there soon. Welcome to the Soyuz, thought Sasha.

Or whatever.

He looked around. The lobby was dim. About half the ceiling lights were burned out. An escalator was sloppily boarded over with plywood. Small groups of Moscow militiamen, presumably on airport duty, stood around joking and smoking in their trimly tailored brown uniforms. A smiling soldier approached the aerobics instructors and tried to sell them his hat. They giggled some more. In bad Russian, the short guide told the soldier that he should know that it was *zaprishchany,* forbidden, for tourists to purchase anything with military insignias. The soldier thanked him for the information, laughed, smiled again at the girls, and then rejoined his mates, who were discussing which girl they'd like most to go to bed with.

Sasha began moving toward the lobby doors. Through the mud-splattered windows he could see minivans and high-slung Ladas and Volgas jockeying for parking spaces outside the terminal, eager to collect passengers for the forty-five-minute ride into Moscow. Horns blew. Cars nudged each other. It was, Sasha thought, like the bumper cars in Coney Island, only no one was laughing. For Westerners, the fare was twenty-five dollars. More if you could get it. Serious money.

Sasha stepped out of the terminal, onto the sidewalk, into Russia.

The chill air promised winter. In a few weeks, maybe less, thought Sasha, who was wearing a dark green corduroy suit, a black turtleneck, and a tan Cerruti raincoat, the Moskva will be frozen. It will be snowing. If I'm still here, I'll have to buy a good hat, a warm coat, boots.

A beat-up gray Volkswagen minivan swung over to the curb in front of Sasha. A short, stocky, dark-haired man wearing jeans, a black leather motorcycle jacket with a Harley-Davidson insignia, and motorcycle boots hopped out and walked up to Sasha.

"Hans Mayduch?" the man asked. That was the name on Sasha's Swiss passport.

"That's right," said Sasha.

"Henry sent me," the man said. "You got any bags?"

"This is it," said Sasha.

"Lenny Kravchuk," the man said, sticking out his hand. Sasha took it. "Aleksandr Eugenev."

They climbed into Kravchuk's van. Kravchuk leaned across Sasha, opened the glove compartment, and pulled out a small bottle of Stolichnaya. He ripped off the top, tossed it out the window, and passed the bottle to Sasha. "Welcome home," Kravchuk said, popping the van into gear and pulling out of the terminal. He slipped a cassette into the boom box on the dashboard; Queen's "Another One Bites the Dust" filled the van, making the windows vibrate.

Sasha took a swig of the vodka. It tasted different, better than in Brooklyn, although he knew it was the same stuff. He handed it back to Kravchuk.

They swung onto the eight-lane Leningrad Highway that connected Sheremetyevo II with Moscow. Sasha lit a Marlboro and offered one to Kravchuk. Kravchuk shook his head no.

"My Marlboros are better than yours," Kravchuk said.

"Oh, yeah?"

"Mine have something extra."

Kravchuk fished a cigarette out of his jacket, lit it, and took a deep drag, holding the smoke in his lungs. "Hashish," he said, exhaling. "Want some?"

"No thanks."

"Azerbaijani blond, man. Excellent stuff."

"Not yet," said Sasha. "I'm getting oriented. I don't want to get disoriented so soon."

Kravchuk shrugged and took another drag. "If I were coming back after living in America for—what, three years?— I'd want to get as fucked up as I could as fast as I could," he said. "That's how you get into it here, man. You get fucked up and then you're in tune with all the fucked-up things going on." He passed the vodka back to Sasha.

They rode for a few minutes without speaking. Sasha absorbed the flatness of the land. He felt the beginnings of an adrenaline rush. I'm no tourist, he thought. I know this jungle.

Queen was replaced by Nirvana's "Smells Like Teen Spirit" on Kravchuk's tape.

"Nirvana. They're the best," said Kravchuk, beating time on the steering wheel as the song's heavy chords chunked out of the boom box's speakers. "Kurt Cobain. He's my man. Looks Russian, too. You know this song?" Kravchuk asked.

Sasha nodded.

"Listen to the end," said Kravchuk. "I think they're saying 'I don't know.' In Russian. I swear it sounds like he's singing 'Ya nee zhnayo, ya nee zhnayo.' You think it's possible?"

"I guess so. Are we going to see Henry now?" asked Sasha.

"No. Henry thinks he should stay away for a few days. He

wants to keep an eye on you, make sure nobody knows you're in town. If they do, he wants to know who they are."

"Using me as bait."

"No, man. You know Henry. He's being careful, is all. Anyway, when we're sure everything's cool, we'll have a blast. Moscow's wide open now, man. Anything you want, you can get it, any time, twenty-four hours a day. New casinos opening up all the time, good restaurants. And women. Good-looking women from all over. Germans. French. Irish. Americans. You got dollars, you got everything."

"You got dollars?" asked Sasha.

"We got everything," Kravchuk said. He patted Sasha's thigh. "I'm telling you, man: Moscow's the place. The center of the whole fucking fucked-up world. And Henry's in the center of the center. In a few weeks, after the election, it'll be official. You came back at the right time."

"What do you mean, after the election? What happens after the election?"

"Henry didn't tell you?"

"Tell me what?"

"Forget it. I'll let him tell you."

"So where are we going?" Sasha asked after taking another swig of the Stolichnaya and passing the bottle to Kravchuk. "You got a place for me in the city?"

"No. We hide you in an apartment, how are we going to see who's interested in you?"

"A hotel?"

"Right."

"The Slavyanskaya Radisson?" asked Sasha, remembering that when he was in Moscow, before leaving for New York, the Radisson, still under construction, was being advertised as Moscow's most luxurious Western-style hotel.

"No, man. The Ukraina."

"Fuck no," Sasha said. "I've been in prison, thank you. I'm not going back."

"Henry's got the whole place wired," said Kravchuk. "Everyone from the manager to the key ladies. Safest place in the world for you, my man. And the easiest way to keep an eye on you and whoever might come around asking questions about you.

"It's not so bad," Kravchuk continued, handing the bottle back to Sasha. "We'll get you a room way up high. Best view in Moscow. You can see the river. You're right across from the Aleksandr casino. Best-looking chicks in Moscow hang there. You can see the fucking White House, man. Windows blown to shit. Powder burns on the walls. Bullet holes. Wild. And I thought Boris Nikolayevich was a pussy. Wrong. He didn't fuck around. Got Rutskoi the fuck out of there. Got the message to all those old Party guys. Like the Who said: Meet the new boss, he's a bad motherfucker. You dig the Who?"

"Sure."

"Hey? Did you know Yeltsin only has three fingers on his left hand?"

Sasha drank some more of the vodka and stared out the window. He was beginning to feel the Stolichnaya. It felt good. The trick, thought Sasha, was to keep your level. Drink enough to relax, not enough to lose your focus. And the trick to that was to drink steadily, slowly. That was the trick to surviving in Russia.

The pine forest around the airport had given way to the crumbling eight- and twelve-story apartment complexes that would continue right up to the Moscow River. The unpaved service road paralleling the highway was dotted with cars cannibalized for parts, broken-down trucks and tractors, piles of rubbish. Here and there, people were buying cabbages and potatoes off the backs of trucks. It all looked poorer to Sasha than it had before he'd left. Could that be? he wondered. Or was he just comparing it to America?

"What's the exchange rate now?" Sasha asked Kravchuk.

"On the street? Depends. You can get two thousand. Don't take less than eighteen hundred. Less than that, you're getting screwed. But fuck that. You need rubles, dollars, just ask, okay? But forget rubles, man. Nobody uses them."

They crossed the river and entered Moscow. They passed the fanciful lime-green-and-white Beloruskaya Vokzal, where the trains left for Minsk and Warsaw. They turned down Tverskaya Ulitsa, which Sasha had always known as Gorky Street.

"When did they change Gorky Street's name?" Sasha asked Kravchuk.

"I don't know," said Kravchuk. "Maybe two, three years ago. Shit, they're changing all the street names. Back to pre-Bolshevik days. Down with the Communists. Down with the Party. Down with Marx, Lenin, Stalin, all the fucking comrades. You know. It's good. But it's fucked up, too. Easy to get lost, man."

The traffic was heavy. Occasionally, among the mud-splattered, beat-up Volgas, Zhigulis, and Ladas, Sasha could see gleaming Mercedes-Benz sport coupés and Honda Accords. They drove through Komsomolskoya Square, and then passed the immense brick pile of the Kievskaya Vokzal, where the trains headed south to the Ukraine. To Sasha, despite the changes, Moscow seemed little changed. Well, he thought, what did you expect? It's only been a few years.

The thirty-five-hundred-room Ukraina, its pseudo-Gothic spires reaching into the sky, loomed ahead like a lunatic spaceship. They turned off Kutuzovskaya Prospekt into the parking lot.

Kravchuk killed the engine. "Here," he said, reaching into his jacket and producing a passport. "Now you're Aleksandr Strahinich, a friendly Croatian businessman on holiday in

Moscow. Your mother was Russian, and you grew up speaking the language. Your visa is inside. So's your Intourist registration card. Give me your old passport and visa."

"What's the story with this Strahinich?" Sasha asked.

"A sad one," said Kravchuk, smiling wolfishly. "He really was on holiday in Moscow. Then he died. Of heart failure. His heart failed when someone stuck a knife in it." Kravchuk laughed. "Not me," he added.

"Where did you get this picture?" Sasha asked, opening the Croatian passport and seeing himself five or six years younger.

Kravchuk shrugged. He took Sasha's Swiss passport and stuck it in his pocket. "Let's go," he said. "Let me do the talking."

They passed through the Ukraina's revolving doors into the hotel's lobby.

It was enormous. Straight ahead was a small glass kiosk selling champagne, chocolates, watches, and caviar. Two long, curving, marble staircases led up to the mezzanine, where the *beriozka,* the hard-currency shop, was located. Behind the kiosk, down at the end of the lobby by the elevators, was a small bar. Dusty men in sweaters, overalls, and cloth caps sat on metal folding chairs, drinking beer and vodka at tiny Formica tables.

Sasha nudged Kravchuk and gestured toward the bar. "Turkish workers," explained Kravchuk. "Fixing up the White House. The good bar is on the twelfth floor, I think. On the tenth floor there's a nice restaurant, Invino. Good-looking waitresses. Short skirts, big tits. Dumb as donkeys."

"And they're staying here, the Turks?" Sasha asked.

"That's right," said Kravchuk. "At night, the place is fucking crawling with hookers. The Turks'll take anything blond. Short, fat, mustaches—they don't care. If it's blond, they'll fuck it. I'd watch my ass if I were you. You're blond."

Kravchuk took Sasha's arm. On their way to the reception desk in a room off the lobby, they passed a half dozen soldiers smoking and lounging on two old leather sofas.

"Guarding the Turks?" asked Sasha.

Kravchuk nodded.

Sasha turned over his passport to a bored young woman, one of six doing nothing at the long desk, and received his hotel card. Kravchuk peered at it. "Is this a good room?" he asked the woman.

"They're all good," the woman said.

"Can I see this gentleman's passport for a moment?" Kravchuk asked.

The woman handed Kravchuk the passport. Kravchuk turned his back on her, slipped a five-dollar bill into the passport, and handed it back.

The woman put the passport on her lap and studied it for a moment. Then she stuck out her hand. Sasha handed her the hotel card and she gave him another one.

"Our best," the woman said. "On the twenty-sixth floor. Far away from the Turks."

"Thank you, dear," said Kravchuk.

"On the fourteenth floor," the woman said, "there are very good blinis. They make them all day."

"Thank you," Sasha said.

"The key lady on your floor is Irena," the woman continued. "Tell her Zhenya says to take care of you."

"I'm going to go now," Kravchuk said, handing Sasha a card. "You need anything, call this number. I'll be in touch."

"When do I see Henry?" asked Sasha.

"Soon. When he thinks the time is right. Don't worry. Welcome home."

Sasha watched Kravchuk leave, then took the elevator up to the twenty-sixth floor. He handed his hotel card to the key lady sitting at her desk opposite the elevator. "My name is

Aleksandr Strahinich," he told her. "Zhenya says you should take care of me."

"What do you want?" asked Irena, a plump, unsmiling woman in her forties wearing too much makeup. She handed Sasha a key card.

"Towels," Sasha said, "lots of towels. Also shampoo, a bottle of Absolut, a bottle of mineral water, some biscuits, and today's *Moscow News*." He handed Irena a twenty-dollar bill. "You need more, Irena, you ask me. Okay?"

The woman smiled. Her teeth were crooked. "You want company?" she asked.

"Maybe later," Sasha said, thinking of blondes with mustaches. "Right now I just want to sleep."

As he walked down the cold and gloomy hallway toward his room, he thought suddenly of Lena. What was her last name? Something like *kolodny*. Cold. Yes, it had been cold in Kiev. That's it. Yelena Kolodyazhnaya.

It had been their first and only date, and they had spent the whole day together, drinking beer and sweet champagne, eating sausages, kissing in doorways, hallways, in the Metro. All day he had had his hands on her.

It grew dark. They went to a movie, a bad one with detectives and unattractive women sitting around talking—blah, blah, blah—and eating. They sat in the back row of the theater. She unzipped his fly and put her hand in his pants. He reached around her, behind her neck, and stuck his hand down under her fuzzy pink sweater, under her brassiere. She was sweating.

She rubbed him, but he was too nervous to come.

"Someone might see us," he whispered in her ear.

"Nobody cares," she whispered back.

He was fifteen, a virgin. He didn't think she was.

When the movie ended, they went to a cafeteria. It was so cold outside, and so hot inside, a cloud of steam had formed. It floated above them, covering the ceiling. A fine, warm mist fell from the cloud like rain. The floor was slick. The tables were wet. Eyeliner ran down Lena's cheek, leaving a thin black tear trail. Sasha was enchanted. His glasses fogged. He took them off.

They talked about school, about their teachers, about their Komsomol leaders. They sat side by side and rubbed each other's legs under the table. Lena, Sasha recalled, had chicken Kiev. Sasha had only enough money to pay for her chicken, so he said he wasn't hungry. When she was finished, they went back outside, out into the cold.

It had begun to snow, a flurry of dry, pinpoint flakes that swirled in the wind. Sasha's lips felt bruised from hours of kissing. His penis was sore and aching. He shuddered as the wind cut through his coat. His ears burned. He turned down the flaps of his cheap, rabbit-fur *shopka,* not caring that it made him look even more like the schoolboy he was.

It was too cold to talk. Silently Lena led him up and down the empty streets. Soon, he thought, he would have to take her home. They would stand in the hallway for another hour—she would never let him inside her parents' apartment—and they would kiss and push against each other, their coats open.

Lena turned up an alley. They were in a cul-de-sac. Tall apartment buildings on two sides, the corrugated metal door of a garage on the other. One tree a few feet in front of the garage.

Lena leaned back against the door and opened her sheepskin coat. Sasha unbuttoned his wool coat and pressed himself against her. The door buckled and boomed, like stage thunder in one of Shakespeare's melodramas.

Sasha jumped back and looked around. The lighted apartment windows were silent, their curtains drawn and still. Lena laughed.

"Nobody cares," she said. Still, she stepped away from the door and leaned against the tree.

Sasha kissed her. She put her hands down his pants and found his aching penis. He had, it seemed to him, been hard for hours. He put his hand up her sweater and squeezed her breast again. His thumb found her tiny nipple. She pushed his hand away.

"I can't stand it," she said. "Let's do it now."

"Here?"

"Where else? Your parents' apartment? Mine? Yes, here. Let's do it."

"It's freezing."

"I'm the one who's going to freeze."

"It's snowing, for chrissakes."

"So? Take me home," said Lena, closing her coat.

"No," Sasha said, deciding, drawing her to him.

Lena turned around. She pulled down her tights. She bent over, bracing herself against the tree.

Sasha unzipped his fly. He took off his glasses and dropped them into his coat pocket. He felt around for her vagina and tried to enter her, unsure of the angle. She reached between her legs and guided him inside.

All Sasha could feel was an empty wetness. Was something wrong? Was he doing something wrong? He grabbed her buttocks, shoved once, then stopped. He was going to come. He knew enough to know it was too soon. The trick, he thought, was to think of something else. "Don't move," he said, and started to count the windows in the alley.

Lena pressed back against him. He came.

For a moment he laid his head on her back, stroking the front of her thighs. Then he pulled out. The head of his penis burned. Had he caught something? Lena stood up, pulled up her tights, turned around, and began smoothing her hair.

Sasha searched for something romantic to say. "I'm not cold anymore," he said.

"See, I told you I would be the one who would freeze," she said brightly.

He took her home on the Metro. He told her he loved her. She said he didn't mean it. He protested that he did. He walked her to her parents' apartment. Then, after kissing her good night, he took the subway home.

The next day, in school, Lena wouldn't look at him. He asked her out several times, but she always had an excuse. She began seeing another boy.

When he was thrown out of Komsomol, Lena stood up to accuse him of anti-Soviet thought. She said he had told nasty jokes about Comrade Brezhnev. Of course he had. Everyone did.

Why had she turned on me? Sasha wondered now as he had then. Because I had hesitated? Because I couldn't find a place to go and we had to screw in an alley? But who ever had a place in the Soyuz? Only married people. And they were never alone either.

Could I imagine two people more different then Yelena Kolodyazhnaya and Madeline Malloy? Sasha wondered. Could I imagine two more different acts of love?

Lena would have had me arrested if I had turned up at her apartment the way I showed up at Madeline Malloy's.

That night, that terrible night, after roaming the streets, after sobering up on the subway to Manhattan, he had found his way to Malloy's apartment. She'd buzzed him up, opened the door, and there she was, wide awake, dressed in an old sweatshirt and panties, holding the box in her hands. "Explain this," she said.

So he told her everything. Well, almost everything. He told her that he was on the beach when Pantera was shot. (But he didn't tell her about the jewelry scam.) He told her about meeting Ebzi Agron. (But not about the killing of the poor pharmacist.) He told her about what had happened to his apartment. (But he didn't mention the pregnant girls.) He almost gave her his real name, but at the last moment he told her it was Aleksandr Petrovich Voynitsky. And as silly as that sounded to his own ears, he saw that she had accepted it, and that emboldened him.

He grew passionate, moved by his own imperfect honesty.

"There are people trying to kill me," he said. "Maybe it's for these coins, maybe not."

"This is probably stolen. It's certainly smuggled," Malloy said. "You've made me an accessory."

"No, no," Sasha protested. He didn't know that it was stolen. Stolen from whom? Who knew? Smuggled? Yes, probably. But so what? People smuggled things all the time. Caviar. Watches. They put them in their pockets and walk through customs. Nobody cares.

"We'll go to the police together," Malloy said.

It was such an American thing to say, Sasha almost wept.

It had taken the rest of the night. When the sun rose, Sasha was still talking. He told her that the Brooklyn police worked for the *Mafiya*. They would send him to jail. He would be murdered there. He told her that giving up the box would be the same as cutting his own throat. He apologized for hiding it in her apartment but pleaded, "It's all I have." He said it over and over, his voice throbbing. "The box is all I have."

Finally he gave her a story for her newspaper. He gave her Boris's name, the unidentified man on the beach. He told her about Kolpashevo. He told her about the thieves-in-law and about *vorovskoy mir*, the thieves' world, and how it was coming to America. He told her about the tattoos, the people's courts, and the code. He told her about the war between Ebzi Agron and Boris Zilberstein. And he promised her a bigger story. When he got back from Russia, he said, they would go to the FBI, not the police, together. And Madeline Malloy would have—how did they say?—an exclusive. Maybe, he said, seeing the agreement forming in her eyes, she would have a book about the Russian *Mafiya*.

It had worked. She had taken him in while he waited for the Professor to forge him a new passport. She had given him Mitch Rose's private number, telling him to call it if he ever needed to find her or if he ever got into serious trouble. She had closed the thin wooden door to her apartment, slid the useless police lock into place, opened her arms, opened her legs, and said, You're safe now.

And for a while, he believed her. He felt protected by her unshakable belief in her own innocence. Who would dare disturb them, surrounded by her expensive furniture, her French rugs, her Japanese television set, her sleek telephone? It seemed to him the very essence of the difference between Russians and Americans, this faith in the power of their possessions to render them invulnerable.

And they made love amid the wealth. He discovered that Madeline Malloy loved to make love like no other woman he had ever known. She would light candles and place them beside the bed. She would take off her clothes slowly, provocatively, while he watched, and anoint herself with sweet smelling, sweet tasting oils. Then she would invite Sasha to worship her with his lips and tongue, reverently working his way up from her toes, up her long, graceful legs, to her groin, her belly, her breasts, and neck. Each night they held a hushed religious service in Madeline Malloy's bedroom, and each night, after hours of intense, prayerful communion, they would fall into a deep, exhausted, peaceful sleep, arms and legs entwined, breathing each other's breaths.

Of course, at other times, when Sasha would wake up in the night and go to the bathroom to sneak a cigarette, he would listen tensely for footsteps in the hall, listen for the signs that would mean that the door was about to burst open, splintering while the police lock stood a futile guard, and people would come in to kill them both. He was not, finally, so American as to share her simple faith.

And yet, he thought, in time, with Madeline Malloy's help, might he not turn into a proper American? A nine-to-five workaday daddy? A *fraier* whose reward each night for toiling all day long was a stroll in the fragrant garden of Maddy Malloy's earthly delights? Maybe that was not such a terrible thing to be. Maybe, in America, it was possible.

I wonder how Lena is making out in the new Ukraine, Sasha thought, slipping the electronic key card into the slot above the doorknob in room 2608. A small green light flashed on and the door clicked open. I wonder if she ever thinks of me? She's probably married. She probably has kids. At least two, maybe more. She probably hates her husband. And I bet she thinks of me. Sometimes. Lying in bed at night, I bet she thinks of the garage door booming like thunder. I bet she thinks of the steaming restaurant, the tree, the snow.

Or maybe not.

❖   ❖   ❖

The room was as hot as the hallway had been cold. Sasha's glasses fogged. He wiped them with his fingers. He pulled the lace curtains apart and threw open the tall French windows. Far below him he could see the Moskva and the white gambling boat berthed across the river on the opposite bank from the Ukraina. What did Kravchuk say the name of the casino was? The Aleksandr? Perhaps I'll walk over the Kalininsky Bridge tonight, have a go at blackjack, Sasha thought. Maybe pick up a girl.

To his right he could see the twin smokestacks of the central heating plant that pumped steam beneath Moscow's streets and was right now turning his room into a sauna. He wondered if its famous slogan—"Communism = Soviet Power + Electrification"—still stood in twelve-foot-high letters on the roof. Farther off, he saw the spires of the Ministry of Foreign Affairs on Smolenskaya Boulevard in a building that was the Ukraina's twin. Another mad Socialist spaceship built by Comrade Stalin, towering menacingly over the Arbat. Later, thought Sasha, I'll go for a walk, see what's changed.

He turned away from the windows. Not a bad room, he thought. High ceiling. A nice rug on the floor. Table and chairs. A telephone. A refrigerator. He clicked on the television, a small Korean Gold Star. He looked around for the remote control. There was none. He flicked through the channels and stopped at a tennis match.

He sat down on the narrow bed. The mattress was thin and bowed. The bed was too short. I can't sleep on this, he thought.

There was a knock at the door. It was Irena with his towels, vodka, water, newspaper, and butter biscuits. "I'll have to go down to the *beriozka* for shampoo," she apologized.

"Thank you. Was twenty enough, Irena?"

"Oh, yes," Irena said enthusiastically. Then she caught herself. "Just enough, yes."

"Good," Sasha said. "But, Irena, I can't sleep on this bed. Can you get me another one?" He pulled another twenty out of his wallet and began folding it.

"I don't know," said Irena, looking worried.

"That's too bad, Irena. And I'll tell you why it's too bad. It's too bad because I like you. And I like this room. But if you can't find me another bed—a longer one, a bigger one, a better one—I'm going to have to say good-bye. I'll have to leave." Sasha stuck the twenty in his pocket.

"I'll find one," Irena said. "But it may take a little time."

"All right. I'll go out, walk around for a few hours. Suddenly, I'm not tired. I look at this bed, I'm reinvigorated. And when I get back, you'll have a new bed for me, right?"

"Absolutely. No problem."

"Good," said Sasha, putting on his coat.

He left the Ukraina and decided to take the subway to the Arbat. The Metro. That's how he'd know he was really back in Moscow.

As he walked down the Ukraina's steps, he noticed a man standing by a kiosk, looking at him. For a moment Sasha returned the man's stare, and the man turned away.

I'm being paranoid, Sasha thought. In Russia, people always notice people coming out of hotels. They want to see what they're wearing. They want to try to see what makes them so special as to be staying in a hotel.

He walked down Ukrainian Boulevard to the Kievskaya Vokzal, the river to his left, taking the pedestrian viaduct under the busy, twelve-lane Dorogomilovskaya Ulitsa. The viaduct was lined with tables piled high with secondhand books. Poetry and history. Plays and novels. People stopped to page through them and chat about them with the vendors. People still read here, Sasha reminded himself. Here, they do not trust what comes out of the television, so they read.

Pages clipped from newspapers were taped to the tiled walls. There were also posters from the various new political parties, ranging from Boris Yeltsin's Russia's Choice, which, Sasha thought, did not offer one, to Vladimir Zhirinovsky's Liberal Democratic Party, which, he knew, was neither. And there he saw it. The Moscow Freedom Party. "Property, Liberty, Law." "Genrikh Tepperman for mayor of Moscow."

There was no picture of Henry. Just a drawing of a knight in armor waving a sword atop a rearing horse. Possibly Peter the Great, but the drawing was poor.

Well, thought Sasha, Henry's lost his mind. He's running for mayor. And on the Czarist ticket. Wonderful.

Suddenly Sasha felt eyes on his back. He looked around. Just people, he thought.

Just my nerves, he thought.

Sasha emerged on the other side of Dorogomilovskaya. The large "M" for Metro guided him to the Kievskaya station.

It was, as always, mobbed. He bought a token for thirty rubles and slipped into the crowd of closed faces, Russian faces, faces that guarded the secrets of lives that were made up of thousands of small secrets. The morning sip of vodka. The bribe to the building manager to get the window fixed. The application for an exit visa.

He let the river of people carry him forward, embracing him in a many-armed hug, as he had thousands of times before. It was familiar, comforting, and he remembered coming to Moscow for the first time and marveling at the Metro—the vaulting ceilings, the grand chandeliers, the size, the magnificence, the quiet efficiency. In the Soyuz, among all the things that broke down and frustrated one's attempts to get by, among all the things that were embarrassingly second-rate, the Metro worked. Say what you would about Moscow, everyone was proud of the Metro, our Metro, the best and the most beautiful in the world.

At the fork where two rivers of people split off, one left to the Circular Line, which traced the Garden Ring Road, the other right and down to the Arbatsko-Pokrovskaya line, a small, skinny, olive-skinned boy leaned against the tiled wall and played the violin, its case at his feet open for kopeks and rubles. Sasha would have liked to stop to listen to the high, sweet tune—a Gypsy song, perhaps, Sasha thought, or maybe even a Jewish one—but the current of people carried him forward to the lip of the steep, narrow escalator that carried one down four stories to the train platform.

Too fast. Wasn't the escalator moving too fast? The hum of the machinery seemed angry, like a swarm of bees trapped between a screen and a windowpane. Had the escalator slipped its gears? It seemed to be plunging into the bowels of the sta-

tion at an absurd rate. Like a cataract. But still, people were
stepping on. Should he? Was he just unused to the Metro after
all these years?

The crowd pushed from behind. Sasha leaned back, trying
to hold his ground, uncertain as to what to do. Someone cursed
him. This was insane, he decided. The escalator was moving
too fast.

He broke free of the crush and pushed to his left, to the
tall stairs between the escalators. As he started climbing down,
the bottom of the escalator below him—and the pile of bodies
there—slowly came into view.

The gears had, indeed, slipped. People were being shot off
the runaway escalator, thrown headlong into the pile, breaking
arms, legs, heads. Men and women were grabbing for the moving rails. A hand grabbed for Sasha, almost knocking him
down. Sasha caught another arm as it swept by, heaved, and
pulled a young man over the side of the escalator onto the
stairs. Sasha reached over the railing and tried to scoop up an
old woman flying by. Her flailing hand hit him in the jaw,
spinning him around. His foot went out from under him and
he slipped down two, three stairs, banging his knees and elbows.

He scrambled to his feet. More and more people were trying to climb off the escalator, trying to get onto the stairs. Now
the machinery sounded like a thousand dentist's drills. He was
knocked down again.

Sasha picked himself up and began to run, taking the
stairs two at a time, weaving through the crowd. People were
shouting, screaming. Above, men and women were still feeding into the escalator.

They're insane, he thought.

At the foot of the stairs, men were pulling bodies off the
pile. A small boy was shrieking. Blood was jetting out of the
wrist where the cruel teeth of the escalator steps had chewed off

and devoured his hand. Sasha saw a woman being dragged along the floor, away from the pile, her shinbone, shockingly white, sticking out through her black stocking.

The lights in the station suddenly dimmed and blinked off, and the escalator began to glide to a stop. There was a moment of silence once the stairs halted, then the screaming began again, louder, more piercing now that it had no competition, more frightening in the dim illumination of the few utility lights glowing weakly on the sides of the train tube. In the gloom, Sasha saw three soldiers running toward the pile. Behind them, he could make out what seemed to be a half dozen more. A train pulled into the station. Its doors opened. There was nothing, he decided, that he could do here.

He stepped into the car, turned around, and faced the platform. A pretty young woman stood in front of the open door, sobbing, covering her mouth with one hand.

"Get in," said Sasha.

The woman looked at him. She shook her head. "I'm sorry," she said.

"For what?" Sasha asked. "For what?"

The doors closed. The train began to move. As the weeping woman slipped from sight, Sasha saw a face come up beside her, a face he recognized. It was the man at the kiosk outside the Ukraina.

As the train slipped into the tunnel, the glass door now revealed Sasha's own reflection.

He studied it. Closed. Frightened.

Staring back at him, he saw a Russian.

11.

IT WAS MITCH ROSE ON THE PHONE. DESPITE HERSELF, MADE-
line Malloy glanced around the office. Naturally, no one was
paying any attention to her. Still, she felt observed. My con-
science, she thought. These days, everything made her feel
guilty.

It's my little Pandora's Box, she thought.

"Did you eat yet?" asked Rose, running the words together in a soft, confidential mumble, as if they were old
friends, longtime lovers.

"No," Malloy said. There was something obscene about
having Rose crooning in her ear.

"So you want to grab some lunch? We could eat at my
club."

"I really have to finish this story, Mitch," said Malloy.

"What is it?"

"A profile of Peter Grushenko, a detective, an investiga-
tor. He's assigned to the Organized Crime Bureau in Brooklyn.
When we broke the story about the guy on the beach, his boss,
Eric Silverman, an assistant district attorney in the Organized

Crime Bureau, he called me. He told me I should talk to
Grushenko. Told me Grushenko wanted to talk to me."

"Grushenko wanted your source?"

"Naturally."

"You give it to him."

"Not yet."

"What'll he give you for it?"

"After the profile, I don't know yet."

"What do you want for it?"

"I'm not sure yet."

"Dangerous ground, Maddy. Let's have lunch, talk about
it. You play squash?"

"No."

"You can watch me. Then we'll eat at the club. So what-
taya say?"

"No thanks, Mitch. Some other time. I really should finish this story."

"You gotta eat, right? You're gonna eat, aren't you?
You're not on some diet?"

"No."

" 'Cause you don't need a diet. You're gorgeous just the
way you are."

Malloy looked around the newsroom. It was already emptying out for lunch. Maybe she should just file a harassment
complaint with the union. Sure. And then go looking for another job at the *Podunk Gazetteer*.

"So where were you going to eat?" Rose asked.

"I was going to get a sandwich in the cafeteria and take it
back to my desk."

"Only schmucks eat at their desk. You don't want people
to think you're a schmuck, right? Meet me downstairs at
twelve. Okay?"

There were only so many times Malloy could comfortably
say no to her boss, the editor of the paper.

"All right."

The phone clicked in her ear. Chalk up another triumph for Mitch Rose, she thought. He pressured one of his reporters into having lunch with him. Big man.

Malloy looked at her screen. What did she want? A good question. At the very least, she knew she wanted a good story, a great story. The story she had run on Boris the Kike had already boosted her status in the newsroom. Now she was someone to deal with. Now she was a rising star. She had followed the Boris story with one about the *vory v zakone,* the thieves-in-law. It had been a clip job with a few quotes from Silverman— the Russian *Mafiya* was a new menace, Agron, Zilberstein, blah, blah, blah—nothing new, but Rose had loved it. And now she had the great Peter Grushenko, Mr. Russian Crime, calling her, agreeing to a profile, which impressed the hell out of the boys at the paper. Politics and crime. That's all they cared about. So this was good, although Grushenko scared her a little. He had told her that he knew she was keeping something from him, and he had warned her that her being a reporter didn't mean shit to him. In fact, he said, he didn't like reporters.

She believed him.

Was she committing a crime by keeping Sasha's box? Of course she was. And the longer she held it, the worse it got.

Was her career that important to her? Yes, she answered herself, it was. She wanted to be Maureen Dowd, Anna Quindlen, and Edna Buchanan rolled into one. She wanted the respect of her peers, respect for her talents. She wanted out of the lifestyle, living pages ghetto, the women's pages no matter what they called it now. But was that all? What else did she want? Sasha? He was sweet, but he was obviously a crook. Did she really want to be mixed up with a crook? Was rough trade her thing? But there didn't seem to be anything rough about

Sasha. He made love like an angel. He was respectful; he was loving. In bed, he was the best she had ever had.

I think I'm being smart, she thought. Am I being too smart?

She had already had one interview with Grushenko in his office in the Municipal Building in downtown Brooklyn, and it had not gone especially well. After she had dodged his questions about how she knew that the other man on the beach had been Boris the Kike, a small-time crook who had been in America all of two days before getting his head blown off, Grushenko had given her his background in a grudging shorthand—born in 1936 in Rostov-on-Don in southern Russia; failed the entrance exam to Moscow University Law School in 1953 (Mikhail Gorbachev would have been his classmate); went to technical school in Rostov; drafted into the army in 1957; mustered out in 1960; joined the Serious Crimes Unit of the Moscow Prosecutor's Office in 1961; came to Brooklyn in 1989 because, he said, that was where all the bastards he had been chasing were showing up.

In other words, he gave her the minimum. No color, no quirks, nothing to grab on to, nothing to write about. Her one success was that Grushenko had agreed to let her spend a day with him.

"It will be very boring, I assure you," he had said, "unless you want to tell me who's been telling you about Pantera and the Kike. Otherwise, we will, most probably, sit here staring at each other. Or maybe I will take you to the station house in Brighton Beach and we can stare at each other there."

Malloy stored the biographical data on her terminal. Unless she lucked into something dramatic while she was hanging out with him, or unless she got Grushenko to open up, she had a weak story. What if she told him there was a third man on the beach? Could she give him that without giving him a name? And what if she gave him Sasha? Could she be such a bitch? What did she owe Sasha? After all, hadn't he stuck her with Pandora's Box?

She met Rose in the *News'* lobby and they cabbed to the Metropolitan Club. Rose showed her around as if he owned the place, then left her in a small bleachers overlooking one of the club's squash courts. Five minutes later, Rose entered the court from a door beneath the bleachers. He wore plain gray sweatpants and an equally plain gray sweatshirt with a white towel wrapped around his neck. He waved up at Malloy and then began banging a ball off the wall. The sound echoed like rifle shots. A minute later he was joined by a tall, slender young man in white shorts and a T-shirt with the club insignia. They began to play.

It was comical watching Rose, his tiny legs churning, outrace his younger opponent to every ball. Rose would maneuver the man around the court and then, inevitably, drop a little dink that the younger, taller man, lurching and tripping over himself, couldn't reach. Rose was humiliating him. It was over quickly.

"Meet me in the dining room," Rose called up to Malloy when the slaughter was over and he had shaken hands with the beaten young man. "I'll shower up and be with you in ten."

The dining room was a dark wood-paneled affair whose opulent surface—white tablecloths, linen napkins embroidered with the club's logo, crystal drinking glasses—belied its mundane menu. There were hamburgers; bacon, lettuce, and tomato sandwiches; Caesar salads. Malloy had decided upon the latter when Rose sat down, his hair combed back wet.

"Here," said Rose, handing her a piece of paper. "You write down your order on this."

"How's the Caesar salad?" Malloy asked.

"Good enough," said Rose. "I mean, this is a WASP joint, right? So basically, the food sucks. They don't care about food. Ever see a fat WASP? They drink.

"So I killed that son of a bitch, didn't I?"

"You sure did, Mitch."

"Christ, I love to *shvitz*. That's why I wear the heavy sweats. Gets all the poisons out. It also gives me an edge. I mean, the guy sees me sweating like a pig, he has to decide, do I want to sweat like that? It makes him think he's gonna have to sweat like me to beat me. So maybe he doesn't feel like it. And if he doesn't, I got him beat before the game starts.

"I mean, this guy I played? Donald Fenwick. Donald Fenwick Junior. A lawyer with Robinson, Silverman. He must be, what, ten years younger than me? And an athlete. Hits harder than me. Got those long WASPy legs. He should kill me. But I got him beat in the head. Oh, I love it so much. I love looking in his eyes, seeing that loser look."

"He looked about twenty years younger than you, Mitch," said Malloy, "which makes it even more impressive, the way you ran him around."

Rose was about to argue the age difference when a short, balding, trim, middle-aged man in a gray pin-striped suit, a blue shirt with a white collar and French cuffs, and a red, white, and blue polka-dot bow tie walked up to their table.

"Maddy, this is Peter Feld. Peter, this is Madeline Malloy, one of my best reporters."

Malloy looked at Rose in pleased surprise. Even if he didn't mean it, it was nice to hear.

"Pleased to meet you, Ms. Malloy," Feld said, slightly goggle-eyed behind thick black horn-rimmed glasses.

"So, what's happening, Peter?" asked Rose.

"About what?" Feld asked.

"About anything," said Rose. "What should we be covering? What should we be writing about? Peter's a lawyer, used to be my financial adviser," Rose said to Malloy, "until he skipped out on me and went to work for Mario, conning the public out of its tax money."

"He means I'm on Governor Cuomo's advisory committee," Feld said. "Doing my public-spirited best."

"I've seen your picture in the paper, Mr. Feld," said Malloy.

"Call me Peter."

"Call me Maddy."

"Peter buys me socks," Rose said. "Show her your socks, Peter."

Feld stepped away from the table and hiked up the leg of his trousers. Golden Renaissance suns with fat cheeks and Cupid lips twinkled above his black loafers.

"My one eccentricity," said Feld. "That and, perhaps, the bow ties. But the ties, I think, are more an affectation than an eccentricity. They make people think I went to Harvard instead of Brooklyn College. What do you think, Maddy? Are they an affectation or an eccentricity?"

Rose cut off any response Malloy might have made. "So, tell me," he said. "What's up? What's news?"

"Actually, Mitch, I just came over to say hello. I've got to run. I'll call you this afternoon. Nice to meet you, Maddy," said Feld, backing away.

"That's why I come here," Rose whispered to Malloy when Feld had left. "You know me. I don't make the big social scene, parties, that bullshit. Can't stand it. But I hang out here, ask people what's going on, the real movers and shakers, the *makhers,* the mavens, they're relaxed, they talk. And they explain things. Shit, that budget stuff puts everybody to sleep, but Peter explains it like it's a football game, the inside stuff, who's handing off to who, who's getting creamed. That's how I keep ahead of my reporters.

"He also knows the international stuff. Been everywhere. Speaks a few languages. His firm, Feld and O'Riley, they've got clients all over the place. Shit, he tells the Japs where to invest.

He'd be a good source for you on Russian stuff. Nice guy, too. The best.

"You know," continued Rose, lowering his voice even more, "I have my suspicions about Peter. He was in the army, early days in Vietnam. Special Services. A Jew in Special Services? I think he was a spook. A spy. CIA. They had to have a few Jews around, keeping the WASPs from bumping into each other, starting a war."

The food arrived. Malloy's salad was soggy. Rose had a tuna-fish sandwich on rye toast and an abstemious glass of Perrier—"designer water," he called it—with a wedge of lime. He was in tremendous shape, Malloy had to admit to herself. And he took care of himself. The product of an astounding vanity, perhaps, but wasn't that better than the fat guts that so many men wore at his age?

"How's the salad?" Rose asked.

"Like you said. Good enough," said Malloy.

"So tell me, Maddy. Tell me about your Russian cop."

"Well, you know that the Russians are getting into the rackets. They run Brighton Beach, and the cops tell me they've basically taken Brooklyn away from the Italians. This assistant DA in Brooklyn tells me that most of their money comes from the gasoline business, dodging taxes, but they're into everything: extortion, drugs, guns, you name it. So the cops are desperate to get a line on them, but they don't know where to begin. I mean, it took years to get Spanish-speaking cops on the force. How many speak Russian? So that's where my guy comes in."

"Your Russian detective."

"Yes. Peter Grushenko."

"Was he a Commie? KGB?"

"Well, he was probably a Party member. I don't think it was possible to be an investigator in Moscow without belonging to the Party. I'm pretty sure he wasn't KGB."

"You think 'probably' he was a Commie. You're 'pretty sure' he wasn't KGB," Rose said sarcastically.

"I know. I'm going to see him again, spend a day with him this time. I know his nickname is Peter the Duck," she said, trying to recover, knowing the sort of detail Rose loved. "He's pretty guarded. When I talked to him in his office, he really didn't open up. He thinks I know more about the shooting on the beach than I'm telling him."

"Do you?"

"Yes."

"What?"

"Mitch, just hypothetically, what if somebody gave someone something that might have something to do with the shooting? What if that someone didn't turn it over to the cops right away?"

"Why not?" asked Rose.

"Someone asked someone not to."

"Evidence in a shooting? Physical evidence? This is hypothetical, right?"

"Right."

"Then, hypothetically, if someone were concealing evidence, the cops would have every right to stick that someone in the can and throw away the key."

"And the paper?"

"You mean if this someone was a reporter, could the paper do anything to keep this reporter out of jail?"

"Yes."

"If this someone was a reporter, the paper couldn't, and wouldn't, do a goddamn thing. Especially if this reporter had been less than forthcoming with her editors. Unless, of course, there was a great story in it. Then all bets are off. You do what you have to."

"A great story?"

"An incredible story. But I don't know any reporters stupid enough to try to play that game. Do you, Maddy?"

"No," said Malloy.

"You sure?" Rose asked, leaning across the table.

Malloy leaned back, putting distance between them.

"So," said Rose, "so this Grushenko didn't open up to you. I can't believe it. What were you wearing?"

"Come on, Mitch."

"I'm serious. You want a guy to talk to you, you use what you got. And you got great legs. As your editor, I advise you to wear a very short skirt when you go out to see him."

"Fine, Mitch."

"You think I'm joking?"

"No. That's the problem."

"What problem?"

"What problem? What problem? Where have you been? You can't just sit there and talk to me about my clothes or my body. You're my boss, for God's sake. It's Clarence Thomas and Anita Hill."

"Oh, come on."

"No, you come on. What you're doing right now is bordering on harassment. You know, when you called me in the office today, the thought crossed my mind that maybe I should file a complaint."

"Jesus Christ, Maddy. Lighten up."

"I'll lighten up when you get off my legs."

Rose cackled.

"Poor choice of words," Malloy said.

"Listen, Maddy," said Rose. "I wouldn't be human if I didn't respond to you like, you know, the man-woman thing. It's got nothing to do with being your editor. I'm just kidding around with you, you know that. I'm married. Happily. For the third time. That's me. I'm old-fashioned. I don't screw around, I get married. And I haven't proposed to you. Yet.

"But what're you doing for dinner tonight?"

"Stop it, Mitch. Please. You're making it worse."

"I'm just kidding."

"Yeah. You know," Malloy said, "you once told me that nothing is ever said entirely in jest."

"I'm so smart."

"So stop coming on to me. I'm flattered, and I know you think you're being charming, but it's inappropriate and it's making me very uncomfortable. Okay?"

"All right," said Rose. "From now on, strictly professional. I promise. But I still think I have the right to advise you on how to dress when you go out to report a story."

"Believe me," Malloy said. "You don't."

"All right. So forget I'm your editor. I'm just a guy. And being just a guy, I think that if you don't dress in a certain way when you go to see your cop, you're making a mistake. There. Is that okay?"

"No, it's not okay."

"Well, fuck me. I give up."

"Let's go, Mitch," said Malloy, standing up.

They took a cab back to the paper. Rose's mood seemed as buoyant as before, but Malloy wondered if she had succeeded in frightening him by mentioning Clarence Thomas, at least enough to get him to tone down his act. He certainly wouldn't want her filing a harassment complaint with the union. That couldn't possibly do him any good with the paper's owners.

Before they separated, Rose to his office, Malloy to her desk, Rose took her elbow.

"What we were talking about before, that someone with evidence?"

"It was just hypothetical, Mitch."

"I know. But, hypothetically, that someone should tell her editor about what she has. Then it's the editor's responsibility, which is why editors get paid the big bucks. You understand?"

"Uh-huh."

"And if, for whatever reason, this someone couldn't speak to her editor, then she should speak to a lawyer, someone like my friend Peter Feld. You understand, Maddy?"

"Yes, Mitch."

"I hope you do," said Rose.

So, Malloy thought, sitting down at her terminal, do I have Peter Feld's number in my Rolodex?

She opened the Grushenko file. She stared at it, not seeing it.

I am, she thought, in the shit. Thanks, Sasha.

12.

To Sasha, the disaster in the Kievskaya Metro seemed like a message. This is no longer your home, it said. This is a more dangerous jungle than the one you just left. The man following him. Could it be Henry keeping an eye on him? He hoped it was. Sasha, who had been looking forward to seeing his old friend, to confronting him about the box of coins, now wondered just who the hell this new Henry Tepperman might be, what trouble he might bring. Hadn't Boris said that he had changed? Hadn't Boris said not to trust him?

A candidate for mayor? Henry? Could it be a joke?

Arbat Street had depressed him. The McDonald's was the same as any McDonald's in Brooklyn. Why would anyone want to eat that crap? Sasha wondered. And at Brooklyn prices, too.

He had stopped into the Ristorante Italia for a beer and had ended up paying five dollars along with the other tourists and the *boyeviki,* the *mafiya* guys, sizing them up. The same prices applied at the Rioni Cafe and at the Prague. A Baskin-Robbins sold ice cream at American prices, as did the Pingvin.

The street was not as crowded as Sasha remembered, and

certainly not as prosperous. There were more beggars, more Gypsies and children selling postcards, pins, and cheap watches to tourists.

Arbat Street isn't for Russians, Sasha thought. Not anymore. It's for rich Germans, rich Japanese, rich Americans. The whole world is rich, except for the Russians. So why should Moscow care about Russians? It's the tourists who have the money.

It was four o'clock, and Sasha felt deeply tired. The vodka he had drunk with Kravchuk had worn off. He took a cab back to the Ukraina after bargaining the driver, who at first took him for a tourist and asked for two thousand, down to five hundred rubles. When he got back to his floor, there was a new key lady, Raisa, who obviously had been told by Irena that Sasha was a good tipper. She told him his new bed had arrived, "the best bed in the hotel." She was positively giddy, bubbling over with offers of caviar, massages, and "company."

Sasha thanked her, gave her a five-dollar bill, and told her he didn't wish to be disturbed. When he opened the door, all he could see was the bed. It was enormous. It devoured the room. The table and chairs, the television set and the dresser, all had been pushed against the windows to make room for it. God only knew where Irena had found it.

The room was, again, too hot. Someone had closed the windows. Sasha climbed over the chairs and stood on the table to open them. Far below him, Moscow's lights were blinking on. He moved a chair next to the bed, put a lamp on it, threw his coat over the small refrigerator, and slipped off his shoes. He opened the refrigerator, took out the vodka, and poured himself a glass. The trick, he reminded himself, was to maintain a certain level.

He took off his glasses and lay down. It was wonderful to stop, to rest, to breathe more slowly, in and out.

It was dark when he awoke. He lay there for a moment, re-
minding himself where he was. He found the lamp and
switched it on. He looked at his watch. It was eleven.

Sasha showered, shaved, and put on a gray tropical-
weight suit from Barney's with a black turtleneck from the
Gap. Raisa told him that he could get blinis on the fourteenth
floor and sandwiches on the eighth floor. The main restaurant
was closed.

Sasha took the elevator to the fourteenth floor, where the
key lady on duty directed him down the hall to the snack bar,
where two women were fixing blinis behind a counter. Otherwise, the room was empty. Sasha had two plates—six blinis,
three with *krasnaya* caviar, three with honey—and fifty grams
of vodka, all for six hundred rubles. He sat at a small, round,
Formica-topped table, smoked two Marlboros, and began to
feel human again.

Money. Had he stopped thinking about money since he
had arrived? When the Communists were in power, everyone
thought about money, but it was like sex: it was considered
rude to talk about it. Now it was everywhere, flaunted like
pornography. And all of Moscow was Times Square. Instead of
people handing out flyers for girlie shows, they handed out flyers concerning investment credits, private banks, and real estate deals. Everyone was either whoring or pimping. This is
not business, Sasha thought. This is not about buying and selling, using your wits for profit. This is about appetite. This is
an orgy.

Sasha shook his head. What you're missing is fun, he told
himself. He thought briefly of telling Raisa the key lady that,
yes, he would like some company tonight, but then he shuddered at the thought of what a whore working the Ukraina
would probably look like. He decided instead to visit the Alek-

sandr, the casino boat tied up just across the river from the hotel.

Walking across the Kalininsky Bridge, Sasha wished he had gone back to his room to get his coat. The night was very clear and very cold. The White House, the Russian parliament building, loomed to his left, its windows boarded up with plywood, its gold clock stopped. On August 19, 1991, Boris Nikolayevich Yeltsin had stood on a tank in front of the White House and defied the Communist putschists, effectively signaling the end of the USSR. On October 5, 1993, as the first democratically elected president of the Russians, Yeltsin ordered his troops to open fire on that same White House, signaling what? Sasha wondered.

Straight ahead, Sasha could see the Kremlin's searchlights vanishing into the starry sky. Anyone who pretended to have answers for this lunatic country was a liar or a fool, thought Sasha. He began to trot. He came off the bridge, turned left, and found the service road down to the embankment.

A Mercedes sport coupé glided past him toward the boat and joined a gaggle of similarly expensive cars parked by the ferry, its fresh coat of whitewash lit up by red, blue, and green spotlights. As Sasha approached, he could hear music coming from the boat, drifting over the river. It sounded scratchy, like something out of an old car radio. He watched a man and a woman get out of the Mercedes and give some money to a man in a tuxedo standing at the foot of the gangplank. To watch their car, Sasha presumed.

"Good evening," the man said to Sasha. "Welcome to the Aleksandr."

"Good evening," Sasha said, noting the man's shiny black hair, the bulge under his coat, and his southern accent. A Georgian, he thought. A thug.

At the top of the gangplank, another man in a tuxedo

stood waiting. This one had no bulge, meaning either that he wasn't armed or that he had a better-fitting holster.

"Welcome aboard," the man said. "Is this your first time on the Aleksandr?"

Sasha nodded.

"My name is Iosif Vissarionovich," the man said. "Yes, just like Stalin. I've heard all the jokes. May I show you around?"

"I can find my way, thank you," said Sasha. "My name is Aleksandr, just like your boat. Aleksandr Strahinich. I'm Croatian."

"Pity what's happening to your country. It's the Americans' fault."

"Yes," Sasha said curtly, not wishing to be drawn into a conversation.

"Yes, well, you go that way, toward the music. The cashiers are to your right as you enter the casino. All drinks are compliments of the house. There are snacks available, too. Of course, we accept only hard currencies. Dollars, pounds, francs, kroners, and marks."

"Thank you, Iosif Vissarionovich."

"If you need anything, I'll be around. Enjoy yourself."

The man turned away from Sasha to greet two men coming up the gangplank, and Sasha entered the casino.

Sasha's pal, Ivan Siskin, used to love to go down to Atlantic City to gamble, and he'd frequently beg Sasha to go with him. Sasha, who enjoyed Siskin's company, would eventually agree. They'd pile into Siskin's Chevrolet with a bottle or two of vodka and a bag of marijuana and drive down for the evening, always starting at the Trump Castle at the foot of Brigantine Bridge, where Siskin would shout, "They treat you like royalty! Like the motherfucking czar!"

Siskin liked the roulette and the free drinks. He drank a lot, played loosely, and made big bets. Sasha's evenings usually went the same way. He'd sit down at a fifteen-dollar-minimum blackjack table with a six-hundred-dollar stake, order an Absolut on the rocks, tip the waitress a five-dollar chip, tip the dealer fifteen, and begin playing in a businesslike fashion, tightly, according to the odds, leaving the table if he lost three hands in a row. The trick, he knew, was to find a cold dealer and avoid the hot ones. Often he would find himself up several hundred dollars. And then something would happen. Slowly, imperceptibly, he would slide into a reverie. He was no longer in Atlantic City; he was in Monte Carlo. He was no longer Aleksandr Volkavich Eugenev; he was Cary Grant, a raffish figure in a white dinner jacket. Suddenly he would be at a fifty-dollar table, doubling down on hunches, dreaming of fabulous riches. He would come back to himself when he realized that the small pile of chips in front of him had vanished. Then he would collect Siskin, and they would spend the ride back to Brooklyn excoriating Donald Trump, America, capitalism, and their own rotten luck. It was fun.

By contrast, the casino in the Aleksandr was a rather shabby affair, poorly lit, drafty, smelling of ammonia and the brackish waters of the Moskva. An Oriental-looking carpet had been laid down over the iron deck, and heavy red velvet curtains covered the portholes. Still, the wind off the river found its way into the room. There were a half dozen blackjack tables with worn-looking blue felt, several chemin de fer tables, and an equal number of roulette wheels and craps tables. Waitresses in high heels, short black skirts, black mesh stockings, and white blouses drifted between the tables, carrying trays of drinks. Over a loudspeaker, Sasha heard the American song "The Lion Sleeps Tonight."

The casino was moderately crowded. The overwhelming majority of the players were young men dressed very much like Sasha in suits and turtlenecks. Many wore gold chains and heavy, expensive wristwatches. The women, Sasha thought, were largely disappointing in their typically Russian print dresses. Here and there Sasha noted a few prostitutes.

Sasha changed two hundred dollars into chips and sat down at a blackjack table. He began to drink. He began to win.

After a while, it seemed to Sasha as if this were what he had been born to do, as if he had spent his whole life in search of this seat at this blackjack table in this casino moored on the Moskva. Dealers came and went, and each one seemed friendlier—and unluckier—than the last. If the dealer had nineteen, Sasha had twenty. If the dealer had twenty, Sasha had twenty-one. If the dealer had blackjack, Sasha had an insurance bet down. And the pile of chips in front of him grew and changed colors like a beneficent genie in a fable.

The moment he felt thirsty, a drink appeared. Whenever he lifted a cigarette to his lips, there was a hand ready to light it. To his right and left gentlemen praised his skill and good fortune. Women, prettier now, better dressed, stood behind him, pressed their breasts against his back, and laughed at his jokes.

Sasha leaned back, took a deep breath, and looked around the casino. It seemed very crowded now, very bright, colorful, and jolly, like a party. He looked at his watch. It was three A.M. Should he count his chips and go back to the hotel? The thought of returning to the gloomy Ukraina repulsed him.

A finger tapped his left shoulder, and Sasha turned to his left. "Stop now," said a voice in his right ear. "Stop before you give it all back."

"What?" Sasha said, spinning to his right.

"Excuse me?" said the player sitting there.

"Nothing," said Sasha, looking back at his cards—a king and a five. Not good. The dealer showed a six. The dealer was weak.

"It's starting," said the voice behind him in a whining taunt.

Sasha turned around on his chair, trying to focus, trying to pick a face out of the blur in front of him.

"I told Lenny you'd be here. Didn't care for that Stalinist dump, the Ukraina?"

Sasha squinted at the small, dark-haired young man standing in front of him.

"Henry?"

"Would you like a card?" the dealer demanded, tapping the table in front of Sasha.

"Yes, sure," said Sasha, hurriedly turning back to his cards.

A queen landed on top of his king-five. Bust.

"Jesus," said Henry Tepperman. "You don't know what the fuck you're doing, do you? You got to give the dealer a chance to bust. Are you drunk?"

"I'm not drunk," Sasha lied, bewildered by Tepperman's sudden materialization and by the fact that he seemed younger than Sasha remembered.

"You are drunk," Tepperman said. "You'd have to be to be so stupid. Look at all the chips in front of you. Now look around. See all the young men who are being so careful about not looking at you? Half of them are thinking about ripping you off and throwing you in the Moskva as soon as you get off the boat. The others aren't planning to wait that long."

Sasha looked around. There was, he had to admit, a wolfish look to most of the young men in the casino.

"You'd know about rip-offs," Sasha said bitterly.

"Uh-oh," said Tepperman. "Sasha's got a hair across his ass. Wait. You can tell me later."

"Cards?" the dealer asked Sasha.

"No," said Tepperman. "He's cashing in. Hey, Lenny."
Lenny Kravchuk appeared, smiling, at Tepperman's side. "I

told you he'd be here. Get his chips and cash them in for him. Then," Tepperman told Kravchuk, "get his stuff out of the Ukraina. He's suffered enough. And ditch the Croat passport. We're going to get him a Russian one. I'm going to pour some coffee into him and then he'll have some of your medicine and then we'll head out to the *dacha*. I have a surprise for you there. Okay, Shurik?"

Sasha nodded. Okay, he thought. We'll go back to your *dacha,* Henry old friend. I want to see your face when I tell you I have your fucking coin box. I want you to pay me well for all my troubles, for my apartment, my girls. I want you to make it right so I can go home to New York without getting killed.

The words in his head echoed so loudly, it made the room spin. I want to go home, Sasha thought.

Henry Tepperman patted his head. "There, there, Shurik," he said. "There, there."

13.

Tuesday, October 26

PETER GRUSHENKO SAT SLUMPED ON THE BOARDWALK BENCH, his hands stuffed deep into his tan raincoat, his legs straight out in front of him, his chin tucked into his chest, his back to the slowly rolling ocean. The sun was high and bright overhead, but the wind was cold and penetrating. The sea already looked like winter: oily, lugubrious, gray, and dense. The boardwalk was empty except for a scattering of old Jews taking the air and a few kids from the projects wearing their hooded sweatshirts and Air Jordans. Grushenko took the newspaper out from beneath his raincoat. What crap.

"Stately, plump Peter Grushenko," Madeline Malloy's article began. What was that "plump"? That was the same as fat. He wasn't fat. He was a big man, yes, but not fat.

Grushenko felt betrayed. The woman had seemed so sympathetic, so interested in what he had to say once he had made up his mind to talk to her. But she had twisted everything.

He returned to the article, reading again.

"He sipped a glass (not a cup) of tea Russian style, placing a lump of sugar between his teeth and sucking the strong, black fluid through it. 'Americans don't know anything about tea,' Detective Grushenko said gruffly, thereby adding tea to his long list of things Americans know nothing about: vodka, and how to drink it; crime, and how to stop it; and, most of all, the Russian Mob, and how to fight it."

She had made him sound mean-spirited, ungrateful, contemptuous of the men he worked with. And anti-American. His wife, Olga, had been in tears this morning, afraid that he would be fired. (Thank God he had said no when Malloy asked to come to his home. If she had described him as fat, what would she have written about Olga?) He had tried to comfort his wife, telling her that nobody cared what the newspapers said, but he wasn't so sure. What would Silverman, the assistant DA, say when he read:

"'In America,' said Grushenko, 'the law is for the criminals. For the good people, there is no law. In the former Soviet Union, for the good people, the citizens, the law protected them. And the criminals, we put them in prison and kept them there. We made them pay.'"

Now he was afraid to go into the office, afraid of that little Jew, Silverman.

What had made him think he could say such things to that woman? Was it because she had told him that there was a third man on the beach? He had heard as much already, and asking around the neighborhood had given him a good idea of who it was.

The Panther's girlfriend, Svetlana Furtseva, had told him that Aleksandr Eugenev, a scam artist Grushenko had met but had never busted, had turned up at her apartment with an American reporter, a girl, obviously Malloy, asking questions about the Panther. (Furtseva had also accused Eugenev of having had the Panther shot. That, Grushenko knew, was nonsense. Even if he had wanted to, Eugenev had neither the clout nor the balls. But still, thought Grushenko, an accusation like that was a good thing to have in his pocket when he caught up with him.)

Emma Bovrilina had told him that Aleksandr Eugenev had come to her Georgian Cafe on the night of the shooting with an American reporter, a woman. Malloy again. Eugenev also had been seen later that night at the Odessa, without Malloy, speaking with Ebzi Agron.

A busy boy, Sasha Eugenev. Here, there, everywhere. But nobody had seen him lately. He seemed to have vanished.

Hiding out? Because he was guilty? Because he was scared?

Grushenko would bet on scared.

I should have walked away when Malloy refused to give me her source on Boris the Kike, he thought. When she denied that she knew anyone named Aleksandr Eugenev. Better, I should have hauled her spoiled American ass down to the station, confronted her with Furtseva and Bovrilina, made her confess that she knew Sasha Eugenev, that she was probably sleeping with Sasha Eugenev, that she probably knew where he was right now. Why didn't I?

Was he afraid that Silverman would lecture him about hassling reporters?

No. Even Silverman wouldn't interfere with a murder investigation. Confess, Peter, he said to himself. It was because she was pretty, wasn't it? You stupid old goat. You thought such a pretty young girl would be scared of you. You couldn't imagine such a pretty young girl causing you trouble.

He folded the paper and put it back in his coat. He took out his handkerchief, blew his nose, and examined the mucus. It was dark green. Wonderful, he thought. The cold has become sinusitis. He pressed his forehead with the tips of his fingers. Yes, it hurt. They're infected. He crumpled the handkerchief and stuffed it back in his pocket.

Of course, he thought, what he had told the reporter was

nothing less than the truth. The police were a joke. Arrest someone, they're out in a few hours, while you're filling out forms for days. That's why so many police refused to arrest people they saw using drugs or bothering citizens. It wasn't worth the trouble. And then, if you did bust someone, you had to treat them as if they were your grandmother's best china. Slap one of them and you were risking your job. So why should the criminals respect them?

Naturally, the Russians in Brighton knew that Grushenko played by different rules. The Russians feared him. They knew what he thought of them. They knew how he had been trained.

But Silverman was always telling him that Brooklyn was not Moscow. As if he didn't know that. Anyway, it was Silverman's fault, telling him to cooperate with that Madeline Malloy. It's not your job to talk to the newspapers, he told himself. That's Silverman's job. It's your job to put Ebzi Agron, Boris Zilberstein, Aleksandr Eugenev, and all the other punks in jail. If you do that, no newspaper article will matter. And maybe that newspaperwoman will be helpful to you despite herself. At the very least, he was now certain that Eugenev was involved in the Panther's shooting. And Eugenev would be easy to crack. All Grushenko had to do was find him.

Grushenko stood up as a tall woman in sunglasses, a black silk windbreaker, tight jeans, and high-heeled black boots wobbled unsteadily across the boardwalk toward his bench.

"You are going to break your leg one of these days," said Grushenko. The woman, her crew-cut hair dyed white, towered over him.

"Beauty knows no pain, honey," she said.

"Where do you buy those big boots? Where do they sell women's boots so big?"

"Why? You looking for a pair? You want to try these?"

Placing her hand on Grushenko's shoulder for balance, she stuck her foot in the air and waggled it coyly.

"Christ," said Grushenko, "they must be size fourteen."

"They're elevens. And you know what they say about big feet, honey. What it means. For a big guy, you've got eenie-weenie feet, don't you? I read about you in the paper this morning, Detective. In the *News*. You're famous."

"I didn't read it."

"Oh, you should. It's very flattering. Even the picture. You look very butch."

"Take off your sunglasses," said Grushenko.

"It's too bright, darling."

"I want to see your eyes," Grushenko said.

She removed her wraparound shades and, hand on hip, struck a fashion model's languid pose.

Grushenko looked up into her bloodshot eyes, seeing the tiny pinpoint pupils. Rabbit eyes.

"You are using again, Terry," he said.

"Just a little pot, darling."

"Bullshit. Show me your arms."

"I'd never mark up my beautiful milky white arms," said Terry.

"What about your ass? Maybe you want to pull down your pants?"

"I thought you'd never ask. You want to come back to my place? I'll show you anything you want."

"What you got I don't want."

"You never know until you try, baby."

"Give me your purse."

"Oh, come on. Even if I was using, which I'm not, do you think I'd be crazy enough to carry when I'm going to see you? You think I'm stupid?"

"What I think about you, Terry, you don't want to know.

And who knows what the hell you would think to do? Give it to me."

"I have rights, you know," Terry said sullenly as she handed Grushenko her purse.

Grushenko popped it open. He pulled out a vial of pills and shook them. "What is this?"

"Valium," said Terry. "For my nerves. To help me sleep. I got a prescription."

Grushenko rooted in the purse. "Oh, ho," he said. "Look what I found."

"Shit," said Terry.

Grushenko pulled out a gravity knife and flicked it open. The blade was four inches long. "Very bad," he said. "This is very bad. Very bad, nasty thing here."

"A girl's gotta protect herself," said Terry.

"This is against law," Grushenko said. "Concealed weapon. I can arrest you for this. I can put you in cell for few days, maybe more. Of course, you are not using, so that doesn't bother you, yes? Sitting in jail. You might like it. Lots of nice men for you to meet."

"What do you want?" asked Terry.

"You are using?"

"A little. Just sniffing. Just dabbling. For my nerves. I swear I'm not shooting."

"So why do you lie to me, Terry?" Grushenko asked. "Don't you know that you can't lie to me? So now you can tell me what that crazy bastard you live with told you about those men who were killed on beach. The third man. That was Sasha Eugenev, wasn't it? Everybody knows that. I want to talk to him. Where is he?"

"I don't know. David already told you he didn't know anything about it."

"Yes, but now I am asking you."

"David didn't tell me anything. He never tells me anything. You Russians. You never tell women anything."

"He is not a Russian. He's a kike, Ukrainian kike. And you are not a woman. All right. We go together. You take me to see him. We ask David together, all right?"

"I don't know where he is. He's out of town."

"All right, Terry. Let's go. We go to station now and I book you for the knife. You will make all the *bolshoi chyorniys,* the big blacks, in the jail very happy. They love blondes."

"I'm telling you the truth, Peter."

"You don't fucking call me Peter," Grushenko exploded. "You call me Detective or Mister Grushenko."

"I don't know where he is, Detective," said Terry. "He went away."

"Another fucking lie. Okay. I am tired of talking to you now. Let's go."

Grushenko took Terry by the elbow, and they began walking across the boardwalk.

"You're not really busting me for that stupid knife, are you?"

"Yes, I am."

"You can't. I can't. I mean, maybe I am using more than a little. I can't sit in a cell. I'll die, I swear it."

"Then you take me to your boyfriend. Now. Then I let you go."

Terry thought about jail, thought about going cold turkey. Her habit was new, courtesy of a new trick who was buying her ass for smack. Another Russian, of course. For a moment, Terry thought of giving Grushenko her new trick, making up a story that would involve him. But this new Ivan had a mean streak. He liked to tie her up, and he liked to hit her. And he was big. Not a smart idea, girl, she told herself. The Cowboy, she knew she could handle.

"All right," said Terry.

They climbed into Grushenko's Buick Regal, parked by Nathan's, and drove back to Brighton Beach. They stopped in front of the Cafe Arbat under the El at 239 Brighton Beach Avenue.

"If he's not inside," said Terry, "I don't know where he is."

"Let's go," Grushenko said.

"No way," said Terry. "You crazy? He sees me with you, he twists my titties off tonight. I'm not going in there with you."

"Okay, Terry," Grushenko said. "You can go."

"Can I have my knife back, Detective?"

"You have big balls, Terry."

"A girl's gotta have something," said Terry. "No knife?"

"No knife."

Terry got out of the car, and Grushenko watched her walk down the street shaking her ass. For a man, he thought, she was not a bad-looking woman. He shook his head. This country, he thought, is making me crazy.

Entering the Arbat, passing the video poker machines in the vestibule, Grushenko saw a black cowboy hat sticking up over the top of a red Leatherette booth next to the bandstand in the back. Behind the stage, a silver double-headed eagle hung on a green velvet curtain. Everyone is a Czarist these days, thought Grushenko. Seventy-five years of socialism and all they know is that those were the good old days.

The Arbat's walls were covered with emerald-green felt. The tablecloths were also green, surrounded by red vinyl chairs. The photographs on the wall—the Kremlin at night, St. Basil's, the Hermitage in St. Petersburg—were hung in gilt frames. Gold, green, and red. Just like the Winter Palace, Grushenko thought. He walked down the aisle and sat down, sliding across the bench opposite David Gatlober. He lit a cigarette and opened a menu.

"I never eat here," said Grushenko. "Anything good?"

"The piroshki," Gatlober said.

"You know," said Grushenko, "I don't really want to eat. I want to talk. They must have an office here, in the back."

"I don't feel like talking, Grushenko. This is America. You want to talk to me, get a warrant."

Grushenko kicked Gatlober hard in the shin below the table. Gatlober yelled. The Arbat's manager came running.

"Hello, Detective," he said. "Any trouble?"

"No trouble, Dmitri," said Grushenko as Gatlober rubbed his leg. "But my friend here doesn't feel well. Do you have an office in the back where we could sit quietly for a while?"

"We don't want any trouble, Detective."

"No trouble, Dmitri. We won't have any trouble, will we, David?" Grushenko asked. Gatlober shook his head, tears in his eyes.

"See, Dmitri?"

"Sure, Detective. Just behind the curtain behind the stage. Across from the toilet. Would you like me to bring you anything there? Some vodka?"

"No, thank you, my friend," said Grushenko. "We won't abuse your hospitality for long."

Grushenko stood and, grabbing him under the arm, lifted Gatlober up from the booth. Grushenko's hand closed around Gatlober's right wrist. "This country is making you soft in the head," Grushenko whispered in Gatlober's ear. "You talk to me with respect. Believe me, if you try to run away, I'll break your arm. I'll break it right off. Then I'll stuff it up your ass, fist first. But you don't need to be frightened. I just want you to tell me about Sasha Eugenev."

"What do you want to know?" asked Gatlober. "I already told you about the three cows he had stashed in that apartment."

"But you didn't tell me why you told me," Grushenko said. "Understand? Now I want to know that. I want to know why you fucked your friend. Understand? And I want you to tell me where he is now."

"No problem," said Gatlober. Aleksandr Volkavitch Eugenev, whom he had not seen since that wild night at the Odessa weeks ago, had already become, for the Cowboy, a somewhat misty, unreal figure out of the dim past. He was back in Russia, for Christ's sake. Who knew if he'd ever come back? And as for Aleksandr Velikhov—the man who had paid him to waste the guys on the beach, the man who had paid him to drop a dime on Sasha Eugenev's girls . . . well, he didn't even like the dude. The way he looked at Terry. KGB fuck. Giving him up was easy.

But why was Grushenko so interested in Sasha Eugenev? the Cowboy wondered. What had Sasha been into?

Staring at Grushenko's meaty face, hating it, the Cowboy decided he would do a little looking around for himself. The Panther's girlfriend, that whore Svetlana, had been telling everyone that when the Panther got shot, Sasha had turned up at her apartment with an American reporter. A reporter? What was that about?

You could never tell, he thought, what Sasha Eugenev might be working on. But whatever it was, it had to be some scam with money in it. If so, maybe Ebzi Agron would be interested. Now that Sasha was gone, maybe it was time for the Cowboy to move on up, to go to work for the *batyushka.* Or for Boris Zilberstein. Zilberstein was young, like him.

"Why didn't you just ask, man?" the Cowboy said. And even as he told the detective that Sasha Eugenev had gone back to Russia, and that some guy named Aleksandr Velikhov had it in for him, the Cowboy resolved to look up the girl reporter and ask her a few questions himself.

It was easy to find people in America, the Cowboy reminded himself. In America they had phone books. And the phone books, incredibly enough, had addresses.

14.

THE SWEAT RAN DOWN SASHA'S FOREHEAD. IT DROPPED, BURN-
ing, into his eyes. He ran his tongue over his lips. They were
cracked. Sticky. He reached for the bottle sitting in the ice
bucket on the sauna's bench. His stomach heaved in anticipa-
tion. Would he vomit? No. The feeling passed.

He swallowed the vodka. It went down smoothly.

I should eat, he thought. When did I last eat?

Days ago, it seemed. For days he had been drinking,
smoking hash, and snorting coke. Coke in the morning, coke
and hash in the afternoon, vodka and hash and cocaine at night.

Oh, yes. There was *studen* in the kitchen last night—cold
meat in clear beef jelly, Alyona's specialty.

Alyona. Alyushka.

He looked at his wrist. No watch. Where's my watch? he
wondered.

Did I sleep last night? How long have I been up?

Once more, he lifted the bottle to his lips. He felt it go
cold down his throat, into his chest. Once again, his stomach
accepted it. He closed his eyes.

What would it be like to be sober? he wondered. He shuddered. He took another drink.

Drunk again. Oh, well. Perhaps Lenny Kravchuk had been right. Perhaps the only way to survive in this new Russia was to be stoned all the time.

About Alyona, he was not surprised. Well, maybe a little. But basically, no. Henry had always fancied his wife. Sasha remembered how Henry would always *dostat* little presents for her. Here, he'd say, here are some Swiss chocolates for Alyona. Here's some American shampoo for Alyona. Don't you think Alyona would like a new *shopka?*

And when they were together, the three of them, Henry would pay more attention to Alyona than he would to Sasha. She's smarter than you, Henry would say, and much better looking. I don't know what she's doing with you.

Of course, neither did Sasha. He had always assumed that she had fallen for his looks and when she got over that she would leave him.

Well, it worked out like I thought it would, didn't it?

"So? What did you expect?" Alyona Romanova had asked him that first night when Henry had brought him to the *dacha* from the casino. It must have been about four A.M. I didn't feel drunk, Sasha recalled, but was I sober? Not likely. Henry had pushed everyone else out of the kitchen, saying, "Let them talk. They're husband and wife, after all."

Romanova was staring a challenge at him. Her eyes, almond shaped and dark, seemed to glitter. She was wearing a black sweater with a boat neck that hung loosely off one shoulder. She had beautiful shoulders, Sasha reminded himself, and a dancer's erect posture. She must have been tired, Sasha thought, but still she held herself as if someone had attached a string to the top of her head and was pulling up on it. Her neck was long, graceful, and strong. He glanced at her feet, turned out in first position. A dancer, he reminded himself. A beautiful, accomplished woman. I forgot. How could I have forgotten?

He poured himself a glass from a two-liter bottle of Italian mineral water standing on the counter and gulped it down. He was terribly thirsty. He spat into the sink. Kravchuk's cocaine had turned his saliva to paste. Alyona was standing with her back to the refrigerator, not leaning against it, her arms folded beneath her breasts.

"So?" Romanova demanded.

"It's good to see you, Alyona Romanova," said Sasha. "You look wonderful."

"Fuck you."

"All right," said Sasha, turning away and pouring himself another glass.

"I mean it. Fuck you."

"All right. You mean it," Sasha said. "Fuck me."

"You're incredible," Romanova said. "How many times did I write to you? What did you write, two letters? Two letters the first year and then nothing."

"I meant . . ."

"You meant what?"

"Nothing. You're right," said Sasha.

"You might as well have gone to the moon, to Mars."

"You're right," said Sasha.

"I could have died. Would you have known?"

"Henry would have told me," Sasha said, and then thought, Not smart, Sasha. Not the right thing to say.

"That's wonderful," said Romanova. "Well, now I feel much better. Do you think you would have made it to my funeral?"

"No. Your parents didn't like me, remember. I suppose Henry's all right because he's rich. If you're going to marry a Yid, you might as well marry a rich one."

"My father died last year."

"I'm sorry."

"No, you're not."

"You're right. I'm not sorry."

"You stink. You really stink."

"You're right. I don't blame you for being angry."

"I'm not angry, Aleksandr Volkavitch. I stopped being angry a long time ago."

"Good. I'd hate to be having this discussion if you were angry."

Sasha poured himself another glass of water. Outside the kitchen he could hear a wind chime. When would the sun come up?

"Is that it?" she asked. "Don't you have anything to say to me?"

"I'm sorry."

"And that's supposed to make everything all right?"

"No. What do you want me to say? I don't blame you for shacking up with Henry? Is that what you want to hear?"

"Blame me?" Romanova said. "You think I should apologize to you?"

"No."

"You should apologize to me."

"I already did."

"I was your wife."

"You're still my wife," said Sasha, "unless you know something I don't."

"You think I'm still your wife? You're incredible."

"All right. Tell me what I should say. What do you want to hear? Tell me, and I'll say it."

"Nothing. Don't say anything to me."

"Look. I'm sorry. I really am sorry. I have no excuse. What can I say? I'm an idiot. You want a divorce? You can have one."

Romanova looked at the floor. "You know," she said, "I really did care for you. I knew, when you left, it was finished.

It hurt. Do you understand? How could you just go away and forget me? Was I that ugly? Was I that boring? Were American women so much more sophisticated? Were they better in bed? Did they know tricks over there I didn't know? But then I got over it. Time passed. I thought I would never see you again."

She stopped. In the silence, Sasha heard the wind chime again.

"Why did you come back, Sasha? Now it hurts all over again."

Sasha took a step forward. Does she want me to embrace her? he wondered.

Romanova looked up and shook her head as if she had read his mind. "I have to go," she said, and left the kitchen.

The sauna door swung open. Sasha felt a rush of cold air.

I'll just keep my eyes closed, he thought. I'll think about making love to Alyona. No, I'll think about making love to Madeline Malloy.

He heard a sigh.

"Now I learn to love this things," said a man's voice. "This saunas. So very cold here."

The young Colombian who's been trying to make a deal with Henry, Sasha thought. Jorge Norton.

"You think about what we talk about?" Norton said in execrable Russian.

What? Sasha opened his eyes, blinking.

Norton wasn't talking to him. He was talking to Lenny Kravchuk, who was sitting next to Norton across from Sasha. Kravchuk, with a towel across his lap, was wearing earphones and holding a Sony Discman. Probably listening to Nirvana, Sasha thought. He noticed that Kravchuk had a small blue Orthodox cross tattooed on his left breast, above his heart. Another prison tattoo, Sasha thought. A thief's tattoo. The cup or crescent moon beneath the cross bar. What did it signify? The

Christian triumph over Islam? A cup to catch Christ's blood? I used to know, Sasha thought, closing his eyes again.

"You think we can work?" said Norton, who was only twenty-two and had been encountering a surprising amount of difficulty trying to recruit Russian couriers for his father's cocaine business. "Very, very good profit," Norton said. "You talk Henry, please?"

"What?" Kravchuk pulled the plugs out of his ears.

"Rubles, dollars," said Norton, brushing his long, jet black hair out of his eyes. He had been feeding Tepperman and his men his best cocaine, getting nothing out of it. What was wrong with them? he thought. Didn't they understand how much money there was to be made? Why had that big shot his father had set him up with in Moscow sent him to Tepperman if Tepperman was not serious? What would his father say if he came back from Russia without a deal?

"Very, very big business," Norton said. "Henry and you talk. Very, very big money," he said, rubbing his thumb against his index finger.

"Where did you learn to speak Russian?" Kravchuk asked the Colombian.

"Harvard," said Norton. "One year. Study Russian. My family. Understand?"

"Understand what? Your fucking family what? Jesus. I can never figure out what the hell you're talking about."

"What? I don't understand. Excuse me."

"Talk English to him, Sasha," Kravchuk said. "He's driving me crazy."

"His English isn't much better," said Sasha.

"Got to be better than his Russian," Kravchuk said.

The door swung open again. Henry Tepperman stood in the opening, dressed in black pants, black loafers, and a black silk shirt buttoned at the throat. Jorge Norton popped to his feet, his brown eyes shining, his handsome, high-cheekboned face alight.

"Sit down, Jorge," Tepperman said in English. "Come on, Shurik," he said to Sasha in Russian. "Get showered, dressed. I want to show you something."

Sasha stood up. He swayed. He felt so weak.

"Time for some more medicine," Tepperman said. "Come on."

"Don't leave me alone with this fucker," said Kravchuk. "He won't shut up."

"Poor baby," Tepperman said. "Come on, Sasha, I'm getting sweated up."

Sasha showered and put on his clothes while Tepperman watched.

"Here," said Tepperman, handing him a vial of cocaine. "This'll straighten you out."

Sasha poured some into the crack between his left thumb and forefinger and snorted it. Maybe it would wake him up.

"You're getting fat," Tepperman said. "And bald."

And you've got a tiny dick, Sasha thought.

"Let's talk about Boris," said Sasha.

"In a minute," Tepperman said. "Let's go."

In Tepperman's living room, Sasha saw Alyona sitting on a sofa next to a fat, stupid-looking young woman. Standing behind them and slowly passing a gaudy Tartar dagger over Alyona's head was a bearded old man dressed like a peasant in muddy, knee-high rubber boots, brown breeches, and a red collarless shirt. The woman was wearing a shapeless print dress faded to the color of boiled potato skins.

"Who the hell is this?" Tepperman asked.

"This is Uncle Zhora and Natalya Ivanova," said Romanova, who was wearing a red-and-white Boston University sweatshirt and black tights. "Say hello to Henry and Aleksandr Volkavitch, Uncle Zhora."

"What kind of a name is Henry?" the man asked, pulling at his gray, tangled beard.

"It's a German name," Romanova explained.

"A German?" grunted Uncle Zhora, sticking the dagger in his belt and coming around the sofa to make himself comfortable beside Romanova. "I healed a German once. In Sevastopol. He came to me with a stomachache. He had a big, fat German gut. I gave him some root tea, and the shit just poured out of him like a river. A river of German shit." He laughed, and Natalya Ivanova laughed with him.

"It was a real river," she echoed.

Sasha caught a whiff of something foul. He edged over to Uncle Zhora. He smelled like a donkey. A donkey who had died after drinking a gallon of vodka and puking all over himself. Sasha backed away.

"I didn't know you had an Uncle Zhora," Tepperman said.

"He's not my uncle," said Romanova. "He's just Uncle Zhora. He's a healer."

The fat woman nodded. "He is touched by God," she said, crossing herself and then sticking a coy finger in Uncle Zhora's ear. Zhora giggled.

"Are you crazy, Alyona?" Tepperman said.

"He came highly recommended," said Romanova.

"By who? For what? What lunatic recommended him? What's he treating you for?" Tepperman asked.

"What do you care?" said Romanova. "Leave us alone."

Uncle Zhora jumped up. "I can't help you," he shouted at Romanova. "You're surrounded by unbelievers." He turned toward Tepperman. "Germans? You mean Yids." He spat. "I can smell them. Children of Satan."

"Children of Satan," Natalya Ivanova repeated, crossing herself again.

"Jesus Christ," said Tepperman.

"Blasphemer!" Uncle Zhora screamed. Then he squatted,

closed his eyes, and farted loudly. He sighed. "Ah, that's better. You know," he said quietly, still squatting, looking up at Tepperman, "you have terrific teeth. Are they real? Would you consider selling them?"

"All right," said Tepperman. "Out. Get out of here, Uncle Shithead."

Romanova stood up. "They're my guests," she said. "You don't insult my guests."

"That's all right, child," said Uncle Zhora, patting Romanova's hand. "We will gladly leave this house of evil where Slavs, true Slavs, are not welcome. Remember: Money cannot buy God's favor, and money cannot relieve your suffering. Come, Natalya. May Christ preserve you, my child," he said to Romanova, "and may He make this putrid blaspheming Yid piss up his own asshole."

Uncle Zhora swept grandly out of the room, followed by Natalya Ivanova, who was giving Tepperman the evil eye over her shoulder.

"What's got into you?" Tepperman asked Romanova.

"You wouldn't understand," said Romanova, following Uncle Zhora and Natalya Ivanova out of the room.

"Your wife gets crazier every day," said Tepperman. "How are you two getting along? She won't tell me anything."

"That's because it's none of your business, Henry," said Sasha.

"You're not mad at me, are you?" Tepperman asked.

"It's not worth talking about, you know?"

"Maybe I should have told you," said Tepperman. "But, you know, it's not the kind of thing you can just mention over the phone."

"Forget it. Let's talk about Boris."

"Right. You know, this thing with Alyona . . ."

"Fuck, Henry. I said I don't want to talk about it."

"No, I mean this Uncle Zhora bullshit. This is what happens when you get involved with a Russian. Sooner or later, they go screwy on you. You remember Anatoly Kashpirovsky? The Ukrainian mesmerist?"

"Kashpirovsky?"

"You know, he used to come to Moscow, perform at the Mossoviet or the Sovremennik Theaters, everyone thought he was KGB."

"So?"

"Well, now he plays football stadiums. He's the biggest thing in Russia. The Ukraine, too. You can't imagine how huge he is. He has these television séances. Everyone watches. He stares into the camera, very intense, like Rasputin. He says, 'Some of you are worried about money.' He says, 'Some of you have pain. Now think of the mountains. Think of the snow on top of the mountain. Think of the cold snow. Move the snow from the mountains into your bodies. Now, you're healed.' It's astonishing."

"What about the people worried about money?"

"I don't know. The thing is, intelligent people, people like Alyona, they believe. Things are falling apart, so they start believing in magic. Anything is better than the reality, you know?"

"And what's that?" asked Sasha.

"The reality? You know the reality. We're very primitive and we're getting more primitive all the time. That's what the Westerners don't understand. They come here, they're talking about democracy, about market economies. And everyone they talk to is very polite. They nod their heads and they say 'Of course,' but they really don't know what the fuck they're talking about. Democracy? That means we should kill all the old Party members, right? Send their wives and children off to the Gulag, right? That means we're allowed to confiscate their apartments and sell them to the Germans. That means we can tear down the old factories and sell the machines for scrap.

What about the people who used to work there? The hell with them. They can beg. That's democracy, right?

"And what about the economy? Oh, the free market will take care of that, the Westerners say. The free market is magic. The free market is like Kashpirovsky. If you believe in it, it'll work. But what the hell is a free market? Is it like Ismailovo, where they sell shashlik, icons, and toasters, where every little stand forks over money to every Ivan who claims he's *mafiya?* Is that the free market? All right. Okay. We'll do it. How about a loan to get us started?

"This country. You can't reform this country. You can't have these alien things, democracy, markets.

"Have you ever been to the Armory in the Kremlin?" asked Tepperman, growing excited. "Ivan's throne? Peter's crown?"

"Sure."

"You remember the czarina's coach, the one with diamonds set into the wooden wheels?"

"I don't remember."

"You have to look. You have to look closely. But they're there. Diamonds in the goddamn wheels. Hundreds of them. Thousands. Rolling over the cobblestones. Think about it. You can't even see them. They're there because the fucking Romanovs had so much money it didn't matter what they did with it. Here are some diamonds. Stick them somewhere. Anywhere. Stick them in the fucking wheels.

"Do you think they thought about them? Maybe when they ran over some poor peasant kid, they thought about the diamonds ripping open his face. Probably not.

"Stalin was the same way. 'Here,' he'd say. He'd put his finger on the map. 'Here, build the railroad here.' And tens of thousands of poor bastards would end up in the middle of nowhere freezing their asses off because Stalin pointed and said, 'Build it here.'

"It's all the same, and it never changes. Diamonds in the wheels. Railroads going from nowhere to nowhere. It's all about power. That's all there is here, and that's all there's ever been. Power. No morality. Just power. It turns people into monsters."

"Nice speech," said Sasha. "Is this why you're running for mayor? To hear yourself talk?"

"Yes and no. I'll tell you a little secret, Shurik. I'm not really running for mayor. I mean, I am, but I'm not."

"In other words, you're collecting money for running, but you're not spending it."

"That's about right. Well, I'm spending a little. Just to make it look good. But it's not about money. Not just about money, anyway. It's about protection. Understand? Nobody'll screw with a political candidate. Not now, not with the Western bankers watching.

"We're all doing it, you know. All the old guys. Misha Kuznetsov, from the Solntsevo mob. He's this close to running for parliament. Andrei Zotsky. The Bricklayer, we used to call him. You remember? He used to control all the construction sites. He's running for city council. They've got their soldiers twisting arms for votes, money. That is, when they're not throwing foreigners out of windows.

"Hey. Listen to this," Tepperman said, laughing. "This American kid walks into a Saab place on Tverskaya last week, wants to buy a thirty-thousand-dollar car. Kid works for some mining company, an engineer, maybe twenty-eight years old, he's making so much money he goes a little crazy. The company warns him not to spread it around, but he's twenty-eight, you know? You remember? He wants a fancy car to impress the girls. So, of course, the dealer says cash. The kid goes to get it. The dealer calls up a friend, the guy follows the kid to his bank, back to the kid's apartment—which was the kid's mistake—throws the kid out the window. Literally throws him out the window, sixteen stories. Splits the money with the dealer. Nice, huh?"

"Beautiful city, Moscow," said Sasha. "Beautiful people. But what about you, Henry? You don't throw people out of windows. You just get their heads blown off smuggling coins."

Tepperman poked Sasha in the chest. "You asshole," he said. "Have you got the box?"

"I got it."

"You schmuck. I said to myself, Sasha wouldn't lie to me. Sasha wouldn't be so fucking stupid. You thought you were being smart, right?"

"I thought we were partners, Henry," Sasha said indignantly. "Boris thought so, too. He told me you were dealing with some KGB prick, the same prick who got me beat up at Kolpashevo. I thought . . ."

"You thought. No wonder people are trying to kill you. You know what's in that box, idiot?"

"Yes."

"No. You think you know, but you don't know."

"Coins. Old coins."

"Schmuck."

"Stop it. All right. The box is probably worth something, too. It's antique."

"That's brilliant. You're really a shrewd thief, Sasha."

"All right. So what's the deal?"

"Uranium."

"What are you talking about?"

"Enriched uranium oxides, ten grams. The chest has a false bottom."

"Seriously? Uranium?" Sasha took off his glasses and began cleaning them against his shirt. He felt overwhelmed, unable to cope. He felt nauseated.

"Where is it?" asked Tepperman. "Where's the box?"

"Uranium?" Sasha asked, thinking of Madeline Malloy. "You mean it's radioactive?"

"No, schmuck. It's shielded. Where is it?"

"It's safe."

"No, it's not. It's in New York?"

"Yes. Look, Henry. Okay. So the box isn't what I thought it was. So what? Sergei Pantera gets shot. Boris gets shot. I thought maybe somebody was trying to shoot me. You don't know what it's like in Brooklyn. Everybody's whacking everybody else all the time. It's like a war. So I picked up the box. When I saw what it was . . ."

"You mean what you thought it was."

"Okay. What I thought it was. I got pissed. I thought we were partners. Then all hell started breaking loose."

"Jesus, Sasha. Somebody's holding it for you?"

"Yes."

"Can you get in touch with them, tell them to give it to somebody?"

"Who?"

"What do you care who?"

"Well, Henry," said Sasha. "Coins or uranium, you know, I think I deserve a share."

"Schmuck. Didn't you hear what I just told you?" Tepperman shouted. "There are people involved who'll crucify us if we don't deliver. Powerful people. I'm talking about governments. KGB. CIA. This is no fucking-around time, Sasha."

"And you're not making any money on the deal?"

"Right now, the trick is to get out alive. You understand? Now you call the person who has the stuff. I'll call Volkov. He'll pick it up and we'll go through with everything as planned."

"I deserve something," Sasha insisted.

"You deserve a hole in the head for not telling me you had the box," said Tepperman. "Causing me all this trouble. Almost getting both of us killed. You make the call."

"You'll take care of me? A commission?"

"I am taking care of you, Sasha. I'm trying to keep you alive."

"I'll make the call."

Later that day, after trying unsuccessfully to reach Madeline Malloy in New York, Sasha was taken by Tepperman to a padlocked garage behind the *dacha.*

The sun was setting. Sasha was cold, but Tepperman, in his silk shirt, seemed comfortable, warmed by an inner heat. Now that he knew where the uranium was, he felt vastly relieved. He'd feel even better, of course, when Aleksandr Volkov picked it up and got the money.

Tepperman fished a key out of his pocket. He swung open the door of the garage and flicked on a light.

Parked inside was a half track with a machine gun mounted on the hood. Resting against the walls were assault rifles, rocket launchers, and mortars. Above them were shelves containing shells and hand grenades.

"Holy shit," said Sasha. "What are you going to do, Henry? Start a war?"

"Maybe. We're going to hit Zagorsk."

"What's in Zagorsk?"

"In Zagorsk, in Sergeev Posad, is the greatest art collection in the world. It's Nazi art, stolen by the Nazis from every museum and collector in Europe. Stolen from every Jew in Europe. We liberated it when the Great Patriotic War ended, and officially, we returned it to its proper owners sometime in the fifties. Naturally, we didn't."

"And you're just going to walk in and steal it."

"Just a few paintings. Maybe some coins. Just a little fortune. I'm not greedy."

"And when does this happen?"

"Soon."

"And you're going to use all this?" Sasha asked, indicating Tepperman's arsenal.

"No," said Tepperman. "Zagorsk will be a snap. You and I could do it ourselves. No guards to speak of. No alarms. No locks. Officially, it doesn't exist. Nobody ever imagined that it could be hit. Who could do it? Where would they go? Where would they hide? This was the Soyuz, remember? No thieves, no crime, just the Party and the army. And now that the Party's gone and the army's in the shitter, it'll be easier than ever."

"So why the hardware?"

"To keep it when the men who think they own it come looking for it. These are the same men who own the uranium, Sasha. And these men do not believe that I haven't stolen it. My guess is that they think you've stolen it for me."

"Me?"

"Yes, you, Shurik."

That night Sasha again failed to reach Madeline Malloy. He would try in the morning. What more could he do? He hit the vodka, cocaine, and hashish hard. He passed out in his bed.

Then, suddenly, he was awake.

"Who's there?"

"It's me," whispered Alyona Romanova, slipping into bed next to him. "Your wife. Glad to see me?"

15.

With a roll of film borrowed from the newspaper's photo department, Madeline Malloy took pictures of Pandora's Box. She shot the fur-wrapped hunters, the rearing, terrified bear. She spread the coins out on a tablecloth and shot them, heads and tails. She unloaded the camera and slipped the film into her pocket. Then she put the coins back in the lacquered box, put the box back in her linen closet, and took the subway uptown to the paper. Sitting at her desk, she took Mitch Rose's advice and called Peter Feld.

Malloy spoke softly. After getting his assurance that their conversation was confidential, she told Feld that she believed she was in possession of a stolen casket of antique coins. If not stolen, then certainly smuggled into the country. And if that wasn't bad enough, there had been a murder involved.

Feld told her he had a pretty good idea of what the casket was. Smuggling Russian art treasures—icons, coins, paintings, amber, even Soviet-era kitsch—had become, he said, big business. The *Mafiyas,* both Russian and Italian, were involved. They moved the goods through legitimate auction houses and sold them to relatively legitimate dealers. In the art world, explained Feld, legitimacy was always relative.

Feld said he had connections with the FBI and the police. He could handle everything. Malloy, he promised, would not get into trouble. All she had to do was turn the box over to him, and he would make everything go away. He wouldn't, he promised, even ask her where she got it.

Malloy took a deep breath. She told him that she didn't want everything to go away. Gripping the phone tightly, whispering, she told him she wanted the story. No story, no box.

Feld promptly agreed. They would meet that night at P.J. Clarke's on Third and Fifty-fifth. She would bring the casket. He would keep her informed. She would have an exclusive when the smuggling ring was cracked. She, and she alone, would be invited to the bust.

Malloy hung up, feeling as if a huge stone had been lifted off her chest.

This was perfect. She didn't have to worry about the box, but she had the pictures for her story. Feld, who was probably CIA, would be a great source. And she hadn't given Sasha up. Nor, she decided, would she. He probably didn't deserve it, but she would keep him out of the story.

Anyway, after breaking her promise, after getting rid of Sasha's box, it was, she thought, the least she could do.

But, she decided, she would have to tell Mitch Rose. She had given Sasha Rose's private number. When Sasha returned, he might use it, and Rose had to be prepared.

Her phone rang. She jumped, stared at it, and then picked it up.

"Can you come to the office now?" It was Mitch Rose. "Bill and I want to talk to you."

Malloy stood up, smoothed her skirt, and tried to swallow. It was difficult. The stone that had been on her chest was back, but now it was lodged in her throat. Had Feld immediately called Rose to tell him that one of his reporters was a crook?

"Hi, Maddy," said Bill Katz, Rose's managing editor, sprawled in a gray conference chair.

Seeing the bearded, rabbinical Katz, Malloy relaxed. If Feld had finked to Rose, Rose would have seen her alone.

"We have a proposition for you, Maddy," Rose said, sitting on the edge of his desk, his feet dangling a full foot off the floor.

"How would you like to get out of features?" asked Katz. "Go news side permanently."

"I'd like that a lot," Malloy said.

"You seem to have a good feel for these Russian stories," Katz said. "You like them?"

"Yes, I do," said Malloy.

"Lot of good stories there. We think they're going to be good copy from now on," Katz said.

"I think so, too," said Malloy.

"So?" asked Rose. "You want the beat? Not to mention the raise that goes with it?"

"Absolutely," Malloy said, her mind racing. She was at the top of the union scale for feature writers; she probably wouldn't make top reporter money, but she'd still be looking at an extra five or ten thousand a year. She'd have to check. Maybe she should take Russian lessons. If and when Sasha came back, it would be easier. Or would it? She hadn't heard back from Peter Grushenko. Would she? Maybe Grushenko had hated the profile. Maybe she shouldn't have called him plump. People rarely liked reading about themselves in the newspaper. The picture the writer created never squared with the picture they had of themselves. People invariably felt betrayed. It came with the territory.

"Good," said Rose. "I'm having a cocktail thing at my

house early tonight for Andy Steinberg, welcoming him to the paper."

"Big coup," Katz said. "Steinberg is hot."

"Steinberg is a pretentious asshole," said Rose.

"Yes, but he's a Pulitzer Prize–winning pretentious asshole," Katz said.

"That's the only kind of asshole I hire," said Rose.

"Thanks, but I don't think I can make it tonight," Malloy said.

"Wrong attitude, Maddy," said Katz.

"What do you think, I'm inviting you to meet Steinberg?" Rose said. "His desk is going to be right next to Bill's. You can listen to them argue about Israel any time you want."

"He's a self-hating Jew," said Katz.

"So what?" Rose said. "He'll sell papers. So what is it, Maddy?" he continued. "Do you think I want you to serve drinks and canapés to my guests? What's so important you can't come?"

"No. I just said—"

"Forget what you said. After I read your Grushenko profile, I called Peter Feld, asked him if he knew any Russians with clout, guys who knew what was going on. He said, funny thing, he knew a guy just like that, and that this guy had been asking about you."

"About me?"

"Yeah, you. Peter said this guy's been reading your stuff. Told me he used to work in the Soviet embassy, culture section, I think. You know what that means. Spook. Takes one to know one, right? Remember what I told you about Peter? Anyway, Peter's going to bring him over tonight. I want you to meet him. Okay? Six o'clock. No dinner. You know where I live? Ninety-third off Central Park West. Number eighteen. Top floor. You'll be there?"

"Peter Feld will be there?"

"What did I just say? You got something going with Peter? No, just kidding."

Which was how, glass of white wine in hand, Madeline Malloy found herself standing in Mitch Rose's living room, listening as Bill Katz and Andrew Steinberg, formerly a columnist for *The Washington Post,* insulted each other.

"You ever live in the Middle East?" Steinberg was asking.

"That's such bullshit," said Katz. "That's what ballplayers say to sportswriters: 'You ever play the game, man?' What difference does that make?"

Rose's top-floor apartment was enormous, easily containing the forty-odd people gathered there, and Malloy felt a Manhattanite's twinge of real estate envy. The L-shaped living room alone was larger than her whole apartment. It had beautiful hardwood floors and skylights hugging the external wall. French doors led outside to a wraparound patio.

"It used to belong to a painter," said Blue Churchill, Rose's third wife. "I'm sorry," she said, "but I saw you looking at the skylights. The painter, his name was Frank Vass, put them in. He painted right here. It doubled as his studio. Have you heard of him?"

"No," said Malloy.

"He was an abstract expressionist. A drunk, poor man. He passed away about ten years ago. That's one of his," she said, pointing at a large red-and-purple canvas that looked like spilled entrails.

"I love it," continued Churchill, a tall, slender, slightly strained looking woman in her early fifties. "It's so vivid, so strong and masculine, yet I find it strangely peaceful."

"It's very powerful," Malloy said. "I don't know about peaceful."

"Do you work at the paper, Miss . . . ?" asked Churchill.

"Yes," Malloy said. "I'm sorry. My name is Madeline Malloy."

"Oh, yes. Of course. Madeline Malloy." Churchill smiled brightly. "Mitchel thinks very highly of your work," she said.

"Thank you."

"Can I get you anything? Some more wine?"

"No, thank you. You have a beautiful home here," said Malloy, wondering what this elegant woman with her perfect manners saw in Mitch Rose.

Her thought seemed magically to summon Rose, who appeared at his wife's side and took her elbow. His head just came up to her chin.

"You boring Maddy, dear?" he said in a whine that was, perhaps, intended to be humorous but succeeded only in being offensive.

Out of his suit, Rose seemed even younger. His pipestem arms, sticking out of a garish Hawaiian shirt, looked like a skinny twelve-year-old's. An open collar revealed a scrawny, relatively unlined neck and a hairless chest. For a blinking moment, Malloy saw the childless Roses as mother and son rather than husband and wife. Perverse, she thought. Maybe that's what she sees in him.

"Such was certainly not my intent," Churchill said.

"Not at all," Malloy chimed in.

"You know," said Rose, "Blue's daddy used to be a preacher, and Blue inherited his style of one-way discourse."

"I don't think that's true, Mitchel," said Churchill.

"I'm teasing you, sweetheart," Rose said. "I'm going to take Maddy away from you. There's someone I want to introduce her to."

"It was a delight meeting you," said Churchill. "Perhaps we can have lunch sometime."

"Call me, please," Malloy said.

"I will," said Churchill.

"She won't," Rose said, leading Malloy away. "She always says things like that. It's such crap."

"She's being polite," said Malloy. "I think she's beautiful."

"Women always say that about other women," Rose said. "It's like they belong to a club or something."

He led Malloy across the room to where Peter Feld, sitting on a bench in front of a big black Steinway piano, was speaking with a tall, blond man wearing an obviously expensive, olive-green double-breasted suit with a dark blue shirt and a red-and-olive tie. For a second, Malloy thought it was Sasha.

"Peter," said Rose, "you remember Maddy Malloy. I've just made her my new man on the Russian beat."

"Of course," Feld said, standing up. "How could I possibly forget. I read your story on Peter Grushenko, Maddy. I thought it was excellent. Very literary. I especially liked the *Ulysses* reference."

"Thank you. Love your socks, Peter."

Feld looked down. Fat van Gogh sunflowers writhed above his black loafers.

"Thank you for noticing, Maddy. May I say you look lovely?"

"You may."

"How come Peter can say you're lovely and get away with it, but if I say it you get all huffy and threaten to sue me?" asked Rose.

"Because you're my boss, Mitch. Anyway, what we were talking about before had nothing to do with compliments."

The man who looked like Sasha coughed.

"I'm sorry," Feld said. "Madeline Malloy, permit me to introduce my friend Aleksandr Velikhov. Aleksandr, this is Madeline Malloy. Aleksandr read your story also."

Velikhov took Malloy's hand. "In the old days," he said in a rumbling baritone, "I would have kissed your hand, yes? Today we shake."

"Today we shake," Malloy said.

"Aleksandr is in America looking at art," said Feld.

"Are you an artist, Mr. Velikhov?" Malloy asked.

"No," he said, laughing. "Not at all. I work for a private bank in Moscow. We are very new. But now, in New York, I am looking for paintings to buy for my bank."

"As an investment?" asked Rose.

"Not really. Certainly we would be happy if the value of our paintings increased, but art is a poor investment. Right now we are just looking to decorate our offices with modern American art. This will represent to our customers that our bank is a progressive, modern place with close relations with America."

"Aleksandr used to work for the Soviet embassy when there was a Soviet embassy," Feld said.

"And what did you do at the Soviet embassy, Mr. Velikhov?" Malloy asked.

"Please call me Aleksandr. I may call you Madeline? Good. I arranged for cultural exchanges," said Velikhov. "We send you Bolshoi, Kirov, ice dancers, painters, poets, you send us Beach Boys, Aerosmith, Billy Joel."

"You're making fun of us," Malloy said.

"Not at all," said Velikhov. "Rock and roll was an important factor in the development of glasnost and perestroika."

"Gorbachev was a rock fan?" Rose asked.

"I do not think so," said Velikhov. "What I meant was—"

"Aleksandr told me he had some problems with your story on the policeman, Maddy," Feld said.

"Oh, no, Peter," said Velikhov. "That is too strong. Questions, perhaps."

"Questions like what?" asked Malloy.

"I don't think that now is a good time for this discussion," Velikhov said. "This is a party, yes?"

"That's what American parties are for," said Rose. "Especially parties with journalists. Come on, Aleksandr, let's hear it."

"Yes, let's hear it," Malloy said.

"Well, it is painful for me to say this, Madeline," said Velikhov, "but I think you have been a little bit fooled by this Grushenko."

"In what way?"

"Well, he tells you he comes to America to chase criminals. This is not true. His career in the Soviet Union was, shall we say, compromised by certain irregularities in his investigations. But this is not so important. The big problem is he tells you that the *Organizatsiya*—what we call *Mafiya*—will soon be the biggest in world. This is definitely not true."

"No?" said Rose.

"Not at all. In fact," said Velikhov, "this Russian *Mafiya* is some invention of journalists. They say everything that happens is *Mafiya*. A man is hit on the head and robbed. That is *Mafiya*. A store burns down. That is *Mafiya*. Someone is arrested for selling drugs. He is *Mafiya*.

"That there are Russian criminals, of course, who can deny that? And, yes, some of them are in New York, and they are very bad, this is true. But they are the lowest kind of criminal, stupid thugs. They are not so organized like the Italian Mafia. They do not have the intelligence for this."

"But Grushenko is not a journalist," Malloy said. "Why would he make this up?"

"Well," said Velikhov, smiling, "it is obvious. If there is a big Russian *Mafiya,* our Peter Grushenko is a big important man. If these are just thieves and drug addicts, then he is simply another policeman. You see?"

"Ego. The old story," Rose said.

"Grushenko didn't strike me as someone concerned about his ego," said Malloy. "Whether or not he was important."

"Everybody's got ego," Rose said. "Except Peter."

"Thank you," said Feld.

"Oh, Jesus," Rose said. Across the room, Bill Katz had just shoved Andrew Steinberg, who had tripped and fallen backward.

"Excuse me," said Rose. "My managing editor is assaulting my new star columnist. I love journalists."

Rose left. Malloy turned back to Feld.

"Peter," she said, "shouldn't we be going to take care of what we discussed before?"

"Do not let me intrude," said Velikhov.

"No," said Feld, who did not want Volkov asking questions and did not want him becoming too interested in Malloy. Perhaps Volkov had not stolen the uranium as Feld suspected he had, but now, with the uranium almost in his hands, there was no need to pay Volkov's commission. And having Volkov think that he had screwed up was, Feld decided, good for their relationship.

"Perhaps tomorrow," Feld continued. "Ms. Malloy and I had a date to discuss her new job."

"Which is?" asked Velikhov.

"She will be covering the Russian émigré community. Isn't that right, Maddy?"

"Yes," she said, not happy that Feld was putting her off. She wanted the box out of her life.

"That will be very interesting," said Velikhov. "Do you speak Russian?"

"No," Malloy said.

"Then it will be somewhat difficult. It will be difficult no matter what. We Russians are suspicious, and, you know, we have no experience with journalists."

"Can you tell me about the Russian *Mafiya?*" asked Malloy.

"What is this obsession you journalists have with criminals?" Velikhov asked. "We are coming to America, artists, scientists, businessmen. We are making a new start, a new country in Russia. All this is interesting, important. But you are interested only in *Mafiyas*. I do not understand."

"What about Ebzi Agron?" Malloy asked Velikhov. "You say there's no Russian *Mafiya*. Isn't he what they call a *batyushka*?"

Velikhov laughed. "Ebzi Agron? Grushenko told you this? Agron is harmless old man. He owns a food shop in Brighton Beach. He is grocer. Would you like to interview him for your newspaper?"

"I tried. I was told he's the real owner of the Odessa nightclub. I called there. I called the International. Both places, they said they had never heard of him."

"Well. I believe I can arrange it if you wish. Would you like that?"

"Very much."

"All right. I am sure Agron would be only too glad to talk to you about these rumors. A *mafiya* boss. He will be amused."

"How do you know Agron?"

"Oh, I know everyone," said Velikhov, smiling broadly, and Malloy was suddenly reminded, again, of Sasha. It was amazing, she thought. Not only did they resemble each other, they shared the same admixture of courtliness and bravado. Perhaps it was simply part of being Russian.

"Do you know someone, a Russian, named Aleksandr Petrovich Voynitsky?" Malloy blurted, instantly regretting it.

Velikhov smiled, and then laughed out loud.

"What?" asked Malloy. "What's so funny?"

"I'm sorry," Velikhov said. "Excuse me. It is just that you have asked me if I know someone named John MacBeth or Joe Hamlet. The Aleksandr is wrong, but the rest . . . Ivan Petrovich Voynitsky. That's Uncle Vanya. You know. Chekhov's lovesick 'Uncle Vanya' Someone has been pulling your leg."

"It's not possible?" Malloy asked, frowning.

"I would say it is highly unlikely. You must understand, Madeline, if you are going to write about the Russian community, about Russians, you must question what you hear, what you are told. Everything with us is complicated, not so simple as, for example, a simple policeman would have you believe."

"Why don't you explain it to me then."

"I would love to do that. Perhaps we can have lunch. We can discuss all things Russian. We can talk about *Mafiyas,* or about ballet, or even rock and roll."

"Why not?" said Malloy.

And, she thought, angry now, to hell with Sasha whatever-his-name-was.

❖   ❖   ❖

After the party, in a cab heading downtown, Peter Feld told Aleksandr Volkov to be careful around the *Daily News* reporter.

"You're just jealous, Peter," said Volkov.

"I know reporters," Feld said, worried for Madeline Malloy. "They never stop being reporters. The good ones, anyway."

"I'm not going to tell her my life story, Peter. I'm just going to tie her to the bed, slap her around a little, fuck her eyes out."

"You should be thinking about our lost package," said Feld, disliking Aleksandr Volkov more than ever and wanting to hear more of his lies to confirm his judgment that he should sever their connection.

"I told you, Peter," Volkov said. "Sasha Eugenev stole the package on orders from Genrikh Tepperman. I'm sure of this. And I'm sure that soon Ebzi Agron will turn up to sell it back to us."

"I want to speak to this Eugenev," Feld said.

"And you will, Peter. As soon as I find him."

"You told me he's in Russia, with Tepperman," said Feld,

wondering how long he would have to put up with Volkov. Sooner or later, Feld was sure, Volkov would get carried away and kill one of his playmates. Already, on three occasions— twice for women and once for a boy who couldn't have been more than fifteen—Feld had had to come running to get them out of Volkov's apartment and into hospitals without involving the police. It took money that nobody missed to keep one of the women and the boy quiet (not that the boy, with his broken jaw and haunted eyes, could have spoken right away), and it took clout that Feld hated to spend to keep the New York City police out of it. A day would come, Feld knew, when he would be too late. That was the way it was with men like Volkov. Every time Feld saved his ass, all he learned was that he could get away with it. So one day there would be a corpse. Then Feld would be faced with a choice: become an accessory after the fact or give Volkov up and risk making the company look bad.

"Why were you working with such an unstable asset?" they'd ask at Langley, even as they were congratulating him on obtaining the uranium. As if the Aleksandr Volkovs of the world were always models of rectitude.

Feld squirmed on his seat. Unfortunately, right now Volkov was his only source for the uranium and plutonium leaking out of the former USSR, the fissionable materials the CIA was so desperate to buy before they ended up in the hands of any one of the outlaw groups and nations shopping for atomic credibility on the world stage. It had been a top-level finding: since, given the level of chaos in the former Soviet Union, stopping the traffic in fissionable materials was deemed to be impossible, the company should become the buyer of first resort. If nothing else, the company had money.

Which was good. It was going to need it. Although most Americans had been jubilant when the Soviet Union had collapsed, Feld and his colleagues were not numbered among them. The game they had played so long—call it cold war—with its well-known rules and its better-known adversaries, had suddenly changed. There was a vacuum where the Soviets had once stood, and now the field was filling up with new, unpredictable players with bizarre agendas and mysterious resources.

The Soviets had kept the Serbs and Croats and Bosnians from each other's throats. They sat on the nationalists in Chechnya, in the Ukraine, and in the other, now unstable republics. The Soviets had kept the Iraqis on a short leash. They had kept the Israelis occupied. They had maintained something like order in Africa, and they had balanced the Chinese in Asia. Now, with its doppelgänger diminished, the CIA found itself overwhelmed. Hundreds of bloody little wars were breaking out all over the world, and for the most part, the American public could care less. The "evil empire" had been destroyed, so now America's traditional know-nothing isolationism was reasserting itself, even as the rest of the world awoke to new global realities.

Most frightening of all was the question of what was brewing inside the former Soviet Union itself. What alliances were forming. What power centers were coalescing. As the ruble plunged, and the *Mafiyas* grew rich, who controlled the bombs, the bombers, the troops, and the submarines? Forget the hardware. Who controlled the roads, the planes, the telephones, the giant's nervous system? And when that system twitched, who might be caught by a flailing arm, a limb in spasm?

We never figured on this, Feld thought. We suspected, but we never really knew how much we needed them.

For the first time since as a young student leader he had been recruited for the company right out of Brooklyn College, Feld felt desperately uncertain. Here he was, buying uranium from sharpies like Genrikh Tepperman to keep it out of the hands of who knew who. The Iraqis? Some band of fanatical German kids screwing themselves silly under posters of Mao and Che? Or were they doing it under posters of Goebbels and Göring?

Feld shook off the nightmare. Do the next right thing, he told himself. Get the uranium from Madeline Malloy, who, thank God, didn't know what she had, and then arrange for the next shipment. Perhaps, if I can speak to this Sasha Eugenev before Volkov kills him, I can find out who's supplying Tepperman and deal directly.

The cab stopped in front of Volkov's building.

"Stop worrying, Peter," said Volkov, getting out of the cab and leaning on Feld's window.

Peter Feld stared at Volkov, wishing him dead, wondering if he should make his wish come true.

"Tepperman is not long for this world, I promise you, Peter. And you'll have your chance at Sasha Eugenev," said Volkov, thinking that any meeting between Peter Feld and Sasha Eugenev was going to be rather unproductive. Conversations with corpses usually were.

"That pretty reporter is going to lead me right to him," he continued. "She's Eugenev's girlfriend. Didn't you know?"

Volkov laughed. "Uncle Vanya. Too funny. Would that make the pretty Miss Malloy Yelena Adreyevna? At least this Eugenev is a literate thief."

As Aleksandr Volkov turned away from Peter Feld, Madeline Malloy was entering her apartment. She switched on the light to find a small, skinny man, naked except for a black cowboy hat on his head, sitting on the carpet in the middle of her living room next to an enormous, broad-shouldered woman with spiky white-blond hair. She was naked, too, except for her panties. Malloy's clothes were spread out around them. The woman stood up. She was smoking a cigarette and holding one of Malloy's slips. There was, Malloy thought, something wrong with her. The man was cradling Sasha's lacquered box in his lap.

Malloy turned to run. In an instant the woman was on her, grabbing her around the waist, lifting her off the floor like a child, carrying her back into the room.

"Don't worry, girlfriend," said Terry. "We're going to have fun. We're going to have a pajama party."

16.

Wednesday, October 27

JORGE NORTON SAT ON THE TOILET IN THE SHAMROCK BAR IN
the Irish House Mall on the Novy Arbat and lit another Marlboro as he felt the cocaine he had just snorted dripping down
his throat. He tapped his index finger against his gums, the
numbness familiar and satisfying. Good stuff. In the next stall,
he could hear two people grunting. Animals, he thought.

He had seen them go in, the stocky young Asian—probably a student—and the redheaded, skyscraper-tall Russian
whore. The whore had been sitting at a table, smoking and
gabbing away on her cellular phone in the crowded bar full of
young foreigners paying five dollars for pints of Guinness,
when the Asian left his friends and walked over to her. They
exchanged a few words Norton couldn't hear, and then she
stood up and they went off to the bathroom together.

Why did all the whores have cellular phones? Norton
wondered. Was it because phone service in Moscow was so bad?
Did the whores run ads with their numbers in the new, sexy
weekly, *Private Life*? Did their pimps insist that they carry
them? Did they think that the phones were chic, Western?

What they were, thought Norton, the cocaine doing fast circles in his head, were a sign: "Fucks for Sale."

Not that they needed signs. Moscow's whores all seemed to have bought their clothing at the *puta*'s boutique: spiked heels, black mesh stockings, short skirts, bustiers or tank tops under their fur coats. Norton loved it. He had never seen so many tall women in his life. Certainly not in Calí, in Colombia, where his father, a cousin of the late Gonzalo Rodriquez Gacha, once known as "the Mexican," was a rising figure in the Calí cocaine cartel. There the whores were mostly Indian, short and dark, and they just lay there while the young Norton used their bodies to figure out why everybody made such a big fuss over this sex business. And not in Cambridge, Massachusetts, where he had, indeed, spent a year going to Harvard. It was his father's idea for him to get out of Colombia, where the war between the Medellín and Calí cartels was producing a riot of killings and kidnappings. It was also his father's idea that he should study Russian.

Colombians, his father explained, could never sell drugs successfully in Europe. European cops busted traveling South Americans on principle. What the cartel needed was an arrangement with the Russian *Mafiya*. Calí would supply the cocaine; the Russians would supply the couriers, dealers, and protection.

There were no whores at Harvard, or at least none he could find. And he never seemed to hit it off with any of the women he did meet. They were so serious, so unfeminine. Indeed, there was so little for him to do in Boston that in spite of himself he actually learned to speak Russian rather better than he had let on at Henry Tepperman's *dacha*.

Norton stood, pulled up his pants, and then climbed up on the toilet to look over the top of the stall. His eyes met the redheaded whore's. She, too, was standing on the toilet, leaning against the stall's wall. The Asian's head bobbed up and down between her legs. She was smoking a cigarette, one hand resting lightly on the top of the dark student's head. She smiled.

Norton jumped off the toilet. Angry, but not knowing why, he banged his fist against the metal wall. It boomed.

"*Pridurok!*" the whore yelled. Asshole.

Norton went back to his seat at the bar and ordered another seven-dollar Absolut and tonic. He hated Moscow. He hated the cold, the grayness, the bad food, the atrocious coffee. He hated the dirt and the bad bed in his room at the Hotel Belgrade. He hated the language with its strange sounds and its incomprehensible letters. Most of all, he hated the Russians. Rude, drunken, supercilious bastards. Like that Prudnikov guy who sent him to Henry Tepperman. Or like Tepperman himself, with all his guns locked in the garage. Tepperman, who was demanding a quarter of a million dollars up front before agreeing to one test deal of a few kilos. Of course, thought Norton, Tepperman was a Jew, which explained a lot.

Norton looked at his gold Rolex, a gift from his father. It was eleven P.M. Should he go back to the hotel? Should he hire a cab to take him back to Tepperman's *dacha* and try again to talk business?

Both possibilities were distasteful to him. A wave of loneliness washed through his body. The miles between Moscow and Calí filled the twenty-two-year-old boy's stomach, creating a gnawing vacuum.

A woman edged through the crowd and leaned against the bar next to him. She had shoulder-length, ash-blond hair and sad, almond-shaped green eyes above high cheekbones. He smiled at her.

"Lonely?" she asked in English.

A thrill ran through Jorge Norton as he heard his heart's cry given voice. He leaned back to get a better look at her body. She was more attractive and better dressed than most of the whores he'd seen. Simple black pumps. Knee-length skirt. A white sweater underneath her black raincoat. Just enough makeup.

"Do you speak Spanish?" Norton asked.

"*Ciertamente,*" she said. "I trained for Intourist as a translator at the Morris Torez Institute for Foreign Languages. He was the outstanding leader of the Communist Party of France." She smiled. "In other words, a real shit."

Norton laughed. It was so nice to hear Spanish again. And spoken fairly well. He looked at his watch. Screw it, he thought. And screw Tepperman. It would be crazy to go into business with someone who used as much cocaine and smoked as much hashish as the Jew did.

"You work for Intourist?" he asked.

"No more," she said. "They don't pay. Now I am in business for myself. As you can see."

"What's your name?" he asked.

"Katya."

"And your family name?"

"You couldn't pronounce it. What's yours?"

"Jorge."

"It sounds so beautiful when you say it," she said.

"How much, Katya?" he asked.

"Two hundred. Dollars, of course."

"That's a lot."

"I'm worth it."

"My hotel?" he asked.

"Oh, no," she said. "People are so nosy at hotels. I have a place near here."

"Let's go," Norton said, throwing a twenty-dollar bill on the bar and sliding off the stool. Standing, he realized that this Katya was a good half-foot taller than he was. He was suddenly aroused.

He followed her down the narrow staircase that led out of

the Irish House Mall onto the Novy Arbat. The street was deserted except for the occasional taxi cruising for a fare. It was bitingly cold. He tried to put his arm around her shoulders, but she was too tall for that to be comfortable for either of them. After a few staggering steps, she shrugged off his arm and took his hand. Norton was grateful.

She led him off Novy Arbat onto a side street. He tried to read the street sign, but it was too hard. They made another turn down what seemed to be an alley.

"Are you near here?" he asked.

"Very near," she said.

They made another turn into a dark cul-de-sac.

"I'm never going to find my way back," said Norton.

Katya stopped and turned to face him. She looked sad.

"You don't have an apartment, right?" he said. "You want to do it here? Outside? No. Not for two hundred. Not in this weather. Come on. Let's go to my hotel."

The next thing he knew he was on his knees, the back of his head throbbing, his world spinning. He bent over, resting his weight on his palms, his head dangling between his arms. He vomited.

"Disgusting," said a harsh Russian voice.

The tip of a shoe caught him in the ribs and knocked him sideways. He rolled over and curled up to protect his face and balls.

"Look at him," the voice said. "Like a hedgehog."

Norton twisted to reach for his wallet. "Here," he said, trying to make out the faces of the two men standing above him. "Take it," he said, holding the wallet out in front of him.

"We don't want your fucking money," said the man, kicking it out of his hand.

"What do you want?" asked Norton, feeling for the switchblade in his pocket.

One of the men threw himself on top of Norton, coming

down hard with his knee in his chest, pinning Norton's right arm to his side. The other one crouched down and grabbed Norton's wrist, pulling his hand out of his pocket. The knife fell to the ground.

"Nice," the man said, picking it up and flicking it open. He held it to Norton's throat.

"You're making a mistake," said Norton. "You don't know who I am."

"Oh, but I do," the man said. "You're a fox. You've come to steal our chickens. You've been hanging around with that Yid, Genrikh Tepperman. You're going to sell drugs to corrupt our country. You see, I know all about you. And you know me."

Norton looked into the man's face. "You were in that man's office. The one who sent me to the Jew. What is this bullshit?"

"Do you want to live?" the man asked.

"Yes," Norton said.

"Then tell me how many guns Tepperman has, how many cars, how many men, everything you know about him."

"All right," said Norton. And he told the man about Tepperman's garage arsenal and about the things he had overheard, after which Major Anatoly Shubentsov cut Jorge Norton's throat and left him in the cul-de-sac while he went to call Viktor Prudnikov and Yuri Drozhdov to report.

The sad-eyed woman whose name really was Katya stayed with the young Colombian, stroking his forehead and comforting him, first in Spanish and then, when he could no longer hear her, in Russian, as he delved ever more deeply into the hard, lonely discipline of dying.

17.

"WAKE UP, LOVEBIRDS."

Sasha opened his eyes. Henry Tepperman was standing over him, smiling. Sasha jerked himself up and swung his legs over the edge of the mattress, feeling for the cold floor. If Henry was going to attack him, he wanted to have his feet planted, ready to defend himself.

"Time to get going," said Tepperman. "Busy, busy day."

Sasha twisted his head to see if Alyona Romanova was still there, hoping she was not. Of course, she was, sitting up and running her hands through her hair.

"Good morning, Henry," she said, yawning.

"Good morning, Alyushka," Tepperman said. "You had a pleasant night, I hope? Sweet dreams?"

"Very sweet," said Romanova, reaching out to run her nails lightly down Sasha's back.

"Stop it," Sasha said, pulling away from her. He stood up. "Whatever you think you're doing," he said, hopping into his pants and addressing both Tepperman and Romanova, "just stop it. I don't want any part of it."

He found his glasses by the bed and put them on. The world snapped into focus and he felt less vulnerable.

"What are you talking about, Sasha?" asked Tepperman.

"Yes. What are you talking about?" Romanova said.

"This game. This game you're playing, whatever it is," said Sasha. "And you, Alyona," he said. "I thought you had more self-respect."

"Don't be so bourgeois," Romanova said. "Do you think Henry sent me? Is that what you're thinking?"

"I think what I think," said Sasha.

"Do you think he tells me what to do?" Romanova continued. "You think he tells me who to sleep with? Is that what you think?"

"Alyona does what she wants, Sasha," said Tepperman. "You know that."

"You're both crazy," Sasha said.

"Poor Sasha," said Romanova. "I understand now, Henry. He thought you would find us in bed and challenge him to a duel. Did you imagine that you and Henry would fight over me? And that I would go to the winner like a prize, like something in Dostoevsky? You really are a little boy, aren't you?"

"This is getting back at me for leaving, isn't it?" Sasha said.

"And how do you figure that?" asked Romanova.

"By making a fool of me," Sasha said.

"America seems to have done that already," said Romanova. "Listen, Sasha. Last night was about forgiving you. I didn't want to hate you—it made me too sad—so I thought about it and I decided to forgive you. Don't you see that?"

"No. I don't."

"Well, think about it," said Romanova, standing up and heading for the bathroom.

"She's something, isn't she," Tepperman said. "A magnif-

icent woman. Oh, she drives me crazy sometimes, but all the
best ones do."

Sasha stared at Tepperman.

"Oh, for Christ's sake," said Tepperman. "Don't give me
that hurt little puppy look. I can't control what's between you
and Alyona. I don't control her, I don't control you. Right?
Isn't that right? She wants to sleep with you, fine. I'm not a
jealous guy. She wants to go back to you, well, what am I going
to do about it? Lock her up? Shoot her? I mean, I won't like it,
it'll be tough for me, but I'll get over it. I'll live. Fuck me, you
know? She's your wife, not mine. Meanwhile, I wasn't kidding.
Alyona can wait. Today is busy, busy. Today, we go into
Moscow for a Freedom Party rally. Then we eat, and then,
tonight, Zagorsk. And you, Sasha. You must try again to reach
that person in New York."

Everything Tepperman was saying, thought Sasha, made
a certain sort of sense, but Henry was so slippery. Was he really
so unmoved by the sight of the two of them in bed? Was he
tired of Alyona? Was he trying to get rid of her? Tepperman
was always up to something. What was he up to now?

Do I want Alyona back? Sasha asked himself. No, not
really. Last night was wonderful, full of nostalgia, but nostalgia, he thought, isn't what it used to be. What I really want
now is to get away, to go back home. To Brooklyn. To Madeline Malloy, if that's still possible.

This new Russia was a madhouse, he thought. And he
certainly didn't want to die in Moscow or in Zagorsk on Tepperman's crazy job.

Sasha remembered the days after they found his grandfather dead on the floor. First, his mother couldn't find a coffin.
This for a hero of the Soviet peoples! Then, when she had
arranged for a used one, taken from a pauper's grave, the First
Grandskaya Hospital Mortuary wouldn't release the body because his mother didn't have his grandfather's passport; it had

been confiscated by the police when they had arrived at the house. The mortuary official had hooked his thumb at the sign behind his head: "The Dead Are Given Out on the Production of Death Certificate, Passport, and Residence Permit." So Sasha's mother had to go to the *chekisti* and pay a bribe of three hundred rubles to get the passport returned. Finally, when they got to the elite Vagankovskoye cemetery, a huge concrete block covered the open grave. His mother paid the workers fifty rubles to move the stone. Sasha watched as they lifted it with a crane and placed it over another open grave. A good business, he recalled thinking.

At least when the Party ran everything, Sasha thought now, you knew who the enemy was. He was easy to spot. He was fat, his cheeks were red from butter, sausage, and vodka, and he wore a gray suit, a fur coat, and an expensive *shopka* of red fox or black sable. He smoked American cigarettes he bought with D-coupons at the Kremlin canteen or with dollars at one of the *beriozkas.* He lived high above the river, where the air was clean, and he rode around the city—be it Moscow, Kiev, or Leningrad—in a Chaika limousine. He always had one hand in your pocket. The other held a knife to your throat.

Now, in this new Russia, who knew? Did the enemy look like his old friend? Like his old wife?

"Who was shooting at me on the beach in Coney Island, Henry?" Sasha asked suddenly, feeling fully sober for the first time since Lenny Kravchuk had picked him up at Sheremetyevo II. "You told me why, now tell me who. Who killed Boris and Pantera? Who trashed my apartment? Let's cut all the crap, Henry. Who wants the box, the uranium?"

"Everybody, Sasha. I want it. The CIA wants it. A man named Viktor Prudnikov, he wants it. For all I know, maybe Ebzi Agron wants it. Maybe Boris fucking Yeltsin wants it."

"That's not what I want to know, Henry. Besides you, who knows I have it?"

"I don't know, Shurik."

"Bullshit. Bullshit, bullshit, bullshit. You think I'm an idiot?" Sasha shouted.

"Look, Sasha." Tepperman paused, shrugged, and took a deep breath. "Oh, fuck it. You want me to guess? Okay. A good guess. Probably Volkov. Aleksandr Volkov."

"Your KGB broker? The guy I got beat up for in Kolpashevo?"

"Apparently, it made a deep impression on him. I think you've been taking another beating for him."

"Explain," said Sasha.

"You ever heard of Viktor Prudnikov?" Tepperman asked.

"What's he got to do with Volkov?"

"Wait. Viktor Nikolayevich Prudnikov. Used to be a director in the Party Control Commission."

"A *vozhd*," said Sasha, using the thief's word for boss.

"A *vozhd* and a prick," Tepperman said. "Well, now he runs a private bank and a few other things. He's a bigshot behind Pamyat; he's tight with a bunch of army and KGB thugs. He's got big ideas. He's selling uranium, Sasha. It's his box.

"Prudnikov approached me about finding a buyer for some of his uranium," Tepperman continued. "He said it was a trial run with more to come. I remembered Volkov. He approached me once, years ago, with the idea of knocking over Zagorsk. Anyway, I thought if anybody can find a buyer, it's Volkov. I was right. Of course, he fucked me. He fucked everybody. If you hadn't been on the beach, if you hadn't have been such a thief, he'd have sold the uranium and been long gone by now. Serves me right for trusting a KGB man."

"So he shot Boris and the Panther."

"If it wasn't you, it was Volkov, yes."

"You thought it was me?"

"Not really, Shurik, but who knew?"

"So this Prudnikov character is pissed at Volkov."

"No, he doesn't give a shit about Volkov. He's after me. He doesn't believe I didn't take it myself."

"Does Volkov know I have the box?"

"I wouldn't bet against it, Sasha. I imagine that's why your apartment was trashed."

Had Volkov followed him to Madeline Malloy's? wondered Sasha. Is that why he couldn't reach her?

"You don't know what you're doing, do you, Henry?" Sasha said. "You really don't know." And he looked at his old friend, feeling, for the first time he could remember, afraid for him.

Lenny Kravchuk appeared in the doorway. "Ready, boss?"

"Ready, Sasha?" Tepperman asked.

"No," said Aleksandr Eugenev, "but I'll come anyway."

As Kravchuk and Tepperman passed cocaine back and forth in the black Mercedes, Sasha sat silently, sipping a bottle of Stolichnaya. Could he believe Tepperman? Well, he had no choice. He had no passport, no visa, he wasn't going anywhere. Except, right now, to one of the meeting halls at Moscow University for the Moscow Freedom Party rally.

Tepperman's car stopped on Universitetsky Prospekt, overlooking Leninskiye Gory, the Lenin Hills. Far beneath him, across the river and to the left, Sasha could see the white buildings of the Central Lenin Stadium, where the 1980 Olympics were held. To the left of the stadium were the gilded cupolas of the Novodevichy Convent. They reminded Sasha of Zagorsk and what awaited him there.

Tepperman's bodyguards in a black Land Rover pulled up behind the Mercedes.

Kravchuk handed Tepperman a hashish cigarette. He took a drag, held in the smoke, and then exhaled, throwing the butt down and grinding it out with his toe. "Let's go," he said.

As it turned out, the rally was poorly attended. No more than forty men and women had gathered in the large room to hear Tepperman speak in front of a Moscow Freedom Party banner with its slogan of "Freedom, Property, Law." Tepperman, however, seemed unperturbed. He mounted a stage flanked by walls bearing white circles where once bas-reliefs of Lenin and Marx had glowered down upon the worn red plush seats.

"I see we are mainly students here," Tepperman began. "That's good. The future of our country lies in your hands. Men like me, old farts, we fucked up good."

There was some appreciative laughter.

"Not," he continued, "that it will be easy for you, you young people. You have been lied to all your lives. You were told you were rich, but you were poor. You were told you were happy, but you were miserable. You were told our country was a democracy, at least for Party members, and you went to the university thinking you had bright, shining futures. Now you look around and you realize you have no work, no prospects, no life. Your money is worthless, and all day long the idiots argue in the parliament. Does it piss you off? Doesn't it piss you off?"

"And where were you, Tepperman?" a student called out. "What were you doing?"

"I'm glad you asked," said Tepperman. "You see me standing here, you think maybe he's another old *apparatchik* like all the rest, another Party member who threw away his pin in August '91, the day after Dzerzhinsky's statue came down, the day after Akhromeyev and Pugo put bullets in their brains. No, I was a *vor*. I was a *stilyag*, a *fartsovshchik*. I lived in the shadow world among the shadow people. I made my own way, and I got rich.

"That's right. I'm a rich man. Does that bother you? It shouldn't. You think the politicians and the intellectuals will lead the new Russia? Where will they lead it? They'll lead it to hell, or back to the Communists, which is the same thing. They'll lead it to the army, to assholes like Zhirinovsky and

Zuganov and Baburin, and you'll all find yourselves carrying Kalashnikovs, shooting your brothers and sisters, fathers and mothers, just like in Stalin's time. No, it's the thieves, the black marketeers, the underground factory owners, and the men who graduated from the prisons of Kharkov and Taganka and Krasnaya Presna who will lead the new Russia. There's nobody left in this poor country who remembers how to make things work."

"You're probably still a thief!" a student shouted.

"You're goddamn right," Tepperman shouted back. "I'm not a prick like you, sitting on my ass in the university. How did you get here? Did your father work for the Party? Did he inform on people? Or did he personally break their necks in the basement at the Lubyanka?"

"Fuck you," another student shouted.

Kravchuk jumped up onto the stage just as a book came flying through the air toward Tepperman's head. Sasha followed Kravchuk.

But no more missiles came. Some laughing, some grumbling, the students began to filter out of the hall.

"You are a serious lunatic, Henry," said Sasha.

"Thank you, Sasha," Tepperman said. "Now, my political duty done, we'll go back to the *dacha,* eat, drink, and get ready."

At eleven-thirty, after an evening of relatively moderate drinking, the caravan of three black Land Rovers and a black Toyota van left Khimki and headed toward Moscow. The cars snaked through the city, down Boulevard Street, past the old TASS headquarters, the Soviet news agency, with the huge iron ball out front bearing the Cyrillic letters *TACC,* past the McDonald's, the Pushkin Monument, and the Moscow Art Theater.

The cars followed Mira Prospekt to Trinity Avenue to the Yaroslavskoye Highway, the route that since the thirteenth century Moscovy pilgrims had taken north to Zagorsk and the monastery of Sergeev Posad.

As soon as they broke free of Moscow, a light, dry snow began to fall. The highway was deserted. The dense forest of spruce and birch closed in on them. A sliver of moon flickered behind the clouds and the trees. From time to time the forest would open, revealing meadows dotted with small wooden shacks, each with its own tiny vegetable garden and outhouse—proletarian *dachas*.

"See, Sasha," said Henry Tepperman, pointing out the window. "There's millions, millions of dollars to be made here. Who knows how much? All that land. Thousands of acres. Hundreds of thousands. Nobody owns it. Those *dachas?* Nobody owns them. What do they call it in America? Development? Someday I will develop all this land. Houses. Stores. People will drive to work in Moscow and come home at night to their country home. Just like in America."

"We'll call it Teppergrad," said Lenny Kravchuk, laughing, a Makarov pistol in his lap. "Gateway to Moscow."

"Why not?" Tepperman said. "Why not? There are a million ways to make money. You hear the story of Colonel Melnik?" he asked Kravchuk.

"No," said Kravchuk.

"Colonel Anatoly Melnik," Tepperman began. "Last month he buys about sixteen thousand bottles of Royal Prina Feinspirit in Germany at one and a half deutsche marks a liter. That's about a quarter of the market rate. It's cheap, see, because—listen to this, Sasha—it's humanitarian aid from our German friends. Like there's not enough booze in Russia.

"Anyway, Melnik packs up a few Mercedes trucks, turns them around in Moscow, has the whole shipment stamped 'mineral water,' takes them back to Dresden, and starts selling them for three deutsche marks a liter. He sells the lot in about two minutes because that's still half the going rate. Doubles his money. Not bad. The schmuck gets caught, of course."

Kravchuk laughed. "Let me guess," he said. "The customs guy who stamped the bottles in Moscow decides Melnik screwed him, so he tips the German cops. Am I right?"

"Right," said Tepperman. "And he did screw the customs guy. Paid him half of what he should have."

"Cheap bastard," Kravchuk said.

"An asshole," agreed Tepperman. "But a nice scam."

After a little over an hour, the blue, star-studded onion domes of Sergeev Posad, standing on a hill above the ancient town of Zagorsk and illuminated by searchlights, rose above them, snowflakes dancing furiously in the beams.

The cars cut their lights, shut off their engines, and glided to a stop beneath the monastery's kremlin wall. The stalls and tables where during the day *matryoshkas* and lacquer boxes were sold to busloads of tourists were deserted. The town of Zagorsk beneath them was silent. The snow was coming harder now, and the wind had picked up. The moon had disappeared. Ten men, nearly invisible in identical black turtleneck sweaters, carrying Israeli-made Uzi submachine guns, jumped down from the Land Rovers and hit the tall iron gate underneath Pilgrim Tower. One guard in a small, onion-domed shack was overpowered, his throat cut. One man secured the entrance. The flashlights went on.

Nine gunmen ran through the gate. Tepperman, Kravchuk, and Sasha trotted after them.

They passed the small, gingerbread Church of St. John the Baptist. A bearded priest, coming out from behind the church, saw them and began shouting, his voice muffled first by the snow and wind and then by the butt of a gun. He dropped to the ground and lay still, bleeding from his ruined mouth. One man split off from the group to stand guard at the refectory, where several priests slept.

The miniature army entered the darkened, five-domed, four-hundred-thirty-year-old Cathedral of the Assumption. Behind the altar, a stone stairway led down to the burial chamber of the Godunovs. At one end of the sepulcher, an iron gate, secured by a chain, barred the way. Kravchuk snipped the chain. Pushing through the gate, another stairway snaked down to a series of climate-controlled chambers, prepared in 1946 to receive the loot stolen for Hitler by Reichsleiter Alfred Rosenberg's EER. It was here that Anatoli Svirdenko had stumbled across the Zagorsk Archive and begun the journey that would lead him to his death in Viktor Prudnikov's basement.

When Kravchuk located a switch and turned on the lights, Sasha found himself in a long, narrow, tiled catacomb with a vaulted roof. Filling both sides of the room, illuminated by sconces set in the walls every fifty feet, hundreds of paintings in gilded frames formed military ranks in tall wooden cradles. In the gaps between the cradles, marble and bronze sculptures stood next to shelves containing illuminated manuscripts, icons, silver plates, pitchers, cups, and filigreed, bejeweled boxes filled with rings, chains, and ancient coins.

"How do you know what to take?" Sasha, dizzy with the riches surrounding him, whispered to Tepperman.

"Why are you whispering?" asked Tepperman.

"I don't know," Sasha said.

"Well, stop it. It makes me nervous. I know what to take because it's all in the records. I just want the cream. The Rubens. The Raphael. *Portrait of a Young Man.* Van Dyck's *Jan Wildens. The Convict Prison.* Van Gogh. The real one. The Roman coins. Just a few. Just a little fortune. Then we'll watch Prudnikov and his dog Drozhdov crawl."

Tepperman's men walked up and down the ranks of paintings, pulling pictures out of their cradles and then putting them back on Tepperman's orders. Sasha saw what he took to be a Gauguin—a dark-skinned woman with flowers in her hair—slide out and then slide back, rejected. He saw what seemed to be a Van Gogh: a farmhouse, a road, some twisted, tortured cypress trees, the distinctive, madly furious brush-strokes.

"Wait," Sasha said as the putative Van Gogh was about to be returned to its cradle.

For a moment, Sasha forgot to be afraid. He ran his hand over the Van Gogh's rude wooden frame. He touched the canvas with the tip of his finger, feeling a small ridge of thickly applied paint.

Over a hundred years ago, thought Sasha, Van Gogh mixed these paints. He built this frame, stretched this canvas, and then he set up his easel alongside a road somewhere in Arles and tried to paint his way out of his private hell.

"All right," he said, and the painting was pushed back into its cradle. Sasha strolled between the cradles, peeking into the past as he went. Here were some darkly varnished paintings from the Renaissance; here, some wild Fauvist pieces, condemned by Hitler as degenerate. Here were some heroic, almost life-size marbles—could they be Roman, Greek?—here some tall, abstract bronzes looking like African fetishes. Giacometti? It made Sasha's head spin. Hundreds of years of art thrown together in one vast, secret collection, buried beneath the onion domes of Sergeev Posad. Untold riches, stolen by the Nazis, then by the Red Army, now controlled by who? Henry Tepperman? Was it possible?

Sasha found himself standing alone between two tall cradles. He was staring at a shelf, containing a small iron box, beneath a tall, eight-armed silver candelabra.

He looked around. He reached inside the box and slipped a few irregularly-shaped coins into his pocket. For a rainy day, he told himself. Sasha stepped away from the wall, away from the cradles. Then, on his left he saw a metal door he hadn't noticed before. It was marked with a circle containing a three-spoked wheel and the word *Radioactive.*

"Hey, Henry," he whispered loudly. "What's this?"

Tepperman came over and stood silently in front of the door for a moment. "That's it," he said. "That's where they do it, hide the uranium."

"What do we do?" asked Sasha.

"We forget about it," Tepperman said, walking away.

As the looting continued, Sasha's nervousness grew. Maybe there were silent alarms. Perhaps, at any moment, armed men would come tumbling down the stairs to kill them.

But the men never came.

The job took no more than an hour. True to his word, Tepperman took only seven paintings, one box of coins, and a candelabra because he liked it. They were loaded into the Toyota van, and the convoy, running without lights, glided back onto the Yaroslavskoye Highway and headed back toward Khimki and the *dacha.*

To Sasha, in the aqua glow of the Land Rover's dashboard, Tepperman's excited face looked absurdly young. He looks, thought Sasha, just as he did when I met him, the sly young currency trader, so many years ago.

Sasha felt a surge of affection for his old friend and mentor. After all, it had been Tepperman who had made it possible for him to leave the Soyuz. It was Tepperman who had always dreamed the biggest dreams, and it was Tepperman who had become a powerful man in the new Russia. From Tepperman, Sasha had learned how to carry himself, how to impress the men who worked for him—the Professor, the Cowboy, the Panther, Ivan Siskin. And look what he's just pulled off. Stick with Henry, Sasha told himself.

Tepperman popped the cork on a bottle of 1985 Dom

Pérignon and quickly put it into his mouth to contain the foam. He failed, sputtering, spraying champagne on Sasha and laughing. Instantly Sasha felt sad that he could not join in Tepperman's laughter. Why is my spirit so heavy? he wondered. What am I afraid of?

What's happening to Madeline Malloy? Sasha asked himself. Why can't I reach her?

"Now," said Tepperman, "I propose a toast."

"You're supposed to propose a toast before you stick the bottle in your mouth, boss," said Kravchuk from behind the wheel.

"That's the way they did it in the old Russia," Tepperman said. "In the new Russia, we drink first, toast second. That's my decree."

"So what's the toast?" asked Sasha.

"I've got a hundred of them," Tepperman said. "How about starting with, 'To Sasha. Forever a thief.' "

"I just came along for the ride," said Sasha.

"Sure. And those coins you stuffed in your pocket? I see everything," said Tepperman as Sasha, caught, coughed. "I hear everything. I am the new czar."

"Hand me the bottle, Your Greediness," Sasha said. "I'm dying of thirst."

They drank and joked, and Tepperman examined Sasha's coins, shrugged, and handed them back. "Keep them," he said. "Maybe they'll be lucky for you." A bottle of vodka appeared after the champagne was finished. Kravchuk handed Sasha one of his hashish cigarettes, and Sasha smoked it down to his fingers.

Tepperman was quiet. Sasha thought that perhaps he had fallen asleep. Then, in the darkness, Tepperman began to speak:

"Remember when I told you about the diamonds in the carriage's wheels at the Kremlin Armory, Sasha? I remember going there as a kid with my class. Big day. All the kids were real excited. We were getting out of school, going to Red Square, visiting old Comrade Lenin. We were going to eat ice cream afterward. Great. Big day.

"The teacher was an ugly bitch. Comrade Fedorovna. Very mean, mean mouth. So we go to the Armory and she shows us the Romanov treasures. The thrones and crowns, the ball gowns with the pearls stitched in, the swords with the emeralds and rubies in the handles. All that crap. And she's smiling. I'd never seen her smile before unless she was smacking one of us in the face. She says, 'See how glorious the Russian peoples are. See how powerful.' And I look at my classmates and they're all tall and straight, taller than me, and they've all got the blond hair and little noses—like you, Sasha, except for the nose—and I thought, This doesn't have anything to do with me. Peter and Ivan, Boris and Catherine, they weren't my czars. It said so right on my passport. It said Jew. The other kids, it said Russian. I didn't really know what Jew meant—I still don't—but I knew I wasn't one of them.

"It was different for you, wasn't it, Lenny? When you went to the Armory, you were home, right? It's your country. That must feel good. So what are you doing hanging out with a couple of Yids?"

"I ask myself that all the time, boss," said Kravchuk.

"Well, excuse me, Lenny," Tepperman said, "but I say fuck 'em. Fuck 'em all. Fuck all the Russians. Fuck the Communists and fuck the Democrats. You know what I mean, Shurik?"

"I do, Henry."

They entered Moscow, and somewhere along the city's deserted streets, Sasha fell into a light sleep, hearing and not hearing Tepperman and Kravchuk chatting, feeling his body being carried through the night, and then struggling to open his eyes as the van came to a stop in front of Tepperman's *dacha*.

And then the night exploded.

18.

HOW LONG HAD IT BEEN? A DAY? TWO DAYS? MADELINE MALLOY heard the telephone ringing. She ignored it. Lying on the chaise in her bedroom, naked, an old quilt wrapped around her, she turned away from the sound, shutting her eyes, shutting her mind.

How long had they stayed? That Russian boy and that grotesque, freakish man with breasts? Malloy had read about people like that. She had seen them at parties, in bars, and on the street, in the Village, in SoHo. But she had never touched one or been touched by one. She had never smelled one.

She got up off the chaise. She looked at her bed. She had watched them do it there. On her bed. On her sheets.

They had made her strip down to her panties and bra and pretend to be in love with the boy. They'd told her what to say and she had. "I love you," she had told the boy. "I want you," she had said.

They had made her put her arms around his skinny waist and kiss his hollow cheeks. The boy had pressed against her, his sharp, pointy pelvic bones grinding into her, hurting her.

Then the freak, wearing her stockings, tearing them, had pretended to be jealous. "Leave him alone, bitch," she had said as if she were Bette Davis in some thirties Hollywood melodrama.

And then the boy with the cowboy hat had pushed Malloy away, knocked her down, and spat on her. Spat in her face.

On my face, Malloy recalled, rubbing her cheek.

The boy had then fallen into the freak's arms. He'd climbed on top of her. Then she'd climbed on top of him.

"We want you to watch, girlfriend," the freak had said while the boy had gone down on her. The freak had been squeezing the boy's head between her thighs, but she'd been looking at Malloy. "Keep those pretty eyes open, honey, or my boyfriend will hurt you."

It had gone on and on.

When they'd left, Malloy had stripped the bed. The sheets, mattress pad, pillowcases, comforter—they all lay in a pile in a corner of the room.

She could wash them. She could burn them. She could give them away.

After that, she had showered. She had showered for a long time, maybe hours, the water as hot as she could stand it. Everywhere they had touched her, there were bruises. Some of them, only she could see. Then she'd fallen asleep on the chaise. When she'd woken up, she'd made tea and taken it back to the chaise to drink. She'd fallen asleep again. That's all she wanted to do now. Sleep.

Before they'd left with Sasha's box, the boy had shown her a knife. He had held it against her face. In a thick Russian accent he had told her that he would come back and cut her if she told anyone about what had happened. He had told her that he hoped she did tell someone because he wanted to cut her. He would rape her, and then he would cut her. He would rape her, and then he would slit her throat.

"Don't worry, honey," the freak had said. "He's a one-woman man. He'll kill you, but he won't fuck you."

The phone rang again. Malloy wondered why she was standing, staring at the bed. Why had she gotten up? What was she going to do? Take another shower? Call the paper? Call Peter Feld? Call the police?

Madeline Malloy walked over to her computer. Naked, she sat down and turned it on. She knew what she had to do. She had to write the story. It was a killer.

19.

FIREBALLS BLOSSOMED. MACHINE-GUN FIRE TORE THROUGH THE
trees. Sasha heard bullets slapping into metal. He heard glass
shattering. He felt the car shudder.

He dove to the Land Rover's floor, reaching up for the
door handle. He pulled it down and pushed open the door,
crawling through it, tumbling onto the hard, snowy ground,
rolling away from the car, away from the house. He caught
sight of the car in front of him burning. The gunfire continued. He couldn't see Kravchuk or Tepperman. He couldn't see
anyone. He could see the snow, the trees. He rolled for the
trees. He bumped into something. A man stood above him.
Sasha was looking into the barrel of a gun.

"Don't move," the man said.

Sasha didn't move.

He lay on his back, the snow falling on his face,
snowflakes turning to water droplets on his glasses. He saw
only the gun barrel. He didn't see the man's face.

He didn't want to see the man's face.

He heard the gunfire, the shouting.

I'm dead, he thought.

What should I think about before dying?

He didn't know.

Should I say a prayer?

What prayer? He didn't know any.

Please, God, don't let me shit my pants.

The gunfire stopped.

Sasha kept staring into the gun barrel.

Will I see the bullet? he wondered.

Will I hear it?

Will I just be gone, like falling asleep, no dreams?

Will it hurt?

The minutes dragged.

Sasha had no idea how long he lay there.

Maybe I'm not dead, he thought.

Tears of relief sprang to his eyes. His body trembled as a new wave of fear shook him like a child. It's too soon to hope, he told himself. The trick, he told himself, is to imagine that you're dead already. Then you won't care.

The man holding the gun was joined by another man.

Sasha looked beyond the gun barrel. He could see two sets of knees turned toward each other.

"Get him up, bring him to the side of the garage," the second man said, his knees turning away.

"Get up," said the first man.

Sasha stood up, keeping his eyes on the ground. No faces, he thought. Let's not see any faces. The man shoved him forward.

"Move," he said.

Sasha moved. He lifted his eyes. He saw a car on fire. He saw bodies on the ground. A crowd of men were shining flashlights at the side of the garage. He slowed. The gun jabbed him in the spine. He moved toward the crowd.

A hand grabbed him by the collar and hurled him forward. Another hand stopped him. An arm went around his neck, forcing his head up. A light blinded him.

"Who's this?" a voice asked. A military voice. The voice of a prison guard, full of meanness, contempt.

"Fuck you," said a woman's voice. Alyona, thought Sasha. A gun went off.

He heard something fall. Not Alyona, he thought. No.

"Bastards!" It was Tepperman.

"Who's this?" The same contemptuous voice as before.

"Aleksandr Volkavitch Eugenev," said Sasha.

"Good," said the voice.

"Bastards!" It was Tepperman again.

"She didn't suffer," the voice said. "For you, we have something different."

The light in Sasha's face switched off. Purple clouds rimmed in orange hung in front of his eyes. He blinked. He blinked again. The clouds swam away. He began to see. He saw Tepperman pressed flat against the garage wall with two men holding his arms up and away from his body. He saw a man approach Tepperman.

Henry Tepperman's eyes went from Alyona Romanova's body sprawled in the snow, a bullet in her brain, to Yuri Drozhdov's smiling face.

This is real, Tepperman thought.

This is happening.

Until he saw the mallet in Drozhdov's hand, he had thought he could deal with them. He had thought he could buy them. He had thought he could convince them that he didn't have the uranium, that he didn't know where it was. He told them about Volkov. It was Volkov, he said. It was all Aleksandr Volkov.

The funny thing was, they finally believed him.

And it didn't matter.

Nothing mattered.

Well, perhaps he had saved Sasha, as he hadn't saved Alyona.

"Now how did they do it?" Drozhdov asked mildly. "I've
seen pictures of the nails going through the wrists, and I've
seen them going through the palms."

"Through the palms," a voice called out.

"All right," said Drozhdov. "Hold him still."

Tepperman shut his eyes.

The tip of a railroad spike touched his right palm.

He jumped, lifting his knees, banging his heels against
the wall, using the wall as leverage, trying to leap away.

I'll fly, he thought. I'll get away.

Held, he went nowhere.

"Hold him still, goddammit," Drozhdov said.

The hands on his wrists tightened. Something—a hand, a
club—thudded into his stomach.

Please, God, he thought.

Again, he felt the spike touch his palm.

He screamed.

Drozhdov swung the mallet.

The railroad spike went through Tepperman's right hand
into the garage wall, crushing bones.

Sasha let his head fall forward. A hand grabbed his hair
and pulled.

"Watch," a voice said.

The second spike went through Tepperman's left hand.

The men stepped away.

Tepperman heard screams. A fire ran from his hands to his
chest and then engulfed his face. He opened his eyes, expecting
to see flames. Instead he saw a whirling circle of white-and-
blue lights surrounded by darkness. Again he heard screams,
but now he laid claim to them, and they tore at his throat.

The agony in his hands suddenly began to retreat. He felt
as if a bucket of ice water had been poured over his head, soak-

ing his whole body. At first he welcomed it. Then his teeth
began to chatter and his body began to shake. Every muscle in
his arms, chest, and legs went into spasm. His bowels exploded, and he felt the shit running down his legs. His knees
buckled. Suddenly, even as the fire in his hands roared again to
vivid life, he was free. Lying on the beautiful ground, he
hugged himself and tried to hide his torn hands beneath his
body.

"Oh, shit," said Drozhdov. When Tepperman collapsed,
the weight of his body had pulled the spikes through the webs
of flesh between his right and left thumbs and forefingers.

"Pick him up," Drozhdov ordered. "We'll try again."

Tepperman felt himself being lifted up. He was so tired.
I'll fly away, he thought. I'll fly way up into the clouds.

My poor Alyona, he thought.

As the men propped Tepperman against the wall, his head
lolled forward. He vomited, and he imagined that his stomach
and intestines, his liver and lungs, were sliding out of his
mouth. He was being emptied. He was being freed of ballast.
It was surprisingly easy, surprisingly pleasurable.

Drozhdov pushed Tepperman's head back against the
wall. "You know? I've always wanted to do this," Drozhdov
said. "Are you having fun? God knows I am."

Tepperman barely felt the spikes going through his
wrists, severing the radial arteries. Somehow it seemed that his
arms and legs had dissolved. He was just a head and torso. He
heard a slow, pounding, rolling thunder in his ears, and one
part of his brain recognized that what he heard was his heart
slowing down, its chambers becoming flaccid as it had less and
less blood to pump. It was that same part of his brain that
wanted to say something to Drozhdov.

"What?" Drozhdov asked. "I can't hear you."

He bent his ear to Tepperman's lips, and then he stood up
and slapped him across the face.

Henry Tepperman felt his head fly off with the blow and, spinning, soar high above the trees. He tried to focus. Then he saw the fires, the lights, the cars, and the people below. His *dacha* seemed very small from his new vantage point.

Then it slipped behind a black cloud and was gone.

Sasha was spun around, away from the corpse hanging from the garage wall, and marched into the forest.

Now they will kill me, he thought. A bullet behind the ear.

Good, he thought. I'm ready.

Proschay, Alyushka. *Proschay,* Henry. *Proschay,* Madeline Malloy and Ivan Siskin and Moscow and Brooklyn and everyone and everything. Farewell.

The snow had stopped. Sasha noticed the trees emerging from the grayness, becoming distinct. Dawn was coming on. The air tasted sweet and cold, like ice cream, like sorbet. The small hairs inside his nostrils bristled. He felt his bones cradled inside their sheaths of sinew and muscle; he felt his muscles sliding beneath his skin. With each step, his calf bunched and relaxed. He marveled at the articulation of his foot, his body's weight rolling forward, his toes splaying inside his shoe to provide both a broad foundation and a launching pad for the next step.

I'm a liar, he thought. I'm not ready.

He was pushed and shoved until he reached a car parked on a dirt road. A small, thin, compact man in his mid-forties was leaning against the door. Sasha was brought to a stop in front of him.

"Aleksandr Volkavitch Eugenev," the man said, "my name is Viktor Nikolayevich Prudnikov. This, I am sure, has been a difficult evening for you. It has been difficult for all of us.

"Don't bother speaking," Prudnikov continued. "I'm sure that you're confused, tired, perhaps even frightened. I understand. But I have good news for you. We're going to send you back to America.

"You should see the look on your face," said Prudnikov, smiling. "Yes, we're going to send you back to America. Your late friend, Genrikh Tepperman, told us that there's a man in New York who has taken something that belongs to us. We believe him. At first, we thought it might be you. Now we do not. But my associates and I feel that you are uniquely qualified to retrieve it for us."

"Who?" asked Sasha, his hoarse voice sounding strange to his own ears.

"His name is Aleksandr Volkov, sometimes Velikhov. Now you must try to get some sleep. We'll give you something to help you."

They led Sasha away.

I'm alive, he told himself.

But for how long? he wondered.

After Sasha was gone, Yuri Drozhdov turned to Prudnikov.

"So you believe Tepperman?"

"Absolutely," said Prudnikov. "I cannot imagine a man in such a position confecting a lie. Can you?"

Drozhdov grunted.

"You're upset, Yuri," Prudnikov said. "What's the matter?"

"Why not have Shubentsov take care of Volkov?" asked Drozhdov. "Volkov'll probably just kill Eugenev."

"So? Volkov will be on his guard against anyone coming from us. If Eugenev gets himself killed, Tolya can take over."

"Why deal with that bastard Volkov again? Why not just eliminate him?"

"Because, Yuri, we need his CIA buyer. Don't be so quick to pass judgment on people who can help us."

"You mean Eugenev?"

"Actually, I was thinking of Volkov."

"He's a thief and a traitor."

"So?"

"And we're sure Eugenev doesn't have our uranium."

"Eugenev? I hardly think so, Yuri. You saw him. I think he was pissing in his pants."

"And if he runs?"

"He won't. We'll keep him for a while, get him healthy, and then tell him he has ten days after he gets to New York to deliver the box to Sotheby's auction house or we'll come looking for him."

"Why ten days?"

"Because he will arrive in New York on December 20, and the auction of space memorabilia and Russian crafts will be held at Sotheby's on December 30. Shubentsov will be holding the title to the box, in case there's any trouble at the auction. Volkov, I'm sure, will be there. And our Sasha will be there also."

"And if somehow he does the job on Volkov?"

"Then he gets to live eleven days. So?" Prudnikov continued. "So tell me, Yuri. What did Tepperman say? What did he say that made you so angry?"

"The bastard," said Drozhdov.

"What did he say?"

"He said, 'I forgive you.' That's what the bastard said."

BOOK III

20.

Monday, December 20

MADELINE MALLOY TURNED OFF THE LIGHTS. SHE PICKED UP A pack of matches, bent over, and lit the squat red candle sitting in a small ceramic dish beside the bed. She stood up and smiled, and as the candlelight played over her face, she pulled her sweater up over her head and tossed it into the shadows. Then she reached behind her and unsnapped her brassiere, letting it fall to the floor.

Still smiling, she unbuttoned her jeans slowly and pulled them down to her ankles. She stepped out of them and kicked them away. She ran her fingers under the waistband of her white cotton panties. Then she pulled them up tightly over her hipbones and caressed herself, beginning at her groin, then moving up over her flat, ridged belly to her small, high breasts. She put her left hand to her mouth, licked her fingers, and then squeezed her right nipple between her thumb and forefinger.

Sasha's mouth went dry. He took a step forward. Malloy shook her head and said, "No. Not yet. Just watch. I want you to watch." Then she slid off her panties and lay back on the bed, pulling up her knees. She lifted her ass and put both hands between her legs. Her knees fell apart. Sasha heard her gasp.

Then Sasha heard another sound, a sound like someone sighing softly, coming from somewhere behind him, in another room.

"There's someone here," he said.

"What do you mean?" asked Malloy, sitting up, covering herself with a sheet.

"I heard someone. I think in the bathroom," Sasha said.

"But there's nobody here," said Malloy.

"I'll check," Sasha said.

He turned away from her and saw Henry Tepperman come into the bedroom, holding out his torn, bloody hands.

"It hurts, Shurik," Tepperman said. Then, to Sasha's horror, he opened his mouth wide and began to shriek.

Madeline Malloy screamed. Sasha tried to scream, but his mouth wouldn't work. All he could get out was a groaning mumble.

"Are you all right?"

Aleksandr Volkavitch Eugenev opened his eyes. An elderly woman was looking at him with concern.

"You had a bad dream," she said. "You were talking in your sleep."

"Yes. Sorry," said Sasha.

"It's all right. You're almost home," she said.

I am? he thought. Disoriented, he looked out the window, and far below him, between the scudding clouds, he saw the twin towers of the World Trade Center reaching up. He fell back against his seat, exhausted.

How long had it been? He hadn't been treated poorly. Sure, they had kept him inside, in a locked room somewhere, except for an hour a day. And nobody had ever spoken to him. But he had had enough to eat. Mostly he'd slept. And as the days turned into weeks, he'd felt he was slowly losing his grip on the world. Lying on his cot, staring into the darkness, he'd tried to conjure up his childhood, the camps, Moscow, Brooklyn, his friends and lovers. He'd tried to remember everything that had ever happened to him. But it had all seemed vague and disconnected, like a bad movie he had seen a long time ago rather than a life he had lived. Everything had been pale and insubstantial. Except for his dreams, when Alyona and Henry would visit him, and he would wake up sweating and screaming.

The plane touched down at JFK.

Sasha passed through customs. In the baggage area, hung with Christmas wreaths, he placed a call to Coney Island Hospital and asked for Susan Lerner, the nurse who had steered infertile couples to him. When he got her on the line, he asked her to help him find Tatyana Semenova, whom he had last seen being loaded into a police van. Perhaps Tatyana could provide him with a place to stay.

The nurse gave him a number. Sasha started to punch it in, then realized it was the number for the old apartment on Fifth Street. Whoever was there now, it surely wouldn't be Tatya.

He hung up. He called Ivan Siskin. A woman's voice answered: Siskin's wife, Marta.

Sasha hung up. He didn't want to talk to Marta, who had never liked him, who had never liked anybody, and who he had no doubt would sell him out to anyone who offered her a dollar. And could Siskin really help him? And would he if he could?

What I need, thought Sasha, is a gun.

A gun to blow my brains out.

Sasha called the *News,* asking for Madeline Malloy.

The phone rang. Then he heard a Christmas jingle, followed by Malloy's voice mail. A voice interrupted. A man's voice.

"Hello?"

"I wish to speak to Madeline Malloy," said Sasha.

"She's not available. If you leave your name and number . . ."

"No, thank you," Sasha said.

"Miss Malloy is out of the office," the voice said. "I can get a message to her."

Something's wrong, Sasha thought, hanging up quickly.

The phone slipped off the hook, dangling at the end of the wire. Sasha retrieved it, felt its weight for a moment, and then, without thinking, banged it hard against the phone box.

The receiver shattered. Wires and silver disks popped out and danced as if the phone were a jack-in-the-box.

Good, he thought. Let's smash everything.

He looked around. He caught people turning away, instinctively avoiding his eyes in the fashion New Yorkers learned from the cradle.

The crazy man.

That's me, thought Sasha.

Avoiding the escalator, which he now regarded with anxious loathing, he took the stairs up to the main terminal and found a men's room. He entered a stall and closed the door.

Fuck this, he thought.

Get our package back, Prudnikov had said.

Fine. If Malloy still had it.

But what if Aleksandr Volkov had it now?

No problem. I'll just ring him up at his apartment, say, Excuse me, Comrade Volkov. My name is Aleksandr Volkavitch Eugenev. May I come over to see you? A man I know, Viktor Nikolayevich Prudnikov, insists that you give me the box I took from the beach that day when Boris the Kike and the Panther had their heads blown off. The box has a false bottom. There's uranium in it. You probably knew that, right? Oh, yes. This man says that if I don't return the box, he'll kill me. He says that if you give me any trouble, I should kill you.

I'm sure you understand.

What? You don't want to? You'd rather shoot me instead?

Come now, Comrade. Fair is fair. I took a beating for you

at Kolpashevo. Now you can take a bullet for me. I'll tell you what. You can choose the spot. In the mouth? Behind the ear? Isn't that the way you KGB bastards used to do it in the basement of the Lubyanka?

What if I run? Sasha thought. Why can't I run to Hollywood? I could sell my story to the movies, make a fortune. One man against the *Mafiya*. Maybe I'll be discovered. Maybe I'll get to play the title role. Michael Caine wore glasses, and look at him. He got all the girls. Why couldn't I be Michael Caine?

Oh, Jesus, thought Sasha. Oh, Jesus. I'm fucked, seriously fucked.

With the side of his fist, Sasha struck the metal wall of the stall. It boomed hollowly. He kicked it. It boomed again. He struck it with his knuckles. A plume of pain shot up his arm. He looked at his hand. His knuckles were red and beginning to swell.

"Hey! What's going on in there?" a voice called.

"Mind your own motherfucking business," Sasha shouted.

His hand was killing him. Good, he thought. Good for you, you stupid prick. I hope it's broken. That would serve you right. You idiot. You fool. You screw up everything. Everything you touch turns to shit.

He looked around for something to break. He kicked at the toilet paper dispenser, catching it flush. The screws pulled out from the wall, and the roll of paper fell to the floor and unspooled. He lifted the toilet seat and slammed it back down against the white bowl. A deep crack appeared in the black plastic next to the hinge. He repeated the process until the seat came off.

You turd. You should stick your head in the bowl and flush yourself to hell.

Instead he swung the black horseshoe of the toilet seat against the tile wall, then hurled it, discuslike, over the stall's door. He heard it crash into the long mirror over the sinks. He heard pie slices of glass tinkle and clunk on the floor.

"Hey, you," another voice said. "Asshole. Come out of there. Slowly. Hands where I can see them."

Sasha opened the stall door.

An airport security guard was standing there, his legs spread, his hand resting on his holstered gun.

Oddly, Sasha felt relieved.

He was led out of the bathroom and taken to a security area. A New York City policeman arrived, placed Sasha under arrest, and drove him to the 113th Precinct. He was booked and allowed a phone call.

He called the paper.

He got Madeline Malloy's voice mail. This time there was no interruption. "Press one when you are finished with your message. Press two to hear your message. Press three to begin again."

Suddenly he could think of nothing to say.

"It's me," he told Malloy's machine. "Sasha. I'm back."

He thought for a moment.

What could he say?

Should he ask her to come and get him?

Hello, I'm back. How are you? That's good. Look, I'm in jail. Come and get me out, please.

And bring the box.

He pressed one.

He was led back to the holding cell. A few hours later he was taken to a room with a folding table and two chairs and told to sit down and wait. The door closed. After a while it opened and Peter Grushenko, who was called as soon as the Queens cops realized they had a Russian in custody, entered carrying a newspaper.

"Look what happened to your girlfriend, thanks to you," Grushenko said, tossing the paper on the table. "It's a very interesting story. You should read it. She's causing a lot of people a lot of trouble. Especially you, Aleksandr Eugenev. Especially you."

21.

"THE RUSSIANS AREN'T COMING," MADELINE MALLOY'S FRONT-page story began.

"The Russians are here.

"Today, the Russian *Mafiya,* or *Organizatsiya,* based in Brooklyn's Brighton Beach section, controls the bootleg gasoline racket.

"It extorts money from legitimate businesses run by law-abiding Russian emigrants.

"According to local police and FBI sources, the *Organizatsiya* is rapidly moving into the drug trade.

"It smuggles art and weapons.

"It launders money.

"It's rich.

"And it's brutal.

"This reporter knows.

"She was stupid.

"She got in its way."

Tuesday, December 21

The short, bosomy brunette in the off-the-shoulder black mesh see-through cocktail dress wriggled happily as Boris Zilberstein introduced her to Ebzi Agron. "Meet Rhonda Grosinger from the Bronx," Zilberstein said in English. Then, switching to Russian, he added, smiling broadly, "Ever see a pair like that? I mean, outside your dreams? They're real, too."

Agron nodded, bent over to kiss Rhonda Grosinger's pink, chubby hand, and smiled past her, taking in Zilberstein's new nightclub, Romanov's, on the corner of Coney Island Avenue and Kings Highway. It was, Agron had to admit to himself, classier than the Odessa. The walls and pillars were a rich, gleaming brown marble. The pink tablecloths felt like real linen. The cigarette girls—all of them young, tall, thin, and busty—were dressed in black tights, green half boots, and red bodices. They looked like Santa's elves moonlighting as hookers. Red, white, and green laser beams shot out of the tops of the Kremlin towers in the mural that dominated one wall. On the sound system, the Leningrad Cowboys, backed by the Red Army Chorus, were pounding out their version of Lynyrd Skynyrd's "Sweet Home Alabama."

How much had Zilberstein poured into this place? Agron wondered. A few million, easy. Anyway, he knew that that's what Zilberstein wanted him to think, what he wanted all the thieves-in-law he had invited to Romanov's opening to think.

"Very nice," Agron said casually. He'd be damned if he'd let Zilberstein see that he was impressed.

"Want to feel them?" Zilberstein asked, laughing, his hand resting on one of Rhonda Grosinger's creamy shoulders.

Agron chuckled sociably. Zilberstein was an asshole, he thought, but Romanov's, and the limousines lined up outside it, was a testament to his success. You had to respect that. You also had to respect his capacity for violence.

Now thirty, Zilberstein had come to Brooklyn from Minsk twelve years ago with his mother and older brother, Vladimir. A Jewish organization had found them a one-bedroom apartment in Brighton Beach and got their mother a job as a seamstress in a Newark, New Jersey, dress factory. The Zilberstein boys went right to work beating up candy store owners for small change, assembling a small gang of like-minded youths. One day, a muscular, middle-aged shop owner from Rostov chased Vladimir Zilberstein out of his store. An hour later Boris walked in alone, beat the man to death with a baseball bat, and then, after pouring gasoline on the body, set the shop on fire.

In short order, the Zilbersteins began doing hits for the Genovese family. Blowing up cars was one favorite Zilberstein technique, and they had a liberal hand with explosives; the storefronts the cars were parked in front of were invariably demolished.

The Genoveses rewarded them with a small heroin franchise in Brooklyn, which the Zilbersteins, using their connections in Minsk, turned into a vertically integrated operation right out of a Harvard Business School case study. They soon owned opium fields in Turkmenistan, a small fleet of cigarette boats on the Caspian Sea, and a processing plant in Baku, in Azerbaijan. They controlled everything from the police chief in the Turkmeni port city of Krasnovodsk to the street dealers in the Flatbush section of Brooklyn. The profits were enormous—so enormous, in fact, that when the Genoveses became jealous and tried to take back the franchise, the Zilbersteins were able to buy enough muscle and weaponry to hold them off.

Of course, Vladimir had had his face shot off in the process, and Boris now had a jagged white scar running along the right side of his jaw, courtesy of a Genovese bullet that missed, but there were compensations. Boris's mother no longer rode the bus to the factory in New Jersey; she drove her own Honda Civic. And although she dressed in perpetual mourning for Vladimir, she was resolutely proud of her Boris.

"My mom's around here somewhere," said Zilberstein, his gesture encompassing the festive Romanov dance floor. "I want to introduce you."

"I can't stay long, Boris," Agron said. "Sorry."

Zilberstein pinched Rhonda Grosinger's ass. She giggled. "Go to our table, darling," he said. "I'll be with you in a minute."

Grosinger kissed his cheek and swiveled away.

In a vaudeville gesture, Zilberstein smacked his own cheeks. "Our Italian friends would die for a piece like that," he said, nodding in the direction of a group of Genovese soldiers who were ostentatiously admiring Grosinger's round, retreating butt.

"So," Zilberstein continued, taking Agron's elbow and pitching his voice low. "What do you think? That newspaper article."

"What newspaper article?"

"I mean that story in the newspaper. About the girl. You know. The one with all our names in it. And that psycho faggot from Odessa, the one with the cowboy hat. You know him, don't you? What's his name?"

"You should be on television, Boris. One of those talk shows, like that black woman who is always on a diet."

"I should. I would be good. More interesting than the rest of the crap on TV. Except football. I love American football. I will miss L.T. I think the Giants are finished. So what was I saying? Oh, yeah. Those coins must be something special," Zilberstein continued. "People getting shot on the beach, reporters getting beat up. So stupid. In America, it's better to shoot a cop than piss off a reporter, don't you think? Hey, Ebzi, what do you think? I was thinking about talking to that reporter. You know, this stuff in the newspapers, it's anti-Semitic, is what it is. Think about it. Some Jews are doing all right, the newspapers call us *mafiya,* Russians. Don't they know that Jews aren't Russians? We're Jews. Maybe we should get, I don't know, Hadassah on their case. The Anti-Defamation League. What do you think?"

Agron sighed. "I want to thank you for inviting me to your party, Boris, but I really have to go."

"I understand. It's so noisy here, so crowded. I'm honored that you came, Ebzi," said Zilberstein, whose dislike of Agron was visceral. A typical Uzbeki, he thought. Fat face. Beady eyes. Stupid, but cunning. Who really knew if he was Jewish? His grandmother was probably raped by an Afghani or a Mongol. She probably liked it.

Well, soon, he thought. Soon we'll be saying *dosvidanya* to the so-called *batyushka.*

"I really am honored," Zilberstein continued. "I wasn't sure you'd come. You know, I thought you might think Romanov's was competing with the Odessa. Which, of course, would be the farthest thing from my mind. If Romanov's hurt the Odessa, I'd be, I don't know, very upset. But I don't think it will. The Odessa is a great old place, a fucking institution, is what it is. It reminds me of home. My mother, all her friends, they love the Odessa. This place, it's too modern for her, too American. All these young people. The loud music. You know who's here tonight?"

Zilberstein scanned the room. "I don't see him now, but Pytor Kartolnov. You know him? Big hockey guy? Plays for the Islanders? He just signed a contract for seven million dollars over five years. I helped him negotiate it. I advised him. We're good friends. The girls are all over him now. Anyway, what was I saying? Oh, yeah. The Odessa. The older folks will always go to the Odessa, just like they do now."

A waitress, dressed like the cigarette girls, passed by carrying a tray of toasted bread rounds covered with sour cream, chives, and large dollops of Sevruga caviar. Zilberstein grabbed two and offered one to Agron.

"I respect you, Ebzi," Zilberstein said through a mouthful of bread and caviar. "You're like a hero to all of us younger guys. Maybe we should have a meeting. You, me, Puzaitzer, Ivankov. You could be the chairman because of your age. We could talk about our image in the press. Maybe organize a, you know, a boycott of the papers that portray a negative image of Russian Jews. The anti-Semitic bastards."

"Ivankov's not Jewish," Agron said. The Sevruga was delicious, but he preferred the bigger taste and larger roe of the beluga.

"So what?" asked Zilberstein, distracted by a cigarette girl whose nipples were peeking out of her bodice. "We're all Russians."

"Forget television, Boris," Agron said. "You should become a politician."

"What?" asked Zilberstein, shouting, leaning forward to hear. The Leningrad Cowboys had given way to Aerosmith.

"A politician."

"Me? Are you serious? I have more self-respect. Okay, Ebzi. Think about it. About a meeting. Oh, yeah. Before you go. Just out of curiosity, I was thinking about looking for that asshole myself. The Cowboy. Who knows? Nobody has seen him since that newspaper story. You know? You know what was funny about that story?"

"What was funny?"

"The box of coins. She never said who gave it to her. Just a man. Isn't that funny? Man brings it to her apartment, she doesn't tell us his name? I mean, she has to know the name. But she doesn't write it. Why? Why would she do that?"

"I don't know, Boris."

"Well, it's funny. But if this is your affair, Ebzi, just tell me, I'll back off. I wouldn't want to step on your toes. I respect you too much for that. Just say the word."

"You do what you want, Boris. You don't need my approval."

"So you wouldn't mind if I interested myself? I wouldn't want to interfere in your affairs. I respect you too much. . . ."

"I know. You said."

Agron left the club and stepped into his black Lincoln Town Car waiting by the curb.

"Where do we have Gatlober stashed?" the *batyushka* asked his driver, a Chechen named Dmitri Duyadev.

"In the Coney Island apartment."

Soon, Agron thought, he would have to settle with Boris Zilberstein. He'd like to do it himself. With his hands.

Agron settled back on his seat.

"Drive," he said. "And for God's sake, watch where you're going."

22.

"YOU'RE GOING TO HAVE ANOTHER DRINK?" PETER FELD ASKED in not-so-mock astonishment. Mitch Rose rarely drank, couldn't hold his liquor, and knew it. Self-knowledge, he had always claimed, was the wellspring of his strength. And it was true. But he was drinking now.

"It's your party; you're buying," said Rose, "so I'm drinking."

The waiter came over, and Rose, already feeling the first cognac, loosely waved his hand over his empty snifter. "Another Delamain," he said. "With a soda back."

"And you, sir?" the waiter asked.

"I'm fine," said Feld.

"You're being stupid," Feld continued when the waiter left to get Rose's drink.

"I'm being a whattayacallit, a journalist," said Rose.

"Spare me, Mitch, all right?"

"I'm being an editor. I'm taking care of my reporter. And you've seen her. She's gorgeous. You wish you could take care of her yourself. You're a dirty old man, Peter."

"That's exactly what I've been trying to tell you," Feld said. "You're not taking care of her. You can't. You think what she went through was bad? That's nothing. There are some very dangerous people out there who want a piece of her. But I can protect her. Where is she, Mitch?"

The waiter returned with Rose's cognac.

"Oh, this is good," he said, taking a sip. "Delamain Vesper. Only stuff I'll drink. Smooth. You know, booze is one of the only things in this world where you can rely on getting what you pay for. What is this stuff? Seventy bucks a bottle? Eighty? I don't know, the wife always buys it for me."

"It's about twelve bucks a pop right here."

"Well, it's delicious. I love it. You know me. I don't really like the taste of alcohol. But this stuff tastes like cream soda. Or butterscotch. I love butterscotch. You know what? We should get wild someday, go out and have a couple of butterscotch sundaes. Get fat. Clog those arteries. Live dangerously."

"Can we focus, Mitch?"

"On what?"

"On Malloy."

"Forget it, Peter. Leave it alone. She's not your concern."

"You know, you've spent all your life in newspapers," Feld said, "and it's made you ignorant."

"Ah, a Brooklyn College education speaks. What does 'ignorant' mean?"

"In this case, it means you don't know what you're doing. I'm serious. You think you know everything. You believe in the power of the press because you make a lot of money, live in a big, fancy apartment, and wear a lot of Armani on your hideous body. But there's no power of the press. It's a myth the press made up about itself."

"I know that, Peter. A. J. Liebling said that the power of the press belongs to thems that own one. Or something like that. I forget. Great line, anyway."

"That's not what I'm talking about. She's going to be subpoenaed, you know? You've got to know that. The DA in Brooklyn, Silverman, he's got a grand jury on the beach shooting that's been twiddling its thumbs until now, until she spilled the beans—irresponsibly, I might add—in your paper, and he's going to call her. And if she holds anything back—I mean, for example, like the name of the man who gave her the box—if he thinks she's holding anything back, he'll crucify her. He's got a wild hair up his ass about reporters. For some reason, he doesn't think they have any right to withhold evidence in a capital murder investigation. He went to Harvard, he's read the Constitution, and he must have missed the part where it says reporters are above the law. But I have some pull with Silverman. I can help."

"You saying he'll throw my pretty Maddy in jail? I don't think so, Peter. I can see the picture on the front page now. We'll shoot her through the bars. She'll look great in denim. Like one of those young, innocent chicks in those prison movies where the warden's a bull dyke with big tits, walks around in high heels and fishnet stockings. *Pussycats in Cellblock Nine.* She'll look brave, but maybe she'll have a little tear in one eye. Brave little Maddy. Big, bad DA Silverman. Shit, his own mother'll disown him."

"He'll throw her in jail, Mitch, and he won't even have to think about it. That's power. And she won't be safe in jail because the other side is powerful, too."

"Jesus. Would you listen to yourself? 'The other side.' Oooh, scary. That's the old cold warrior speaking. I always knew you were a spook. Hey. Earth to Peter: The war's over, man. We won."

Peter Feld signaled the waiter. "I think I will have another of these," he said, pointing to his empty beer glass.

The two old friends stared at each other.

"Listen, Mitch," Feld said when the waiter had come and gone. "What do you think the cold war was about?"

"I'm guessing that was a rhetorical question, right?"

"You think the cold war was between communism and capitalism, between the United States and the Soviet Union, between the CIA and the KGB?" Feld asked.

"You forgot d), none of the above," said Rose, "and I bet that's the answer. I was always good on tests."

"I'm trying to tell you something. Would you be serious for a second?"

"All right," Rose said, furrowing his brow and smirking. More than ever, thought Feld, he looked like a dissolute bar mitzvah boy.

"The cold war," began Feld, "was fought between the governing elites and their own populations. You understand? It was about maintaining control on the home front. The CIA and the KGB were partners. I'm only just beginning to realize this myself. Communism and capitalism? They were just team names. Mets and Yankees. Jets and Giants. We were supposed to root for one side or the other while the real game was going on behind our backs."

"And the real game was . . . ?"

"Well, who benefited from the cold war? The men who owned the factories that made the guns and planes and ships, the men who sold the oil, the men who sat on the boards and massaged the money, the men who owned the Congress and the Kremlin. And they didn't want anybody asking 'What's in it for me?' Because the answer was always nothing.

"Remember *Sputnik*? Muttnik? The Soviets shoot two dogs, Strelka and Belka—hey, how do you like that? I remember their names—into space, and everybody freaks out. Gotta get the kids interested in science and math. Gotta beat the Reds to the moon. So the aerospace industry gets a jump start, which it badly needed, MIT starts churning out drones to man the labs, and the economy takes off.

"By the way. Heard of anyone walking on the moon lately?

"Remember the missile gap? Any time the markets got slow, we just revved up the cold war. Any time your citizens started getting out of line, rev it up.

"It was a brilliant idea. It was a war, meaning the factories were kept humming, meaning everybody followed orders, but most of the time, nobody got hurt. That was the beauty part. No moms crying on the news. At least not directly. You could kill proxies, stand-ins. The Politburo told the Russians, 'We have to protect ourselves from the imperialists by killing the Afghanis.' Or the Poles or the Czechs. Or whoever. We told the people, 'We gotta protect ourselves from the Commies by killing the Vietnamese, the—what was the name of that flyshit island we invaded?—Grenada?"

"Americans got killed in Vietnam. Russians got killed in Afghanistan."

"Well," Feld said, "it didn't always work perfectly. People got carried away. And when that happened, it caused a lot of trouble at home. But my point is, nothing's changed. I'm telling you, Mitch: it's still business as usual. Same guys in charge, they're just changing front men, stooges, just thinking up a new game to keep everybody in line, to keep everybody from asking 'What's in it for me?' You think the game is over? We won? Don't be naive. It's never over. It's just going through a transition period. The rules are changing. And that's a dangerous situation."

"You sound like a man who's worried about losing his job," said Rose.

"I knew you'd understand," Feld said.

"Look," said Feld, trying again, "I need to see Malloy. Isn't that enough? Don't you trust me?"

"No," Rose said. "No. I don't. That's the truth. I like you, Peter. You're a good guy. But why should I trust you? I don't even know who the fuck you are. I don't know what the fuck you want. And that's okay. We're not teenage girls, we gotta tell each other our secrets. We're adults, grown men. We do what we want. We go out for lunch, we gossip about people we know, we piss and moan about this and that. We do our jobs. But we don't talk about our wives, and we don't swap spit.

"You have your agenda. That's fine. But don't ask me to believe that you're acting out of some grand philosophy, or out of some great affection for me or Madeline Malloy. It insults my intelligence. You want to tell me what you want, what you're really doing, then maybe we can talk. The rest, this cold war bullshit, it's just that. Just two white guys sitting around talking. Okay?"

"Okay," said Feld. "Forget the cold war. What about the Russians? Everybody thinks that now the Commies are gone, the Russians are our cuddly friends. Listen, Mitch. The Russians are empire builders. The greatest the world has ever known after, maybe, the Romans. Around the middle of the seventeenth century they controlled an area about the size of Texas around a one-horse town called Moscow. They had Poland to the west, Tartary to the east, and Astrakhan and Circassia to the south. And over the next few hundred years they conquered more land, and eliminated more people, than any nation the world has ever seen. They crushed the Mongols, for chrissakes, and they were some tough mothers. You think because the Commies are gone they're going to stop? You think they're going to let the Ukrainians, the Litvaks, the Kazakhs, the Ingush, the Azeris, the Chechens, and the rest go their own way? You're dreaming."

"Who gives a shit?" Rose said. "I mean, really Peter, who gives a shit? I've never even heard of these guys. Ingush? Give

me a break. I should worry about Ingush? What are they? Es-
kimos? Come on. Talk to me when they invade Alaska. This is
getting tiresome. I always hated history."

Feld gave up. "Can I call her on the phone?" he asked.

"No."

"Why?"

"You'll have the line bugged, next thing I know, guys in
suits'll be busting down the door. Forget it."

"What if I give you my word that nothing like that would
happen?"

Rose stood up and swayed slightly. "Nothing personal,
Peter," he said, finishing off his Delamain. "Delicious. Thanks
for the cognac."

"Ask her," said Feld. "Ask her if she wants to talk to me.
I know she does."

"I'll ask her," Rose said. "But if she asks me what I think,
I'll advise her against it."

Feld grabbed Rose's wrist. "Okay, Mitch. You talk to me.
She told you, didn't she? She told you who gave her the box.
She told you how she really got involved. What did she tell
you, Mitch?"

"Getting rough, Peter?" Rose asked quietly.

Feld released Rose.

"What she knows," Rose said, "was in the paper. You
read all about it along with about a million other New Yorkers. I can't be exact; I haven't checked my circulation figures
lately.

"You know," said Rose, pulling on his overcoat, "she's
going to be a hell of a reporter. She's going to be a star. Probably end up leaving me for the *Times*. I train them, I get them
started, and just when they get going good, those fuckers scoop
them up."

After Rose left, Feld finished his beer and went to a pay
phone to call Aleksandr Volkov. Rose was right, Feld thought

as Volkov came on the line. He had tried to do the right thing, but now it was time to do his job. There was nothing more important than recovering the uranium. It was time to step back and let Volkov handle things his own way.

23.

Thursday, December 23

THE TIGHTNESS IN TERRY'S CHEST WAS ALREADY EASING, THE muscles in her stomach were beginning to relax. She was home, safe, and in a minute she would be high.

She closed the door behind her and locked it. Then she shrugged off her black faux fur jacket, letting it drop to the floor in the hallway. She went into the kitchen. She shooed her cat off a folding chair and sat at a small card table. She pulled off her boots and socks. She stood up, slipped off her jeans, and sat back down wearing only a black turtleneck sweater and black panties. She picked up her jeans and fished in the pocket for the small glassine envelope stamped with the dealer's logo—a red star. She ripped it open and poured twenty-five dollar's worth of white heroin into a scorched and blackened tablespoon. Using an eyedropper, she mixed the heroin with a few drops of tapwater. After lighting two matches at once, she held them under the spoon and watched the heroin dissolve and the solution bubble. The cat jumped on her lap, its nails digging into her thighs. Terry didn't move. She waved out the flame just after it burned her fingertips. She put the spoon on the table. She slapped the back of the cat's head. It yowled and hopped to the floor, its claws clicking on the linoleum as it ran out of the room. Terry stuck her singed fingertips in her mouth.

The solution bubbled down. Terry delicately placed a small cotton ball in the spoon, picked up her syringe, and drew the heroin up through the filtering cotton. She squinted at the syringe, holding it up to the light, trying to see if any cotton threads had been pulled inside. There was nothing more painful than a bone cruncher—shooting cotton into your veins. She didn't think she saw anything, but, of course, you could never be absolutely sure.

Holding the syringe in her mouth, she crossed her left leg over her right thigh and turned her ankle down and out, forcing the big vein to the surface. She palpated it. It was still soft, thank God, not yet thrombosed. She was getting excited.

She took the syringe out of her mouth, flicked it with a long red nail to get any remaining air bubbles up to the top, and then slowly squeezed a single drop out of the tip of the needle. Like a cock, she thought. Like a drop of come.

She took a deep breath, held it, bent over, and, holding her foot back with her left hand, slid the needle under the skin, into—she hoped—the vein and depressed the plunger a quarter of an inch. Then, after slipping her thumb under the plunger's flange, she pulled back, exhaling as she saw a bright red plume of blood flower in the tube. She was in the vein, not through it. She pushed and pulled the plunger, in and out, half an inch at a time, playing, mixing her blood with the heroin solution in the syringe, getting every last drop, every infinitesimal and hugely needed grain of relief into her body.

She put the empty syringe on the table, bent over, and licked a droplet of blood off her ankle. She sat up, lit a cigarette, and began examining her foot.

The polish on her toes was chipping.

Got to take care of that.

She leaned back.

An ash from her cigarette fell on her sweater.

She brushed it off, took the cigarette out of her mouth, opened the lacquer casket from which the Cowboy had taken the coins, and dropped the burning cigarette inside. She closed the lid.

Fuck it, she thought.

She felt the drug's lovely, healing warmth rising, blossoming, radiating up from her ankle, washing into her groin, splashing into her belly, filling her chest, her mouth. A sudden wave of nausea closed her throat. Her stomach heaved. She stood up and bent over the sink, gagging.

Beer cans. Cigarette butts. Plates. Forks, knives, and spoons. What was that green stuff on the plates? she wondered. When did we eat green stuff?

The nausea passed. She spat.

She touched her forehead. It was moist.

Jesus, she thought. This is great shit.

The hell with the Cowboy, she thought. He wants to come back, fuck him. He's too much trouble. Gets us in the newspapers. We should have killed the bitch. Scares me half to death, then disappears with the coins. Leaves me alone. No money. Gotta get some money. Fuck him. Or don't fuck him anymore. That'll drive him nuts.

Terry smiled. Her face felt hot. Her eyelids were becoming heavy.

Still standing, still bent over the sink, she began to drift.

Someone was knocking on the door.

She opened her eyes.

Green stuff. Now what the fuck was that?

Someone was knocking.

"I know you're in there, Terry."

Go away, Terry thought. Vanish. Fade away and radiate.

"It's Sasha. David's friend. Open up."

"I don't know any Sasha," Terry called out, her voice clotted. Jesus, I sound like Brenda Vaccaro, she thought. Only I'm better looking. I'm exquisite.

"I just want to talk, Terry. Let me in. I have some money for you."

Money? thought Terry. A trick? No way she could get it up now, but so what? Maybe this Sasha, whoever he was, got off on something else. S&M. B&D. Maybe he liked golden showers. Maybe he wanted to dress in her clothes. All those Russians were freaks.

Gotta pull myself together, she thought.

"Just a minute, honey," she said.

She floated down the hallway, bumping against the wall as she went. She turned into the bathroom and looked at herself in the mirror. God, I haven't taken my beard off. Okay, a little pancake will take care of that. She sat on the toilet seat. So tired. The hell with this.

"Now's not a good time, honey," she called out. "Come back later. Mama's going to take a little nap. Freshen up. Come back in two hours."

Three would be better, she thought.

Sasha hammered on the door. "Open up, Terry. I've got lots of money for you. David sent me. He said make sure Terry has money. He sent me with money for you."

David? The Cowboy? Since when does he send me tricks? He's pimping now, the little bastard? Little bastard, disappearing on me like that. I'm not going to fuck him anymore. Serve him right.

Now what was I doing? Terry wondered. Where did I leave my butts? Where are my pants?

She stood up, looked around, and began walking back to the kitchen.

Sasha knocked again.

"I told you," Terry said, stopping. "I'm tired. Come back later.

"Money, Terry. I've got money."

"Slip it under the door."

"He said to put it in your hand."

Terry sat on the jacket she had left on the floor in the hallway, opposite the door. Who was this asshole? she wondered, bugging her, dragging her high. The fur felt good on her thighs. She closed her eyes, summoning the drug. The drug came running.

"Terry?" Sasha called.

The cat hopped onto her lap and snuggled against her. She scratched it behind the ears.

"Fuck off," she said. "I'm not interested."

Sasha kicked the door. He stepped back and threw his shoulder into it. He bounced back. How do they do it in the movies? he asked himself. What's the trick?

There's no trick, stupid, he answered. That's the movies.

Should he just wait on the stairs?

Not a good idea. He'd taken a chance coming here. He'd taken a chance of bumping into the Cowboy, whom he did not want to deal with. Better to keep moving.

"I'll come back in an hour," Sasha called. "You hear me, Terry?"

On the other side of the door, Terry was stroking her cat and examining her toenails again. They still needed polish.

◈   ◈   ◈

Aleksandr Volkavitch Eugenev went back down the stairs and out into the cold. His sunglasses immediately fogged.

What was wrong with the bitch? he wondered. Probably stoned. He had heard that she was a junkie. Maybe she would straighten up in an hour, Sasha thought. Maybe not.

He rubbed his face. He needed a shave. He needed a bath. He needed a rest. For the last three nights he had slept on the subway, riding uptown and down, moving when the cops told him to, eating hot dogs, knishes, and candy, walking the streets, his thoughts going around in circles.

He knew he should avoid Brighton, but how could he? He knew he should avoid everyone he knew, but how could he do that? Ultimately he had made up his mind. He had to do what he could to recover the box. It was the only way. Of course, there was no way to be sure that the Cowboy still had the box that, according to Madeline Malloy's story in the newspaper, he had taken from her. But he had to start somewhere. And he could not reach Malloy.

Damn the Cowboy and that freak Terry. What Maddy Malloy had described in her story had made him sick. And it was his fault for involving her, his fault for betraying her.

She trusted me and I used her, Sasha thought. Just like they taught me to in the Soyuz.

You're a good little Soviet, he scolded himself bitterly.

At the police station in Queens, Peter Grushenko had told him that he knew that he had been on the beach when the Panther and Boris the Kike had been killed. He knew, he had said, that Sasha had taken the coin box Malloy had written about and stashed it with Malloy. He didn't have evidence, but he knew. Now they were both in the shit. He'd told Sasha that a grand jury in Brooklyn was hearing charges against him, against Madeline Malloy, and that if he didn't cooperate, if he didn't agree to help Grushenko find the Cowboy and the box, he would be held as a material witness for as long as it took the grand jury to hand down an indictment. And that, Grushenko had pointed out, could be a very long time indeed.

Then there was the matter of the pregnant girls in the apartment.

"Selling babies is a serious crime," Grushenko had said.

With one thing and another Grushenko had said, the best Sasha could hope for was to get his ass shipped back to Russia.

"Right now, I'm the only friend you have," Peter the Duck had said. "And in my opinion, the street would be safer for you than jail. It's your choice. Help me, or sit here until one of your friends decides it's too risky to let you live. Help me, and I'll see what I can do about saving your Yiddish ass."

Sasha had had to agree with Grushenko. Jail was not a long-term proposition. Viktor Prudnikov had given him ten days until the auction at Sotheby's, and he had already used up four.

I deserve to die, thought Sasha. Everything I touch turns to shit. Everyone I touch gets fucked.

But he didn't want to die.

He didn't want to miss Prudnikov's deadline.

"I won't be able to find the Cowboy wearing you like a fur coat," Sasha had said.

"Don't worry," Grushenko had said. "You'll never know I'm there. But I'll be watching, Aleksandr Eugenev. You can count on that."

Sasha turned up the collar of his coat, not only for the protection, but also for the anonymity it offered. Peter the Duck was certainly keeping an eye on him. Sooner or later he would have to get in touch with Anatoly Shubentsov. And Aleksandr Volkov. Who knew what Volkov knew or where he was?

And what if I do get the box for Prudnikov and deliver it to Sotheby's in time for the auction?

Will Shubentsov be waiting there to tie up a loose end named Aleksandr Volkavitch Eugenev?

Will Aleksandr Volkov?

If I'm lucky, maybe Grushenko'll be there with Immigration and send me back to Russia. If I'm lucky, maybe I could get a job cleaning out the toilets at the Ukraina.

Underneath the El, where the sun never shined, it was

bitterly cold. Men and women in their heavy coats and fur hats jammed Brighton Beach Avenue, shopping for Christmas, for Chanukah. Menorahs and Christmas trees shared store windows.

He was home, in Brighton, and that fact made him feel both secure and anxious. There, he thought, down Sixth Street, was the Cowboy's apartment, with Terry high as a kite inside. On Fifth, Ivan Siskin and Marta were probably fighting. The Professor lived on Coney Island Avenue. In the opposite direction, on Brighton Beach Avenue, was the International with all its cozy, wonderful smells. A block down was Goldman the fence's shop and a few blocks farther, toward Kings Highway, the Odessa. There was the Cafe Arbat, where all the young dudes hung out, and the Georgian Cafe, with Emma Bovrilina's heavenly *hinkali*. I could walk in anywhere, and people will know me. They'll say, *Zdrahstvootye,* Sasha. How are you? Where have you been?

Which, of course, was the problem.

Too many people know me.

A few months ago I felt like a prince, Sasha thought. It was warm; I was chatting up Madeline Malloy in the International; I was about to make a few grand off the Panther, not to mention the girls' babies. I was as comfortable as a bear in his lair.

So why did I have to pick up that goddamned box? Sasha asked himself.

Because you're a thief, he answered.

Sasha stopped. The El roared overhead, but for a few moments he was back in Zagorsk and in his hand were several antique coins. "Maybe they'll be lucky for you," Henry Tepperman had said.

Maybe, thought Sasha. Maybe they will.

Sasha walked toward Coney Island Avenue, watching the neighborhood changing from Russian to Hispanic to Orthodox

Jewish. It was amazing how fast it happened. On one block, the signs were in Cyrillic. On the next, they were in Spanish. Then Yiddish.

Sasha turned up Coney, leaving the El behind. He was chilled. He was exhausted.

He found his way to the Professor's building and rang the bell. To his relief, the door opened.

He walked up the narrow stairway to the Professor's floor and knocked on his door.

It swung open.

"Sasha!" said Moses Filonovsky, the Professor. "You're back!"

"I'm back," Sasha said, walking past the Professor and sitting next to his phone.

"You want some tea?" the Professor asked. "Some bread and jam? I have some good prune butter. Vodka? Pickles? Take off your coat. I hear Henry is dead. Is it true?"

"It's true," said Sasha. "I'll tell you about it later. Right now, tea would be good. Bread would be good. It all sounds good. You all right?"

"Yes. All right. I'm all right. But I hate this place. You wouldn't believe it, Sasha. Every day, somebody else gets shot, murdered. The Panther was only the beginning. Remember Bekker the doctor?"

"Something happened to Bekker?"

"Dead."

"How?"

"They say he was drunk and fell in front of a car. I don't believe it, do you? You know Bekker. He didn't drink. And those drugs he put in his arm, they didn't make him drunk. No. It's that Zilberstein. He's fighting with Agron, although nobody says so. And all the newcomers are going with Zilberstein. He has the drug business, and the drug business is quick money. Everybody has to look behind them now, someone doesn't come up and hit them over the head. For no reason. Or run them over in the street like Bekker."

"Why kill Bekker?" Sasha asked. He would miss Bekker. It was, Sasha thought, as if his past were being erased, his identity slowly vanishing.

First Boris. Then Alyona Romanova and Henry. Now the only people he had left in Russia were those murderers who had crucified Henry. And now his new life in America was disappearing before his eyes. With Bekker gone, another connection was disconnected.

If you lose your past, Sasha wondered, do you become a ghost?

It would be good to be a ghost, he thought.

"Why Bekker?" Sasha repeated.

"Bekker was important to Ebzi," said the Professor. "Bekker took care of everything. Somebody got shot, Bekker patched them up and kept his mouth shut. Somebody died, Bekker wrote up a death certificate that said the right things. Somebody's girlfriend got pregnant, Bekker took care of it. I liked Bekker."

"So did I," Sasha said. "He was a funny guy. What about Ivan Siskin?"

"He's all right, except for that wife of his. I don't know how he stands it. She walked into the Arbat the other night around one in the morning. Yelled at him to come home, and he went, like a dog, in front of everybody."

"You working?"

"Licenses. Passports. Small stuff for the new people. But now it's fucking Christmas and all the radio plays is that fucking Christmas music and it's making me crazy. You want a drink? I have some vodka in the icebox."

"Not now. Maybe later. Thanks."

"I'm going to have some."

"I need to make some phone calls, Professor. All right? And I need to rest."

"Of course. I've missed you, Sasha."

"I'm in trouble."

"I assumed."

"I don't want to get you in trouble," said Sasha.

"I don't want you to get me in trouble, either. But right now, make your calls, drink your tea, eat, rest. After, I know a place where you can stay. There's a family, the Abramovitzes from good old Kiev. Myron and Ivana. They're *fraiers*. No connections to nobody. They wouldn't cross the street against a red light. I made a driver's license for the woman a few months ago. Sometimes I go there, the woman gives me a glass of tea. They have a boy, Ari, he's a genius. We play speed chess together and I never win. I mean, he crushes me. Ten years old, he plays like a man. He absolutely crushes me. When he's not studying chess, he's with the piano or the computer. An extraordinary boy. They're a nice family."

"You know," the Professor said, "you should get married, have a family."

"And get a job? Be a *fraier*?"

"So? Things are different here, Sasha. They could be different here. Being a thief in America, it's, it's . . ."

Moses Filonovsky groped for a word, for a new and alien concept. "It's not necessary," he concluded.

Sasha looked at the old man, who, apart from his skills as a forger, had never impressed him as anything but a simple crook. Here was a man who had spent most of his life in the camps, who had never read anything or, Sasha had believed, thought about anything except his next score or his next meal. But now the Professor's words resonated, echoing and clarifying his own thoughts.

Could Filonovsky be right? And, even if he was right, was there anything Sasha could do about it?

Aleksandr Volkavitch Eugenev was a thief. At one time—could Sasha remember when?—that seemed the best, the only thing, to be. And now?

"Anyway," the Professor continued, "it's good to have a woman. I never did, and look at me—a lonely old fart who drinks too much vodka and knocks on his neighbors' doors to borrow their families. You're still a young man, Sasha."

"No," said Sasha. "Only compared to you."

"You should have married that nice girl—what was her name?—Tatyana. You liked her, I know. She told you where to get off. She didn't take any of your shit."

"A nice girl? You mean the Tatyana who was always getting knocked up?"

"So? She was still a nice girl. And," said the Professor, smirking, "she had a great rear end."

"Have you seen her?" Sasha asked.

"Not since the baby," the Professor said. "She moved away. Maybe to Queens."

"What was it?" asked Sasha.

"The baby? It was a boy. Another black one."

"I knew it," Sasha said. "Tatyana," he said, shaking his head. "You must be crazy."

"No," said the Professor. "You're the crazy one."

Sasha checked his watch and decided to give Terry a little more time to sober up. He reached into his pocket and removed the coins he had taken from Zagorsk. I need protection, he thought. Maybe these will buy it for me. Then he opened his wallet and took out a small piece of paper with a number on it, the number Madeline Malloy had given him, Mitch Rose's number.

24.

FAT SAM GOLDMAN WAS NOT HAPPY TO SEE THE TALL BLOND transsexual teetering through the door of his shop and shakily navigating her way past the tables crowded with tchotchkes: silver cigarette cases and samovars, crystal goblets and mille-fleur paperweights, lamps, silverware, and seashell ashtrays. Goldman's higher-ticket items—television sets, fur coats, couches—were stored in the basement. Most of it was legit, some of it was not, but all of it was priced to move. If you needed it, Sam Goldman had it. And if he didn't have it, he could arrange to buy it or have it stolen.

Goldman's shop was protected—he supplied half the Six-tieth Precinct with snow tires in winter and air conditioners in summer. The cops would come in, punch his shoulder, and ask, "What have you got for nothing today, Sam? What's going cheap?" And because the cops actually paid for the goods, they didn't think of it as being dirty. But that protection went only so far, and Goldman was pretty sure it didn't include the blonde and her boyfriend, who had just been written up in the *News*.

"What the fuck are you doing here?" demanded Goldman, pitching his voice so that the customer inspecting knock-off Tiffany lamps couldn't hear him. "Don't you know you're hot?"

"How much'll you give me for this?" Terry asked, pulling a lacquered box out of a brown paper shopping bag.

Goldman quickly stepped around the counter and walked over to the woman looking at the lamps. "I'm sorry, lady," he said. "Something's come up. I gotta close now."

"Oh, that's too bad," said the woman. "Will you be open tomorrow?"

"Yeah, bright and early," Goldman said.

He escorted the woman to the door, locked it behind her, pulled down the shade, and turned the Open sign around to Closed. He walked back to Terry.

"Are you nuts?" said Goldman. "Don't you read the papers?"

"How much, Sam?"

Goldman picked up the box. It was lovely, he thought, a real treasure. The painting on the curved top was a pastoral scene of peasants scything hay. On each of the four sides, intricately decorated oval vignettes showed a bear hunt, each vignette containing snowy pine forests and fur-wrapped hunters riding sleds. On one of the end sides, the bear, standing on its rear legs, its mouth open, its red tongue hanging out, was surrounded.

Goldman put the box on the counter and opened it. It was empty. The green felt was burned in several places.

"Where are the coins?" he asked.

"No coins," Terry said. "Just the box."

"You been using this as an ashtray? What a *khazer* you are. You know what a *khazer* is? A *khazer* is a pig."

"You should talk. How much, honey?"

Goldman took his unlit cigar out of his mouth and examined the chewed, ragged end. If he sold the box to a collector, he thought, he could clear a few thousand. If he put it up for auction, maybe he could get more. It was a bit beat up, but it smelled of quality.

He looked at Terry, noting her red eyes, her trembling hands, her five o'clock shadow inadequately disguised by a layer of white powder.

"This cigar," he said to Terry, "is worth more than this box. And this is not an expensive cigar. It's the coins, not the fucking box. What are you, stupid?"

"Come on, Sam," said Terry, taking off her sunglasses and leaning across the counter. "Don't Jew me. I'm sick. I need to buy some antibiotics."

"You're sick all right," Goldman said, reaching for his wallet. "Fifty bucks. That's two bags."

"Sam, that's not right. You know this box is valuable. It's antique, Russian. Beautiful. Look at the painting. Look at the hinge. It's gold."

"It's brass. And you look. You look around, sweetheart. Everyfuckingthing here's Russian. Every fucking Russian who comes to Brighton unloads the family jewels here, and it's all crap. Birch boxes. Lacquer boxes. Want to see lacquer boxes? I got fifty in the basement better looking than this. I got amber up the ass. I got enough samovars to make tea until doomsday. And *matryoshkas*. The whole fucking country made nothing but tchotchkes. And those big, fat, ugly steel watches. And here, look at these cigarette burns. I'm going to have to reline this.

"Look. Tell you what I'm gonna do," Goldman continued. "I'm gonna give you a hundred bucks. Not for the box, that's garbage. I'm not gonna make a nickel off it. But I'm gonna give you a hundred bucks anyway to take care of yourself, get cleaned up, get a meal, because I'm a nice guy. And I don't expect nothing back except, anybody asks, you say Sam Goldman is a good guy. Okay?"

"You're a fucking prince."

"Watch your mouth, sweetheart."

Goldman took five twenties out of his wallet and laid them on the counter. Terry scooped up the bills and stuck them in her jeans.

"Don't you know you're hot?" asked Goldman. "You're in some deep shit. You and that boyfriend of yours. I'm surprised you haven't been picked up yet."

"There weren't any names in that story."

"Oh, that's right. You're so inconspicuous. There are a million six-foot-tall drag queens walking around."

"You'd be surprised, Sam," said Terry. "And I'm no drag queen."

Goldman watched the big blonde sashay out the door. You're a soft touch, he told himself. Now the thing was to get rid of the box as fast as possible. Maybe it was too hot to sell, too hot to auction. Maybe he should forget the money. Maybe he should just give the box to Ebzi Agron as a gift. That would put him in solid with the *batyushka.*

But first he had to reline it. He was sure he had some green felt lying around someplace.

He took the box down to the basement.

❖   ❖   ❖

There was nobody home at the apartment on Ninth where Terry usually went to score. A junkie picking his nose and nodding in the hallway said that they had gone into the city, who knew when they'd be back?

Terry poked her head into the Cafe Arbat and didn't see anyone she knew among the faces turning to stare at her. Just Russians, looking her up and down. A dozen pairs of flat, empty eyes, looking at her as if she were some kind of insect.

As she stood in the Arbat's entrance, it struck her that

that was what was so different about them. They didn't look at her the way people looked at other human beings. Terry was used to seeing disgust or anger, curiosity or lust, in people's eyes. But when the Russians looked at her, their eyes were empty. And it wasn't, she thought, because of what she was. It was because of what she wasn't—Russian. If you're not one of them, Terry thought, you're nothing. You're not really alive. That's why it's so easy for them to kill.

Even the Cowboy. Sometimes she would feel his eyes on her, and it was like being splashed with ice water. No warmth. No recognition. No feeling of any kind.

And the Cowboy loved her.

Of course, she thought, the Cowboy was nuts.

The heroin was dying inside her, and she was beginning to feel sick, depressed. Her nose was starting to run, and the cold was seeping into her bones.

The problem, Terry thought, is that I'm always buying one bag at a time. I never have enough money to put together a decent stash.

Too bad that croaker Bekker got himself run over. Twenty-five bucks and he would have written me a script for twenty or thirty Percodan to take the edge off. He was always good for a prescription.

I'm getting fucked up again, she thought. What am I up to? Four bags a day? You know it's five, girl. Who are you trying to kid?

Of course, the shit I've been getting has been stepped on so many times, I might as well be shooting milk sugar. If I could get the good shit, I'd only be doing three bags.

Goddamn the Cowboy, she thought, heading back to her apartment.

Inside, Terry went to the kitchen and began playing with her works. She picked up the syringe, wondering if there might be a few grains of heroin left in the tube. She found the glassine envelope on the floor and licked the bitter insides.

Then she went into the bedroom, turned on the television, adjusted the coat hanger that served as its antenna, threw herself onto the bed, and began looking at the ads in *Cosmopolitan*. The cat jumped up on the pillow next to her and began to purr.

There was a knock on the door.

"Terry. It's Sasha."

Good, thought Terry. The trick. I'll ask for a hundred, score four bags, and still have a hundred left. I'll do one bag right away, maybe another to sleep on. Maybe I'll just use half tonight, go to sleep, and use the other half to get straight when I wake up. Then I'll have three whole bags for tomorrow. That'll give me plenty of time to turn a few tricks and score some more. Or maybe I'll start cutting down tomorrow. Cut those bags in half. Make them last two days. Find a new doctor for a Percodan script. That's what you should do, girl. That's getting your shit together, she told herself.

As long as I got this, she thought, patting her ass, who needs the Cowboy?

"Just a sec, honey," called Terry.

She opened the door.

Aleksandr Volkov stepped through.

"How you doing, baby?" he said, his mouth smiling, his eyes flat and empty.

He closed the door behind him.

◈   ◈   ◈

Peter Grushenko, accompanied by two patrolmen, broke into Terry's apartment the next morning and found her lying on her back in bed, her panties down around her ankles, her swollen tongue hanging purple out of her mouth, her nose broken, her lips cut, her eyes open and blackened, a garrote of picture-hanging wire cutting into the flaccid, already decomposing flesh around her neck. Her skin was livid, the blood, pulled by gravity, settling in her back, her buttocks. There was blood caked and drying on the pillow, blood caked and drying on the sheet under her ass.

"What I don't understand," one patrolman said, "is why anyone would ever want to make it with that."

"She probably looked better when she wasn't so fucking dead," said the other patrolman.

"Not much, I'll bet," the first said.

"She had nice little tits, though," said the second.

"Hey. What's with this 'she' crap? You see that between his legs? You know what that is?"

"Shut up, please," said Peter Grushenko. He bent down beside the bed, took a pencil out of his pocket, and poked at the pair of sunglasses lying on the floor, Porsche sunglasses.

Grushenko got down on his hands and knees, inspecting the glasses, reading Aleksandr Eugenev's name, lovingly inscribed.

Grushenko cursed and stood up.

"One of you, get the lab people down here," he said. "Put on your gloves now, please. Try very hard not to touch anything, all right? And have the desk get in touch with Silverman at Organized Crime. We are going to want a warrant for the arrest of an Aleksandr Eugenev, address unknown. And let's get reporters. I want him to know we're looking for him."

Grushenko blew his nose and turned away. Now I'm going to look real stupid, he thought. I had him and I let him go.

He turned back to Terry. She really did look bad, he thought, and wished briefly that he could clean her up before the police photographers came. But, of course, he didn't.

25.

Friday, December 24

ARIEL ABRAMOVITZ SAT ON HIS BED UNDERNEATH A POSTER OF
Michael Jordan. Jordan, his tongue hanging out, was dunking
a basketball. On the wall opposite Jordan was a poster of
Patrick Ewing similarly engaged.

"You like Michael Jordan?" Sasha asked.

"He's okay," said Ari, an olive-skinned, skinny ten-year-
old. He had high cheekbones, brown, almond-shaped eyes,
large ears that stuck out, and a colorfully knitted yarmulke attached with a bobby pin to the top of his head. His dark brown
hair was straight and flopped over his forehead and eyes. Someday, Sasha thought, he would be a handsome man. Now, he was
a funny-looking kid in gray sweatpants and a blue New York
Knicks sweatshirt.

"Who do you like better?" Sasha asked. "Jordan or
Ewing?"

"I don't know. Jordan, I guess. No, Ewing. 'Cause I like
the Knicks. Are you going to stay long?"

"I don't know," said Sasha. "Not too long."

After word of the warrant for his arrest hit the street,

Sasha agreed with the Professor that it was no longer safe for him to stay there. It would be easy for Grushenko to look up everyone connected with him.

The Professor made a call, and the Abramovitzes had agreed to put him up.

And Peter the Duck wasn't his only worry. Terry, Sasha thought, was probably killed by Volkov, who was continuing his habit of setting Sasha up to take the fall. That meant that Volkov either had the box or soon would, because he surely would have found out from Terry where it was. And that meant that Sasha would be unable to fulfill Viktor Prudnikov's directive to deliver the box to Sotheby's and to Major Anatoly Shubentsov unless he could find Volkov and take it away from him, a course of action Sasha deemed likely to be hazardous to the already fragile state of his health.

The trick, thought Sasha, is to find someone to take it away from Volkov for me.

But why would anyone do that? Sasha asked himself. Why would anyone do anything for Aleksandr Volkavitch Eugenev, a man who was seriously fucked?

"You're Moses's cousin?"

Sasha had to think for a moment, then realized the boy was speaking of the Professor. "Yes. That's right."

"Want to play speed chess?"

"All right," said Sasha.

The boy hopped off the bed and set up the board on the floor. He scooped up two plastic pawns, made a great show of shifting them from hand to hand behind his back, and then held his two small fists straight out in front of him. Sasha slapped Ari's left hand, and the boy opened it to reveal the black pawn. Ariel moved his white king's pawn two squares and slapped the chess clock. Sasha's move.

They sat cross-legged on the floor, the small red-and-black folding board between them. With Jordan and Ewing watching, Ari played the Austrian Attack—a broad front dominating the center, followed by a pawn blitz on Black's castled king. It was an opening designed to take advantage of weaker players. It worked. Within twelve moves—three minutes—the boy, slamming down his pieces with authority, pummeling the timer on the chess clock, had demolished Sasha's position and had his king on the run.

After some dilatory, desultory moves, Sasha resigned, tipping over his king.

"Again?" Sasha asked, beginning to set up the board.

"Nah. You're not very good," said Ari.

"Thanks a lot."

"Well, it's true. Even Moses is better."

"You know," said Sasha, "sometimes we don't say things even if they are true, especially if it makes someone feel bad."

The boy thought about this for a moment, knitting his brow and pursing his lips. "That sounds like something people say to kids," he said.

"Well, you're a kid, aren't you?"

"Yeah," Ari said. "But I'm not stupid."

Then he rolled underneath his bed and emerged with a Nerf ball.

"Want to shoot hoops?" Ari asked, indicating the basket above his bedroom door. "Best out of ten?"

"Okay," said Sasha.

Ari carefully marked off the distance from the hoop, drew a line on the rug with his toe, and tossed the ball to Sasha.

This time, Sasha won.

"You're better at hoops," Ari said, throwing himself on his bed. Sasha sat next to him.

"It's easier for me," Sasha said apologetically. "I'm a lot taller than you."

"That's the trouble with basketball," Ari said. "You have to be tall. I don't think I'm ever going to be tall."

"No?"

"My mama's short and so's my papa. That's genetics."

"You never know," said Sasha.

"I know."

The boy rolled over on his back, his hands beneath his head. He stared at the ceiling.

"Are you on the run?" he asked.

"Why would you say something like that?" asked Sasha, unsurprised. Clearly Ariel Ambramovitz was as the Professor advertised. "Did your parents say something to you?"

"Nobody told me anything," Ari said. "Nobody ever tells me anything. I'm a kid. But, I don't know, the way you look. You look like you're in trouble."

"And what does that look like?"

"You know. Worried."

"Well, I am in a little trouble, Ari. It's true."

"The police are looking for you?"

"The police, other people. You won't tell anyone, will you? This is very serious stuff."

"I can keep a secret. I'm very mature for my age. So? What are you going to do?"

"I don't know, Ari. What would you do?"

"I'd disappear."

"Good idea. But it's not so easy for a grown-up."

"Yes, it is," Ari said enthusiastically. "Actually, it's easier for a grown-up than a kid. People are always asking kids 'Where are your parents?' 'What are you doing?' 'Shouldn't you be in school, little boy?' And kids can't get money. And anyway, even if I got a plane ticket, I'm only ten, and I look younger. I'd need a letter from my parents to fly alone."

"Tough, huh?"

"Yeah. But nobody asks grown-ups anything. Nobody tells them what to do."

"Maybe you're right. So, if you were a grown-up," Sasha asked, "what would you do? How would you disappear?"

"I'd become another person," said Ari.

"You've given this a lot of thought," Sasha said, recognizing a kindred soul.

"Yes, I have," said Ari. "I think about it a lot."

"Why? Are you in trouble? Are people looking for you?"

"All the time," Ari said. "In school. On the street. All these kids, you know, are always hassling me. Because I'm short, and because I'm smart, and because . . ." Ari touched his yarmulke. "And because of this."

"There aren't other Jews in your school?"

"Sure, but they don't all wear *kippas*. And the ones who do, they're wussies."

"Wussies?"

"Yeah. You know."

"I can guess. So how would you become another person?"

"Easy. First I'd find another kid like me, around my age, someone somewhere where we'd never bump into each other."

"What do you mean?"

"It's easier to become someone else if someone else already exists. You know. If they have stuff like birth certificates and school records and, and, stuff."

"Then what?"

"Then I just put my name and my picture on their stuff."

"And how do you get their stuff?"

"Easy. With the computer."

"Show me," said Sasha. "I like computers."

"Me too," Ari said, jumping off the bed and sitting at his computer terminal.

"Nice," said Sasha, looking over the boy's shoulder.

"It's a Quantex," Ari said. "Got four hundred twenty megabytes on the hard drive, eight megabytes of RAM."

"You have an Internet link?" asked Sasha as Ari logged on.

"Of course," Ari said, exasperated. "I got Delphi. It's text based, menu driven, but it's got full Internet access and it's cheap, so my parents are willing to pay. I got a serious modem, too—fourteen thousand baud. I got PC Paintbrush for Windows for downloading GIF and JPG files off the Net; a sixteen-bit sound card, stereo speakers, and . . . Want to play a neat game I found? There's this games BBS, all the really hot designers post on it. It's called Dork."

"Maybe later, Ari," said Sasha. "I did not follow that business about GIF and JPG files."

"Pictures," Ari said. "That's for downloading pictures. Want to do it?"

"Right now, why don't you show me how I could disappear."

"Okay," Ari said. "Do you know anybody around your age who you could be?"

"As a matter of fact," said Sasha, "I do."

"Where would his stuff be?" Ari asked. "Driver's license, birth certificate, Social Security number?"

"In Russia."

"Cool," said Ari.

His hands flew over the keyboard, and a list of phone numbers appeared on the screen. He pressed Enter, and a ringing sounded through his speakers, followed by a beeping, followed by the familiar electronic crash of two computers shaking hands. Ari entered his log-in, then his password. The Delphi main menu filled the screen.

Ari thought for a moment, his hands poised over his keyboard.

"A lot of Russian kids are in a USENET forum, alt.Info-Russ," he said, more to himself than to Sasha. "I know a kid from school, Smarty, a major criminal. What time is it?"

"Four o'clock," said Sasha.

"He'll probably be on-line," Ari said. "Let's see."

Sasha watched as Ari surfed the Internet. Smarty, who was indeed on-line, sent them to the University of Buffalo, where someone named Ivan directed them to a FIDONET bulletin board where there were postings from the Commonwealth of Independent States and the Baltics.

"That might work," Ari said.

"What might work?" asked Sasha.

"An FTP. Loc.Gov.1./Soviet Archives. In Moscow."

"What's an FTP?"

"File transfer protocol," Ari said. "It lets you search for files in other computers and then copy them. We can telnet there, but we need an access code if we're going to download anything. We also need it if we're going to get any pictures."

"How do we get that?"

Ariel thought for a moment. "Let's go back to Smarty. Maybe he's got a friend over there who's a hacker."

Smarty did. *Bolshoi Pteetsuh.* His name was Big Bird. He lived in Moscow. He was older than Ari. He was twelve.

And he had lots of codes.

In a few moments, as names and numbers began scrolling down Ariel Abramovitz's screen, Russia, thousands of miles away, began to fill the small bedroom in Brooklyn.

Sasha could almost smell it.

"We're in," said Ari. "We're in Russia. Cool. Give me a name."

Sasha did.

They worked all night. When the sun rose, Sasha took a long, hot shower and emerged, reborn.

Good-bye, Aleksandr Volkavitch Eugenev, he thought. You were never good for much of anything anyway.

He dressed, then went into the kitchen and made French toast for Ariel and his family.

After breakfast he placed a call to the Airport Hilton and asked for Major Anatoly Shubentsov.

The phone rang.

Shubentsov picked up.

"This is Aleksandr Volkov," Sasha said.

"What do you want?" asked Shubentsov.

"I want to see you," Sasha said.

"Do you have the package?" asked Shubentsov.

"No," Sasha said, "but I know who does."

26.

SALLY HANDS HAD BEEN GLAD TO HELP WHEN MITCH ROSE HAD asked if she could put Madeline Malloy up at her apartment for a few weeks. For one, she liked Malloy, even though her recent eminence at the paper was slightly unnerving. Hands knew instinctively that only so many spots were reserved for women in the paper's psychological hierarchy, and it was unsettling to see all the attention Malloy had been receiving from Mitch Rose, Bill Katz, Charlie O'Brien, and the others. Were they thinking about bringing Malloy onto the city desk? Was there room for two female assistant metro editors? Two young, attractive metro editors? Hands didn't think so.

Of course, she felt bad about what had happened to Maddy Malloy. It must have been horrible. On the other hand, she was jealous of Malloy's story, run off the front page.

But, Hands had to admit, it was exciting and flattering to be involved in something so obviously important. Usually she felt like a token at the news meetings, rarely taken seriously, rarely listened to, a butt for Mitch Rose's terrible sexist cracks. But maybe now her own star was rising. At least this proved that the boys, as she always thought of them, saw something in her.

And Malloy seemed so messed up. She was either quiet and depressed, not talking, or borderline hysterical. That morning, for example, they were drinking tea when suddenly, for no reason, she had burst into tears. Hands had put her arms around her and just held her. It felt good to be able to help.

On the other hand, having Malloy staying at her place meant that Mitch Rose kept dropping by, and Rose made Hands exquisitely uncomfortable. Here was this powerful figure, the editor of the paper, her boss, and instead of acting like he was supposed to, like the so cool Jason Robards in *All the President's Men* or even like a stereotypically gruff newspaper editor, he insisted upon behaving like her bratty younger brother. She knew that that was how he wanted her to respond to him; she knew that she was supposed to tease him back, act like his big sister and tell him to shut up when he got out of line. But she couldn't. For God's sake, he was old enough to be her father. She knew. She had gained access to his personnel file. He was sixty-two, soon to be sixty-three. Jesus, in two years he'd be retiring.

And right now he was sitting cross-legged on her couch, his shirtsleeves rolled up, looking like a jazzed-up rat sniffing cheese.

"Sally," Rose said, "why don't we order in some pizza. Sound good to you, Maddy?"

Madeline Malloy was sitting on Hands's "reading chaise" across from Rose, turning the pages of the current *Vogue*.

"Fine," she said without looking up.

"Pepperoni? Onions? Mushrooms? Extra cheese?" Hands asked.

"Everything," said Rose. "And lots of anchovies."

"You're just trying to gross me out," Hands said, forcing herself to banter. "Nobody eats anchovies."

"I do," said Rose. "I love them. Have them stick them on one side of the pie. I'll even give you a bite if you ask me nice. What about you, Maddy?"

"Whatever," Malloy said.

Hands went into the kitchen to call in the order. Before returning to the living room, she stopped to listen, leaning against the kitchen wall. Well, she thought, for God's sake, I'm a reporter.

She could hear her mother's old mantel clock ticking on the table next to the chaise. She could hear the pages of *Vogue* being turned. She stepped back into the room. Neither Rose nor Malloy had moved.

"Twenty minutes," Hands said. "That means thirty if we're lucky."

"You got any wine, Sally?" asked Rose.

"Just white," Hands said.

"Yuppie wine. White wine isn't really wine unless it's champagne."

"What does that mean?" asked Hands.

"Forget it," Rose said. "The point is, you can't eat pizza with white wine. We need dago red, Chianti, in the straw basket. Is there a liquor store around here, Sally?"

"Just around the corner. I'll go," she offered.

"Here," said Rose, standing up and pulling out his wallet. "Here's a twenty. Get the good stuff."

Hands froze, calculating furiously. Should she say "I got it," like a grown-up, like Rose's equal? No, she thought. That would be stupid. She wasn't his equal. And he'd insist. That would be embarrassing. Anyway, this was newspaper business, so the editor should pay for the wine. And the pizza? Yes. And the change? Would he ask for the change? Should she just hand him the change? With the receipt? Was he going to expense the wine? Would giving him the receipt be intimating that he was cheap? Maybe she could stick the receipt under the corny straw on the corny Chianti. Then he could take it if he wanted to. And what if the change was just a dollar? What if it was a quarter? Should she hand him a quarter? How could she do that? But what if he went away thinking she had walked off with his change? How would he know it was just a quarter?

Hands suddenly realized that Rose was still standing in front of her, waiting, the twenty dangling from his hand.

"Okay," she said quickly, taking the twenty, wondering if it had been the right thing to do, glad to get away.

"You all right?" Rose asked Malloy when Hands had left.

"I'm okay, Mitch," said Malloy, putting aside the magazine and folding her hands in her lap.

"We have to talk, Maddy."

"All right."

"Okay.

"This isn't so bad, is it?" Rose said after a moment. "Nice place. A little college-y bohemian, but nice."

"You spoke to Peter Feld," said Malloy.

"Yes. I told you. I spoke to Peter Feld. I told him to fuck off. But I'm changing my mind."

"Why?"

"Look, Maddy. Right now, the story is dead. The coins are out there, the cops are looking for them, but you can't report on it, you can't move the story forward sitting in Sally's apartment, not talking to anyone. And this is your story. You got to cover it. I mean, I can assign Mancuso, but it won't be the same. This is prize-winning stuff, Maddy. This is a career maker. You got to go for it."

"Okay."

"And sooner or later you're going to be served with a subpoena and you're going to have to testify. There's no getting around it. So, my thinking is, the best thing for you would be to get everything into the paper, everything you know, everything you can get. Then, when you go in front of the grand jury, all you have to do is quote from your articles. Then the DA thanks you and you go home. No smart-ass questions, no heat. If they ask, you can hand them your notebook because you know there's nothing in it that's not in your stories. Understand?"

"Okay."

"So the best thing is for you to go back to work. You don't have to go back to your apartment just yet—in fact, I think you should find a new one—but going back to work, yeah. And that means, until this is all straightened out, you're going to need some watching, some watching over. And I can't do that. But Peter Feld can. He can talk to the cops; he has his own resources. And I trust him. He's a good guy."

"All right, Mitch. Call him."

"You gotta put this behind you, Maddy. I know that sounds stupid, a fucking cliché, but it's true."

"I said okay, Mitch."

"Okay. You sure you're okay? Because you don't sound okay."

"I'm okay."

"Maybe you should see a doctor."

"I saw a doctor."

"I know. I mean a shrink. Someone who specializes in trauma."

"I'm okay."

"Okay. Well, I'm going to call Peter."

Rose left the room, and Malloy picked up *Vogue*. Everything Rose had just said made sense, but it was a hollow sense. What it meant, she knew, was describing Sasha in the paper. She knew he was back; she knew he had been calling, not leaving a number. Maybe it would be better not to speak to him. She didn't owe him anything. She had slept with him, hid him, lied for him, and all she had gotten in return was a visit from those freaks and, probably, a date in court. And her life was still in danger. If she put it all in the paper, got it all out, it would be over and done with. Finally. Could she do that? That would be the smart thing to do, the wise thing. Would she?

She didn't know.

Rose returned, smiling.

"I talked to Peter. He's going to give you a bodyguard. That guy who was with him at my party for Steinberg."

"Okay."

"There's another thing I want to ask you before Sally gets back," Rose said.

"What?"

"I got a phone call yesterday. On my personal line. The guy said you gave it to him. He said he had to see you. He said his name is Sasha. Is this *the* Sasha? Your mystery man?"

"Yes," she said.

"He said he'd call back. You want to see him?"

"Yes," she said.

All right, so she wasn't smart.

27.

Saturday, December 25

EBZI AGRON FINISHED HIS AFTERNOON TEA, KISSED HIS WIFE, picked up the canvas bag containing the beautiful lacquered box Sam Goldman had given him as a token of his esteem, and trotted down the steps of his Manhattan Beach home. He paused at the bottom, looked up and down the block, and then, satisfied that none of Zilberstein's assassins were lurking in the bushes, he closed his eyes and inhaled slowly, deeply, tasting the sweetness of fog and the acrid tang of ocean. That, above all the rest—more than the antique coins that the Cowboy had turned over to him, more than the box that he was going to Goldman's to sell for a hundred percent profit, more than even the simple miracle of his continued survival—was amazing to him. That at the advanced age of fifty-six, Ebzi Agron lived by the sea. His father had never seen the sea, nor had his father's father. In Uzbekistan, he thought, I never even dreamed about it. Now, I smell it every day and I love it like a sailor. Isn't that strange? he thought. Isn't life wonderful?

The *batyushka* opened his eyes. The black Lincoln Town Car was waiting, its engine running.

Agron banged once on the Lincoln's trunk.

His driver popped the lock, and Agron put the bag in the trunk.

"So. Sam Goldman's shop," said Agron, getting in and unbuttoning his overcoat. "And turn down the heat. It's like a *banya* in here."

Smoothly the car pulled away from the curb.

The radio came on, a jazzy version of "Jingle Bells."

"Turn that the fuck off," Agron said.

The radio went off.

"Fucking Christmas," said Agron.

He stared at the tightly curled black hair on the back of his driver's head. Dmitri Duyadev, a lovely example of your average Chechen, the *batyushka* thought. Russia's Sicilians. This one would stick a blade between your ribs with his left hand while he shook your hand with his right. Allah would, of course, forgive him. Allah always forgave the Chechens their murders. After all, their victim was, in all likelihood, merely a Christian. Or a Jew. But this Chechen was a good driver, a useful person to have around.

The car slid through the lowering mist, over the small metal bridge that crossed the channel that led to the gray-green, oily sea. The plates on the bridge rattled as the car humped over them. The sound echoed. Christmas Day. Not a soul to be seen. The streets were deserted, hushed.

The car turned down Emmons Avenue, passing the tackle shops and clam shacks—closed for the season—past the hulking Moorish wreck of Lundy's, the once famous, now long forgotten seafood restaurant and nightclub, and then cut across to Brighton Beach Avenue, stopping in front of Goldman's Antiques beneath the El.

The windows were dark. Duyadev cut the engine and opened the door for Agron as the streetlights on the empty avenue flashed on. Agron motioned him ahead, leaving the box locked in the trunk. No one in Brighton, Agron knew, would bother the *batyushka*'s car.

They walked down an alley to a side door. Duyadev pressed the buzzer. It rang in the basement, where Sam Goldman was sitting on a chair, his head back, a handkerchief pressed against his nose, trying to stop the bleeding. The blond man was toying with his gun in a meaningful way.

"That must be him," Goldman said through swollen lips. It hurt to talk.

When the man had walked into his shop, Sam Goldman, who was passionately committed to doing business on Christmas Day, could have sworn it was Aleksandr Eugenev. He had the same thinning blond hair, the same muscular build, the same jaunty air. He was even wearing sunglasses. So Goldman had smiled. On the few occasions he had done business with Sasha Eugenev, he had provided good stuff, and he had been reasonable about price. Oh, sure, they had *hondeled.* Goldman would have been disappointed if they hadn't bargained a little. A little give, a little take. But unlike so many of the street thieves he dealt with—dopers, most of them—Goldman knew that Eugenev knew that Goldman was essentially fair, that it was in his interest to be fair, and that Goldman was not trying to screw him. Most important, he knew that Eugenev was a professional, and if Eugenev was ever pinched, he wouldn't be shouting out Goldman's name to the cops.

So Goldman had smiled. "Hey, Sasha," he had said. "Haven't seen you around. How's tricks?"

The man had shut the door behind him and turned the Open sign around to Closed. As he'd walked toward Goldman, Goldman's smile had faded.

"Hey," Goldman had said. "Who the fuck are you?"

"I'm Aleksandr Eugenev," the man said.

"The fuck you are," Goldman said.

"All right," Aleksandr Volkov said. "So I'm not Aleksandr Eugenev."

Then he opened his coat and pulled out a gun. "But I want the box he stole from me."

"What box?" Goldman said.

With a stiff, outstretched arm, Volkov leaned across the counter and jammed the barrel of his gun into Goldman's upper lip, splitting it.

"The box the queen sold you," Volkov said.

"How—" Goldman began to say, and swallowed the "did you know?" He regretted it instantly. Did he really want to know how the man knew? No.

"A little birdie told me," Volkov said. "Where is it?"

At first Volkov had not believed that Goldman no longer had the lacquered box.

That had been unpleasant.

Finally, after Goldman, on his knees, begged to be allowed to call Agron, Volkov stopped hitting him. He told him to tell Agron that he would buy the box from him. But first he had to see it.

And now, Goldman hoped, that was Agron at the side door.

"We'll go up together," Volkov said. "You first."

Sam Goldman was used to being in tight spots. As a teenager he had loved the thrill of sneaking into homes and stores. It had made him feel like Superman. With his super-vision, he could see a wallet or a watch lying on a night table in the dark, and with his super-hearing he could tell whether it was a man, woman, or a child breathing behind a closed door in a bedroom down the hall.

Eventually Goldman had branched out, and eventually he'd done time for knocking over a gas station. In prison Goldman had learned how to crack safes, and, more important, he had learned that crime was a business, not a game. The core idea was to minimize your risks while maximizing your take. If you worked with professionals in a professional manner, you stood to make a good living. If you worked with jerks, with people who thought they were Superman, you ended up in the crowbar hotel, fighting off the shower queers and muscle queens.

After prison Goldman had worked at being professional. He'd taken time off between jobs so as not to attract attention, so as not to advertise his MO to the cops. He'd chosen his partners carefully. He'd refused to carry a piece, and he'd taken a straight gig as a furniture repairman (he had worked in the prison wood shop) in order to establish himself as a taxpayer, a member of the community. When he'd turned forty, he'd opened his own secondhand furniture shop. Not long after that, he'd given up burglary and its concomitant risks to become a full-time fence.

Now, his face swollen, his nose bleeding, he wondered whether he had made such a wise career decision after all.

He went up the stairs and around to the door off the alley. Through the peephole, standing under a small spotlight, he saw Ebzi Agron's moon face. He opened the door and Dmitri Duyadev stepped through, pushing Goldman back against the wall. Goldman felt a gun at his gut.

"Hey," said Goldman, who felt strongly that he had already exceeded his day's quota for pistol whippings.

"It's all right, Dmitri," Agron said, stepping into the hallway.

The gun went away.

"What the hell happened to you?" asked Agron, seeing Goldman's battered face.

"Never mind," Volkov said, stepping around Goldman to confront Agron.

Duyadev stepped between Volkov and Agron.

"And who are you who did this to my friend Sam Goldman?" asked Agron.

"You don't remember me? My name is Aleksandr Velikhov. We spoke at the Odessa some months ago."

Agron peered into Volkov's face for a long moment. Then he smiled. "The uranium," he said.

"Uranium?" said Goldman.

Both Agron and Volkov turned to look at Goldman. Goldman shrugged and backed away.

"You have the box?" Volkov asked.

"It's an empty box," said Agron.

"Do you have it?"

"It's not empty?" Agron asked.

"Do you have it?" asked Volkov.

"Do you have the money?" Agron asked.

"The box first," said Volkov.

"No, no, no, my friend," Agron said, laughing. "I look at Mr. Goldman's face and I see that you are a violent man."

"I'm like you, a businessman," Volkov said.

Agron turned to Goldman. "Sam, do you have anything to drink here? How can we do business without vodka?"

"Downstairs," said Goldman.

"Shall we go?" Agron said.

"Why not?" said Volkov.

The four men went down into Goldman's basement. Volkov sat on an armchair covered with a sheet.

"Dmitri," Agron said, "give me my present."

Duyadev handed Agron a brown paper bag.

"So? A table, Sam?" Agron said. "We need a table. And another chair."

Goldman pulled a small card table over to where Volkov was sitting, and then he retrieved a heavy mahogany library chair for Agron. He placed a bottle of Stolichnaya on the table between them. Then he stepped back into the basement's shadows. He would have liked to disappear, but he was acutely aware of the Chechen keeping an eye on him. An obvious killer, thought Goldman. And this Volkov, a sadist. Not to mention Agron, who, he had heard, liked to beat people to death with his bare hands. I'm surrounded by psychos, he thought.

Agron reached into the paper bag and pulled out a loaf of brown bread and a sausage wrapped in waxed paper.

"A knife. I forgot a knife. Dmitri?"

Duyadev handed Agron a six-inch stiletto.

"Look what he gives me," said Agron, holding the knife for Volkov to see. Volkov smiled thinly. "I see you wiped it clean," Agron said, elaborately examining the blade. "No blood. Just joking. Oh, well, you can take the boy out of Chechnya . . . I brought you some *salo,*" Agron said, cutting a slice of the loaf made from salted and peppered pork fat. "Even though we are in America, especially as we are in America, we must eat and drink over our business like true Russians. Vodka, bread, *salo.* If we eat and drink over it, it will turn out good."

They ate and drank and wished each other good health. *Zu vahsheh zduhrawvyeh!*

Agron offered Volkov a cigarette and lit it for him.

Volkov exhaled and waved away the smoke. "You have something that belongs to me," he said. "That's all right. You came by it honestly, and you deserve something for recovering it."

"It seems I did not know what I had," said Agron.

"So now you do," Volkov said.

"Now I do," said Agron.

"So? In itself, it is worthless," Volkov said. "You have to have a buyer. You don't find a buyer for this on the street. But I have a buyer. A good one."

"I could find one."

"Perhaps. Perhaps not," said Volkov.

"You have a figure in mind?" Agron asked.

"A figure is less important to me than an agreement," Volkov said. "But I must see the box. Look. Look around you. Look at your Chechen. I'm clearly no threat."

Agron nodded. "All right. Dmitri. In the car. The bag. Bring it here."

Duyadev left. Agron poured two more shots for himself and Volkov. They drank.

The Chechen returned, handing the canvas bag to Agron. Agron took the lacquered box out of the bag, admired it briefly, and handed it to Volkov. Volkov put it on his lap and opened it.

"See," said Agron. "Empty."

"The knife?" Volkov said.

Agron handed him Duyadev's stiletto.

Aleksandr Volkov admired the knife for a moment. It felt good in his hand.

He took a deep breath. This, he thought, had been a long time coming. He closed his eyes. Ebzi Agron, he thought, could now play the role he had intended for him months before. They could split Peter Feld's money, and Sasha Eugenev would take the fall, not only for stealing the uranium, but for murdering the big blond queen. Feld would probably want him to leave Eugenev alone, to let the police take him. But that, Volkov felt, would be too risky. Better to take care of Eugenev himself.

Volkov opened his eyes. He made a slit in the box's lining and then tore it off. He reached in and felt for the slightly raised circle of wood that, when rotated, would release the catch on the false bottom.

He found it.

He opened it.

The box was empty.

The basement seemed to spin in a gyre, the empty box a yawning vacuum at its center. Volkov stood up, dizzy with disappointment. The box fell off his lap onto the basement floor.

"Where's the canister?" he demanded, rage rising in his throat.

Agron turned to Goldman. "Sam?"

"I don't know what you're talking about, either of you," said Goldman, terrified. "When Terry brought it in, I relined the box. It was empty. Lots of these old coin boxes have false bottoms for jewels, money, you know. So I looked for a catch. I found it. But there was nothing there, I swear. Nothing. *Gornit. Gornit mit a nit.*"

"Why didn't you say so before?" Agron asked.

"I did," said Goldman. "Didn't I? Anyway, you did. You told him it was empty. It was empty. I knew it was empty. When Terry brought it in, I—it was burned. She was using it for an ashtray, for chrissakes. But it was empty. What can I say?"

"I believe him," Agron said. "Don't worry, Sam. You're getting all upset. We believe you. So," he said, turning to Volkov, "what kind of game is this?"

"If you vouch for this one," said Volkov, indicating Goldman—and, he added to himself silently, if the Jewish *batyushka* hasn't stolen it himself—"there are only two possibilities: the one with the cowboy hat, or Aleksandr Eugenev."

"The Cowboy is easy," Agron said, "although I can't imagine him holding out on me. So. Sam. You have a phone down here?"

Goldman nodded and pointed Agron to a wall phone by the stairs. Agron dialed a number.

"The Cowboy," Agron said. Then, after a moment, "Hedgehogs, that's what you are . . . Yes? . . . So? . . . You do that. Quickly." Agron hung up and turned around.

"He's gone," he said. "But we'll find him soon. Where can

he go? He's crazy, you know. And now he's out of his mind
with grief for that, I don't know, what would you call it, Sam?"

"I don't know, Ebzi," said Goldman.

"Exactly. So. Dmitri. Get the box," Agron said.

"Wait," said Volkov. "The box is mine."

"I don't think so," Agron said slowly. "I have a receipt
from Sam here. I also have Dmitri. Do you still want to buy it
from me? Make me an offer."

"Listen," said Volkov. "We could still make some money."

"I am listening," Agron said.

"Do you want me to go?" asked Sam Goldman. "I don't
want to be in the way."

"No, Sam," Agron said. "Don't worry. Go on," he said to
Volkov.

"My buyer, he doesn't have to know. Say we can't find Eugenev. Or, say we do, and for some reason we can't recover the
uranium. We can still auction the box as was originally
planned. You have a receipt from Goldman, correct?"

Agron nodded.

"That makes you the legal owner. You have clear title.
That makes my buyer happy. I'm happy because all I was ever
supposed to do was facilitate the transfer of the box. Well,
that's what I'm doing. And best of all, it's all legit. It will be a
cash transaction. You contact Sotheby's. They know the piece
from last time. There's still time to get an insert put in the auction catalog."

"Your buyer will be unhappy when he opens the box."

"That's my concern," said Volkov.

"What about Eugenev? The police want him," Agron
said.

"We need to get to him before the police do," said Volkov.

"Yes," Agron said. "I think we should get busy."

"I agree," said Volkov. He stepped toward Sam Goldman,
smiling. He drew his gun from his pocket, and before Gold-

man could register the enormity of the disaster about to befall him, Volkov fired.

A small hole—like a large beauty mark or mole—suddenly appeared an inch above Goldman's left eyebrow. The back of his head exploded as the bullet exited. Goldman flew backward, twisting to the left, his body describing a flat sort of arc in the air, like a man executing a difficult, demanding dive off a high board. He was dead before he hit the floor, his face relaxing into a mask of abstracted concentration.

Ebzi Agron held up a restraining hand to Duyadev, who had drawn his own gun, and then the *batyushka* walked over to Sam Goldman's body. He stood next to Volkov, staring down at the corpse.

"I understand," Agron said quietly, "but that doesn't mean I approve. This was something that should have been discussed between us two. If we are to be partners, there has to be a certain give and take. Here, there may have been options, other courses of action. I don't like this kind of violence in my neighborhood. It's not good for business."

"I'm sure you can handle it," said Volkov. "Anyway, the police are looking for Aleksandr Eugenev. This looks like his work to me."

"Maybe." Agron paused. "Sam," the *batyushka* said. "He was a pretty good guy."

Volkov shrugged. "I didn't really know him," he said.

28.

Monday, December 27

MITCH ROSE LEANED AGAINST THE DOOR TO HIS OFFICE, SURVEYing his quiet newsroom. It was getting on his nerves.

A newsroom wasn't supposed to be this quiet. A newsroom was supposed to be noisy. You were supposed to hear typewriters clacking, wire machines clicking, phones ringing. Reporters and editors were supposed to be talking, arguing, spitting in each other's faces.

How the hell else would you know you were working at a newspaper?

This might as well be an insurance office, he thought. Or a bank.

The typewriters were gone, the wire machines were gone, and no one talked anymore.

People sat mesmerized, narcotized, at their computer terminals and sent each other messages.

No wonder his reporters never seemed to ask enough questions, never seemed to talk to enough people.

They were out of practice. They'd forgotten how to talk.

And no wonder they never wanted to leave the office. No wonder you had to force them out.

They were computer nerds. They were afraid of people. Reporters who were afraid of people, he thought, shaking his head.

And no one argued anymore. No one shouted and no one screamed. It just wasn't done. If you shouted at a reporter, they'd grieve it to the union. If you shouted at a female reporter, you'd be hit with a harassment suit.

And no one kept booze in the bottom drawer of their desks.

Hell, no one had desks with drawers. They had workstations. They had their phone numbers in their computers, their notes in their computers, they had their brains in their computers.

Where was Bill Katz? Rose wondered. Bill remembered. Bill had a bottle of brandy—for emergencies—in his desk. Bill was old enough to remember.

Rose was feeling old today.

Who were these people? he thought, seeing his reporters peering at their screens, whispering into their telephones.

Kids. Earnest kids. College educated, sober, and boring.

For chrissakes, no one even smoked. Who ever heard of a reporter without a butt in his mouth or an editor without a cigar? Every editor Rose had ever worked for had smoked a cigar. Big, fat, smelly ones. The bigger the cigar, the more powerful the editor.

Where are my cigars? Rose asked himself. Where are my reporters, my editors? Where's my goddamn newspaper?

I'm getting ready to give it up, Rose thought. Getting ready to retire. Getting ready to take the big nap on the dirt farm.

I'm sixty-two. I can still get it up, but who cares? I'm sixty-two. Fuck.

Now the fotogs, thought Rose as he saw a tall blond man in sunglasses, jeans, and an olive drab fatigue jacket with a camera slung around his neck make his way through the newsroom, the fotogs haven't changed. They still dress like bums; they still have their cameras hanging around their necks. They still go out on the street to get the story.

But who is that guy? Rose wondered as he saw the photographer stop in front of Madeline Malloy's desk. He saw Malloy stand up and back away.

"Hey!" called Mitch Rose, trotting toward Malloy. "What's going on?"

Men and women looked up from the computer screens. Madeline Malloy turned to her editor, her face pale.

"It's all right," she said. "This is Sasha. Sasha's my unlucky charm, Mitch. The one who called you. Sorry I can't make a proper introduction. I'm not sure I know his last name. He told me it was Voynitsky, but apparently, for a Russian, that's like saying your name is Hamlet. Your name isn't Voynitsky, is it, Uncle Vanya?"

"No," Sasha said sheepishly. "I'm sorry."

"I thought you trusted me," said Malloy. "My mistake. Your mistake."

"Did you let him up?" Rose asked.

"No," said Malloy. "Sasha likes surprises. He's a drop-in kind of guy, not big on social niceties."

"How did you get into my newsroom? Who let you up?" Rose asked Sasha.

Bill Katz appeared at Madeline Malloy's side. He put his arm around her shoulders protectively. "What's the matter?" he asked gruffly. "What's going on, Mitch?"

"We have an uninvited guest," said Rose. "I'm not sure whether he's welcome or not. So, you didn't answer me, Sasha Whatever-your-name-is. How did you get up here?"

Sasha shrugged. The Professor had picked up some old

clothes for him in an Army-Navy store, and he had borrowed
Ariel Abramovitz's Canon camera. Then, arriving at the paper,
he had nodded to the security guard as if they were old friends
too busy to exchange greetings, and the guard had nodded
back. It had been that simple.

"It was easy," Sasha said.

"I thought you were going to call me back," said Rose.

"It was not convenient," Sasha said. "Do you have a place
where Madeline Malloy and I can talk?"

Rose looked to Malloy. She nodded.

"You can use my office," said Rose.

"You be nice now," Katz said to Sasha.

When Rose had left them alone in his office, Sasha allowed himself a moment to inspect Madeline Malloy. She was
sitting on the edge of the editor's big desk, her shoulders
hunched, her head hanging, her legs crossed at the ankles, her
hands clasped in her lap. She seemed intent upon not looking
at him, staring instead at the featureless, gray carpeted floor.
She was wearing baggy brown corduroy pants with an oversize,
bright red chenille turtleneck sweater, the sleeves pushed up to
her elbows. She wore no rings, no bracelets. Her skin, always
pale, was fish white. She wasn't wearing makeup. Perhaps,
Sasha thought, she had lost some weight, weight she could ill
afford to lose. Still, she looked beautiful. But despite the cheery
color of her sweater, she seemed, he thought, terrifically tired
and terribly sad. More than sad. Despairing. He felt an urge to
comfort her, to stroke her black hair, her thin arms, and tell her
everything was all right. But there was no invitation in her
body, no hint of welcome. He sensed a closing off of what had
once been open to him. So he stood where he was, in the middle of Rose's office, shifting his weight like a schoolboy, and
did not move.

"I am sorry, Maddy," he began, clearing his throat. It
seemed to him that he was always apologizing to women. For

a moment his stomach felt empty, and the sound of Alyona Romanova's body falling to the snow in Henry's driveway filled his ears.

I still haven't mourned her, he thought. My wife. There hasn't been time.

"Do you want to tell me about it?" Sasha asked, shaking off the memory. "I know those two, the Cowboy and his girlfriend who is not a girl. You know she's dead. Murdered. You know the police think I did it."

"Then you're Aleksandr Volkavitch Eugenev. Peter Grushenko called me to tell me she, he, was dead. It was nice of him, really. He told me that's who you were. He told me he had a warrant for your arrest."

"That's not my name," said Sasha.

"Did you kill her? Did you?" Malloy asked, looking up.

"No."

"Really? Why should I believe you? Why shouldn't I call the cops right now? Every minute I spend talking to you makes me an accomplice. So maybe you didn't murder that transsexual, but you did something. Jesus. You know what I'm doing now? Do you?"

Sasha shook his head.

"I'm harboring a fugitive. That's what we call it. Harboring a fugitive."

"No, you're not," said Sasha. "The warrant is not for me. It is not in my name."

"It is for you. They just might not have the name right. So? So tell me. Why shouldn't I call the police?"

"I can't give you a good reason, Maddy Malloy. I know there is no reason for you to trust me. I am sorry for that."

"And that's all you're sorry for?" Malloy asked.

"No. I am sorry for what happened to you," said Sasha. "It must have been terrible."

Malloy started to say something and then swallowed and resumed staring at the floor.

"I am sorry for having involved you," Sasha continued. "Maybe, most of all, I am sorry for not being completely honest with you."

"What's your name, Sasha?"

"I could tell you," Sasha said. "And if you want me to, I will. But perhaps it would be better for you if I did not."

"You mean better for you," said Malloy. "Jesus Christ, Sasha," she said, her voice rising, her blue eyes wide, bright, and fierce. "Can't you be straight with me for one blessed second? I've protected you. I hid your goddamn box. I've kept you out of my stories. I've lied to my editor; I've lied to the police; I've lied to the goddamn CIA. I've lied in my stories. And you know what? I don't know why. I really don't know. I've thought about it and thought about it. Could it just be because I let you sleep with me? Because I couldn't imagine that anyone I slept with could be such a complete loss? Could I be such a hopeless girl? Is that it? Do you know, Sasha? Can you tell me? Can you tell me why I've let my life turn to shit? Can you tell me why I'm probably going to end up in jail because of you?"

Malloy was shouting.

"I don't know, Maddy Malloy," said Sasha, checking the door to see if anyone was going to come bursting in.

"I'm not going to cry," Malloy said quietly, more to herself than to Sasha. "You don't cry in the editor's office. You don't cry at the newspaper."

Sasha took off his glasses and rubbed them against his fatigue jacket. I don't have enough words to apologize to this woman, he thought. Not in English. Not in Russian. All I can do is try to save my life, and maybe hers.

"What did you mean, Maddy, you lied to the CIA?" he asked.

"I can't believe you," said Malloy.

"I understand."

"No," Malloy said. "You don't. You stand there and ask me questions? How can you ask me questions when you don't answer mine?"

"What do you want to know, Maddy?"

"What's your name?"

"I'll tell you, Maddy. Just answer me one question. What do you mean you lied to the CIA? Believe me. This is important."

Malloy turned and walked around Rose's desk. She sat on his chair and put her feet up on his desk.

"I'm doing it again," Malloy said. "I'm putting up with your bullshit. All right. Apparently, I can't help myself. All right. A man my editor knows, Peter Feld. According to my editor, he's CIA. He never said so, but I think he is, too. He was very interested in your precious coin box. I was going to give it to him when . . ." Malloy shuddered.

"Anyway," she continued, "after it was gone, after they took it, he wanted to know who gave it to me. So did Peter Grushenko, for that matter. You know him?"

Sasha nodded.

"Of course you do. So, long story short, I didn't tell them. And I don't know why. He's actually very nice. Feld. Even after I didn't tell him what he wanted to know, he gave me a bodyguard."

"A bodyguard?"

"You know something, Sasha? Everyone is very nice. Feld. The bodyguard. Even Peter Grushenko, who hates me. Everyone is nice except you, Sasha. You're a bastard. It's that simple."

"Where is this bodyguard?"

"Oh, he's around. And you know something funny? He looks like you. He even has your name."

"Sasha?"

"Yes."

"Everyone is named Sasha."

"So I noticed."

"What's his last name?"

"Velikhov. He told me things about you."

"What did he tell you, Maddy?" asked Sasha, guessing that he knew.

"Well, he told me you were KGB. But the most important thing is, he told me your name."

Sasha nodded. Old habits die hard, he thought. "So? What did he say it was?" he asked.

"No way. I want to see if you can keep up your streak of never telling me the truth. I want to see if you're going to lie to me again."

"You shouldn't trust these people," Sasha said.

"That's really funny coming from you."

"I want you to do something for me, Maddy Malloy."

"Oh, no. I'm finished doing things for you."

"This you will like. I want you to write a story in your newspaper." Sasha paused. The news that Sam Goldman had been killed, coupled with the rumor that the Professor had picked up that Ebzi Agron was searching for the Cowboy, gave Sasha hope that either the box or the uranium was still missing. If it was, he might be able to bring Volkov, or Velikhov, or whatever he was calling himself, to Shubentsov at the auction, at Sotheby's. The trick would be convincing Shubentsov that Volkov was the thief Eugenev. If he could do that, he might just be able to walk away alive. If not, Shubentsov would certainly eliminate him, as he had promised to over the phone when Sasha had reached him at the Airport Hilton.

The trick, thought Sasha, would be to create enough uncertainty, enough confusion.

"I have the box," said Sasha.

"Then give it to me," said Malloy. "I'll write the story, turn you in to the police, and you'll have done me the only favor you can. You can keep me from going to jail."

"You're not going to go to jail, Madeline Malloy. Believe me, I've done nothing. Nothing wrong. Not this time. But listen. I want you to write that the box everyone is looking for will be with the stuff that will be auctioned at Sotheby's on Thursday. And I want you to tell that CIA man personally that I will be there."

"I can't do that," Malloy said. "How can I write something you tell me? I can't believe anything you say. How do I even know you have the box?"

Sasha reached into his pocket and took out the coins he had taken from Zagorsk. He put them on Rose's desk.

Malloy put her feet down and reached across the desk. She picked up the coins, looked at them, and handed them back to Sasha.

"All right," she said. "So maybe you have the box. Now, what about your name?"

"One final thing, Maddy Malloy," said Sasha. "Do not please go to that auction. All right?"

"Your name?"

Sasha reached into his wallet and took out the KGB identity card Ariel Abramovitz had downloaded and the Professor had forged.

"That's my name," said Sasha. "Aleksandr Volkov."

"Well, hooray. The streak is broken. So, Mr. Volkov," Malloy said, "where do we go from here?"

"Give this to your CIA friend, Mr. Feld," said Sasha, handing her a piece of paper. "I believe we have much to say to each other. And you can also give it to your bodyguard, Velikhov. I believe he will also wish to speak with me."

"What is it?"

"It's an E-mail address. Tell them the bidding is about to begin."

29.

When the buzzer went off, Ivan Siskin was drinking a beer in his living room, watching the Giants driving for a covering touchdown—or at least a field goal—in the final minutes of a Monday night game against the Philadelphia Eagles.

Then Phil Simms, the Giants quarterback, threw an interception.

"Goddammit!" shouted Siskin, who had a nickel—five hundred dollars—on the Giants, giving three and a half points. The Giants were ahead 17–14, meaning that Siskin was losing by half a point.

The buzzer sounded again.

"It's fixed. I know it's fixed," said Siskin, shouting at the television. "The bookies fix it every time. Why the fuck were you throwing?" he yelled at Simms, who was trotting off the field with his head down.

The buzzing continued.

"For chrissakes, Marta," said Siskin. "Answer the fucking door."

"Your wheelchair broken?" Marta called from the kitchen.

"Shit," muttered Siskin, getting up from the couch and pushing the intercom.

"Who is it?" he asked in Russian.

"It's me," David Gatlober said.

"Shit," said Siskin after he pushed the button to let the Cowboy in.

"Who is it?" Marta asked, coming into the living room.

"Gatlober," said Siskin.

Marta made a face. "I don't want him in here," she said. "I don't want him in my home. He'll bring the police."

"He won't stay long," said Siskin. "Now shut up."

"Don't tell me to shut up."

"Go away, Marta. Please?"

Marta left the room. Gatlober knocked on the door. Siskin opened it.

"Hello, David," Siskin said softly.

The Cowboy stood motionless in Siskin's doorway.

"You want to come in, David?" asked Siskin. "Have a beer?"

The Cowboy shook his head. He looked terrible, Siskin thought. His eyes were red and bleary, his skin was blotchy, his hair, sticking out from under his black cowboy hat, was stringy and oily and wet. His green down parka was also wet, as well as stained and torn. One sleeve was patched carelessly with silver duct tape. He stank like a wino.

"Is it snowing?" Siskin asked.

The Cowboy nodded.

"I'm sorry about Terry," Siskin said. "Terrible thing."

"Where is he?" asked the Cowboy, blinking, his voice clotted.

"I don't know," Siskin said.

The Cowboy whirled and punched the door frame.

"I swear I don't know," Siskin said quickly, backing away. "Really. I swear. I haven't got any fucking idea."

"I'm going to cut his balls off," the Cowboy said.

"You can't even be sure it was Sasha," said Siskin. "I mean, just because the cops say so? Since when do the cops know what they're talking about? You think he killed Sam Goldman, too? I hear the cops are also blaming him for Goldman."

"I don't care about Goldman."

"Well, think about it, David. Something's going on. Something big. Too big for Sasha."

"Don't bullshit me, Vanya," the Cowboy said. "You just tell me where he is. I don't want to hurt you."

"I know, David. I know. I believe you. Look. I've got an idea. Let's go down to the Arbat. I'll buy you a drink, something to eat. On me. We'll talk this out. What a good idea, yes? Let me get my coat."

"Is he at the Professor's?"

"I don't know. I swear. I haven't heard a thing. I didn't even know he was back in Brooklyn until I heard about, you know, what happened to Terry."

The Cowboy looked up into Siskin's face. "I'm going to find him," he said. "And if I find out you lied to me, after him, I'm coming back to do you. You understand me, man? I just don't give a shit anymore."

"Come on, David. Think. You know Sasha. Sasha couldn't kill anyone. Anyway, we're friends."

"Sure," the Cowboy said. "Friends. I know what you called me behind my back. I know. You, Sasha, everybody. But you don't know, you know? You don't know anything."

"All I know is we're friends. Come on. Let's go."

The Cowboy seemed to tremble, and then he took a quick step toward Siskin. Siskin's knees buckled instantly. He cringed, shutting his eyes. He lifted his right arm to ward off a blow; he cupped his testicles with his left hand.

"I hate all of you fuckers," he heard the Cowboy say. He

opened his eyes. The Cowboy was walking back down the dark hallway. Siskin closed the door and bolted it. He felt sick, his head pounding with sudden adrenaline. Marta came out of the kitchen.

"Is he gone?" she asked.

Ivan Siskin collapsed on the couch.

He looked away from Marta to the television. The Eagles had the ball. The clock was ticking down. The Giants weren't going to cover. He was going to lose five hundred bucks.

It seemed the least of his problems.

◈   ◈   ◈

The elevator door closed. The Cowboy leaned back and slid down the elevator wall into a crouch. He moaned. He put his palms on the floor and rocked on the balls of his feet. His throat ached. He balled his hands into tight fists and pounded his knees. Tears came to his eyes. He wanted to scream. He wanted to scream and never stop.

I can't stand this, he thought. The vodka doesn't help. Nothing helps. It's too much.

All he knew was that he had to find Sasha. Ebzi Agron had promised to deliver Sasha to him, but he couldn't wait anymore. That was why he had slipped out of the Coney Island apartment. He couldn't wait. His pain, he knew, his awful, demanding pain, the pain the vodka and the drugs couldn't touch, would not go away until he could make Sasha feel it. Here, he wanted to say to him, here's how I feel. Feel my pain, Aleksandr Eugenev. Feel it on your flesh. Feel it in your balls. Maybe he would carve Terry's name into Sasha's chest. Maybe he would open his fucking chest and carve it into his heart, his living heart. That would be fitting, he thought. That would be revenge.

Oh, if only he had shot him that day on the beach. If only

he had blown his brains out. If only there had been three corpses instead of two. Then Terry would be alive now. Then Terry would be by his side.

The Cowboy's body shook. He wanted Sasha. He needed Sasha.

The elevator doors opened onto the dim lobby. A tall man in a dark overcoat was standing near the entrance to the lobby.

Could it be one of Ebzi Agron's men, come to collect me? the Cowboy wondered.

The hell with Agron, thought the Cowboy.

The man moved toward the Cowboy.

It was Sasha.

Good, the Cowboy thought, quickly looking around the empty lobby. I'll do it right here.

He reached for the knife in his pocket, a gravity knife like the one he had given Terry. He slipped it out and held it against his thigh, cupping it with his right hand.

"Hello, you prick," the Cowboy said.

"You don't want to do that," said the man. "Put the knife away."

"Sasha?" the Cowboy asked, confused.

The man came closer.

"Not the one you want," Aleksandr Volkov said.

"I remember you," said the Cowboy. "You're the KGB guy."

"I'm sorry about what happened to your girlfriend," Volkov said. "She was very beautiful."

The Cowboy felt his throat constrict. Again, tears came to his eyes.

Volkov reached out and carefully placed his hand lightly on the Cowboy's shoulder. This is right, he thought. This is what the little pervert needs. He needs to be grounded. He felt the Cowboy tremble. Suddenly the Cowboy wrapped his arms around him, his cheek pressed against Volkov's chest. The Cowboy's hat fell to the floor.

"There, there," said Volkov, pleased, as the Cowboy wept. He patted the Cowboy's greasy head. "There, there," he said. He looked over the Cowboy's shoulder, wrinkling his nose against the smell. Christ, he stank. An image came to him. Terry's long white legs kicking like a frog's as the piano wire bit into her throat. He smiled. It had been sweet. It had almost made up for her not having the box.

After a moment, the Cowboy stepped back and picked up his hat.

"I want Aleksandr Eugenev," the Cowboy said.

"I want to help you," said Volkov. "He's a fucker and he deserves to die. But I need to ask you something."

"What?"

"The coin box you took from that reporter. Did you take something from it?"

The Cowboy rubbed his eyes. "I don't remember," he said.

"Listen to me, David Gatlober. We're on the same side. I want to help you. You understand? Now tell me the truth."

"You mean the coins?" the Cowboy asked, blowing his nose on his sleeve. "The coins in the box? Ebzi Agron's got them. He gave me a grand for them."

"I don't care about the coins," said Volkov. "You can keep the money. I want to know if anything else was inside the box, under the lining."

"What do you mean?"

Look at him, Volkov thought. Look at the snot on his sleeve. Look at those weak red eyes, that hooked nose, that sallow skin. How pathetic, he thought. I should put this little Yid out of his misery right now.

"There was nothing else in the box?" Volkov asked, casually slipping his hand into his coat pocket, feeling for his gun.

"I don't know what you're talking about," said the Cowboy. "I don't know where the box is. I mean, I left it, I left it with Terry, in the apartment."

"All right," Volkov said.

"Don't the police have it?"

"No," said Volkov. "The police do not have it."

"Then maybe it's still at the apartment."

"It's not."

"Then that fucker must have taken it."

"He must have. So. You want Eugenev?" Volkov asked, taking his hand out of his pocket. It would be amusing, he thought, to see what this lovesick little maniac would do to Sasha Eugenev. It would be fun to arrange it. It would be fun to watch.

The Cowboy nodded.

"All right," Volkov said. "Where should we start?"

"The Professor's," said the Cowboy.

"The Professor?"

"A friend of Eugenev's. An old man. We call him the Professor because he's so stupid."

"And where is this Professor?" Volkov asked.

"On Coney Island Avenue." He gave Volkov the address.

"Let's go," said Volkov.

They got into Volkov's red Saab, parked on Fifth Street. He pulled onto Brighton Beach Avenue.

Underneath the El, the traffic crawled as heavily laden, bundled-up postholiday shoppers dashed back and forth from one side of the narrow avenue to the other, splashing in the instant slush, their labored breath steaming. It had begun to snow heavily—wet, fat flakes, lit up by the streetlights, swirling down from the tracks above; wind blowing newspapers and paper bags and candy wrappers along the sidewalk, street, and gutter. Petulant horns blew. People in fur coats, *shopkas,* gloves, and boots pushed and shoved and cursed floridly in the dying holiday spirit.

The Saab inched along. The radio was playing a song, something about a boy with a drum. Then two men coming from the passenger side stepped in front of Volkov's car. One held up his hand for Volkov to stop. He was smiling, shrugging his shoulders, mouthing apologies. Volkov put in the clutch and slipped the car into neutral. He rolled down his window and reached into his pocket for a Marlboro. He pushed in the cigarette lighter on the dashboard. Maybe the smoke and the cold air, he thought, would disguise Gatlober's smell.

"You want one?" Volkov said, offering the pack to the Cowboy.

The Cowboy shook his head no.

The other man began waving an unmarked white delivery van into an empty parking space by the curb in front of the Saab.

The van pulled in front of Volkov's car. Then it stopped.

The smiling man put his hand down and stopped smiling.

The Cowboy said something. Volkov saw the two men split, one going left, the other right.

Volkov popped the lock on his door as the van's back flew open. Three men jumped out and started running toward him. He saw them lift their guns. He threw his left shoulder hard against his door, simultaneously pulling the handle toward him with his right hand. As he tumbled into the street, he heard several shotgun blasts, followed by breaking glass, followed by screams.

Volkov rolled underneath a car parked by the curb. Lying on his back, feeling the wet seeping into his pants, his head turned to the side, he heard more horns, people shouting. He saw feet running on the slush-covered sidewalk. He got out his gun and held it against his chest. The unlit cigarette was still in his mouth. He spat it out. He counted to ten, then rolled out from underneath the car. He crouched behind it and looked both ways, up and down the sidewalk. People were lying on the ground, sitting on the sidewalk. He got to his feet and threw himself over the car's hood, his gun extended in front of him.

He saw the van's door closing and the van swinging into traffic, making a U-turn, smoke pouring from its exhaust, smashing the rear bumper of the car in front of it. He saw his shiny red Saab, its doors open, its windshield blown out. He heard sirens.

He cursed. He had expected Gatlober to be on the front seat, dead, and that would have been disappointing.

But the Cowboy was gone.

And that was worse.

◈   ◈   ◈

The van headed back down Brighton Beach Avenue, turning on Ocean. It went up Ocean Avenue, turned off on Avenue J, and pulled into an alley driveway behind a small grocery store in this predominantly Hasidic section of Brooklyn.

The Cowboy was hustled blindfolded out of the back of the van and down into the store's basement. A man with a jagged white scar on his jaw was waiting for him.

"You know me?" he asked the Cowboy.

"You're Boris Zilberstein," the Cowboy said.

"Good," said Zilberstein, pleased. "Any trouble?" he asked one of his soldiers.

"No. We had to take him away from a guy, though."

"Who?" asked Zilberstein.

"I don't know," a man said.

"I think it was a guy I've seen around. A thief named Sasha Eugenev," said another. "Looked like him, anyway."

"One of Agron's?" Zilberstein asked.

"Probably."

"Well, if Agron's chasing this guy, having him picked up, that means he doesn't have it," said Zilberstein.

He turned to the Cowboy. "You know me," he said. "You know I don't fuck around. So I'm not going to fuck around. Where's the coin box?"

The Cowboy thought for a moment. "Eugenev has it," he said.

The Cowboy spat. "Goddamn Sasha Eugenev," he said.

Ariel Abramovitz ran into the living room, where Sasha was drinking tea and watching the news with the boy's parents.

"Look at that," said Myron Abramovitz as a reporter holding a microphone stood in front of a red Saab with its windows blown out, its roof collecting snow. "Shooting in the street. Madness. Right outside our door. We're going to move, Ivana. It's not safe here anymore."

"Don't run," Ivana Abramovitz said to Ariel. "You're all the time running. You'll make yourself an injury."

"There's a message for you, Sasha," said Ari. "I was talking and this guy just broke in. Real rude."

Sasha followed Ari to his bedroom and sat at the computer. The top of Ari's screen displayed a conversation concerning a girl in Ari's school named Natalie. The question seemed to be, did she have breasts or was she wearing falsies?

Sasha looked at Ari.

Ari shrugged.

Halfway down the screen, set off by two backward slashes, was a message: /YOU DON'T HAVE SHIT, EUGENEV/ The sender was identified as 2662,1226@compuserve.com.

"Is this person still on-line?" Sasha asked.

"Can't tell," said Ari.

"How do I answer?"

"Backward slash, send, my user name, ariel@delphi.com, then enter."

/CHECK OUT TOMORROW'S PAPER AND MEET ME AT SOTHEBY'S, FUCKER/ Sasha typed.

He stared at the screen. Five minutes passed. There was no answer.

"What if he's not on-line?" Sasha asked.

"Then he won't get it," said Ariel. "Better send him an E-mail message, too."

Sasha did. Now, he thought, we'll see.

"Hey, Ari," Sasha said. "Are you finished talking about Natalie's breasts? I'd like to look up a friend. Okay?"

"Okay," said Ari.

Sasha logged on to the Internet, then the USENET, and called up the alt.sex sig for the Amazon Women Forum.

/HELLO, LOLA/ he typed. /MISSED ME?/

Just then another message flashed on the screen.

/THIS IS PETER FELD. WHO THE HELL ARE YOU?/

30.

Tuesday, December 28

MADELINE MALLOY'S ARTICLE RAN ON AN INSIDE PAGE IN THE
paper's "Arts and Entertainment" section. It wasn't a big story.
After the sale of memorabilia from the Soviet space program—
a chess set that had been aboard *Soyuz* 3, Yuri Gagarin's watch,
autographed photographs of the cosmonauts, space suits, moon
rocks, survival kits (including knives and fishing tackle in case
the cosmonauts set down in "unprecalculated areas"), and, of
course, the inevitable *matryoshkas,* these from aboard *Salyut* 7—
a collection of Russian treasures and folk crafts were to be auctioned Thursday, December 30, at Sotheby's, on York Avenue
and Seventy-second Street. Among the icons and paintings, she
wrote, would be a lovely example of the Russian art of decorated, lacquered boxes.

The space auction was to be held at ten o'clock in the
morning, the treasures at two-fifteen.

The story ran with Malloy's photograph of the box Boris
the Kike had brought to America on a shockingly warm Indian
summer day in September.

And for such a small story, it was read with a great deal of interest in a number of quarters.

◈   ◈   ◈

Major Anatoly Ilyich Shubentsov tossed the newspaper onto the bed and lit a cigarette. He had been waiting for a signal ever since Friday, when Aleksandr Volkov had reached him at the Airport Hilton to tell him that Sasha Eugenev had the box and would be bringing it to Sotheby's to hand it off to his CIA handlers. Volkov told Shubentsov that he would meet him there to help the major recover the box.

Shubentsov had been relieved to get the call. If nothing else, it meant that he would be able to go home soon.

He hated America.

From the moment his plane had landed in New York, Shubentsov had felt surrounded by enemies. The people in the terminal. The customs officer. The desk clerk who had checked him in at the Airport Hilton. The Arab cabdriver who had charged thirty-five dollars to take him into Manhattan when Shubentsov visited the Russian embassy and who, after ripping him off, still expected a tip.

Any one of them, or all of them, Shubentsov thought, could have been CIA. How would he know? How could he tell who was carrying a concealed gun, a knife? Most Americans, he knew, were armed. Most Americans, he knew, were criminals and drug addicts.

And then there were the blacks. They were everywhere. As were the Latins, the Chinese, and the Jews. He had not fully realized, not until he had seen it with his own eyes, that America was such a mongrel nation.

How did we lose to these people?

We never got a chance to fight, that's why, thought

Shubentsov. We lost to an enemy we could never get in our sights.

Shubentsov put out his cigarette and picked up the newspaper. He turned again to the article, the bile rising in his throat. What the story didn't say, Shubentsov thought, was that the surviving cosmonauts, those former heroes of the former Soviet Union, were being forced to sell their engraved watches, their precious photographs, their clothes, and their memories to the capitalists at Sotheby's because they were starving. The space program was no more. There were no jobs, no money. Engineers and scientists, like soldiers, were not needed in Boris Yeltsin's new Russia, a Russia in thrall to the Western powers. The political triumph of the Americans and the Jews, the betrayals of Gorbachev and his fellow conspirators, had transformed the greatest achievement of Soviet science into a pile of trash and its heroes into beggars.

The great Gagarin's watch! No doubt being sold by his widow, Valentina, to buy food. As a young soldier, barely nineteen, Shubentsov had been stationed at Star City, the famous cosmonaut training center hidden in the birch woods northeast of Moscow. He had been there on that awful day in 1968 when Gagarin went down in his jet. He remembered how, one by one, he and his comrades had filed, weeping, into Gagarin's office. He remembered the clock on the cosmonaut's desk that had mysteriously stopped at the exact moment of the crash. He remembered the opening words of the telegram from Chairman Nikita Sergeevich Khrushchev framed on Gagarin's office wall: "Your glorious deed will be remembered through the ages as an example of courage, bravery, and heroism for the sake of mankind."

From Murmansk to Petropavlovsk, the whole country had mourned the eagle of *Vostok 1*, the first man in space, Yuri Alekseyevich Gagarin. And now his watch, depicting his capsule orbiting the earth every sixty seconds and presented, if

Shubentsov's memory served, to Gagarin by the workers of the First Moscow Watch Factory, would soon be in the hands of some greasy Yid, who would, no doubt, sell it to another, and another, just as the honor of the whole Soviet peoples had been bought and sold by traitors and Jews.

Shubentsov moved the gun he had picked up at the embassy off the street map of New York City he had purchased after that taxi ride and began studying it.

If he was going to Sotheby's on Thursday, he was not, he thought, going to be cheated again.

◈   ◈   ◈

Aleksandr Volkov finished his Stoly rocks and eyed the blonde sitting at the bar in The Auction House on East Eighty-ninth Street. Fine features, fair skin, long legs, a boyish figure. His type. His meat. And she seemed to be alone.

Christ, he needed some distraction.

After losing the Cowboy, after having his car shot up, he had called Madeline Malloy, who had told him about Aleksandr Eugenev's visit and had given him an E-mail address.

Was Eugenev bluffing?

Did he really have the uranium?

Well, if he didn't, who did?

Was he trying to sell it to Peter Feld?

Damn Feld, he thought. Feld was not returning his calls. Feld seemed to have disappeared.

Had he made a deal with Eugenev already?

Would they both be at Sotheby's?

The blonde was looking his way. She smiled. He smiled back. He checked his watch. Six o'clock. Quitting time.

Volkov folded the newspaper with Malloy's article under his arm and walked past the blonde to the pay phone next to the rest rooms.

He called Madeline Malloy.

"Madeline," he said when she picked up, "this is Aleksandr Velikhov."

"Did you reach him?" Malloy asked.

"You mean Volkov? I used that address he gave you. I received no answer. He admitted his name was Aleksandr Volkov?"

"Yes."

Volkov shook his head. What could Eugenev be up to?

"Listen, Madeline," he said. "You are planning to go to that auction?"

"Of course."

"Then I will go with you, all right?"

"All right."

"We will meet at the paper? Say, one o'clock?"

"Fine."

"Madeline, have you spoken with Peter Feld?"

"Yes, I have."

"Did you give Volkov's computer address to Peter Feld?"

"Yes, I did."

"That's good," said Volkov.

When he emerged from the phone booth, the blonde at the bar was gone.

It's for the best, Volkov thought. Maybe he needed distraction, but he needed Aleksandr Eugenev more.

He left the bar and hailed a cab.

There was still time, he thought, to find Eugenev before the auction.

"Brighton Beach," he told the driver, and gave him the address the Cowboy have given him: Moses Filonovsky's address. The Professor.

"Come on, honey. It's late. I'm tired," said Rhonda Grosinger. She drew a wet circle on the top of the table with her index finger, then plucked the cherry out of her whiskey sour, placing it lightly between her teeth. Boris Zilberstein was watching the waiters push their mops across Romanov's marble floor while others were putting the chairs up on top of the tables.

The two times I love best, he thought. Opening, when the air is clean and everything sparkles, and closing, when the people are gone and you can sit and listen to the echoes.

Grosinger punched Zilberstein's arm. He looked at her, saw the cherry, and smiled. She sucked the cherry into her mouth and bit into it. A drop of red juice appeared at the corner of her mouth. She licked it off lasciviously.

Zilberstein winced. She was a cute piece of ass, yes, but she had no sophistication, no class.

"Come on, honey," Grosinger said. "Let's go home."

"In a minute, darling," said Zilberstein. "In a minute."

Grosinger pulled a thin brown filtered cigarette out of her purse and lit it. Zilberstein frowned.

"I thought you were going to stop," he said. "I hate seeing you smoke."

She looked away.

The laser beams atop the Kremlin towers switched off; the bronze sconces along the Romanov's walls dimmed. A thin, blue ribbon of smoke spiraled up from Grosinger's cigarette and twisted in the air.

One of Zilberstein's soldiers came over and whispered in his boss's ear. Zilberstein nodded. The soldier waved toward the entrance, and Zilberstein watched as a thin man with curly black hair approached. When he got to the table, Zilberstein turned to Grosinger.

"Why don't you do whatever women do in the toilet, darling," he said. "I have a little business here."

"So what?" said Grosinger. "You're gonna talk Russian. I don't understand Russian, remember?"

"Rhonda. Please."

"I'm getting a headache," Grosinger said, dropping her cigarette in the ashtray, where it smoldered.

"I'm sorry," Zilberstein said, reaching over to stub it out. "I promise. By the time you get back, I'll be ready. This won't take long."

Grosinger stood up, straightened her dress, and went off to the bathroom, her heels clicking on the floor, her calves rounding with each step.

"So?" said Zilberstein, looking up at the thin man.

"Agron wants the Cowboy," the man said. "He's willing to pay."

"If I had him, which I don't, how much would Ebzi pay?"

"Five thousand."

"*Bupkis,*" said Zilberstein. "What's your name?"

"Dmitri Duyadev."

"Chechen?"

The man nodded.

"Well, *bupkis* means beans, Dmitri. That means nothing. That means you can go tell the *batyushka* to go shit. Tell him *gay kocken.* He insults me. Can you remember that?"

The man nodded.

"Good. Tell him. And if you ever want to go to work for an up-and-coming organization, you get in touch with me. I respect Chechens. I value them. Not like Agron. Well, you know what Uzbekis are like."

"The *batyushka* has treated me well," Duyadev said.

"What does he pay you? No, don't tell me. He pays you two hundred, two fifty, a week. Maybe three. No more. In my *organizatskiya,* a man like you, he makes six, seven hundred. I understand generosity. I reward loyalty."

Zilberstein watched the Chechen's face. Perhaps his eyes

had widened slightly. Perhaps not. It was always difficult to read Chechens. But at least this one was still listening.

"Look, my friend," continued Zilberstein, encouraged by the Chechen's silence, "you think about it. Agron's days, well, he's an old man, isn't he? Any day now, he could have a heart attack. Then what will happen to his friends? I'll tell you. They'll come running to me. But I only have so much work. Sure, I'll be able to give some of them jobs here, sweeping floors, cleaning toilets, but others, I'll have to say, Sorry, where were you when I needed you? And then what will happen to them? Where will they go? How will they support their families? Who will protect them?

"You think about it," Zilberstein said, extending his hand. "You can always call me here."

Duyadev took his hand, shook it once, and left.

He'll call, thought Zilberstein. He'll call tomorrow, maybe even tonight. Chechens are all traitors.

He bent over and picked up the damp copy of Tuesday's *News* lying on the floor. He turned again to Madeline Malloy's article and studied the photograph of the box that the Cowboy had already identified for him.

It didn't look like much, he thought, but it seemed to mean a lot to Ebzi Agron. That was enough reason to take it, just as he would, he promised himself, eventually take everything that belonged to the old *batyushka,* including his life.

Grosinger emerged from the bathroom. "Can we go now?" she asked, one small hand on her ample hip.

I can do better, thought Boris Zilberstein, suddenly annoyed by Grosinger's nagging, her smoking, her high, whining voice. I can do much better. This is, after all, America. This is, he thought, standing up and offering his hand to Rhonda Grosinger, a land of opportunity.

31.

Thursday, December 30

SASHA DUCKED INTO THE RIVER EAST GOURMET DELI AND Grocery (Open 24 Hours) on York Avenue and East Seventieth Street. His glasses fogged. Drops of water ran down the lenses. He was cold and wet, and he needed coffee. The coffee, he knew, would be better at Sotheby's, but it was too early to go there. He had forty-five minutes before the auction began, forty-five minutes before he'd find out whether or not Volkov had taken his bait, forty-five minutes to kill before he engaged his fate.

It was snowing outside, heavily now, and the huge city plows ground slowly up York Avenue, three abreast, past New York Hospital, the Hospital for Special Surgery, and the Helmsley Medical Tower, creating slushy mountains and ridges for the doctors, nurses, and patients of hospital row to navigate as best they could.

The River East's coffee was weak and turned a pearly gray when Sasha dribbled a small container of cream into it. He took a sip through the paper cup's plastic top and gagged. He stepped outside and poured the coffee onto the snow, watching the coffee-tinted hot water tunnel through the icy crust that covered the sidewalk.

He checked his watch. A quarter to two. The auction was to begin at two-fifteen.

He walked up York, breathing shallowly, his hands sweating inside his gloves. Through the swirling snow he could make out the American flag, whipped by the wind, flying next to the Union Jack over the glass doors in front of the huge gray concrete bulk of Sotheby's.

Sasha pushed through the doors and stomped his feet to shake off the snow and slush. In a glass case, directly in front of him, a large poster bearing the legend "Russian Space History" in block letters showed a yellow rocket silhouetted against a black sky, smoke and flame pouring out of its tail. A smaller poster, marked "Important Russian Treasures," featured a smiling, red-cheeked *matryoshka*. A sign beneath it read "Auction, Main Sales Room, Thursday, 30 December, 2:15." Sasha took off his gloves, jammed them into his coat pocket, and walked past the guard at the door, past the coatroom to his left, and down the stairs to the snack bar.

Sasha loved Sotheby's. Whenever Henry had given him a painting to sell, Sasha had always arrived early and stayed late, no matter when his particular lot was knocked down. He loved coming in off the noisy avenue and relaxing in the hush provided by the thick gray carpets and sound-absorbing baffles in the selling rooms and galleries. He loved the small green enameled oval pins, bearing the name *Sotheby's* inscribed in gold, worn by the elderly, blue-suited black guards. He loved the warm lighting and the slightly musty smell of old art and old furniture, a smell that bespoke old money, confident money, money that knew all the world's secrets and didn't need to boast about it. And simply by being there, Sasha always felt that he was partaking of those secrets, enabled by some mysterious alchemy to translate the subtle susurrus of money whis-

pering around and through the galleries and selling rooms like
an underground stream.

Most of all, Sasha loved the all-knowing, gentle efficiency
of the place, so unlike his two homes, Russia and Brooklyn. In
neither place would you ever find the trim, attractive, smiling
young women in tailored tweeds who worked behind the coun-
ters, selling catalogs and books, their voices soft and musical,
or the impeccably suited auctioneers with their old school ties
and elegant English accents, or even the gray-haired black
guards whose composed, erect, old-world postures were leav-
ened by a down-home friendliness.

I do well here, thought Sasha. And why not? Buying and
selling. Isn't that what I have always been about, and what I
could not be about in the Soyuz? When that teenage Aleksandr
Volkavitch Eugenev walked up and down the aisles of the
Berlin-Warsaw-Kiev express with a case full of rubles, buying
Japanese watches from the Russian tourists (was that a thousand years ago?), didn't I know my customers? Didn't I know
the market? And later, after Kolpashevo, when I was in
Moscow, changing money at the Intourist Hotel and the
Rossiya, did I cheat anyone? Certainly no more than anyone
else on the black market.

I was a businessman. And this, thought Sasha, his eyes
sweeping Sotheby's lower gallery for anyone who looked as
though he could be Major Anatoly Ilyich Shubentsov, this
place is the temple of business, the very sanctum sanctorum.

At the snack bar, across from the Purchase-Payment desk,
people were waiting in line to buy cappuccino or espresso, Pel-
legrino or Orangina, cucumber-and-tomato sandwiches or fo-
caccia with mozzarella. Sasha bought a paper cup of cappuccino
and again looked around for Shubentsov, whom he hoped to
find before Aleksandr Volkov found him.

Sasha had to urinate. He walked into the toilet. The floor
was muddy from people's boots. Even here, he thought, even in

Sotheby's, the toilet floor, like toilet floors the world over, gets dirty. You may love all this, he told himself, you may love the richness and the comfort, but don't trust it. Don't trust anything or anyone.

For a moment he thought of Boris the Kike, bent over the privy at Kolpashevo, digging in the shit for his meager treasures—a bottle of home-brewed *samogon,* a few coins.

Sasha left the bathroom.

Middle-aged men and women wandered through the galleries. They stopped in front of gilt-framed paintings, chatted about the auction or the state of their health, checked their catalogs for price and provenance, glad to be out of the weather, glad to be warm, dry, and snug in a palace of understated but universally understood privilege.

"Aleksandr Volkov?"

Sasha spun around. A powerfully built man with a gray crew cut stood in front of him, his feet planted, his posture daring anyone to try to move him from his chosen spot.

Sasha nodded.

"Identification," Major Anatoly Shubentsov demanded.

Sasha took out his wallet and showed Shubentsov the same KGB card he had shown Malloy. If Shubentsov had asked, Sasha could have shown him a Moscow driver's license, an old internal passport, and even a New York City driver's license, all in the name of Aleksandr Volkov, all bearing his own face, all courtesy of Ariel Abramovitz and the Professor.

"Is he here?" asked Shubentsov, returning Sasha's card. "Eugenev?"

"I don't think so," said Sasha. "He will be."

"He'd better be," Shubentsov said. He put his hand in his coat pocket, making sure he still had the title to the box and the letter from Viktor Prudnikov naming him as the agent for the sale. Then he felt inside his coat, lightly touching the Walther PPK he had picked up at the embassy. He had not quite believed it when Sasha had told him that there were no metal detectors at the door, that the guards were unarmed, but it had turned out to be true. These Americans, Shubentsov thought, shaking his head. So comfortable in their wealth. So drunk with power. So arrogant.

"Let's go upstairs," said Sasha.

Sasha and Shubentsov joined the small crowd heading up the carpeted stairs to the Main Sales Room off the South Gallery. At the top of the stairs, a huge floral arrangement of French tulips, freesia, cherry blossoms, and spruce sprigs perfumed the air.

"This way," Sasha said, leading Shubentsov to the sales desk, which displayed the various catalogs for that month's auctions. Sasha picked up the catalog titled "Russian Treasures" and opened it. He removed a typed insert marked "Late Additions to Sale" and showed Shubentsov the paragraph, reproduced from the September catalog, describing Lot 3A: "Lacquered Box, by Ivan Golikov, 1886–1937. *From the Monastery at Sergeev Posad, in Zagorsk.* A bear hunt on the sides; pastoral on the top. In black, gold, green, and red. After the 1917 Bolshevik uprising, the production of icons was forbidden, and many artists, especially in the Golden Ring town of Palekh, took to painting lacquered boxes. After varnishing the box, the artists painted their scenes of battles, hunts, and fairy tales and then applied a series of translucent coats of paint over the finished design, thereby creating the brilliant shine that marks the genre. Ivan Golikov, of Palekh, a friend of Maxim Gorky's, was a master of this classic Russian art form. $5,000–7,500."

People carrying their registered, numbered bidding paddles were now filtering into the spacious, high-ceilinged Main Sales Room, sitting on the padded metal folding chairs arranged in rows. At the front of the room, before a low stage, was a hooded wooden lectern bearing Sotheby's seal—a circle containing a simple drawing of the two-story London book-shop owned by Sotheby's founder, Samuel Baker. Beneath the building, the legend read "Founded 1744." Baker had died in 1788, leaving his burgeoning business of auctioning rare books to his nephew, John Sotheby.

Above the lectern, suspended above the stage, was an electronic board that was now keeping time and would later keep track of the bidding while simultaneously converting the dollar bids into their equivalent British pounds, French francs, Swiss francs, German deutsche marks, Italian lire, and Japanese yen. On the stage itself, to the left of the lectern, was a raised, circular platform, curtained off in the rear, where the art was displayed. To the right of the first few rows of chairs, a dozen black telephones sat atop a long table.

Sasha and Shubentsov took up positions at the rear of the room, off to the right, where they could see people entering and where they could see, above them, the windows of the offices that encircled and overlooked the Main Sales Room. A silver-haired man in a maroon corduroy jacket standing to Sasha's left was telling an elderly woman, "I feel fine. I'm going through lots of tests, but I feel fine. The electrical connection between my ear and my brain is going bad, that's all."

Where's Volkov? Sasha thought, scanning the room. What happens if he doesn't show?

The electrical connection between my ear and brain will be disconnected, he answered himself. Permanently.

He glanced at Shubentsov, who was frowning at the auctioneer taking his place behind the lectern, flanked on either side by the two men and two women who would assist him in spotting and recording bids.

Sasha turned back toward the stage. The auctioneer was examining a piece of paper, making marks on it with a pencil. A squat, broad-shouldered man in the third row, directly in front of the lectern, stood up, turned toward Sasha, and waved.

"Who's that?" asked Shubentsov.

"Ebzi Agron," Sasha said. *"Mafiya."*

"He looks like a fucking Tartar," said Shubentsov. "A Kazakh or an Uzbeki. Why is he here?"

"I don't know," Sasha said. Agron. What was Agron's interest in the box? he wondered. Who was the *batyushka* allied with? Peter Feld? Volkov?

Is Agron here instead of Volkov? That, thought Sasha, would be very bad.

Sasha looked up at the office windows above the room. A few faces were appearing at the windows, looking down, waiting for the auction to begin.

He checked his watch. It was two-fifteen. The auctioneer, wearing a gray suit, a blue shirt, a rose tie with a muted pattern, and tortoiseshell glasses, took a sip of water from a paper cup and then rapped on the lectern. The audience quieted.

"Are we ready to compete vigorously?" the auctioneer asked in a mellifluous English accent. He smiled fleetingly. Then, decorously, he cleared his throat.

"I direct your attention to article ten of the Conditions of Sale, which are reproduced in the front of your sales catalogs. You are responsible for state and local taxes. I know, I know. That's the bad news, but, I hope, the only bad news. Bidding is by paddle. Hold them up high, thank you. All right?

"Lot one," the auctioneer announced. The small platform to the auctioneer's left rotated, and from behind the curtain a small icon on an easel came into view. "I have forty-five hundred," the auctioneer began. "Forty-seven five. Five thousand. I have five thousand two hundred and fifty all the way back in the last row. Well, sort of the last row. A bit ragged back there. I have fifty-five hundred. I have six thousand ahead of you on the telephone," the auctioneer said, nodding in the direction of the phone bank, where three young women, all blond, held receivers to their ears.

"Any advance? . . . Six thousand. Fair warning."

The auctioneer looked around the room one last time and then rapped on the lectern. "Six thousand, on the phone," he said, looking toward one of the blond women.

"That's M148," she said, putting down the phone and identifying the anonymous absentee bidder as the auctioneer's assistants made note of it.

The auctioneer began the bidding on Lot 2, another icon.

And there she was. Stepping into the room, Sasha saw Madeline Malloy. Christ, he thought, and at the same time unsurprised that she would ignore his warning to stay away. She stopped, looked around, and saw him. She started walking toward him, tall and elegant in a brown velvet jacket over a white shirt, matching brown tights, and knee-high brown boots. Sasha had never seen her dressed so well. Following her, he saw a tall man with wet, thinning blond hair, wearing a knee-length blue wool overcoat and rimless glasses.

He does look like me, Sasha thought.

That's excellent.

He turned and whispered to Shubentsov, "He's here."

"Hello, Sasha," said Madeline Malloy, her eyes preternaturally bright with excitement. If Sasha hadn't known her better, he would have sworn she was high on cocaine.

Shubentsov pushed past Sasha. "So," he said to Volkov in Russian. "The box is here? You have it? I have all the necessary papers."

"Who's this?" Volkov asked Sasha.

"This," said Sasha, "is Major Anatoly Shubentsov. He represents Viktor Prudnikov, in Moscow. Major Shubentsov, this is Aleksandr Eugenev, the thief who stole your box."

"Would you please speak English?" Malloy asked.

"He's lying," Volkov said in Russian. "Is this why you brought me here?" he asked Sasha. "This comedy? You don't have the uranium? So? Where the fuck is it?"

"Please. What are you saying?" asked Malloy.

The auctioneer rapped on the lectern. Lot 2 had been knocked down.

"We're next," Sasha said, turning away from Volkov. "Lot 3 A."

The Golikov box appeared through the curtains.

"You are not Aleksandr Eugenev?" Shubentsov asked Volkov.

"I have fifty-five hundred," said the auctioneer. "Six thousand."

"My name is Velikhov," Volkov said. He jerked his thumb toward Sasha. "He's Eugenev. A Yid and a thief."

"Not true," said Shubentsov. "He's Aleksandr Volkov."

"The hell he is," Volkov said.

"Sasha," said Madeline Malloy, "would you please tell me what's going on?"

"Seven thousand on the phone," said the auctioneer. "Fair warning.

"I have seven five," the auctioneer said, indicating a paddle in the front row. "Seven five. Fair warning."

The auctioneer rapped on the lectern. A small, thin man wearing a polka-dot bow tie with brilliant polka-dot socks stood and began gathering up his coat. The display platform turned, and the box disappeared behind the curtains. A Sotheby's worker on the other side of the curtain, in an empty corridor behind the Sales Room, lifted it off the platform. A man came up behind him and put a gun to the back of his head. The worker handed the man the box.

"*Spaseebah,*" the man said, handing it over to Boris Zilberstein.

Zilberstein opened it, turned it over, and shook it. "What the fuck is this?" he said. "This is just a goddamn box."

"It sold for seven thousand five hundred bucks," Zilberstein's soldier said.

"So what?" said Zilberstein. "I didn't come here for a fucking seven-thousand-dollar box. Sam Goldman, the Panther, they didn't get whacked for a fucking seven-thousand-dollar box."

Zilberstein put the Golikov box on the floor and brought his heel down on it. The box splintered.

"Fuck this," Zilberstein said. "I want that Sasha guy. I want him now. Give the word."

The soldier lifted a walkie-talkie to his lips.

In the Sales Room, Shubentsov turned to Sasha. "What's going on, Volkov?"

"The box has been sold for seven thousand five hundred," Sasha said, "to a man named Peter Feld, I believe. A man working with Eugenev."

"Stop that," Volkov said. "This is Eugenev," he said, grabbing Sasha's sleeve. Then Volkov leaned over and put his lips to Sasha's ear. "You're a dead man, Aleksandr Eugenev," he said. "When we get outside, I'm going to shoot you down like a dog."

Sasha pushed Volkov away.

"So?" Shubentsov held Sasha's arm. "You'll bring me the box now? You'll take me to the real buyer with the real money?"

"Your business is with this man, Aleksandr Eugenev," said Sasha. "I told you I would bring you to him. Now I'm finished."

Ebzi Agron stood up and, followed by another man, edged out of his row and began walking toward them.

"That man, he knows you?" Shubentsov asked Sasha.

"No," Sasha said. "He's mistaken me for Eugenev here. We look alike. You should come with me now, Maddy," he said, turning and touching Malloy's shoulder.

"Look," said Volkov to Shubentsov, reaching for his wallet. "My name is Velikhov. This man is a thief. This man, Eu-

genev. A Jew. Can't you see he's a Jew? He must have the uranium, understand? There's no uranium in the box. It's gone.
Eugenev has it."

Malloy shook Sasha off. "I'm not going anywhere until—"

The windows in the offices above the Sales Room dissolved in a shower of glass. Automatic fire riddled the gray baffles above their heads.

People threw themselves off their chairs, screaming, div-
ing for the floor. The auctioneer crouched down behind the
lectern. The man walking behind Ebzi Agron pulled out a gun
as his boss hit the floor. A bullet caught the man in the chest,
knocking him backward. Sasha grabbed Madeline Malloy
around her waist. "Get low," he said, pushing her forward,
wondering if Viktor Prudnikov had grown impatient and had,
as it seemed, sent an army to kill him.

The firing continued. People began running, crawling, to
get out of the room, to get away from the hellish noise. Sasha,
still pushing Malloy in front of him, keeping low, found himself in the lobby outside the Sales Room, where the catalog girls
were crouching behind the desk, their hands over their ears,
their eyes shut, their mouths open. Someone had knocked over
the flowers. Crushed tulips and cherry blossoms littered the
floor. Sasha grabbed Malloy's hand and pulled her down the
stairs to the first floor and then out through the glass doors.

The cold and snow hit their faces. Peter Feld came up beside them. Before Sasha could say anything, a hand fell on his
shoulder, a gun pressed against the small of his back. Sasha let
go of Madeline Malloy's hand. "Run!" he shouted, pushing
Malloy away. The back of Sasha's head suddenly burst into
flame. His knees buckled, and for a second the world went
dark.

He blinked and fought to remain standing, to remain
conscious. He could feel himself being propelled forward. He
focused and saw an unmarked white delivery van standing at

the curb. Its back doors swung open. Sasha was pushed inside. Two men were waiting for him. He was grabbed and thrown to the floor. Looking up, Sasha saw Peter Feld running toward the van. "Get Maddy!" Sasha yelled at him. The doors closed. The van took off, its tires spinning on the ice, as Major Anatoly Shubentsov, emerging from the auction house, stood panting in the snow.

Ebzi Agron had also made his way out of Sotheby's. He ran for the black Town Car waiting around the corner on East Seventy-second Street, its engine idling. He pulled open the door and threw himself onto the backseat.

"Jesus Christ," he said, pulling out a handkerchief and wiping his face. What madness. The Zilberstein touch, he thought. Well, enough is enough. Time to kill the bastard.

Dmitri Duyadev turned around and quickly squeezed off five shots, hitting Agron in the hand, the jaw, the neck, and just below the sternum. The last bullet missed, burying itself in the plush seat, as the *batyushka* toppled sideways and slipped to the car's floor. Duyadev turned off the engine, stepped out of the car, locked it, and began walking crosstown toward the Lexington Avenue express to Brooklyn.

◈   ◈   ◈

The doors of the van opened. Sasha's two silent guards each grabbed one of his arms and threw him out of the back. He stumbled on the ice and fell sprawling, banging his chin. He looked up and down the deserted, snowy street. He was in Coney Island.

"Get up," a voice ordered. Sasha stood up. The sky, he saw, was turning a grimmer shade of gray. He turned. He was standing in front of a bumper car rink.

A man grabbed Sasha beneath the arm and hustled him up a ramp, past the red, white, and blue bumper cars huddled, as if for warmth, in the middle of the track. Sasha was pushed through a door and then up a flight of metal stairs. A door opened. He stepped into a small, bare, second-floor room whose filthy windows overlooked the boardwalk and the sea.

The door closed.

He was alone.

But not for long.

The door opened and Aleksandr Volkov came sprawling through, followed by Boris Zilberstein and three other men, one of whom was wearing a black cowboy hat.

"This is the bastard!" shouted a red-faced Volkov, pointing at Sasha. "This is Eugenev. Not me, you idiots. He stole the box off the beach. He stole the uranium."

Volkov turned on Zilberstein. "That's what this is all about, you stupid shit. Millions of dollars' worth of uranium oxides. Not a fucking box. Uranium. You know. You make big bombs out of it.

"The CIA wanted to buy it, you idiot. The CIfuckingA. And then this son of a bitch, Aleksandr Volkavitch Eugenev"—Volkov slowed down to pronounce Sasha's name—"he stole it, and he took it out of the goddamn box before that fucking queen ever took it to Sam Goldman's. Then he gave it to that miserable bitch newspaper reporter. You killed her, didn't you? Tell me at least that the bitch is dead."

"Weren't you the man in the car with the Cowboy? Weren't you the man in the Saab?" Zilberstein asked.

"Of course I was," said Volkov.

"Then you're Sasha Eugenev," Zilberstein said. "Didn't you tell me, Grigory," said Zilberstein, turning to one of his men, "that you took the Cowboy away from Sasha Eugenev?"

Grigory nodded. "That's right."

"You're all idiots. You," Volkov said, pointing to the Cowboy. "You tell them. Tell them he's Eugenev."

"How did you know Terry took the box to Goldman's?" the Cowboy asked.

"Because she told me, you pathetic little shit."

"When, when did she tell you?" asked the Cowboy. "She was killed the same day she took it to Goldman's. So when did she tell you?"

Volkov turned away from the Cowboy. "Look," he said, reaching for his wallet, not finding it, shouting, "Fuck! Your idiots took it. Look, for chrissakes. My identification. Aleksandr Velikhov, First Private Bank of Moscow."

Grigory handed Zilberstein Volkov's wallet.

Zilberstein looked at it, then handed it to Volkov.

"Are you insane?" Zilberstein asked. "Identification. You have identification, too, don't you," he said to Sasha.

Sasha nodded. "My name is Aleksandr Volkov," he said, staring at the Cowboy. "His is Aleksandr Eugenev. Look."

From his pocket, Sasha took out a driver's license. "He dropped this at Sotheby's," he said. "I picked it up."

"You fucking did not," Volkov said.

"Look," said Sasha, handing Zilberstein a New York City driver's license for Aleksandr Volkavitch Eugenev, bearing Volkov's face, which had been downloaded by Ariel Abramovitz from a GIF file in the Soviet archives and pasted up and laminated by the Professor.

Zilberstein handed the card to Volkov.

Volkov looked at it and threw it at Sasha.

The door opened. Peter Feld was brought in.

"Who the hell is this?" Zilberstein asked.

"A friend of his," said the soldier accompanying Feld, jerking his thumb at Sasha. "He tried to climb into the van with him, so I thought I'd bring him along. He came quietly."

"So," Zilberstein said in English, "tell me, which one of these sweethearts is Aleksandr Eugenev?"

Peter Feld looked from Sasha to Volkov. He smiled. "That's Aleksandr Eugenev," he said, pointing at Volkov.

"You bastard," said Volkov.

Zilberstein nodded at his soldiers. They grabbed Volkov, threw him onto a chair, and held him down.

"He's fucking CIA," Volkov shouted in Russian.

"Shut him the fuck up," Zilberstein said. "I'm tired of listening to him."

One of Zilberstein's men shoved a rag into Volkov's mouth.

"He said you were CIA," said Zilberstein.

"That's right," Feld said. "And I have a proposition for you."

"Talk," said Zilberstein.

"He works for me," Feld said, indicating Sasha. "I take him out of here. You," he said to Zilberstein, "you're going to go into the uranium business with me."

"Perhaps. Perhaps I'm interested. What about this Eugenev asshole?" Zilberstein asked.

Feld shrugged.

"He's mine," the Cowboy said, smiling for the first time since Terry's death. "He's all mine."

◈　　◈　　◈

In the morning, a group of boys from the projects found a cruelly mutilated, castrated body beneath the boardwalk. In the pants pocket the police found a driver's license identifying the corpse as one Aleksandr Volkavitch Eugenev, wanted for the murder of Terry Reynolds, a transvestite transsexual, and wanted as a suspect in the shooting death of Sam Goldman, a local shop owner.

Detective Peter Grushenko insisted that the body was not, in fact, Aleksandr Eugenev's and that Eugenev must still be at large. But when Moses Filonovsky's body was found in his apartment later that day, shot behind the ear, Grushenko's captain decided that having one dead murderer in the morgue was better than having three unsolved murder cases on the books. Indeed, as the captain told reporters that afternoon, the dead Eugenev qualified as a serial killer and was probably the shooter in the Coney Island beach deaths of last September, although that case, officially, at least, remained open.

Two weeks later the body of David Gatlober, aka the Cowboy, was found in the trunk of a car parked on Brighton Beach Avenue. There were three shriveled testicles in his pocket.

"Are you going to blame that on Aleksandr Eugenev, too?" Peter the Duck asked his captain.

Shortly afterward, Peter Grushenko retired. He and his wife, Olga, moved to Miami Beach.

32.

Friday, December 31
New Year's Eve

SASHA AND PETER FELD KNOCKED ON THE DOOR OF THE APARTment on Eighth Street, one block off Brighton Beach Avenue. A woman opened the door.

"Where is Svetlana Furtseva?" asked Sasha.

"Moved," the woman said.

"When?" asked Sasha.

"Months ago," the woman said.

"I know this is unusual," said Sasha, "but I believe Furtseva may have left something. In the bathroom. May my friend and I come in and take a look?"

The woman shrugged and stepped out of the way.

Sasha and Feld walked through the apartment that was like so many others in Brighton. Framed photographs on every surface; *matryoshkas;* a samovar in the kitchen. The smell of boiled cabbage.

They walked into the bathroom. Sasha lifted the lid of the toilet tank.

He reached in.

He pulled out a palm-size lead container.

He handed it to Peter Feld.

"Boris the Kike always said it was the best place to hide anything," Sasha said. "I was taking a leak at Sotheby's when I thought, maybe, maybe that's where it was."

"Why?" Feld asked. "Why didn't he just deliver it to Volkov like he was supposed to?"

Sasha shrugged. "Boris didn't trust anyone. He was just being cautious. That's what they teach you in the camps. And maybe, maybe he wanted to cut me in. Maybe he was trying to do me a favor. He was a good guy."

Outside, in the cold, Feld turned to Sasha.

"I need a Russian to liaison with Zilberstein," he said. "And I need someone to go to Russia and make arrangements with Viktor Prudnikov. Interested?"

"Not me," said Sasha. "I don't work for murderers."

"You wouldn't be working for Prudnikov. You'd be working for me."

Sasha turned away. The night was clear and cold, the stars bright.

"I'm not a murderer," Feld said.

"No?" said Sasha.

"Well, what can I do?" Feld asked. "I owe you. Do you need money?"

Sasha thought of the coins in his pocket, the lucky coins from Zagorsk.

"No," he said. "No money. I'm a Russian, so I need papers, what else? Always papers. New papers. And I need a new place to live," said Sasha. "Not New York. There's nothing here now. Someplace else. Maybe California. I need to be someone else. I don't want to be Aleksandr Volkov anymore."

"Why not?" Feld asked. "Volkov's dead. In some ways, it's very convenient to be a dead man. There are certain advantages."

"I don't want to be dead," said Sasha. "So. Can you do this for me?"

"Who do you want to be?" Peter Feld asked.

Sasha fell silent. The trick, he thought, was to be somebody with more future than past. That was always Aleksandr Eugenev's problem. Too much past, not enough future. Now who could that be? he wondered.

He was still thinking about that when, shortly after the new year had begun, he rang the bell at Madeline Malloy's apartment.

The intercom came to life.

"Who is it?" asked Malloy.